LURKING
SHADOWS

LURKING SHADOWS

SHADOWS

Shadow Tales in
Classic Short Fiction

Edited by Chad Arment

COACHWHIP PUBLICATIONS
Greenville, Ohio

Lurking Shadows, edited by Chad Arment
© 2022 Coachwhip Publications edition

CoachwhipBooks.com
Cover: Shadow © Le Minuet

ISBN 1-61646-534-4
ISBN-13 978-1-61646-534-6

Contents

The Shadow

Hans Christian Andersen

1847

In very hot climates, where the heat of the sun has great power, people are usually as brown as mahogany; and in the hottest countries they are negroes with black skins. A learned man once travelled into one of these warm climates, from the cold regions of the north, and thought he could roam about as he did at home; but he soon had to change his opinion. He found that, like all sensible people, he must remain in the house during the whole day, with every window and door closed, so that it looked as if all in the house were asleep or absent. The houses of the narrow street in which he lived were so lofty that the sun shone upon them from morning till evening, and it became quite unbearable. This learned man from the cold regions was young as well as clever; but it seemed to him as if he were sitting in an oven, and he became quite exhausted and weak, and grew so thin that his shadow shriveled up, and became much smaller than it had been at home. The sun took away even what was left of it, and he saw nothing of it till the evening, after sunset. It was really a pleasure, as soon as the lights were brought into the room, to see the shadow stretch itself against the wall, even to the ceiling, so tall was it; and it really wanted a good stretch to recover its strength. The learned man would sometimes go out into the balcony to stretch himself also; and as soon as the stars came forth in the clear, beautiful sky, he felt revived. People at this hour began to make their appearance in all the balconies in the street; for in warm climates every window has a balcony in which they can breathe the fresh evening air, which is very necessary, even to those who are used to a heat that makes them as brown as mahogany; so that the street presented a very lively appearance. Here were shoemakers, and tailors, and all sorts of people sitting. In the street beneath, they brought out tables and chairs, lighted candles by hundreds, talked and sang, and were very merry. There were people walking, carriages driving, and mules trotting along, with their bells on the harness, "tingle, tingle," as they went. Then the dead were carried to the grave with the sound of solemn music, and the tolling of the church bells. It was indeed a scene of varied life in the street. One house only, which was just opposite to the one in which the foreign learned man lived, formed a contrast to all this, for it was quite still; and yet somebody dwelt there, for flowers stood in the balcony, blooming beautifully in the hot sun; and this could not have been unless they had been watered carefully. Therefore some one must be in the house to do this. The doors leading to the balcony were half opened in the evening; and although in the front room all was dark, music could be heard from the interior of the house. The foreign learned man considered this music very delightful; but perhaps he fancied it; for everything in these warm countries pleased him, except the heat of the sun. The foreign landlord said he did not know who had taken the opposite house—nobody was to be seen there; and as to the music, he thought it seemed very tedious, to him most uncommonly so.

"It is just as if some one were practicing a piece that he could not manage; it was always the same piece. He thinks, I suppose, that he will be able to manage it at last; but I do not think so, however long he may play it."

Once the foreigner woke in the night. He slept with the door open which led to the balcony; the wind had raised the curtain before it, and there appeared a wonderful brightness over all in the balcony of the opposite house. The flowers seemed like flames of the most gorgeous colors, and among the flowers stood a beautiful slender maiden. It was to him as if light streamed from her, and dazzled his eyes; but then he had only just opened them, as he awoke from his sleep. With one spring he was out of bed, and crept softly behind the curtain. But she was gone—the brightness had disappeared; the flowers no longer appeared like flames, although still as beautiful as ever. The door stood ajar, and from an inner room sounded music so sweet and so lovely, that it produced the most enchanting thoughts, and acted on the senses with magic power. Who could live there? Where was the real entrance? for, both in the street and in the lane at the side, the whole ground floor was a continuation of shops; and people could not always be passing through them.

One evening the foreigner sat in the balcony. A light was burning in his own room, just behind him. It was quite natural, therefore, that his shadow should fall on the wall of the opposite house; so that, as he sat amongst the flowers on his balcony, when he moved, his shadow moved also.

"I think my shadow is the only living thing to be seen opposite," said the learned man; "see how pleasantly it sits among the flowers. The door is only ajar; the shadow ought to be clever enough to step in and look about him, and then to come back and tell me what he has seen. You could make yourself useful in this way," said he, jokingly; "be so good as to step in now, will you?" and then he nodded to the shadow, and the shadow nodded in return. "Now go, but don't stay away altogether."

Then the foreigner stood up, and the shadow on the opposite balcony stood up also; the foreigner turned round, the

shadow turned; and if any one had observed, they might
have seen it go straight into the half-opened door of the
opposite balcony, as the learned man re-entered his own
room, and let the curtain fall. The next morning he went
out to take his coffee and read the newspapers.

"How is this?" he exclaimed, as he stood in the sunshine. "I have lost my shadow. So it really did go away
yesterday evening, and it has not returned. This is very
annoying."

And it certainly did vex him, not so much because the
shadow was gone, but because he knew there was a story
of a man without a shadow. All the people at home, in
his country, knew this story; and when he returned, and
related his own adventures, they would say it was only an
imitation; and he had no desire for such things to be said
of him. So he decided not to speak of it at all, which was
a very sensible determination.

In the evening he went out again on his balcony, taking care to place the light behind him; for he knew that
a shadow always wants his master for a screen; but he
could not entice him out. He made himself little, and he
made himself tall; but there was no shadow, and no shadow came. He said, "Hem, a-hem;" but it was all useless.
This was very vexatious; but in warm countries everything
grows very quickly; and, after a week had passed, he saw,
to his great joy, that a new shadow was growing from his
feet, when he walked in the sunshine; so that the root
must have remained. After three weeks, he had quite a
respectable shadow, which, during his return journey to
northern lands, continued to grow, and became at last so
large that he might very well have spared half of it. When
this learned man arrived at home, he wrote books about
the true, the good, and the beautiful, which are to be
found in this world; and so days and years passed—many,
many years.

One evening, as he sat in his study, a very gentle tap was heard at the door. "Come in," said he; but no one came. He opened the door, and there stood before him a man so remarkably thin that he felt seriously troubled at his appearance. He was, however, very well dressed, and looked like a gentleman. "To whom have I the honor of speaking?" said he.

"Ah, I hoped you would recognize me," said the elegant stranger; "I have gained so much that I have a body of flesh, and clothes to wear. You never expected to see me in such a condition. Do you not recognize your old shadow? Ah, you never expected that I should return to you again. All has been prosperous with me since I was with you last; I have become rich in every way, and, were I inclined to purchase my freedom from service, I could easily do so." And as he spoke he rattled between his fingers a number of costly trinkets which hung to a thick gold watch-chain he wore round his neck. Diamond rings sparkled on his fingers, and it was all real.

"I cannot recover from my astonishment," said the learned man. "What does all this mean?"

"Something rather unusual," said the shadow; "but you are yourself an uncommon man, and you know very well that I have followed in your footsteps ever since your childhood. As soon as you found I had travelled enough to be trusted alone, I went my own way, and I am now in the most brilliant circumstances. But I felt a kind of longing to see you once more before you die, and I wanted to see this place again, for there is always a clinging to the land of one's birth. I know that you have now another shadow; do I owe you anything? If so, have the goodness to say what it is."

"No! Is it really you?" said the learned man. "Well, this is most remarkable; I never supposed it possible that a man's old shadow could become a human being."

"Just tell me what I owe you," said the shadow, "for I do not like to be in debt to any man."

"How can you talk in that manner?" said the learned man. "What question of debt can there be between us? You are as free as any one. I rejoice exceedingly to hear of your good fortune. Sit down, old friend, and tell me a little of how it happened, and what you saw in the house opposite to me while we were in those hot climates,"

"Yes, I will tell you all about it," said the shadow, sitting down; "but then you must promise me never to tell in this city, wherever you may meet me, that I have been your shadow. I am thinking of being married, for I have more than sufficient to support a family."

"Make yourself quite easy," said the learned man; "I will tell no one who you really are. Here is my hand,—I promise, and a word is sufficient between man and man."

"Between man and a shadow," said the shadow; for he could not help saying so.

It was really most remarkable how very much he had become a man in appearance. He was dressed in a suit of the very finest black cloth, polished boots, and an opera crush hat, which could be folded together so that nothing could be seen but the crown and the rim, besides the trinkets, the gold chain, and the diamond rings already spoken of. The shadow was, in fact, very well dressed, and this made a man of him. "Now I will relate to you what you wish to know," said the shadow, placing his foot with the polished leather boot as firmly as possible on the arm of the new shadow of the learned man, which lay at his feet like a poodle dog. This was done, it might be from pride, or perhaps that the new shadow might cling to him, but the prostrate shadow remained quite quiet and at rest, in order that it might listen, for it wanted to know how a shadow could be sent away by its master, and become a man itself. "Do you know," said the shadow, "that in the

house opposite to you lived the most glorious creature in
the world? It was poetry. I remained there three weeks,
and it was more like three thousand years, for I read all
that has ever been written in poetry or prose; and I may
say, in truth, that I saw and learnt everything."

"Poetry!" exclaimed the learned man. "Yes, she lives as
a hermit in great cities. Poetry! Well, I saw her once for a
very short moment, while sleep weighed down my eyelids.
She flashed upon me from the balcony like the radiant
aurora borealis, surrounded with flowers like flames of
fire. Tell me, you were on the balcony that evening; you
went through the door, and what did you see?"

"I found myself in an ante-room," said the shadow.
"You still sat opposite to me, looking into the room. There
was no light, or at least it seemed in partial darkness, for
the doors of a whole suite of rooms stood open, and they
were brilliantly lighted. The blaze of light would have
killed me, had I approached too near the maiden herself;
but I was cautious, and took time, which is what every one
ought to do.

"And what didst thou see?" asked the learned man.

"I saw everything, as you shall hear. But—it really is not
pride on my part, as a free man and possessing the knowledge that I do, besides my position, not to speak of my
wealth—I wish you would say you to me, instead of thou."

"I beg your pardon," said the learned man; "it is an old
habit, which it is difficult to break. You are quite right;
I will try to think of it. But now tell me everything that
you saw."

"Everything," said the shadow; "for I saw and know
everything."

"What was the appearance of the inner rooms?" asked
the scholar. "Was it there like a cool grove, or like a holy
temple? Were the chambers like a starry sky seen from the
top of a high mountain?"

"It was all that you describe," said the shadow; "but I did not go quite in—I remained in the twilight of the ante-room—but I was in a very good position,—I could see and hear all that was going on in the court of poetry."

"But what did you see? Did the gods of ancient times pass through the rooms? Did old heroes fight their battles over again? Were there lovely children at play, who related their dreams?"

"I tell you I have been there, and therefore you may be sure that I saw everything that was to be seen. If you had gone there you would not have remained a human being, whereas I became one; and at the same moment I became aware of my inner being, my inborn affinity to the nature of poetry. It is true I did not think much about it while I was with you, but you will remember that I was always much larger at sunrise and sunset, and in the moonlight even more visible than yourself, but I did not then understand my inner existence. In the ante-room it was revealed to me. I became a man; I came out in full maturity. But you had left the warm countries. As a man, I felt ashamed to go about without boots or clothes, and that exterior finish by which man is known. So I went my own way; I can tell you, for you will not put it in a book. I hid myself under the cloak of a cake woman, but she little thought who she concealed. It was not till evening that I ventured out. I ran about the streets in the moonlight. I drew myself up to my full height upon the walls, which tickled my back very pleasantly. I ran here and there, looked through the highest windows into the rooms, and over the roofs. I looked in, and saw what nobody else could see, or indeed ought to see; in fact, it is a bad world, and I would not care to be a man, but that men are of some importance. I saw the most miserable things going on between husbands and wives, parents and children,—sweet, incomparable children. I have seen what no human being has the power of knowing, although they would all be very glad to know—the evil conduct of their neighbors. Had I written a newspaper, how eagerly it would have been read! Instead of which, I wrote direct to the persons themselves, and great alarm arose in all the towns I visited. They had so much fear of me, and yet how dearly they loved me. The professor made me a professor. The tailor made me new clothes; I am well provided for in that way. The overseer of the mint struck coins for me. The women declared that I was handsome, and so I became the man you now see me. And now I must say adieu. Here is my card. I live on the sunny side of the street, and always stay at home in rainy weather." And the shadow departed.

"This is all very remarkable," said the learned man.

Years passed, days and years went by, and the shadow came again. "How are you going on now?" he asked.

"Ah!" said the learned man, "I am writing about the true, the beautiful, and the good; but no one cares to hear anything about it. I am quite in despair, for I take it to heart very much."

"That is what I never do," said the shadow; "I am growing quite fat and stout, which every one ought to be. You do not understand the world; you will make yourself ill about it; you ought to travel; I am going on a journey in the summer, will you go with me? I should like a travelling companion; will you travel with me as my shadow? It will give me great pleasure, and I will pay all expenses."

"Are you going to travel far?" asked the learned man.

"That is a matter of opinion," replied the shadow. "At all events, a journey will do you good, and if you will be my shadow, then all your journey shall be paid."

"It appears to me very absurd," said the learned man.

"But it is the way of the world," replied the shadow, "and always will be." Then he went away.

Everything went wrong with the learned man. Sorrow and trouble pursued him, and what he said about the good, the beautiful, and the true, was of as much value to most people as a nutmeg would be to a cow. At length he fell ill. "You really look like a shadow," people said to him, and then a cold shudder would pass over him, for he had his own thoughts on the subject.

"You really ought to go to some watering-place," said the shadow on his next visit. "There is no other chance for you. I will take you with me, for the sake of old acquaintance. I will pay the expenses of your journey, and you shall write a description of it to amuse us by the way. I should like to go to a watering-place; my beard does not grow as it ought, which is from weakness, and I must have a beard. Now do be sensible and accept my proposal; we shall travel as intimate friends."

And at last they started together. The shadow was master now, and the master became the shadow. They drove together, and rode and walked in company with each other, side by side, or one in front and the other behind, according to the position of the sun. The shadow always knew when to take the place of honor, but the learned man took no notice of it, for he had a good heart, and was exceedingly mild and friendly.

One day the master said to the shadow, "We have grown up together from our childhood, and now that we have become travelling companions, shall we not drink to our good fellowship, and say thee and thou to each other."

"What you say is very straightforward and kindly meant," said the shadow, who was now really master. "I will be equally kind and straightforward. You are a learned man, and know how wonderful human nature is. There are some men who cannot endure the smell of brown paper; it makes them ill. Others will feel a shuddering sensation to their very marrow, if a nail is scratched on a pane of glass. I myself have a similar kind of feeling when I hear any one say thou to me. I feel crushed by it, as I used to feel in my former position with you. You will perceive that this is a matter of feeling, not pride. I cannot allow you to say thou to me; I will gladly say it to you, and therefore your wish will be half fulfilled." Then the shadow addressed his former master as thou.

"It is going rather too far," said the latter, "that I am to say you when I speak to him, and he is to say thou to me." However, he was obliged to submit.

They arrived at length at the baths, where there were many strangers, and among them a beautiful princess, whose real disease consisted in being too sharp-sighted, which made every one very uneasy. She saw at once that the new comer was very different to every one else. "They say he is here to make his beard grow," she thought; "but I know the real cause, he is unable to cast a shadow." Then she became very curious on the matter, and one day, while on the promenade, she entered into conversation with the strange gentleman. Being a princess, she was not obliged to stand upon much ceremony, so she said to him without hesitation, "Your illness consists in not being able to cast a shadow."

"Your royal highness must be on the high-road to recovery from your illness," said he. "I know your complaint arose from being too sharp-sighted, and in this case it has entirely failed. I happen to have a most unusual shadow. Have you not seen a person who is always at my side? Persons often give their servants finer cloth for their liveries than for their own clothes, and so I have dressed out my shadow like a man; nay, you may observe that I have even given him a shadow of his own; it is rather expensive, but I like to have things about me that are peculiar."

"How is this?" thought the princess; "am I really cured? This must be the best watering-place in existence. Water in our times has certainly wonderful power. But I will not leave this place yet, just as it begins to be amusing. This foreign prince—for he must be a prince—pleases me above all things. I only hope his beard won't grow, or he will leave at once."

In the evening, the princess and the shadow danced together in the large assembly rooms. She was light, but he was lighter still; she had never seen such a dancer before. She told him from what country she had come, and found he knew it and had been there, but not while she was at home. He had looked into the windows of her father's palace, both the upper and the lower windows; he had seen many things, and could therefore answer the princess, and make allusions which quite astonished her. She thought he must be the cleverest man in all the world, and felt the greatest respect for his knowledge. When she danced with him again she fell in love with him, which the shadow quickly discovered, for she had with her eyes looked him through and through. They danced once more, and she was nearly telling him, but she had some discretion; she thought of her country, her kingdom, and the number of people over whom she would one day have to rule. "He is a clever man," she thought to herself, "which is a good thing, and he dances admirably, which is also good. But has he well-grounded knowledge? that is an important question, and I must try him." Then she asked him a most difficult question, she herself could not have answered it, and the shadow made a most unaccountable grimace.

"You cannot answer that," said the princess.

"I learnt something about it in my childhood," he replied; "and believe that even my very shadow, standing over there by the door, could answer it."

"Your shadow," said the princess; "indeed that would be very remarkable."

"I do not say so, positively," observed the shadow; "but I am inclined to believe that he can do so. He has followed me for so many years, and has heard so much from me, that I think it is very likely. But your royal highness must allow me to observe, that he is very proud of being considered a man, and to put him in a good humor, so that he may answer correctly, he must be treated as a man."

"I shall be very pleased to do so," said the princess. So she walked up to the learned man, who stood in the doorway, and spoke to him of the sun, and the moon, of the green forests, and of people near home and far off; and the learned man conversed with her pleasantly and sensibly.

"What a wonderful man he must be, to have such a clever shadow!" thought she. "If I were to choose him it would be a real blessing to my country and my subjects, and I will do it." So the princess and the shadow were soon engaged to each other, but no one was to be told a word about it, till she returned to her kingdom.

"No one shall know," said the shadow; "not even my own shadow;" and he had very particular reasons for saying so.

After a time the princess returned to the land over which she reigned, and the shadow accompanied her.

"Listen, my friend," said the shadow to the learned man; "now that I am as fortunate and as powerful as any man can be, I will do something unusually good for you. You shall live in my palace, drive with me in the royal carriage, and have a hundred thousand dollars a year; but you must allow every one to call you a shadow, and never venture to say that you have been a man. And once a year, when I sit in my balcony in the sunshine, you must lie at my feet as becomes a shadow to do; for I must tell you I am going to marry the princess, and our wedding will take place this evening."

"Now, really this is too ridiculous," said the learned man. "I cannot, and will not, submit to such folly. It would be cheating the whole country, and the princess also. I will disclose everything, and say that I am the man, and that you are only a shadow dressed up in men's clothes."

"No one would believe you," said the shadow; "be reasonable, now, or I will call the guards."

"I will go straight to the princess," said the learned man.

"But I shall be there first," replied the shadow, "and you will be sent to prison." And so it turned out, for the guards readily obeyed him, as they knew he was going to marry the king's daughter.

"You tremble," said the princess, when the shadow appeared before her. "Has anything happened? you must not be ill to-day, for this evening our wedding will take place."

"I have gone through the most terrible affair that could possibly happen," said the shadow; "only imagine, my shadow has gone mad; I suppose such a poor, shallow brain, could not bear much; he fancies that he has become a real man, and that I am his shadow."

"How very terrible," cried the princess; "is he locked up?"

"Oh yes, certainly; for I fear he will never recover."

"Poor shadow!" said the princess; "it is very unfortunate for him; it would really be a good deed to free him from his frail existence; and, indeed, when I think how often people take the part of the lower class against the higher, in these days, it would be policy to put him out of the way quietly."

"It is certainly rather hard upon him, for he was a faithful servant," said the shadow; and he pretended to sigh.

"Yours is a noble character," said the princess, and bowed herself before him.

In the evening the whole town was illuminated, and cannons fired "boom," and the soldiers presented arms. It was, indeed, a grand wedding. The princess and the shadow stepped out on the balcony to show themselves, and to receive one cheer more. But the learned man heard nothing of all these festivities, for he had already been executed.

Shadow—A Parable

Edgar Allan Poe

1845

Yea, though I walk through the valley
of the *Shadow:*

Psalm of David.

Ye who read are still among the living; but I who write
shall have long since gone my way into the region of shadows. For indeed strange things shall happen, and secret
things be known, and many centuries shall pass away, ere
these memorials be seen of men. And, when seen, there
will be some to disbelieve, and some to doubt, and yet a
few who will find much to ponder upon in the characters
here graven with a stylus of iron.

The year had been a year of terror, and of feelings more
intense than terror for which there is no name upon the
earth. For many prodigies and signs had taken place, and
far and wide, over sea and land, the black wings of the
Pestilence were spread abroad. To those, nevertheless,
cunning in the stars, it was not unknown that the heavens
wore an aspect of ill; and to me, the Greek Oinos, among
others, it was evident that now had arrived the alternation
of that seven hundred and ninety-fourth year when, at the
entrance of Aries, the planet Jupiter is conjoined with the
red ring of the terrible Saturnus. The peculiar spirit of
the skies, if I mistake not greatly, made itself manifest,

not only in the physical orb of the earth, but in the souls, imaginations, and meditations of mankind.

Over some flasks of the red Chian wine, within the walls of a noble hall, in a dim city called Ptolemais, we sat, at night, a company of seven. And to our chamber there was no entrance save by a lofty door of brass: and the door was fashioned by the artisan Corinnos, and, being of rare workmanship, was fastened from within. Black draperies, likewise, in the gloomy room, shut out from our view the moon, the lurid stars, and the peopleless streets— but the boding and the memory of Evil they would not be so excluded. There were things around us and about of which I can render no distinct account—things material and spiritual—heaviness in the atmosphere—a sense of suffocation—anxiety—and, above all, that terrible state of existence which the nervous experience when the senses are keenly living and awake, and meanwhile the powers of thought lie dormant. A dead weight hung upon us. It hung upon our limbs—upon the household furniture— upon the goblets from which we drank; and all things were depressed, and borne down thereby—all things save only the flames of the seven lamps which illumined our revel. Uprearing themselves in tall slender lines of light, they thus remained burning all pallid and motionless; and in the mirror which their lustre formed upon the round table of ebony at which we sat, each of us there assembled beheld the pallor of his own countenance, and the unquiet glare in the downcast eyes of his companions. Yet we laughed and were merry in our proper way—which was hysterical; and sang the songs of Anacreon—which are madness; and drank deeply—although the purple wine reminded us of blood. For there was yet another tenant of our chamber in the person of young Zoilus. Dead, and at full length he lay, enshrouded; the genius and the demon of the scene. Alas! he bore no portion in our mirth,

save that his countenance, distorted with the plague, and
his eyes, in which Death had but half extinguished the
fire of the pestilence, seemed to take such interest in our
merriment as the dead may haply take in the merriment
of those who are to die. But although I, Oinos, felt that
the eyes of the departed were upon me, still I forced myself not to perceive the bitterness of their expression, and
gazing down steadily into the depths of the ebony mirror,
sang with a loud and sonorous voice the songs of the son
of Teios. But gradually my songs they ceased, and their
echoes, rolling afar off among the sable draperies of the
chamber, became weak, and undistinguishable, and so
faded away. And lo! from among those sable draperies
where the sounds of the song departed, there came forth a
dark and undefined shadow—a shadow such as the moon,
when low in heaven, might fashion from the figure of a
man: but it was the shadow neither of man nor of God,
nor of any familiar thing. And quivering awhile among the
draperies of the room, it at length rested in full view upon
the surface of the door of brass. But the shadow was vague,
and formless, and indefinite, and was the shadow neither
of man nor of God—neither God of Greece, nor God of
Chaldaea, nor any Egyptian God. And the shadow rested
upon the brazen doorway, and under the arch of the enta-
blature of the door, and moved not, nor spoke any word,
but there became stationary and remained. And the door
whereupon the shadow rested was, if I remember aright,
over against the feet of the young Zoilus enshrouded. But
we, the seven there assembled, having seen the shadow as
it came out from among the draperies, dared not steadily
behold it, but cast down our eyes, and gazed continually
into the depths of the mirror of ebony. And at length
I, Oinos, speaking some low words, demanded of the
shadow its dwelling and its appellation. And the shadow
answered, "I am SHADOW, and my dwelling is near to the

Catacombs of Ptolemais, and hard by those dim plains of Helusion which border upon the foul Charonian canal." And then did we, the seven, start from our seats in horror, and stand trembling, and shuddering, and aghast, for the tones in the voice of the shadow were not the tones of any one being, but of a multitude of beings, and, varying in their cadences from syllable to syllable fell duskly upon our ears in the well-remembered and familiar accents of many thousand departed friends.

The Man without a Shadow: A New Version
Fitz James O'Brien
1852

Fortunate fellow that I am! I have lost my shadow!

But do not imagine that, like the poor Peter Schlemihl, I have sold it to the Devil! Heaven forbid that any Devil should be stupid or extravagant enough to buy such a Shadow!

No; as it came, so it has departed, a thing of mystery, an awful bore.

It is not my natural shadow I speak of; but an unnatural, an impertinent Shadow, which of late attached itself to my person, and could not be shaken off whether in the glare of sunshine or the pale moonlight, in the rays of volatile gas or of explosive camphine.

I first observed it about six weeks ago. I knew it was a shadow, for I never could detect anything real or true about it; nevertheless, to look at it, one would have taken it for a man, or, at the least, a monkey. I have had my doubts in the latter point. But no! I will not insult monkeydom by the suspicion. It was only a Shadow—no more.

When I first observed it at a friend's house, I tried to find out what it was; but my friend knew as little as myself. It had followed him from another friend's, and that friend said it had followed him from somewhere else. Of its origin nothing was known. Like all Shadows, its nature was involved in obscurity. At any attempt to throw light upon it, it disappeared entirely—like other Shadows.

Still it was a very troublesome Shadow, and very different from my own dear aboriginal Shadow which so closely resembled me in outline, that no one would fail to detect my relationship; but this new strange Shadow was not a bit like me. It was my opposite in every respect—even at dinner. And it was not only a troublesome, but an expensive Shadow; for when I dined, it dined with me, and when the bill came, the waiter charged for the Shadow as if for a human being—and truly it had a most astonishing semblance of eating and drinking about it! Whatever I took it took, when I drank wine it drank wine—nay, it drank even more than I drank myself, for Shadows are generally larger than the objects which shun them. I should almost have questioned whether it was a Shadow, had it not in all respects aped my movements and reflections. If I said it was a hot day, the Shadow said it was a hot day, or I fancied it said so. If I wiped my forehead, the Shadow seemed to do the same. If I put my hand in my pocket to pay for cigars, the Shadow did the same—only being a Shadow, it never brought out any money to pay for them, which is a peculiarity of Shadows.

When I praised anything the Shadow praised, and when I condemned the Shadow condemned—at least so its attitude seemed to imply. When I was going up town the Shadow was going up town, and when I inclined towards the Battery the Shadow was likewise attracted thither. Wherever I went, the Shadow went too. What I did, the Shadow did. What I thought the Shadow thought, and what I swore the Shadow swore. Of its Shadowy nature, there could surely be no question.

It is now a whole week since it left me. When I last saw it I was dressing to go out, and the Shadow of course had precisely at that epoch occasion to dress too; so it put on one of my clean shirts (as I did myself), and went out with me. At the door it borrowed a five dollar bill, and—vanished. It is the nature of Shadows to vanish. I have since heard that the same Shadow has vanished from more than one boarding house in the most shadowy manner.

May the reader never be haunted by Shadows!

I have a scientific theory, by the way, with reference to these visitors from Shadow-land. It is, that they are the spiritual manifestations of departed (i.e. emigrated) Do-dos. I mean to suggest the idea at the next meeting of the Royal Society, in London.

The Shadow of a Shade

Tom Hood

1869

My sister Lettie has lived with me ever since I had a home of my own. She was my little housekeeper before I married. Now she is my wife's constant companion, and the 'darling auntie' of my children, who go to her for comfort, advice, and aid in all their little troubles and perplexities.

But, though she has a comfortable home, and loving hearts around her, she wears a grave, melancholy look on her face, which puzzles acquaintances and grieves friends.

A disappointment! Yes, the old story of a lost lover is the reason for Lettie's looks. She has had good offers often; but since she lost the first love of her heart she has never indulged in the happy dream of loving and being loved.

George Mason was a cousin of my wife's—a sailor by profession. He and Lettie met one another at our wedding, and fell in love at first sight. George's father had seen service before him on the great mysterious sea, and had been especially known as a good Arctic sailor, having shared in more than one expedition in search of the North Pole and the North-West Passage.

It was not a matter of surprise to me, therefore, when George volunteered to go out in the *Pioneer,* which was being fitted out for a cruise in search of Franklin and his missing expedition.

There was a fascination about such an undertaking that I felt I could not have resisted had I been in his place. Of course, Lettie did not like the idea at all, but he silenced her by telling her that men who volunteered for Arctic search were never lost sight of, and that he should not make as much advance in his profession in a dozen years as he would in the year or so of this expedition.

I cannot say that Lettie, even after this, was quite satisfied with the notion of his going, but, at all events, she did not argue against it any longer. But the grave look, which is now habitual with her, but was a rare thing in her young and happy days, passed over her face sometimes when she thought no one was looking.

My younger brother, Harry, was at this time an academy student. He was only a beginner then.

Now he is pretty well known in the art world, and his pictures command fair prices. Like all beginners in art, he was full of fancies and theories. He would have been a pre-Raphaelite, only pre-Raphaelism had not been invented then. His peculiar craze was for what he styled the Venetian School. Now, it chanced that George had a fine Italian-looking head, and Harry persuaded him to sit to him for his portrait. It was a fair likeness, but a very moderate work of art. The background was so very dark, and George's naval costume so very deep in colour, that the face came out too white and staring. It was a three-quarter picture; but only one hand showed in it, leaning on the hilt of a sword. As George said, he looked much more like the commander of a Venetian galley than a modern mate.

However, the picture pleased Lettie, who did not care much about art provided the resemblance was good. So the picture was duly framed—in a tremendously heavy frame, of Harry's ordering—and hung up in the dining-room.

And now the time for George's departure was growing nearer. The *Pioneer* was nearly ready to sail, and her crew only waited orders. The officers grew acquainted with each other before sailing, which was an advantage. George took up very warmly with the surgeon, Vincent Grieve, and, with my permission, brought him to dinner once or twice.

"Poor chap, he has no friends nearer than the High-lands, and it's precious lonely work."

"Bring him by all means, George! You know that any friends of yours will be welcome here."

So Vincent Grieve came. I am bound to say I was not favourably impressed by him, and almost wished I had not consented to his coming. He was a tall, pale, fair young man, with a hard Scotch face and a cold, grey eye. There was something in his expression, too, that was unpleas-ant—something cruel or crafty, or both.

I considered that it was very bad taste for him to pay such marked attention to Lettie, coming, as he did, as the friend of her fiancé. He kept by her constantly and anti-cipated George in all the little attentions which a lover delights to pay. I think George was a little put out about it, though he said nothing, attributing his friend's offence to lack of breeding.

Lettie did not like it at all. She knew that she was not to have George with her much longer, and she was anxious to have him to herself as much as possible. But as Grieve was her lover's friend she bore the infliction with the best possible patience.

The surgeon did not seem to perceive in the least that he was interfering where he had no business. He was quite self-possessed and happy, with one exception. The portrait of George seemed to annoy him. He had uttered a little impatient exclamation when he first saw it which drew my attention to him; and I noticed that he tried to avoid looking at it. At last, when dinner came, he was told to sit exactly facing the picture. He hesitated for an instant and then sat down, but almost immediately rose again.

"It's very childish and that sort of thing," he stammered, "but I cannot sit opposite that picture."

"It is not high art," I said, "and may irritate a critical eye."

"I know nothing about art," he answered, "but it is one of those unpleasant pictures whose eyes follow you about the room. I have an inherited horror of such pictures. My mother married against her father's will, and when I was born she was so ill she was hardly expected to live. When she was sufficiently recovered to speak without delirious rambling she implored them to remove a picture of my grandfather that hung in the room, and which she vowed made threatening faces at her. It's superstitious, but constitutional—I have a horror of such paintings!"

I believe George thought this was a ruse of his friend's to get a seat next to Lettie; but I felt sure it was not, for I had seen the alarmed expression of his face.

At night, when George and his friend were leaving, I took an opportunity to ask the former, half in a joke, if he should bring the surgeon to see us again. George made a very hearty assertion to the contrary, adding that he was pleasant enough company among men at an inn, or on board ship, but not where ladies were concerned.

But the mischief was done. Vincent Grieve took advantage of the introduction and did not wait to be invited again. He called the next day, and nearly every day after. He was a more frequent visitor than George now, for George was obliged to attend to his duties, and they kept him on board the *Pioneer* pretty constantly, whereas the surgeon, having seen to the supply of drugs, etc., was pretty well at liberty. Lettie avoided him as much as possible, but he generally brought, or professed to bring, some little message from George to her, so that he had an excuse for asking to see her.

On the occasion of his last visit—the day before the *Pioneer* sailed—Lettie came to me in great distress. The young cub had actually the audacity to tell her he loved her. He knew, he said, about her engagement to George, but that did not prevent another man from loving her too. A man could no more help falling in love than he could help taking a fever. Lettie stood upon her dignity and rebuked him severely; but he told her he could see no harm in telling her of his passion, though he knew it was a hopeless one.

"A thousand things may happen," he said at last, "to bring your engagement with George Mason to an end. Then perhaps you will not forget that another loves you!"

I was very angry, and was forthwith going to give him my opinion on his conduct, when Lettie told me he was gone, that she had bade him go and had forbidden him the house. She only told me in order to protect herself, for she did not intend to say anything to George, for fear it should lead to a duel or some other violence.

That was the last we saw of Vincent Grieve before the *Pioneer* sailed.

George came the same evening, and was with us till daybreak, when he had to tear himself away and join his ship.

After shaking hands with him at the door, in the cold, grey, drizzly dawn, I turned back into the dining-room, where poor Lettie was sobbing on the sofa.

I could not help starting when I looked at George's portrait, which hung above her. The strange light of daybreak could hardly account for the extraordinary pallor of the face. I went close to it and looked hard at it. I saw that it was covered with moisture, and imagined that that possibly made it look so pale. As for the moisture, I supposed poor Lettie had been kissing the beloved's portrait, and that the moisture was caused by her tears.

It was not till a long time after, when I was jestingly telling Harry how his picture had been caressed, that I learnt the error of my conjecture. Lettie assured me most solemnly that I was mistaken in supposing she had kissed it.

"It was the varnish blooming, I expect," said Harry. And thus the subject was dismissed, for I said no more, though I knew well enough, in spite of my not being an artist, that the bloom of varnish was quite another sort of thing.

The *Pioneer* sailed. We received—or, rater, Lettie received—two letters from George, which he had taken the opportunity of sending by homeward-bound whalers. In the second he said it was hardly likely he should have an opportunity of sending another, as they were sailing into high latitudes—into the solitary sea, to which none but expedition ships ever penetrated. They were all in high spirits, he said, for they had encountered very little ice and hoped to find clear water further north than usual. Moreover, he added, Grieve had held a sinecure so far, for there had not been a single case of illness on board.

Then came a long silence, and a year crept away very slowly for poor Lettie. Once we heard of the expedition from the papers. They were reported as pushing on and progressing favourably by a wandering tribe of Esquimaux with whom the captain of a Russian vessel fell in. They had laid the ship up for the winter, and were taking the boats on sledges, and believed they had met with traces of the lost crews that seemed to show they were on the right track.

The winter passed again, and spring came. It was a balmy, bright spring such as we get occasionally, even in this changeable and uncertain climate of ours.

One evening we were sitting in the dining-room with the window open, for, although we had long given up fires, the room was so oppressively warm that we were glad of the breath of the cool evening breeze.

Lettie was working. Poor child, though she never murmured, she was evidently pining at George's long absence. Harry was leaning out of the window, studying the evening effect on the fruit blossom, which was wonderfully early and plentiful, the season was so mild. I was sitting at the table, near the lamp, reading the paper.

Suddenly there swept into the room a chill. It was not a gust of cold wind, for the curtain by the open window did not swerve in the least. But the deathly cold pervaded the room—came, and was gone in an instant. Lettie shuddered, as I did, with the intense icy feeling.

She looked up. "How curiously cold it has got all in a minute," she said.

"We are having a taste of poor George's Polar weather," I said with a smile.

At the same moment I instinctively glanced towards his portrait. What I saw struck me dumb. A rush of blood, at fever heat, dispelled the numbing influence of the chill breath that had seemed to freeze me.

I have said the lamp was lighted; but it was only that I might read with comfort, for the violet twilight was still so full of sunset that the room was not dark. But as I looked at the picture I saw it had undergone a strange change. I saw it as plainly as possible. It was no delusion, coined for the eye by the brain.

I saw, in the place of George's head, a grinning skull! I stared at it hard; but it was no trick of fancy. I could see the hollow orbits, the gleaming teeth, the fleshless cheekbones—it was the head of death!

Without saying a word, I rose from my chair and walked straight up to the painting. As I drew nearer a sort of mist seemed to pass before it; and as I stood close to it, I saw only the face of George. The spectral skull had vanished.

"Poor George!" I said unconsciously.

Lettie looked up. The tone of my voice had alarmed her, the expression of my face did not reassure her.

"What do you mean? Have you heard anything? Oh, Robert, in mercy tell me!"

She got up and came over to me and, laying her hands on my arm, looked up into my face imploringly.

"No, my dear; how should I hear? Only I could not help thinking of the privation and discomfort he must have gone through. I was reminded of it by the cold—"

"Cold!" said Harry, who had left the window by this time. "Cold! what on earth are you talking about? Cold, such an evening as this! You must have had a touch of ague, I should think."

"Both Lettie and I felt it bitterly cold a minute or two ago. Did not you feel it?"

"Not a bit; and as I was three parts out of the window I ought to have felt it if anyone did."

It was curious, but that strange chill had been felt only in the room. It was not the night wind, but some supernatural breath connected with the dread apparition I had seen. It was, indeed, the chill of polar winter—the icy shadow of the frozen North.

"What is the day of the month, Harry?" I asked.

"Today—the 23rd, I think," he answered; then added, taking up the newspaper I had been reading: "Yes, here you are. Tuesday, February the 23rd, if the *Daily News* tells truth, which I suppose it does. Newspapers can afford to tell the truth about dates, whatever they may do about art." Harry had been rather roughly handled by the critic of a morning paper for one of his pictures a few days before, and he was a little angry with journalism generally.

Presently Lettie left the room, and I told Harry what I had felt and seen, and told him to take note of the date, for I feared that some mischance had befallen George.

"I'll put it down in my pocket-book, Bob. But you and Lettie must have had a touch of the cold shivers, and your stomach or fancy misled you—they're the same thing, you know. Besides, as regards the picture, there's nothing in that! There is a skull there, of course. As Tennyson says:

'Any face, however full,
  Padded round with flesh and fat,
  Is but modelled on a skull.'

The skull's there—just as in even good figure-subject the nude is there under the costumes. You fancy that is a mere coat of paint. Nothing of the kind! Art lives, sir! That is just as much a real head as yours is with all the muscles and bones, just the same. That's what makes the difference between art and rubbish."

This was a favourite theory of Harry's, who had not yet developed from the dreamer into the worker. As I did not care to argue with him, I allowed the subject to drop after we had written down the date in our pocket-books. Lettie sent down word presently that she did not feel well and had gone to bed. My wife came down presently and asked what had happened. She had been up with the children and had gone in to see what was the matter with Lettie.

"I think it was very imprudent to sit with the window open, dear. I know the evenings are warm, but the night air strikes cold at times—at any rate, Lettie seems to have caught a violent cold, for she is shivering very much. I am afraid she has got a chill from the open windows."

I did not say anything to her then, except that both Lettie and I had felt a sudden coldness; for I did not care to enter into an explanation again, for I could see Harry was inclined to laugh at me for being so superstitious.

At night, however, in our own room, I told my wife what had occurred, and what my apprehensions were. She was so upset and alarmed that I almost repented having done so.

The next morning Lettie was better again, and as we did not either of us refer to the events of the preceding night the circumstance appeared to be forgotten by us all.

But from that day I was ever inwardly dreading the arrival of bad news. And at last it came, as I expected.

One morning, just as I was coming downstairs to breakfast, there came a knock at the door, and Harry made his appearance. It was a very early visit from him, for he generally used to spend his mornings at the studio, and drop in on his way home at night.

He was looking pale and agitated.

"Lettie's not down, is she, yet?" he asked; and then, before I could answer, added another question:

"What newspaper do you take?"

"The *Daily News*," I answered. "Why?"

"She's not down?"

"No."

"Thank God! Look here!"

He took a paper from his pocket and gave it to me, pointing out a short paragraph at the bottom of one of the columns.

I knew what was coming the moment he spoke about Lettie.

The paragraph was headed, 'Fatal Accident to one of the Officers of the *Pioneer* Expedition Ship'. It stated that news had been received at the Admiralty stating that the expedition had failed to find the missing crews, but had come upon some traces of them. Want of stores and necessaries had compelled them to turn back without following those traces up; but the commander was anxious, as soon as the ship could be refitted, to go out and take up the trail where he left it. An unfortunate accident had deprived him of one of his most promising officers, Lieutenant

Mason, who was precipitated from an iceberg and killed while out shooting with the surgeon. He was beloved by all, and his death had flung a gloom over the gallant little troop of explorers.

"It's not in the *News* today, thank goodness, Bob," said Harry, who had been searching that paper while I was reading the one he brought—"but you must keep a sharp look-out for some days and not let Lettie see it when it appears, as it is certain to do sooner or later."

Then we both of us looked at each other with tears in our eyes. "Poor George!—poor Lettie!" we sighed softly.

"But she must be told at some time or other?" I said despairingly.

"I suppose so," said Harry; "but it would kill her to come on it suddenly like this. Where's your wife?"

She was with the children, but I sent up for her and told her the ill-tidings.

She had a hard struggle to conceal her emotion, for Lettie's sake. But the tears would flow in spite of her efforts.

"How shall I ever find courage to tell her?" she asked. "Hush!" said Harry, suddenly grasping her arm and looking towards the door.

I turned. There stood Lettie, with her face pale as death, with her lips apart, and with a blind look about her eyes. She had come in without our hearing her. We never learnt how much of the story she had overheard; but it was enough to tell her the worst. We all sprang towards her; but she only waved us away, turned round, and went upstairs again without saying a word. My wife hastened up after her and found her on her knees by the bed, insensible.

The doctor was sent for, and restoratives were promptly administered. She came to herself again, but lay dangerously ill for some weeks from the shock.

It was about a month after she was well enough to come downstairs again that I saw in the paper an announcement of the arrival of the *Pioneer*. The news had no interest for any of us now, so I said nothing about it. The mere mention of the vessel's name would have caused the poor girl pain.

One afternoon shortly after this, as I was writing a letter, there came a loud knock at the front door. I looked up from my writing and listened; for the voice which enquired if I was in sounded strange, but yet not altogether unfamiliar. As I looked up, puzzling whose it could he, my eye rested accidentally upon poor George's portrait. Was I dreaming or awake?

I have told you that the one hand was resting on a sword. I could see now distinctly that the forefinger was raised, as if in warning. I looked at it hard, to assure myself it was no fancy, and then I perceived, standing out bright and distinct on the pale face, two large drops, as if of blood.

I walked up to it, expecting the appearance to vanish, as the skull had done. It did not vanish; but the uplifted finger resolved itself into a little white moth which had settled on the canvas. The red drops were fluid, and certainly not blood, though I was at a loss for the time to account for them.

The moth seemed to be in a torpid state, so I took it off the picture and placed it under an inverted wine-glass on the mantelpiece. All this took less time to do than to describe. As I turned from the mantelpiece the servant brought in a card, saying the gentleman was waiting in the hall to know if I would see him.

On the card was the name of 'Vincent Grieve, of the exploring vessel *Pioneer*'.

"Thank Heaven, Lettie is out," thought I; and then added aloud to the servant, "Show him in here; and Jane, if your mistress and Miss Lettie come in before the gentle-man goes, tell them I have someone with me on business and do not wish to be disturbed."

I went to the door to meet Grieve. As he crossed the threshold, and before he could have seen the portrait, he stopped, shuddered and turned white, even to his thin lips.

"Cover that picture before I come in," he said hurriedly, in a low voice. "You remember the effect it had upon me. Now, with the memory of poor Mason, it would be worse than ever."

I could understand his feelings better now than at first; for I had come to look on the picture with some awe my-self. So I took the cloth off a little round table that stood under the window and hung it over the portrait.

When I had done so Grieve came in. He was greatly altered. He was thinner and paler than ever; hollow-eyed and hollow-checked. He had acquired a strange stoop, too, and his eyes had lost the crafty look for a look of terror, like that of a hunted beast. I noticed that he kept glancing sideways every instant, as if unconsciously. It looked as if he heard someone behind him.

I had never liked the man; but now I felt an insur-mountable repugnance to him—so great a repugnance that, when I came to think of it, I felt pleased that the incident of covering the picture at his request had led to my not shaking hands with him.

I felt that I could not speak otherwise than coldly to him; indeed, I had to speak with painful plainness.

I told him that, of course, I was glad to see him back, but that I could not ask him to continue to visit us. I should be glad to hear the particulars of poor George's death, but that I could not let him see my sister, and hint-ed, as delicately as I could, at the impropriety of which he had been guilty when he last visited.

He took it all very quietly, only giving a long, weary sigh when I told him I must beg him not to repeat his visit. He looked so weak and ill that I was obliged to ask him to take a glass of wine——an offer which he seemed to accept with great pleasure.

I got out the sherry and biscuits and placed them on the table between us, and he took a glass and drank it off greedily.

It was not without some difficulty that I could get him to tell me of George's death. He related, with evident reluctance, how they had gone out to shoot a white bear which they had seen on an iceberg stranded along the shore. The top of the berg was ridged like the roof of a house, sloping down on one side to the edge of a tremendous overhanging precipice. They had scrambled along the ridge in order to get nearer the game, when George incautiously ventured on the sloping side.

"I called out to him", said Grieve, "and begged him to come back, but too late. The surface was as smooth and slippery as glass. He tried to turn back, but slipped and fell. And then began a horrible scene. Slowly, slowly, but with ever-increasing motion, he began to slide down towards the edge. There was nothing to grasp at—no irregularity or projection on the smooth face of the ice. I tore off my coat, and hastily attaching it to the stock of my gun, pushed the latter towards him; but it did not reach far enough. Before I could lengthen it, by tying my cravat to it, he had slid yet further away, and more quickly. I shouted in agony; but there was no one within hearing.

He, too, saw his fate was sealed; and he could only tell me to bring his last farewell to you, and—and to her!"— Here Grieve's voice broke—"and it was all over! He clung to the edge of the precipice instinctively for one second, and was gone!"

Just as Grieve uttered the last word, his jaw fell; his eyeballs seemed ready to start from his head; he sprang to his feet, pointed at something behind me, and then flinging up his arms, fell, with a scream, as if he had been shot. He was seized with an epileptic fit.

I instinctively looked behind me as I hurried to raise him from the floor. The cloth had fallen from the picture, where the face of George, made paler than ever by the gouts of red, looked sternly down.

I rang the bell. Luckily, Harry had come in; and, when the servant told him what was the matter, he came in and assisted me in restoring Grieve to consciousness. Of course, I covered the painting up again.

When he was quite himself again, Grieve told me he was subject to fits occasionally.

He seemed very anxious to learn if he had said or done anything extraordinary while he was in the fit, and appeared reassured when I said he had not. He apologized for the trouble he had given, and said as soon as he was strong enough he would take his leave. He was leaning on the mantelpiece as he said this. The little white moth caught his eye.

"So you have had someone else from the *Pioneer* here before me?" he said, nervously.

I answered in the negative, asking what made him think so.

"Why, this little white moth is never found in such southern latitudes. It is one of the last signs of life northward. Where did you get it?"

"I caught it here, in this room," I answered.

"That is very strange. I never heard of such a thing before. We shall hear of showers of blood soon, I should not wonder."

"What do you mean?" I asked.

"Oh, these little fellows emit little drops of a red-look-ing fluid at certain seasons, and sometimes so plentifully that the superstitious think it is a shower of blood. I have seen the snow quite stained in places. Take care of it, it is a rarity in the south."

I noticed, after he left, which he did almost imme-diately, that there was a drop of red fluid on the marble under the wine-glass. The blood-stain on the picture was accounted for; but how came the moth here?

And there was another strange thing about the man, which I had scarcely been able to assure myself of in the room, where there were cross-lights, but about which there was no possible mistake, when I saw him walking away up the street.

"Harry, here—quick!" I called to my brother, who at once came to the window. "You're an artist, tell me, is there anything strange about that man?"

"No; nothing that I can see," said Harry, but then sud-denly, in an altered tone, added, "Yes, there is. By Jove, he has a double shadow!"

That was the explanation of his sidelong glances, of the habitual stoop. There was a something always at his side, which none could see, but which cast a shadow.

He turned, presently, and saw us at the window. Instantly, he crossed the road to the shady side of the street. I told Harry all that had passed, and we agreed that it would be as well not to say a word to Lettie.

Two days later, when I returned from a visit to Harry's studio, I found the whole house in confusion.

I learnt from Lettie that while my wife was upstairs, Grieve had called, had not waited for the servant to announce him, but had walked straight into the dining-room, where Lettie was sitting.

She noticed that he avoided looking at the picture, and, to make sure of not seeing it, had seated himself on the sofa just beneath it. He had then, in spite of Lettie's angry remonstrances, renewed his offer of love, strengthening it finally by assuring her that poor George with his dying breath had implored him to seek her, and watch over her, and marry her.

"I was so indignant I hardly knew how to answer him," said Lettie. "When, suddenly, just as he uttered the last words, there came a twang like the breaking of a guitar—and—I hardly know how to describe it—but the portrait had fallen, and the corner of the heavy frame had struck him on the head, cutting it open, and rendering him insensible."

They had carried him upstairs, by the direction of the doctor, for whom my wife at once sent on hearing what had occurred. He was laid on the couch in my dressing-room, where I went to see him. I intended to reproach him for coming to the house, despite my prohibition, but I found him delirious. The doctor said it was a queer case; for, though the blow was a severe one, it was hardly enough to account for the symptoms of brain-fever. When he learnt that Grieve had but just returned in the *Pioneer* from the North, he said it was possible that the privation and hardship had told on his constitution and sown the seeds of the malady.

We sent for a nurse, who was to sit up with him, by the doctor's directions.

The rest of my story is soon told. In the middle of the night I was roused by a loud scream. I slipped on my clothes, and rushed out to find the nurse, with Lettie in her arms, in a faint. We carried her into her room, and then the nurse explained the mystery to us.

It appears that about midnight Grieve sat up in bed, and began to talk. And he said such terrible things that the nurse became alarmed. Nor was she much reassured when she became aware that the light of her single candle flung what seemed to be two shadows of the sick man on the wall.

Terrified beyond measure, she had crept into Lettie's room, and confided her fears to her; and Lettie, who was a courageous and kindly girl, dressed herself, and said she would sit with her.

She, too, saw the double shadow—but what she heard was far more terrible.

Grieve was sitting up in bed, gazing at the unseen figure to which the shadow belonged. In a voice that trembled with emotion, he begged the haunting spirit to leave him, and prayed its forgiveness.

"You know the crime was not premeditated. It was a sudden temptation of the devil that made me strike the blow, and fling you over the precipice. It was the devil tempting me with the recollection of her exquisite face— of the tender love that might have been mine, but for you. But she will not listen to me. See, she turns away from me, as if she knew I was your murderer, George Mason!"

It was Lettie who repeated in a horrified whisper this awful confession.

I could see it all now! As I was about to tell Lettie of the many strange things I had concealed from her, the nurse, who had gone to see her patient, came running back in alarm.

Vincent Grieve had disappeared. He had risen in his delirious terror, had opened the window, and leaped out. Two days later his body was found in the river.

A curtain hangs now before poor George's portrait, though it is no longer connected with any supernatural marvels; and never, since the night of Vincent Grieve's death, have we seen aught of that most mysterious haunting presence—the Shadow of a Shade.

A Story of a Shadow
Rebecca Harding Davis
1872

The house stands in a quiet by-street in Philadelphia. After being vacant for many years it was bought by C. W. Knapp, a widower, and teacher of quiz-classes in one of the medical colleges, who took his mother and child there to live. A few months later his cousin, a Miss Demar, from Ohio, came to visit him, and soon perceived the singular hold the house had upon him.

"There are inexplicable passages in the Bible," she said, speaking of the matter afterward, "which refer to certain buildings as possessing life of their own. They had human diseases, and were blessed and cursed like men by the priesthood. This house reminded me of those Jewish buildings. It affected me from the day I entered it as an inferior grade of life would do; an animal's—a dog's, for instance. Of course, looking at it rationally, the impression became the merest absurdity; but it always came back, do what I would. It was not a disagreeable impression in itself."

She said nothing of this fancy to Mr. Knapp, accounting for his interest in his new possession on more rational grounds.

"To ordinary eyes it's an ordinary house enough," he used to say as they came home together in the evening twilight. "There it is: dull red brick, based and capped with brown stone; shutters dark and heavy; high stoop. Yet the moment my eye rested on it I said, 'There's a house could tell a story if it would.' I was on tenter-hooks until I found whether mother would like it. I think she's very comfortable in it, Mary, eh?"—anxiously.

"Very comfortable, Charley."

Knapp scans it complacently as they come up the street. The yellow sunset flames up behind it in the cold sky, throwing it into bold relief; in front the row of maples rustle cheerfully their few red, ragged leaves in the nipping air. Nobody but Mary Demar knew how that pile of dull red bricks had suddenly barred his life and absorbed all his hopes and plans. She looks curiously at the stout little man beside her, with his jaunty black dress and felt hat set on the back of his head, the broad rim making a frame for the fat, high-colored face, and twinkling blue eyes under their spectacles. They had been intimate as brothers all of their lives. She knew how the money had been saved, penny by penny, since he was a boy, on which he married. For since he was a boy there had been but one woman in the world for Charley Knapp, and when she was gone, even his most casual acquaintance knew that it was impossible he would ever marry again. Miss Demar had come to him a year ago, when she heard his wife was dead. She found him quiet and silent. "I am stifling here," he said to her. "I'll take what money I have and go out of the country with the boy. My only chance is to get away out of doors." Yet she had scarcely reached home when she heard that he had put all his savings into this house, and settled down for life.

"You changed your mind about going abroad, Charley?" she said now, gently.

He did not answer for a moment. "Yes. Well, mother was alone, and fancied I would be out of temptation if she had me in charge. Cain vagabondizing over the world was the only idea my journey suggested to her, so I gave it up."

His sorrow, then, was to be a sealed subject even to her. Mary was rebuffed, but the rebuff pleased her. She leaned more heavily upon his arm. Knapp's thinking, as usual, went on in his face, to be seen of all men, while he kept time to it by whistling under his breath and rattling his cane on the tree-boxes. He always carried a noise with him, like any other overgrown boy.

"It's curious, though," he broke out at last, "how that journey I did not take clings to me. Sometimes now, when I go into the halls, I think that here the sea was lost, and the nights on deck, the moon whitening the rim of water; and when we are at breakfast in the pretty dining-room I think how it swallowed up China and her wall and pagodas, and California canyons, Yosemite, and all. It's damnably selfish in me, but it makes me like the house. There are bits of the whole world built into the walls for me. Then," energetically, "it's such a home for her and Tom! When it's time for the boy to rough it at school, there's the garden to bring him back to Nature. Why, the smell of those bean-pods and grass after a rain would make the worst man choke in his wickedness! I've been thinking, too, as soon as he's old enough to want his friends about him, I'd run those side rooms into one, for dancing. He'll be a social fellow, Tom. I see that in his eye. When the dog marries there'll be plenty of room for him to bring his wife home—and their children, if God sends them any. Here we are, '130!'" glancing up over the door. "To think it's nothing but a pile of bricks and a number to people. Hey, Mary?"

"It would certainly be very inconsistent if the house were not numbered," said his mother, who was waiting inside. "The mat, Charles, my dear! Have some care for the carpets." Charley caught her in his arms and whisked her round. She began to laugh, but choked it off with a sigh. She was her son duplicated in caps and petticoats. Nature meant her to be dumpy and good-tempered, but her face had been twisted by some bastard notion of godliness into a perpetual penitence and woeful looking-for of judgment. She also protested against the sins of the world by a nasal twang—the ghost of a bagpipe. It was in play now. "Some of your boon companions are here for supper, as usual, Charles."

Knapp peeped through the open parlor door at a couple of half-fledged medical students guiltily conscious of their neckties and best coats. "All right, boys! I'll bring Tom and be with you in a moment!" He met Mary a moment afterward, with Tom astride of his shoulders. "They'll bore you horribly," anxiously. "But you'll not mind. There's such a lot of fellows like that in the college—strangers—got no mother here, nor friends, d'ye see—no place open for them but the theatres or rum-shops. I try to make it like home here. They're a little heavy, to be sure. But you'll like the boys, even the flashiest and most priggish among them."

"I'll come down and give you some music, Charley."

"All right."

Mrs. Knapp came into Mary's room and dumped herself with a wretched thud on a chair. "So it goes! Billiards, chess, pipes, night after night. They've not got to drinking yet, but what is tobacco but a mean makeshift for liquor? You'll say why don't I talk to Charles? But what does Charles care for *my* opinion? He has these men roystering with him for breakfast, dinner, and supper. He's introduced them to young girls, and says he hopes love affairs will come of it. Love affairs! Yes; and even with that the half's not told. Why, he has brought actors here. They wore their street clothes, to be sure, and did not play any of their fantastic tricks before me, I assure you. But to think it is not fifteen months since poor Sophy was laid to rest! Ah, child, now you see what man's love is worth!"

Miss Demar nodded, twisting her long hair about her head.

"Up from the ear, Mary—there. Not that Charles wasn't a sincere mourner at first. But I did hope Sophy's death would have been a call to his Master's service. I intended him always for a missionary, you know."

"Yes."

"Yes, Charles has been my cross. The Lord knows wherewith to try us," wiping her eyes. Miss Demar turned to speak, but changing her mind put on her collar. "Not but that he's a good son, Mary; but when I think of him as unregenerate, all his kindness to the poor but filthy rags— Now there's your aunt Johns. She gave up her son to carry the banner of the Cross to Africa. But when Charles wanted to leave me, it was to go gaping about at hills and sunsets and Papistical pictures—"

It was at this moment that Miss Demar, who had been standing motionless for a few seconds, turned on her with a startled face. "What is it that is in this house?" she said.

"You saw it?" Mrs. Knapp started up, looking from side to side. "I'm sure I don't know what you mean," petulantly. "There's a story that a child was killed here, or a bride—some ridiculous report that has hung about the house for years. You've heard the story and fancied you saw something."

"No, I never heard it; and I really saw nothing." Miss Demar, ashamed of having betrayed herself, tried to go on with her dressing, but her fingers shook and the blood burned in them.

Like most American women, Mary Demar's nerves lay on the surface, charged like the wires of an electric battery; but she had steady eyes and a broad chest, and usually managed to keep them in order. As soon as the dribble of talk behind her stopped, and she was left alone, she sat down to reason with herself. She had literally seen and heard nothing. In the midst of her annoyance with Charley's mother there had come upon her the sudden consciousness of a something present in the house, which was apart from its bricks and mortar and from its human inmates—some strength, vehement and kindly, which, as if for a whim, had turned her face to face with the poor old woman, showed her gray hairs, the honest love for her boy under her bigotry, the grave not far from her. It might have been Charley's self taking part with his mother.

"It certainly was not *I*," said Miss Demar with a shrug. "Such charity is not in me."

She began after that to ask questions carelessly about the house and its history, wondering herself at the hold the matter had taken upon her. Mary Demar had been betrothed for years to a man whom she loved with her whole heart. It was but a few days ago that she had dis-covered a fact in his early life which made him unfit to be her husband. It was not natural that idle vagaries about an old house should interest her now. Yet she could not shake them off; there was, too, an unaccountable feeling that this mystery concerned her personally.

"What do you know of this house?" she asked of Charley one evening as they were watching the sunset from the garden.

"Nothing. When the searches were made to establish a clear title, oddly enough it was impossible to find out when it was built or by whom. People had a vague dis-like to living in it; it lay vacant for years in this crowded neighborhood. Old Seth—Kenyon's protégé, you know—"

Miss Demar's countenance changed suddenly. "Yes, I know Seth."

"He has some ancient ghost story about it. The vaguest nonsense! To my notion it's the most cheerful place I was ever in. This garden, for instance."

Now the garden was a straight, long strip of ground, enclosed by a high, solid fence, which shaded the trim parterres of their neighbors—a strange, solitary place, which seemed to have brought its alien air into the city. The damp grass yielding to their feet was brown with the field clover; wild honeysuckles and grapes, such as tangle the hedges in unused lanes, grew along the borders; rows of hollyhocks stood like sentinels, turning their watchful faces toward the house; the common June roses, which all summer long sweeten and redden forgotten graves in country churchyards, sent their perfume up to it. Even the flowers had a friendly message for Knapp's home. The lighted windows shone coldly from garret to basement on one end of the dusky garden; beyond the other end a little way, the Schuylkill rolled, laden with craft, down to the bay; the tall masts of the clustered ships struck fine black lines up into the yellow evening sky. The air was damp but quiet; even the floating white ball of dandelion seed scarcely moved in it over their heads.

"I wish I could hear that ghost story," said Miss Demar.

"Very well. We'll go down to Seth," glancing at a little brick house beyond the garden. "By the by, Kenyon will be surprised to find us so near the old man."

Miss Demar stopped. "You don't mean— Is Mr. Kenyon coming here?"

"Now don't be vexed, Mary. 'Pon my soul, I never said come. I only wrote on business yesterday, and mentioned that you were here. Why not? One always thinks of you two as so nearly husband and wife that these petty formalities seem out of place to my notion. It's half a year to the wedding, and the poor devil's there, working night and day to be ready for it. Why shouldn't he have a glimpse of you to keep his heart up?"

"It was a kind thought of you, Charley," said Miss Demar after a pause. Her coldness irritated Knapp. He always

had doubted whether she was quite competent to appre-
ciate a man like Kenyon. Charley was very fond of Mary,
but she was only a younger brother to him. He had knuck-
led with her at marbles and talked over his business to
her ever since they were grown. Coming too close, he had
grown blind to the beauty in her thin, singular face, and
to the indescribable sway which she held over other men.

"Here she is, with her admirable sense, downright as a
sledge-hammer," he thought, as they walked over the grass,
"and Kenyon full of subtle delicate fancies. He'll be dashed
to pieces against her admirable sense. It's the old story of
the clay and porcelain pitcher again." The next minute,
full of remorse at his own harsh judgment of her, he caught
her hand and drew it affectionately through his arm.

"What is it, Moll?" He fancied she looked worn and
tired.

"I was thinking of Seth." She stopped, hesitated.
Knapp's instincts were keen; whatever question she was
about to ask, he said, for some reason imported much to
her. "What do you know of him, Charley?"

"Very little. Less than I ought, for Kenyon put him in a
manner under my care, years ago. But the old fellow heeds
no charity and keeps his affairs to himself. Scotch-Irish,
you know. I used to look in on him now and then, until we
moved into this house. Now of course I see him every day."

"You do not know then what—what connection there
was between him and Mr. Kenyon? Would he be likely to
know anything of John's early life?"

"No, certainly not. Kenyon, as you know, is from
Carolina; his family dies out with him. High-blooded,
high-handed old race, the Kenyons, I've heard. I've often
told John both his virtues and his faults were those of
civilization pushed too far. It's odd, isn't it, that American families won't bear high culture for several generations? The physical stock gives out unless inferior blood is

brought in." Knapp began to stammer, remembering suddenly that Miss Demar could hardly claim to belong to
her lover's Brahmin caste. "What could Seth know about
him?" he added hurriedly. "Lived all his life in that shanty.
Kenyon and I met him accidentally on the street here one
day, and John mentioned him as a person who had done
him a kindness." Miss Demar stopped at this, coming into
the path before him in her breathless eagerness to hear. "A
kindness—where was I? What the deuce can this matter
to you Mary? He said, if I remember rightly, something
about an annuity he paid him, and asked me to have an
oversight of the old fellow, and if he were in want to send
him word."

"Mr. Kenyon is charitable," bitterly.

"Why do you use that tone about him? What possible
sinister motive could he have in his kindness to the old
man?"

Miss Demar was silent. But Knapp noticed the glitter in her half-shut eye, and an unusual steadiness in her
walk. With all her sense she had a temper of which Charley stood in wholesome awe. He quickened his pace, and
began to talk with a sudden gust of cheerfulness. "Now I
do suppose Kenyon did not dwell on the subject because
it was a matter of charity, and for the same reason I never
mentioned it to Seth. There he goes. Hello, Seth!"

"You need not call him. I've changed my mind. I'm going into the house."

"God bless me, these women! Don't hurt the old fellow's feelings, Moll."

Miss Demar turned at that and came back. She was
miserable, and in a passion that she was miserable. Charley, man-like, only thought how lack of temper improved
her looks. No doubt Kenyon would think her delicate face
lovely with the hair rumpled about it, and her dark eyes
full of unshed tears. The old sailmaker, meanwhile, came

hobbling up with a broad smile, carrying a bucket of coals in either hand. He was generally watching the garden for Knapp in the evening, to "have a conferrence on the political sitooation," in which Seth doled out the views of his oracle, the "Review," of which he chewed the cud perpetually.

"We came to find you, Seth. I want you to raise the best ghost you can out of the house yonder for this young lady."

Seth bowed, but his mouth suddenly dropped at the corners. "You ben't afeard of sperrits then, Mr. Knapp?"

"Not much. But—what is it, Mary!"

Miss Demar drew up her shawl and stood erect. She, stooping forward, looking at Seth as he leaned on the gate, the low light bringing his short heavy body and square head into full relief, as if she would have dragged the secret of his life out. He nodded to her, smiling.

"Miss Demar were in my house the other evening, and we discussed different matters. But not sperrits."

She laughed and said "No," with a sudden light-heart-edness. Now that she was face to face with the old man, the dread that haunted her appeared utterly fantastic and impossible. He was just at home from his day's work, and, instead of going to bed as the other workmen did, had washed and brushed himself. A scuffed black suit of Knapp's was stretched over his broad, rawboned body, the big wrists and ankles grinning bare with a grim sort of protest. A thin fringe of white hair and whisker was brushed with a soldierly air about his high-featured face, red and rasped with soap, on the top of which an old beaver hat of Charley's was set jauntily. At every turn the body and brain of the old man betrayed, she fancied, the lifelong, dreadful drainage of poverty—betrayed it in nothing so much as in his aping the habits and gestures of gentlemen, and in the pitiful swagger with which he wore his begged clothes.

And this man she had believed to be John Kenyon's father.

Until Knapp told it to her a few moments ago, she had never heard this story of the family to which Kenyon belonged. But without it she recognized the absurdity of any connection between her lover and the sailmaker. Kenyon was a quiet homely man, thorough-bred as no other whom she had ever met. His enemies might question his intellect or kindliness; but whatever else he might be, that he was the product of generations of affluence and culture was a fact so patent that no one could doubt it—not the stranger who passed him on the street. His extravagance, his domineering temper, his morbid fastidiousness of taste, were all diseased outgrowths from that one cause, as Knapp had shrewdly noted.

Miss Demar forgot the proof which half an hour ago had seemed so inexorably sure to her. When she was in Seth's house the other evening a small photograph had fallen from one of his books into her lap. It was undoubtedly that of Kenyon as a much younger man. On the back a few lines were scrawled signed "Your son." There could be no question of the writing. She knew it better than her own. There was, too, the odd subtle likeness in the old man's face to the younger one, which came at times in an uneasy dropping of the eye or pose of the head. It was not there now. Miss Demar, when she missed it, blushed and trembled as though her lover had kissed her, and was unbelieving and happy.

When she turned to Charley and the old man she found them fully launched on the ghost story.

"You see, Miss Demar," said Seth, "it's an old neighborhood on the bank here, and them sort of stories hang

around old houses like spiders' webs agen the wall. Yon's
the room," pointing to a chamber on whose windows the
rising moon began to glitter. "There's no figger seen there,
howsoever, nor sound heard." So intent was he on his story
that he spat deliberately on each of his palms as if he were
moistening his thread, and rubbed them, while slowly
eying his hearers.

"What is there, then?"

"A shadder, sir," solemnly. "To them as is left alone in
that room there comes a shadder on the wall. Nothing more."

"The murdered man, I suppose," said Mary cheerfully.
Seth did not relish her cheerfulness. "I've no knowledge
of my own what it is, ma'am. But I've heerd say that every
man has a ghost that follers him—the shadder of them that
he has wronged. It comes into sight to him on that wall."

"By George!" laughed Knapp. "I'll put Kenyon there to
sleep when he comes, Mary. He shall have a fair tug with
his ghost."

"Kenyon?" said Seth, and then was quickly silent. Miss
Demar watched him.

"You have no more to tell us of the ghost, then?" she
said, to try him. He turned a countenance to her which
might have been cut out of wood, it was so vacant.

"Miss Demar spoke to you, Seth."

"I beg your pardon ma'am. My wits was wool-gatherin'.
Regardin' the ghost? No, I know nothin' more. I believe
I'll be goin' now," taking up his bucket. But he lingered,
fingering the gate-latch.

"I'll send you the morning's paper over, Seth."

"Much obleeged, sir. You said," in a forced deliberate
tone, "that a gentleman was to sleep in that room—Mr.
Kenyon. Is he with you now? You'll excuse me for askin',"
he added hastily, "but I—I had some acquaintance with
him fifteen years ago."

"To be sure you had! Why, you've no idea how kindly Mr. Kenyon spoke of you to me, Seth—charged me to have an oversight over you, and so on. You were able to oblige him once in some way, I think he mentioned?"

"Did he put it in that way?" with a queer flickering smile. "No, it was no obligation."

"Well, Mr. Kenyon is a warm-hearted man, and very likely to exaggerate any little service. You couldn't have a more generous friend in your old age. And you're well on to seventy now, Seth."

The old man straightened his back, and put his hand mechanically to his hips. "I'm quite able to work for the little I eat," he said quietly. "I'll not be likely to need money from Mr. Kenyon. I'd be sorry if you gave him that impression. But when he comes, if you'll mention to him—" He stopped for a full minute. "If you'll mention to him that Seth Barnes is livin' yet, in the house where he used to know him, I'll be obleeged to you. You'll leave it to his own free will to come or not—if you please, sir?"

"Certainly, Seth, certainly. But Kenyon's the last man in the world to be uncivil to an old friend because he has not prospered like himself. You mistake him, Barnes."

Seth nodded gravely and, buckets in hand, limped away. "Well, really," said Knapp, "I thought Kenyon paid the old fellow an annuity. There must have been a mistake about it; I did not tell him John was coming to-night. I had a telegram from him; he'll be here in an hour, I thought I'd surprise you"—feeling with a certain pleasure that Miss Demar trembled and that her hand was cold. Her common sense was not so invincible, after all.

"We'll sit here and wait for him." He drew her to a bench, and remained silent. But Miss Demar was restless and impatient. She must keep off the one fact that filled the future for her. Tomorrow would prove whether Kenyon was a true man or the basest of frauds. She had but him in the world; she was an orphan, without kinsfolk.

Knapp sat smoking, nursing one foot on his knee, and glancing, she noticed, now and then, up at the two windows on which the moon cast a mysterious glitter.

"Confess that there is some reality in Seth's ghost story to you, after all, Charley," touching his arm.

"Nonsense! I never heard that story of the shadow. I did not even know it was to that room they had fastened the ghost. There is a curious fact about that room—a coincidence. Not that I believe in such rubbish as spirits, you know—"

"Of course not. But tell me the story."

"Two or three months after we moved into the house, I brought Russell Sands home one night. You remember him, don't you?"

"Very well. A slight fair-haired boy, with an innocent face, like a girl's?"

"Yes, that was Russell. Thorough mother's boy. Not a prig, or goodish either—as manly, spirited a little fellow as lived. That was four or five years ago. His mother was a widow, and she had but him." Knapp shifted his foot to the other knee, stroking it for a minute or two. "Well," hurriedly, "I lost sight of him for years, until I found him one night, as I was coming home, lying drunk on a market-house stall. He had grown out of all likeness to himself into a swollen bloated animal. He did not know me; I was glad of that. I brought him home and put him in that room to bed, and I went down below to smoke. About one o'clock (I was sitting quite quiet, somehow I couldn't sleep) I heard a noise overhead, a sudden gasp, as of fright or horror, and then there was a long silence. Presently the door of his chamber opened and Russell came down the stairs. He was perfectly sober, to my astonishment—quite master of himself. I shook hands with him and brought

him in. He did not ask how he came there; sat down and
talked in his usual self-possessed way on politics and the
news of the day; but he was terribly shaken, and I saw
there was some under-thought kept down, which now and
then threatened to master him. I went down to the kitchen
and broiled a bit of steak and made a strong cup of coffee
for him, but he couldn't eat. He said, 'You'll sit up with
me until morning, Uncle Charley? I would prefer not to
be alone.' That was the only reference either of us made
to his condition. The college boys have fallen into the way
of calling me that, you see, and I like it; it makes them
somehow free to ask help when they need it. But Russell is
a man to whom you could not offer help. When the first
streak of dawn came, he got up. I had brushed the mud
off his overcoat without his knowledge. We stood in the
front door together. The morning wind was keen. 'It will
be a pleasant day,' he said, trying to be careless and easy. 'I
thank you sincerely, Mr. Knapp, for your—your hospitality.' I looked up at the great broad-shouldered fellow, and
thought how death was dragging him down, and not a soul
to stretch a hand to him. But I had to be guarded. I took
hold of one of the lapels of his coat. 'Can I do anything
for you—in any way, Russell?' I said, 'I'm an old friend
of your father's, you know, my lad.' 'No, I thank you,' he
said dryly; but he stood looking abstractedly down the
street, and turned presently. 'A curious thing happened to
me last night,' trying to bluff it off with a careless laugh,
but I saw the poor boy wanted to open his heart to me if
he knew how. 'Did you ever hear that that room of yours
was an uncanny sort of place? I woke suddenly with my
eyes on the blank wall, and do you know the picture that
hangs there I could have sworn was myself? As I used to be
five years ago—not *this*,' with a gesture of terrible meaning over his face and bloated figure—'the Russell Sands
now dead.' 'He's not dead,' I broke out, for I could keep

quiet no longer. 'You can go back to your old self, dear boy, if you will.' 'O God! if I could believe that!' he cried, with a sort of sob. But in a moment or two he was cool and quiet again, buttoned up his coat, and talked of the weather until he bade me good-by. He held my hand a minute. 'There is no use talking of these things,' he said, 'but if ever I can go back to the boy I once was, I'll come to you, Uncle Charley.'"

"Well, and then?" said Mary.

"He went away with that. For a long time I could find no trace of him; but I heard of him finally out West. Kenyon had secured a place for him where he could free himself from his old associates, and had seen him last July. He reported the poor boy as hard at work; thin as a rail, his jaws sunken like death's, but his eyes clear and steady. It had been a long battle, but Kenyon thought he had won it. 'See Mr. Knapp when you go back,' he said; 'tell him I'm not ready to meet him yet, but I mean to come. I'll come!' wrenching his hand with a nervous laugh."

"Don't put him in the haunted chamber when he comes. Don't let him see the picture again and find that his fancy was only a fancy."

Knapp laughed uneasily. "Now there is where the curious part of the story comes in. The wall is a blank wall. *There was no picture there.*"

"Then it was the shadow of the man he had wronged the most that he saw." Miss Demar rose.

"Tut, tut! Now, Molly, you don't pretend to believe that folly of Seth's?" She took a turn up the long path for lack of argument. But to Miss Demar the point of the story lay in the part Kenyon had taken in it. She thought she had looked at him on every side, as journalist, treasurer, clerk, *homme de société,* and lover; but doing good? a philanthropist? The role was a new one. She sat down to think it over.

"He went to John?" she said when Knapp came back.

"Yes. Men are very apt to go to Kenyon who are in scrapes. Especially lately. He was the first mover in that scheme for aiding discharged convicts, you know?"

Of course he was! Of course he was the one to whom all men would turn for aid. A gush of tears choked her throat and eyes. The idea of Kenyon's benevolence was new to her a minute ago, but it had sprouted up already, like Jack's scarlet beans, as high as heaven.

"No men," began Knapp, vehemently, "has a tenderer heart than— There he is!"

There he was: a sallow, thin man, carefully dressed in white linen, picking his steps down the walk to avoid the dust. Miss Demar tried to rise, but her knees shook under her, and a gusty heat went through her limbs. Charley was off like a flash, leading him down, wrenching his hand, watching him with any amount of inarticulate clucks and chuckles. How underbred and unmanly he always was beside Kenyon! Miss Demar also thought of the porcelain pitcher and the clay jug.

"Here she is! here she is! It's dark here, and your eyes are dulled coming out of the glare of the gas."

He brought Kenyon up to Miss Demar, and then was bolting off with a mumbled apology, when a second glance made him stay. He felt somehow that they would rather not be left alone. "A lover's quarrel, eh?" to himself. "There's a seat, Kenyon. Cursedly hot to-day, travelling, wasn't it? You're just off the cars?"

"No. I came in the afternoon train. I waited to shake off a little of the dust before I came up."

This was not the fiery, impulsive lover of a year ago. Knapp's face burned with the slight to Mary. There was, too, a certain uneasy guardedness about Kenyon which was utterly new in his usual simple, unaffected manner. Knapp, to cover it, rushed into the first subject that came to him.

"I was just giving Mary the account of Russell Sands. You think his reformation is complete?"

"I trust so. Sands can be of great use to our party in that part of Iowa. Just the magnetic sort of power about him that collects and leads weaker young men. I mean to make a lever of him out there as soon as I am sure he can be relied upon. I had that in view in sending him there."

"Politics is a bad field to put a man in who is trying to save himself from the devil of drink," said Knapp hastily.

"Yes. I suppose it is," carelessly. "But what would you do? Clever young fellows who choose that most disgusting mode of suicide are so common this winter in Washington that one grows hardened to them and their fate; while as to the importance of this next election there can be but one opinion."

"By the way, I hear, Kenyon, that if our party go in you are sure of an office here that pays—pays—'pon my soul I forget what, but something stu-pendous. What's in it, eh?"

Kenyon, who had leaned forward and kept his eyes on Miss Demur's face, dimly seen through the darkness, during this speech, waited with a curious anxiety for her to speak. But when she did not, he replied in a dry business tone: "Some such offer was made to me, but I rejected it. I'm in a condition to set my own terms. They must give me an appointment abroad—one that pays equally well, too."

There was that malignant influence astir among them which sometimes makes each pause in the conversation appear significant and oppressive.

Knapp broke the silence each time with a more awkward effort.

"You did not use to care for the loaves and fishes, John," forcing a laugh.

"I've altered, then," dryly. "At my age one grows tired of giving the whole of life to grubbing for the means to sustain it. What a curious place you have *here,*" changing his tone. "There's something unnatural in it; something—I hardly know what it is," looking about him. "The dust and dampness, probably. But this house always affected me strangely."

"Why, my dear fellow, I lived in Germantown when you were here last. You never saw this house before."

"I think I have," said Kenyon quietly, though cursing himself inwardly for his mistake; for he had come fully prepared to face and escape the danger of detection. Knapp's house he knew was near to his father's. What more likely than that Miss Demar should meet the old man and discover his secret?

Kenyon had thrown up all his engagements this morning, and started at a half-hour's notice, though it was the last day of Congress and the culmination of all his plots and wire-pulling for the year was at hand. What was success if this chance robbed him of her? What did she know? He was on guard as never before in his life—eye, ear, every nerve under control, and watching. He could see her face but indistinctly; she had spoken but once to him.

His ready tongue failed him; he sat silent.

"By the way," began Knapp again desperately, "I was talking to Mary just now of your winter's work—discharged convicts, you know."

"Pray do not induce Miss Demar to mistake me for a philanthropist, Charley."

"You did not mean to use them for 'levers,' eh?"

"Not precisely. But I went into the work to strengthen my popularity."

"I don't believe it! You shall not so wrong yourself!"

Miss Demar rose in a heat and walked hastily away. Kenyon rose also, and sat down again. The words thrilled him as with an electric fire.

"She knows nothing. She is safe," he thought. He gave a short, uncadenced laugh. "But it is true for all that," turning to Knapp. "I loathe demagoguism, but I am a demagogue. I hate work, yet I drudge harder than any man in Washington. I used to be *honest,* as men go, but now I cringe and fawn and lie—all for money."

Knapp looked at him in dismay.

"You did not use to care for it."

"I care for her. I care to earn a few years in which to sit down with her, with money and ease to enjoy the world before I go out of it. I mean to wash my hands in innocency as soon as I have the appointment and sit down, as I said, to take 'mine ease in mine inn.'"

Knapp coughed uneasily, jerking at his waistcoat as if it did not fit him. He had keenness enough to see that Kenyon's life had been a fierce, breathless race for one end, and that some obstacle to-night was about to balk him. He knew him to be always a gusty, uncertain fellow, with a temperament either at high tide or dead low ebb, as anybody could see, but he was not used to talk about it to other people. The mental pang must have been extreme that wrenched this vehement egotism from him.

"What in God's name can I do for him?" Knapp repeated blankly to himself.

For ordinary men whose troubles grew out of broken bones or empty pockets he had cures enough, but he looked upon Kenyon as of a different order of being from himself. It was Pegasus, he thought, coming to a cow-doctor for help.

He stood rattling some pennies in his pockets, looking at Kenyon's thin face under the broad Panama hat, turned toward Miss Demar with a cynical, sad smile.

"We'd better join Molly, eh?"

"One minute. There's an old man, Barnes, lives hereabouts somewhere?"

"In the alley—not ten steps from the gate. I told them you'd not forget him—I told him and Mary both. I'm deucedly glad you asked for Seth, do you know, Kenyon?"

"Miss Demar has seen him, then?"

"Oh, of course. He comes to the gate every night for the 'Review.' He has just gone."

"Reads the 'Review' yet, does he?"

Kenyon stopped. For the moment he forgot Knapp, Miss Demar, himself. He only remembered how the old man used to sit waiting at night until he had learned his lesson for school from the "dog-eared" spelling-book, to take his turn at it while the boy played teacher. There was the little kitchen, ship-shape and neat as a man-of-war's deck, the crackling coal fire, the pot of mush simmering on one side for supper when they had finished. How anxious and red the old man's face was as he stammered dully over the unconquerable three syllables. How dull he always was! Kenyon remembered how his boy's heart used to ache and sicken when he first began to understand that his father was dull and poor, and all that it meant to be either. He had dashed the book down one day and caught the old man about the neck, crying out in his impotent rage:

"Why should other men be what they are, and you this, dad? How could God be so unjust as to make such a difference between men?"

"I don't see as He does," the sailmaker said gently. "However, you are to go beyond them all, Jack, and as soon as I can read I mean to take the paper and go through it reg'lar. I'll keep posted that way, so as I'll not shame you."

That was twenty long years ago. The old man was poring over it yet! Did he hope that his boy would come back to him, late as it was? He had sent back the money again and again without a word. He was waiting for something better than money. Kenyon glanced down to the low house, the red roof of which was just seen above the fence. If he ever went back it must be now. If he married under a false name, so it must stand; the old man must remain thrust aside until the end. What if he went now? What if he crossed the alley and went to the old man sitting alone by his fire? Although he had put this thing away from him for twenty years, so whimsical and perverse was the man, that his heart throbbed and his eyes were wet at the thought; the next, they had reached Miss Demar.

"I found them in the dark for you." She held out a branch of wet, fragrant roses toward him.

The night almost hid her from him. She seemed to belong to and to crown its passionate warmth, its strength, its solemn beauty. So set apart did she seem from all other women, that he thought how, if the whole world was lost in the night, he could straightway find her, as she had found the roses for him. He took her hand in his.

Charley sauntered up to the porch and smoked a cigar while the lovers passed slowly down the dusky alleys of the garden. A night-jar flapped its wet wings in Kenyon's face; the damp air was heavy with the scent of the roses she had given him; from one of the ships on the river came broken snatches of music which the distance softened into sweetness and sadness.

When they came back to the house and into the light of the gas, the politician's sallow face, which had warped lately into a shrewd cunning, glowed with a finer beauty than Miss Demar's. A word from the woman he loved caused his legs to tremble like a sensitive boy's; there was a fiery impatience in his eye which reminded Charley of a racer that is stayed within a stride of his goal.

"If you get this appointment, you can marry at once?" he said as he led Kenyon to his room.

"Yes. Nothing shall come between us now."

Charley wrung his hand, and bade him a hasty good-night. The next moment he was back. "I say, Kenyon,

pardon me, but you never looked into this matter of spir-
itualism, did you?"

"I? No; it was always a repugnant subject to me. But
did it never occur to you, old fellow, that your habit of
hurling new ideas at a man was confusing?"

"I don't know," absently. "Repugnant? Now that's just
what it is to me. But—you don't think it possible that disembodied spirits could manifest themselves in a room—in
any way—by means of matter, then? Yet there are some
things—things which those who are pure, you know, John,
have worn or touched, which seem to me to be alive with
their presence. Yet—"

He stopped, turned to the window, his double chin
quivering. "Well, it's all a puzzle," turning presently and
looking wistfully about the room. "When I think about
the different lives in men and horses and vegetables, I get
perplexed. How can I say, into this matter a soul has gone,
and in that there is none? Why should not a human spirit
linger in a house, for instance, and affect the matter in
it, as it affected the matter in his body? Now, why not?"
again looking about the dim chamber with the same curious hesitation.

"I can't tell you why not. I only know it never does."

Kenyon laughed good-humoredly, impatient as he was
to be left alone.

"Of course it never does. Bless me, I forgot what a bore
this must all be to you. I only thought I'd warn you—but
no matter. It's all trumpery gossip, no doubt." And still
muttering to himself he burst out of the room and went
stumbling down the stairs. Kenyon threw a quick glance
about the room, as he threw off his coat and bools and sat
down by the window. He had a vague impression when he
came into it that there was some one in it besides Knapp
and himself. He saw his mistake. It was a small, cheerful

chamber, with no fireplace, its windows opening to the west. The walls were a pale green; a well-darned carpet on the floor, and a half-worn cottage suit of furniture of the same color ranged against the walls. Just the room one might look for in Knapp's house—commonplace, cheery, with the stamp of poverty on every part of it. Knapp knocked at the door that instant and dashed in with a fresh pitcher of water, went out with a final good night, came back again to thrust his hand into the bed and punch the pillows. "There. All right. I was afraid they hadn't put on the new mattress. Good night. God bless you."

Knapp's whole life and nature, with all their cheerfulness, Kenyon thought, were commonplace—bore the poverty stamp. For himself—it would be different! Another step, and he would have turned his back on poverty and self-denial forever. God, who made the man, only knew how he loathed them both; with what panting, breathless delight, as he sat there, he looked into the world he was about to enter, where love was the first blessing and money almost its equal; the world to which he had been climbing since he was a ragged boy in yonder alley; full of luxurious houses, art, music, delicate viands, rare wines, beautiful women delicately dressed. "There is no reason why she should not consent to an immediate marriage," he thought. "My appointment is sure: then for France or Italy. I'll shake the dust of the country off my feet forever."

What made him spring up suddenly and, going to the window, turn to the house in the alley where the old man's light still burned? Leaning with his knuckles on the sill, he looked down into it steadily. Men who knew him in the office of the "Age," or in caucus, would not have recognized this face that he wore. He recovered himself presently.

"Bah! It can never be. If she guessed the truth, she would spurn me under her feet." Yet he could not put away the fancy that the old man was sitting there, watching the windows of this room—waiting—waiting; that he would watch there all night believing that his boy would come to him.

"If a man sets himself a high aim in life, he must put all obstacles out of his way; it is unavoidable"—as he began to prepare for bed. But when he caught sight of his ghastly face in the glass, he started back, and did not go near it again. He did not care to know how much it cost him to put this obstacle out of his way.

The sounds on the streets had died into silence. In some room below he heard Knapp's mother grumbling and scolding, and Charley's unwearied, cheerful little cackle in reply; then Tom woke with the colic, and Charley trotted to and fro—to and fro, carrying him for hours, until all the house was asleep and quiet. Long afterward, Kenyon, standing by the darkened window, saw Knapp go out into the garden for a moment's coolness and rest before he slept. He walked up and down slowly. The stars had come out, and threw faintly the lines of the bushy paths out from the darkness, massing into unbroken shadow the houses to the right. Beyond, a lamp at a mast-head here and there showed where the water flowed. The little man, thinking himself quite alone in the night, began to sing some old tune softly in his thin, chirrupy voice:

> "Here in the body pent,
>   Absent from thee I roam.
> And nightly pitch my moving tent
>   A day's march nearer home."

There was a slight pause, and he went on:

> "I want a true regard,
>   A single steady aim,
> Unmoved by suffering and reward,
>   To Thee and Thy great name."

Kenyon drew back. What dreadful Presence was this so near to commonplace Knapp, with his little body and little soul, of which he knew nothing? Kenyon's brain was feverish and strained. A new, vague idea entered readily among the thoughts that racked him: the something above the night—above him, his struggle, or his love—the infinite life before which his world of rare books, aesthetic dressing, and good eating sank into nothingness.

Knapp went into the house, and the night sank back into silence.

In the door of the little house in the alley an old man stood looking up to the darkened windows of his son's room. "It is too late; he will never come now," he said.

Kenyon lay upon the bed, his eyes covered with his hand. But he did not sleep.

The sun was not up. There was no sign of morning beyond the cold wind that shook the wet trees to and fro, and a gray lightening of the banked clouds over the river. Of all his unhealthy, unquiet life, this night had been to Kenyon the most unhealthy and the fiercest in its struggle. That first cold wind of dawn came with a wholesome freshness. He sat up, rubbed his aching eyes. It was time to be done with shadows and to go down into the real world. He wiped the hot sweat from his forehead and looked about as a man does after a sleepless night, his eyes falling at last by chance on the opposite wall to his bed. He had not thought the light strong enough to throw a shadow, but the reflection of the drifting clouds made strange shimmering figures on the blank surface. The clouds—what else could they be? The shadows slowly moved, approached each other, grew compact. Kenyon leaned forward; one could almost fancy that they took human forms. The strange illusion annoyed him; he drew down the curtains over the windows; the wind waved them fitfully. It was their shadows that he saw now; or was it— Good God! what was this that faced him, beckoning to him with strange and solemn gestures, showing him—

The blood ebbed back to his heart; he stood stiffly erect, his hands behind him, as he was used to stand when he faced an enemy in debate whom he recognized as stronger than himself. There was silence over all the city in that last hour of the night. The silence was nowhere more profound than in this little chamber through which the strange wind blew violently, yet without sound.

What Kenyon saw in that room he never told. Whether his old boy's life came back to him, or the life yet to come, what truth was pressed home to his calloused scheming brain, no man ever knew.

Death and disaster meet a man sometimes on his journey, and bring him for a brief moment face to face with himself, his friend, and God. When Kenyon left his chamber at dawn his face wore the look of one who voluntarily had met them and wrenched their secret from them.

He went down the garden and crossed the alley. Seth was stooping over the fire warming his chilled hands. He was going to his work, and did not mean to come back until Kenyon was gone. "He'd have come last night if he meant ever to own me," he told himself again and again. "I'll think of the boy as dead now. Better we'd both died when he was a boy."

A shadow struck across the doorway. The next moment a man stood before him, put his hands on his shoulders.

"Father! It's I, father."

Seth was not strong. He staggered under the first touch of his boy. "Jack?" he cried—"Jack?"

His son led him to a bench. The old man covered his face with his hands, but in a little while he looked up and motioned Kenyon to a chair. "It's your old seat, my lad. I'm glad to see you in it agen," he said, quietly untying his

gingham cravat. His high-featured face had strangely lost
its color.

Kenyon sat cowed, humiliated. This twenty years of
neglect rose before him; the more inexorably as Seth neither by word nor look recalled them. The delicacy which
kept the old man silent from showing even the reproach
of joy had different birth from his own fine taste in books
and music and wine. He felt that with all the old man's
passionate love for the boy he had lost, he would weigh
and measure the man who had come back to him. He knew,
too, having finer intuitions than Miss Demar, that the
man who thus measured him was weightier than he, stood
on firmer ground, was built up of larger, more liberal
elements.

In the heat of his passionate contrition and old, awakened love, he felt all the sacrifices he must make for his
father could be borne. "You will come to Washington to
me at once," he said. "We will have our home alone together. Nothing shall part us again."

"I think you're wrong there, Jack," Seth said gently,
"My ways are not your ways. You shall come to me when
you will, but I'll live out my life as I've begun. Old trees
grow best on their own rooting."

Kenyon was silent. He was not sure of his own rooting; ho was not sure of himself, of the work he had done
or the work he had planned to do. Was it all a sham? Had
he grasped only shadows, while Knapp, with his mediocre
brain, and this ignorant laborer, had laid hold on reality?

To-day he would be done with shams, though it would
cost all he had worked or cared for in life.

"Will you come with me a moment, father?" He led him
quickly over to the garden, where Miss Demur stood gath-
ering flowers for the breakfast table. He gave one passionate glance at the rare beauty in her face, at the fine soul

that looked smiling from her eyes to welcome him, before he let the bar fall between them which could not be raised.

"Miss Demar, this is my father."

The smile deepened. She put out her hand cordially but calmly. "I knew he was your father long ago, Mr. Kenyon. Have you told him who I am?"

"Mary?"

"Will you welcome a daughter as well as a son?" she said, all flushed and glowing. When the old man laid his hand on her head she, too, had a glimpse beneath the beggar's clothes and vulgar words.

They lingered long in the solitary garden. Apart from the morning light and dewy freshness there was a curious calm in it. The house had, as it still has, a strange trick of falling into silence in the midst of the busiest summer's day.

"What unaccountable stories hang about this old place," said Miss Demar to her lover. She could not restrain her curiosity as to his experiences of the night before.

But his face was inscrutable. "Where such a man as that lives," he said, glancing at Knapp, "no morbid shadows would linger long, I fancy. Yet I can believe that under his roof stronger men than he would be haunted by the ghosts of what they might have been. Their best selves would come to meet them."

But he never told her more than that.

The Shadow in the Corner

Mary Elizabeth Braddon

1879

Wildheath Grange stood a little way back from the road, with a barren stretch of heath behind it, and a few tall fir-trees, with straggling wind-tossed heads, for its only shelter. It was a lonely house on a lonely road, little better than a lane, leading across a desolate waste of sandy fields to the sea-shore; and it was a house that bore a bad name among the natives of the village of Holcroft, which was the nearest place where humanity might be found.

It was a good old house, nevertheless, substantially built in the days when there was no stint of stone and timber—a good old grey stone house, with many gables, deep window seats, and a wide staircase, long dark passages, hidden doors in queer corners, closets as large as some modern rooms, and cellars in which a company of soldiers might have lain perdu.

This spacious old mansion was given over to rats and mice, loneliness, echoes, and the occupation of three elderly people; Michael Bascom, whose forbears had been landowners of importance in the neighbourhood, and his two servants, Daniel Skegg and his wife, who had served the owner of that grim old house ever since he left the university, where he had lived fifteen years of his life—five as student, and ten as professor of natural science.

At three-and-thirty Michael Bascom had seemed a middle-aged man; at fifty-six he looked and moved and spoke like on old man. During that interval of twenty-three years he had lived alone in Wildheath Grange, and the country people told each other that the house had made him what he was. This was a fanciful and superstitious notion on their part, doubtless; yet it would not have been difficult to have traced a certain affinity between the dull grey building and the man who lived in it. Both seemed alike remote from the common cares and interests of humanity; both had an air of settled melancholy, engendered by perpetual solitude; both had the same faded complexion, the same look of slow decay.

Yet lonely as Michael Bascom's life was at Wildheath Grange, he would not for any consideration have altered its tenor. He had been glad to exchange the comparative seclusion of college rooms for the unbroken solitude of Wildheath. He was a fanatic in his love of scientific research, and his quiet days were filled to the brim with labours that seldom failed to interest and satisfy him. There were periods of depression, occasional hours of doubt, when the goal towards which he strove seemed unattainable, and his spirit fainted within him. Happily such times were rare with him. He had a dogged power of continuity which ought to have carried him to the highest pinnacle of achievement, and which perhaps might ultimately have won for him a grand name and a world-wide renown, but for a catastrophe which burdened the declining years of his harmless life with an unconquerable remorse.

One autumn morning—when he had lived just three-and-twenty years at Wildheath, and had only lately begun to perceive that his faithful butler and body servant, who was middle-aged when he first employed him, was actually getting old—Mr. Bascom's breakfast meditations over the latest treatise on the atomic theory were interrupted by an abrupt demand from that very Daniel Skegg. The man was accustomed to wait upon his master in the most absolute silence, and his sudden breaking out into speech was almost as startling as if the bust of Socrates above the bookcase had burst into human language.

"It's no use," said Daniel; "my missus must have a girl!"

"A what?" demanded Mr. Bascom, without taking his eyes from the line he had been reading.

"A girl—a girl to trot about and wash up, and help the old lady. She's getting weak on her legs, poor soul. We've none of us grown younger in the last twenty years."

"Twenty years!" echoed Michael Bascom scornfully. "What is twenty years in the formation of a stratum—what even in the growth of an oak—the cooling of a volcano!"

"Not much, perhaps, but it's apt to tell upon the bones of a human being."

"The manganese staining to be seen upon some skulls would certainly indicate—" began the scientist dreamily.

"I wish my bones were only as free from rheumatics as they were twenty years ago," pursued Daniel testily; "and then perhaps I should make light of twenty years. Howsoever, the long and the short of it is, my missus must have a girl. She can't go on trotting up and down these everlasting passages, and standing in that stony scullery year after year, just as if she was a young woman. She must have a girl to help."

"Let her have twenty girls," said Mr. Bascom, going back to his book.

"What's the use of talking like that, sir? Twenty girls, indeed! We shall have rare work to get one."

"Because the neighbourhood is sparsely populated?" interrogated Mr. Bascom, still reading.

"No, sir. Because this house is known to be haunted."

Michael Bascom laid down his book, and turned a look of grave reproach upon his servant.

"Skegg," he said in a severe voice, "I thought you had lived long enough with me to be superior to any folly of that kind."

"I don't say that I believe in ghosts," answered Daniel with a semi-apologetic air; "but the country people do. There's not a mortal among 'em that will venture across our threshold after nightfall."

"Merely because Anthony Bascom, who led a wild life in London, and lost his money and land, came home here broken-hearted, and is supposed to have destroyed himself in this house—the only remnant of property that was left him out of a fine estate."

"Supposed to have destroyed himself!" cried Skegg; "why the fact is as well known as the death of Queen Elizabeth, or the great fire of London. Why, wasn't he buried at the cross-roads between here and Holcroft!"

"An idle tradition, for which you could produce no substantial proof," retorted Mr. Bascom.

"I don't know about proof: but the country people believe it as firmly as they believe their Gospel."

"If their faith in the Gospel was a little stronger they need not trouble themselves about Anthony Bascom."

"Well," grumbled Daniel, as he began to clear the table, "a girl of some kind we must get, but she'll have to be a foreigner, or a girl that's hard driven for a place."

When Daniel Skegg said a foreigner, he did not mean the native of some distant land, but a girl who had not been born and bred at Holcroft. Daniel, had been raised and reared in that insignificant hamlet, and, small and dull as the spot was, he considered it the centre of the earth, and the world beyond it only margin.

Michael Bascom was too deep in the atomic theory to give a second thought to the necessities of an old servant. Mrs. Skegg was an individual with whom he rarely came in contact. She lived for the most part in a gloomy region at the north end of the house, where she ruled over the solitude of a kitchen, that looked almost as big as a cathedral, and numerous offices of the scullery, larder, and pantry class, where she carried on a perpetual warfare with spiders and beetles, and wore her old life out in the labour of sweeping and scrubbing. She was a woman of severe aspect, dogmatic piety, and a bitter tongue. She was a good plain cook, and ministered diligently to her master's wants. He was not an epicure, but liked his life to be smooth and easy, and the equilibrium of his mental power would have been disturbed by a bad dinner.

He heard no more about the proposed addition to his household for a space of ten days, when Daniel Skegg again startled him amidst his studious repose by the abrupt announcement:

"I've got a girl!"

"Oh," said Michael Bascom; "have you?" and he went on with his book.

This time he was reading an essay on phosphorus and its functions in relation to the human brain.

"Yes," pursued Daniel in his usual grumbling tone; "she was a waif and stray, or I shouldn't have got her. If she'd been a native she'd never have come to us."

"I hope she's respectable," said Michael.

"Respectable! That's the only fault she has, poor thing. She's too good for the place. She's never been in service before, but she says she's willing to work, and I daresay my old woman will be able to break her in. Her father was a small tradesman at Yarmouth, He died a month ago, and left this poor thing homeless. Mrs. Midge, at Holcroft, is her aunt, and she said to the girl, Come and stay with me till you get a place; and the girl has been staying with Mrs. Midge for the last three weeks, trying to hear of a place. When Mrs. Midge heard that my missus wanted a girl to help, she thought it would be the very thing for her niece

Maria. Luckily Maria had heard nothing about this house, so the poor innocent dropped me a curtsey, and said she'd be thankful to come, and would do her best to learn her duty. She'd had an easy time of it with her father, who had educated her above her station, like a fool as he was," growled Daniel.

"By your own account I'm afraid you've made a bad bargain," said Michael. "You don't want a young lady to clean kettles and pans."

"If she was a young duchess my old woman would make her work," retorted Skegg decisively.

"And pray where are you going to put this girl?" asked Mr. Bascom, rather irritably; "I can't have a strange young woman tramping up and down the passages outside my room. You know what a wretched sleeper I am, Skegg. A mouse behind the wainscot is enough to wake me."

"I've thought of that," answered the butler, with his look of ineffable wisdom. "I'm not going to put her on your floor. She's to sleep in the attics."

"Which room?"

"The big one at the north end of the house. That's the only ceiling that doesn't let water. She might as well sleep in a shower-bath as in any of the other attics."

"The room at the north end," repeated Mr. Bascom thoughtfully; "isn't that—?"

"Of course it is," snapped Skegg; "but she doesn't know anything about it."

Mr. Bascom went back to his books, and forgot all about the orphan from Yarmouth, until one morning on entering his study he was startled by the appearance of a strange girl, in a neat black and white cotton gown, busy dusting the volumes which were stacked in blocks upon his spacious writing-table—and doing it with such deft and careful hands that he had no inclination to be angry at this unwonted liberty. Old Mrs. Skegg had religiously refrained from all such dusting, on the plea that she did not wish to interfere with the master's ways. One of the master's ways, therefore, had been to inhale a good deal of dust in the course of his studies.

The girl was a slim little thing, with a pale and somewhat old-fashioned face, flaxen hair, braided under a neat muslin cap, a very fair complexion, and light blue eyes. They were the lightest blue eyes Michael Bascom had ever seen, but there was a sweetness and gentleness in their expression which atoned for their insipid colour.

"I hope you do not object to my dusting your books, sir," she said, dropping a curtsey.

She spoke with a quaint precision which struck Michael Bascom as a pretty thing in its way.

"No; I don't object to cleanliness, so long as my books and papers are not disturbed. If you take a volume off my desk, replace it on the spot you took it from. That's all I ask."

"I will be very careful, sir."

"When did you come here?"

"Only this morning, sir."

The student seated himself at his desk, and the girl withdrew, drifting out of the room as noiselessly as a flower blown across the threshold. Michael Bascom looked after her curiously. He had seen very little of youthful womanhood in his dry-as-dust career, and he wondered at this girl as at a creature of a species hitherto unknown to him. How fairly and delicately she was fashioned; what a translucent skin; what soft and pleasing accents issued from those rose-tinted lips. A pretty thing, assuredly, this kitchen wench! A pity that in all this busy world there could be no better work found for her than the scouring of pots and pans.

Absorbed in considerations about dry bones, Mr. Bascom thought no more of the pale-faced handmaiden. He saw her no more about his rooms. Whatever work she did there was done early in the morning, before the scholar's breakfast.

She had been a week in the house, when he met her one day in the hall. He was struck by the change in her appearance.

The girlish lips had lost their rose-bud hue; the pale blue eyes had a frightened look, and there were dark rings round them, as in one whose nights had been sleepless, or troubled by evil dreams.

Michael Bascom was so startled by an undefinable look in the girl's face that, reserved as he was by habit and nature, he expanded so far as to ask her what ailed her.

"There is something amiss, I am sure," he said. "What is it?"

"Nothing, sir," she faltered, looking still more scared at his question. "Indeed, it is nothing; or nothing worth troubling you about."

"Nonsense. Do you suppose, because I live among books, I have no sympathy with my fellow-creatures? Tell me what is wrong with you, child. You have been grieving about the father you have lately lost, I suppose."

"No, sir; it is not that. I shall never leave off being sorry for that. It is a grief which will last me all my life."

"What, there is something else then?" asked Michael impatiently. "I see; you are not happy here. Hard work does not suit you. I thought as much."

"Oh, sir, please don't think that," cried the girl, very earnestly. "Indeed I am glad to work—glad to be in service; it is only—"

She faltered and broke down, the tears rolling slowly from her sorrowful eyes, despite her effort to keep them back.

"Only what?" cried Michael, growing angry. "The girl is full of secrets and mysteries. What do you mean, wench?"

"I—I know it is very foolish, sir; but I am afraid of the room where I sleep."

"Afraid! Why?"

"Shall I tell you the truth, sir? Will you promise not to be angry?"

"I will not be angry if you will only speak plainly; but you provoke me by these hesitations and suppressions."

"And please, sir, do not tell Mrs. Skegg that I have told you. She would scold me, or perhaps even send me away."

"Mrs. Skegg shall not scold you. Go on, child."

"You may not know the room where I sleep, sir; it is a large room at one end of the house, looking towards the sea. I can see the dark line of water from the window, and I wonder sometimes to think that it is the same ocean I used to see when I was a child at Yarmouth. It is very lonely, sir, at the top of the house. Mr. and Mrs. Skegg sleep in a little room near the kitchen, you know, sir, and I am quite alone on the top floor."

"Skegg told me you had been educated in advance of your position in life, Maria. I should have thought the first effect of a good education would have been to make you superior to any foolish fancies about empty rooms."

"Oh, pray sir, do not think it is any fault in my education. Father took such pains with me; he spared no expense in giving me as good an education as a tradesman's daughter need wish for. And he was a religious man, sir. He did not believe"—here she paused with a suppressed shudder—"in the spirits of the dead appearing to the living since the days of miracles, when the ghost of Samuel appeared to Saul. He never put any foolish ideas into my head, sir. I hadn't a thought of fear when I first lay down to rest in the big lonely room upstairs."

"Well, what then?"

"But on the very first night," the girl went on breathlessly, "I felt weighed down in my sleep as if there were some heavy burden laid upon my chest. It was not a bad dream, but it was a sense of trouble that followed me all through my sleep; and just at daybreak—it begins to be light a little after six—I woke suddenly, with the cold perspiration pouring down my face, and knew that there was something dreadful in the room."

"What do you mean by something dreadful. Did you see anything?"

"Not much, sir; but it froze the blood in my veins, and I knew it was this that had been following me and weighing upon me all through my sleep. In the corner between the fire-place and the wardrobe, I saw a shadow—a dim, shapeless shadow—"

"Produced by an angle of the wardrobe, I daresay."

"No, sir. I could see the shadow of the wardrobe, distinct and sharp, as if it had been painted on the wall. This shadow was in the corner—a strange, shapeless mass; or, if it had any shape at all, it seemed—"

"What?" asked Michael eagerly.

"The shape of a dead body hanging against the wall!"

Michael Bascom grew strangely pale, yet he affected utter incredulity.

"Poor child," he said kindly; "you have been fretting about your father until your nerves are in a weak state, and you are full of fancies. A shadow in the corner, indeed; why, at daybreak, every corner is full of shadows. My old coat, flung upon a chair, will make you as good a ghost as you need care to see."

"Oh, sir, I have tried to think it is my fancy. But I have had the same burden weighing me down every night. I have seen the same shadow every morning."

"But when broad daylight comes, can you not see what stuff your shadow is made of?"

"No, sir; the shadow goes before it is broad daylight."

"Of course, just like other shadows. Come, come, get these silly notions out of your head, or you will never do for the work-a-day world. I could easily speak to Mrs. Skegg, and make her give you another room, if I wanted to encourage you in your folly. But that would be about the worst thing I could do for you. Besides, she tells me that all the other rooms on that floor are damp; and, no doubt, if she shifted you into one of them, you would discover another shadow in another corner, and get rheumatism into the bargain. No, my good girl, you must try to prove yourself the better for a superior education."

"I will do my best, sir," Maria answered meekly, dropping a curtsey.

Maria went back to the kitchen sorely depressed. It was a dreary life she led at Wildheath Grange—dreary by day, awful by night; for the vague burden and the shapeless shadow, which seemed so slight a matter to the elderly scholar, were unspeakably terrible to her. Nobody had told her that the house was haunted; yet she walked about those echoing passages wrapped round with a cloud of fear. She had no pity from Daniel Skegg and his wife. Those two pious souls had made up their minds that the character of the house should be upheld, so far as Maria went. To her, as a foreigner, the Grange should be maintained to be an immaculate dwelling, tainted by no sulphurous blast from the under world. A willing, biddable girl had become a necessary element in the existence of Mrs. Skegg. That girl had been found and that girl must be kept. Any fancies of a supernatural character must be put down with a high hand.

"Ghosts, indeed!" cried the amiable Skegg. "Read your Bible, Maria, and don't talk no more about ghosts."

"There are ghosts in the Bible," said Maria, with a shiver at the recollection of certain awful passages in the Scripture she knew so well.

"Ah, they was in their right place, or they wouldn't ha' been there," retorted Mrs. Skegg. "You ain't agoin' to pick holes in your Bible, I hope, Mariar, at your time of life."

Maria sat down quietly in her corner by the kitchen fire, and turned over the leaves of her dead father's Bible till she came to the chapters they two had loved best and oftenest read together. He had been a simple-minded, straightforward man, the Yarmouth cabinet-maker—a man full of aspirations after good, innately refined, instinctively religious. He and his motherless girl had spent their lives alone together, in the neat little home, which Maria had so soon learnt to cherish and beautify; and they had loved each other with an almost romantic love. They had had the same tastes, the same ideas. Very little had sufficed to make them happy. But inexorable death parted father and daughter, in one of those sharp sudden partings which are like the shock of an earthquake—instantaneous ruin, desolation and despair.

Maria's fragile form had bent before the tempest. She had lived through a trouble that might have crushed a stronger nature. Her deep religious convictions, and her belief that this cruel parting would not be for ever, had sustained her. She faced life, and its cares and duties, with a gentle patience which was the noblest form of courage.

Michael Bascom told himself that the servant-girl's foolish fancy about the room that had been given her was not a matter for serious consideration. Yet the idea dwelt in his mind unpleasantly, and disturbed him at his labours. The exact sciences require the complete power of a man's brain, his undistracted attention; and on this particular evening Michael found that he was only giving his work a part of his attention. The girl's pale face, the girl's tremulous tones, thrust themselves into the foreground of his thoughts.

He closed his book with a fretful sigh, wheeled his large arm-chair round to the fire, and gave himself up to contemplation. To attempt study with so disturbed a mind was useless. It was a dull grey evening, early in November; the student's reading-lamp was lighted, but the shutters were not yet shut, nor the curtains drawn. He could see the leaden sky outside his windows, the fir-tree tops tossing in the angry wind. He could hear the wintry blast whistling amidst the gables, before it rushed off seaward with a savage howl that sounded like a war-whoop.

Michael Bascom shivered, and drew nearer the fire.

"It's childish, foolish nonsense," he said to himself, "yet it's strange she should have that fancy about the shadow; for they say Anthony Bascom destroyed himself in that room. I remember hearing it when I was a boy, from an old servant whose mother was housekeeper at the great house in Anthony's time. I never heard how he died, poor fellow—whether he poisoned himself, or shot himself, or cut his throat; but I've been told that was the room. Old Skegg has heard it too. I could see that by his manner when he told me the girl was to sleep there."

He sat for a long time, till the grey of evening outside his study windows changed to the black of night, and the war whoop of the wind died away to a low complaining murmur. He sat looking into the fire, and letting his thoughts wander back to the past and the traditions he had heard in his boyhood.

That was a sad, foolish story of his great-uncle, Anthony Bascom: the pitiful story of a wasted fortune and a wasted life. A riotous collegiate career at Cambridge, a racing-stable at Newmarket, an imprudent marriage, a dissipated life in London, a runaway wife, an estate forfeited to Jew money-lenders, and then the fatal end.

Michael had often heard that dismal story; how, when Anthony Bascom's fair false wife had left him, when his credit was exhausted, and his friends had grown tired of him, and all was gone except Wildheath Grange, Anthony, the broken-down man of fashion, had come to that lonely house unexpectedly one night, and had ordered his bed to be got ready for him in the room where he used to sleep when he came to the place for the wild duck shooting, in his boyhood. His old blunderbuss was still hanging over the mantelpiece, where he had left it when he came into the property, and could afford to buy the newest thing in fowling-pieces. He had not been to Wildheath for fifteen years; nay, for a good many of those years he had almost forgotten that the dreary old house belonged to him.

The woman who had been housekeeper at Bascom Park, till house and lands had passed into the hands of the Jews, was at this time the sole occupant of Wildheath. She cooked some supper for her master, and made him as comfortable as she could in the long untenanted dining-room; but she was distressed to find, when she cleared the table after he had gone upstairs to bed, that he had eaten hardly anything.

Next morning she got his breakfast ready in the same room, which she managed to make brighter and cheerier than it had looked overnight. Brooms, dusting-brushes, and a good fire did much to improve the aspect of things. But the morning wore on to noon, and the old house-keeper listened in vain for her master's footfall on the stairs. Noon waned to late afternoon. She had made no attempt to disturb him, thinking that he had worn him-self out by a tedious journey on horseback, and that he was sleeping the sleep of exhaustion. But when the brief November day clouded with the first shadows of twilight, the old woman grew seriously alarmed, and went upstairs to her master's door, where she waited in vain for any reply to her repeated calls and knockings.

The door was locked on the inside, and the housekeep-er was not strong enough to break it open. She rushed downstairs again full of fear, and ran bare-headed out into the lonely road. There was no habitation nearer than the turnpike on the old coach road, from which this side road branched off to the sea. There was scanty hope of a chance passer-by. The old woman ran along the road, hardly know-ing whither she was going or what she was going to do, but with a vague idea that she must get somebody to help her.

Chance favoured her. A cart, laden with sea-weed, came lumbering slowly along from the level line of sands yon-der where the land melted into water. A heavy lumbering farm-labourer walked beside the cart.

"For God's sake, come in and burst open my master's door!" she entreated, seizing the man by the arm. "He's lying dead, or in a fit, and I can't get to help him."

"All right, missus," answered the man, as if such an invitation were a matter of daily occurrence. "Whoa, Dob-bin; stond still, horse, and be donged to thee."

Dobbin was glad enough to be brought to anchor on the patch of waste grass in front of the Grange garden. His master followed the housekeeper upstairs, and shattered the old-fashioned box-lock with one blow of his ponder-ous fist.

The old woman's worst fear was realised. Anthony Bas-com was dead. But the mode and manner of his death Michael had never been able to learn. The housekeeper's daughter, who told him the story, was an old woman when he was a boy. She had only shaken her head, and looked unutterable things, when he questioned her too closely. She had never even admitted that the old squire had com-mitted suicide. Yet the tradition of his self-destruction was rooted in the minds of the natives of Holcroft: and there was a settled belief that his ghost, at certain times and seasons, haunted Wildheath Grange.

Now Michael Bascom was a stern materialist. For him the universe, with all its inhabitants, was but a stupen-dous machine, governed by inexorable laws. To such a man the idea of a ghost was simply absurd—as absurd as the assertion that two and two make five, or that a circle can be formed of a straight line. Yet he had a kind of dilettante interest in the idea of a mind which could believe in ghosts. The subject offered a curious psychological study. This poor little pale girl, now, had evidently got some supernatural terror into her head, which could only be conquered by rational treatment.

"I know what I ought to do," Michael Bascom said to himself suddenly. "I'll occupy that room myself to-night, and demonstrate to this foolish girl that her notion about the shadow is nothing more than a silly fancy, bred of timidity and low spirits. An ounce of proof is better than a pound of argument. If I can prove to her that I have spent a night in the room, and seen no such shadow, she will understand what an idle thing superstition is."

Daniel came in presently to shut the shutters.

"Tell your wife to make up my bed in the room where Maria has been sleeping, and to put her into one of the rooms on the first floor for to-night, Skegg," said Mr. Bascom.

"Sir?"

Mr. Bascom repeated his order.

"That silly wench has been complaining to you about her room," Skegg exclaimed indignantly. "She doesn't deserve to be well fed and cared for in a comfortable home. She ought to go to the workhouse."

"Don't be angry with the poor girl, Skegg. She has taken a foolish fancy into her head, and I want to show her how silly she is," said Mr. Bascom.

"And you want to sleep in his—in that room yourself," said the butler.

"Precisely."

"Well," mused Skegg, "if he does walk—which I don't believe—he was your own flesh and blood; and I don't suppose he'll do you any hurt."

When Daniel Skegg went back to the kitchen he railed mercilessly at poor Maria, who sat pale and silent in her corner by the hearth, darning old Mrs. Skegg's grey worsted stockings, which were the roughest and harshest covering that ever human foot clothed itself withal. "Was there ever such a whimsical, fine, lady-like miss," demanded Daniel, "to come into a gentleman's house, and drive him out of his own bedroom to sleep in an attic, with her nonsenses and vagaries." If this was the result of being educated above one's station, Daniel declared that he was thankful he had never got so far in his schooling as to read words of two syllables without spelling. Education might be hanged, for him, if this was all it led to.

"I am very sorry," faltered Maria, weeping silently over her work. "Indeed, Mr. Skegg, I made no complaint. My master questioned me, and I told him the truth. That was all."

"All!" exclaimed Mr. Skegg irately; "all, indeed! I should think it was enough."

Poor Maria held her peace. Her mind, fluttered by Daniel's unkindness, had wandered away from that bleak big kitchen to the lost home of the past—the snug little parlor where she and her father had sat beside the cosey hearth on such a night as this; she with her smart workbox and her plain sewing, he with the newspaper he loved to read; the petted cat purring on the rug, the kettle singing on the bright brass trivet, the tea tray pleasantly suggestive of the most comfortable meal in the day.

Oh, those happy nights, that dear companionship! Were they really gone for ever, leaving nothing behind them but unkindness and servitude?

Michael Bascom retired later than usual that night. He was in the habit of sitting at his books long after every other lamp but his own had been extinguished. The Skeggs had subsided into silence and darkness in their dreary ground-floor bed-chamber. To-night his studies were of a peculiarly interesting kind, and belonged to the order of recreative reading rather than of hard work. He was deep in the history of that mysterious people who had their dwelling-place in the Swiss lakes, and was much exercised by certain speculations and theories about them.

The old eight-day clock on the stairs was striking two as, Michael slowly ascended, candle in hand, to the hitherto unknown region of the attics. At the top of the staircase he found himself facing a dark narrow passage which led northwards, a passage that was in itself sufficient to strike terror to a superstitious mind, so black and uncanny did it look.

"Poor child," mused Mr. Bascom, thinking of Maria; "this attic floor is rather dreary, and for a young mind prone to fancies—"

He had opened the door of the north room by this time, and stood looking about him.

It was a large room, with a ceiling that sloped on one side, but was fairly lofty upon the other; an old-fashioned room, full of old-fashioned furniture—big, ponderous, clumsy—associated with a day that was gone and people that were dead. A walnut-wood wardrobe stared him in the face—a wardrobe with brass handles, which gleamed out of the darkness like diabolical eyes. There was a tall four-post bedstead, which had been cut down on one side to accommodate the slope of the ceiling, and which had a misshapen and deformed aspect in consequence. There was an old mahogany bureau, that smelt of secrets. There were some heavy old chairs with rush bottoms, moldy with age, and much worn. There was a corner washstand, with a big basin and a small jug—the odds and ends of past years. Carpet there was none, save a narrow strip beside the bed.

"It is a dismal room," mused Michael, with the same touch of pity for Maria's weakness which he had felt on the landing just now.

To him it mattered nothing where he slept; but having let himself down to a lower level by his interest in the Swiss lake-people, he was in a manner humanized by the lightness of his evening's reading, and was even inclined to compassionate the feebleness of a foolish girl.

He went to bed, determined to sleep his soundest. The bed was comfortable, well supplied with blankets, rather luxurious than otherwise, and the scholar had that agreeable sense of fatigue which promises profound and restful slumber.

He dropped off to sleep quickly, but woke with a start ten minutes afterwards. What was this consciousness of a burden of care that had awakened him—this sense of all-pervading trouble that weighed upon his spirits and oppressed his heart—this icy horror of some terrible crisis in life through which he must inevitably pass? To him these feelings were as novel as they were painful. His life had flowed on with smooth and sluggish tide, unbroken by so much as a ripple of sorrow. Yet to-night he felt all the pangs of unavailing remorse; the agonizing memory of a life wasted; the stings of humiliation and disgrace, shame, ruin; the foreshadowing of a hideous death, which he had doomed himself to die by his own hand. These were the horrors that pressed him round and weighed him down as he lay in Anthony Bascom's room.

Yes, even he, the man who could recognize nothing in nature, or in nature's God, better or higher than an irresponsible and invariable machine governed by mechanical laws, was fain to admit that here he found himself face to face with a psychological mystery. This trouble, which came between him and sleep, was the trouble that had

pursued Anthony Bascom on the last night of his life. So
had the suicide felt as he lay in that lonely room, perhaps
striving to rest his wearied brain with one last earthly
sleep before he passed to the unknown intermediate land
where all is darkness and slumber. And that troubled mind
had haunted the room ever since. It was not the ghost of
the man's body that returned to the spot where he had
suffered and perished, but the ghost of his mind—his very
self; no meaningless simulacrum of the clothes he wore,
and the figure that filled them.

Michael Bascom was not the man to abandon his high
ground of sceptical philosophy without a struggle. He
tried his hardest to conquer this oppression that weighed
upon mind and sense. Again and again he succeeded in
composing himself to sleep, but only to wake again and
again to the same torturing thoughts, the same remorse,
the same despair. So the night passed in unutterable weariness; for though he told himself that the trouble was not
his trouble, that there was no reality in the burden, no
reason for the remorse, these vivid fancies were as painful
as realities, and took as strong a hold upon him.

The first streak of light crept in at the window—dim,
and cold, and grey; then came twilight, and he looked at
the corner between the wardrobe and the door.

Yes; there was the shadow: not the shadow of the wardrobe only—that was clear enough, but a vague and shapeless something which darkened the dull brown wall; so
faint, so shadowy, that he could form no conjecture as to
its nature, or the thing it represented. He determined to
watch this shadow till broad daylight; but the weariness of
the night had exhausted him, and before the first dimness
of dawn had passed away he had fallen fast asleep, and was
tasting the blessed balm of undisturbed slumber. When
he woke the winter sun was shining in at the lattice, and

the room had lost its gloomy aspect. It looked old-fashioned, and grey, and brown, and shabby; but the depth of
its gloom had fled with the shadows and the darkness of
night.

Mr. Bascom rose refreshed by a sound sleep, which had
lasted nearly three hours. He remembered the wretched
feelings which had gone before that renovating slumber;
but he recalled his strange sensations only to despise them,
and he despised himself for having attached any importance to them.

"Indigestion very likely," he told himself; "or perhaps
mere fancy, engendered of that foolish girl's story. The
wisest of us is more under the dominion of imagination
than he would care to confess. Well, Maria shall not sleep
in this room any more. There is no particular reason why
she should, and she shall not be made unhappy to please
old Skegg and his wife."

When he had dressed himself in his usual leisurely way,
Mr. Bascom walked up to the corner where he had seen or
imagined the shadow, and examined the spot carefully.

At first sight he could discover nothing of a mysterious
character. There was no door in the papered wall, no trace
of a door that had been there in the past. There was no
trap-door in the worm-eaten boards. There was no dark
ineradicable stain to hint at murder. There was not the
faintest suggestion of a secret or a mystery.

He looked up at the ceiling. That was sound enough,
save for a dirty patch here and there where the rain had
blistered it.

Yes; there was something—an insignificant thing, yet
with a suggestion of grimness which startled him.

About a foot below the ceiling he saw a large iron hook
projecting from the wall, just above the spot where he had
seen the shadow of a vaguely defined form. He mounted

on a chair the better to examine this hook, and to understand, if he could, the purpose for which it had been put
there.

It was old and rusty. It must have been there for many
years. Who could have placed it there, and why? It was not
the kind of hook upon which one would hang a picture or
one's garments. It was placed in an obscure corner. Had
Anthony Bascom put it there on the night he died, or did
he find it there ready for a fatal use?

"If I were a superstitious man," thought Michael; "I
should be inclined to believe that Anthony Bascom hung
himself from that rusty old hook."

"Sleep well, sir?" asked Daniel, as he waited upon his
master at breakfast.

"Admirably," answered Michael, determined not to
gratify the man's curiosity.

He had always resented the idea that Wildheath Grange
was haunted.

"Oh, indeed, sir. You were so late that I fancied—"

"Late, yes! I slept so well that I overshot my usual hour
for waking. But, by-the-way, Skegg, as that poor girl objects to the room, let her sleep somewhere else. It can't
make any difference to us, and it may make some difference to her."

"Humph!" muttered Daniel in his grumpy way; "you
didn't see anything queer up there, did you?"

"See anything? Of course not."

"Well, then, why should she see things? It's all her silly
fiddle-faddle."

"Never mind, let her sleep in another room."

"There ain't another room on the top floor that's dry."

"Then let her sleep on the floor below. She creeps about
quietly enough, poor little timid thing. She won't disturb me."

Daniel grunted, and his master understood the grunt to mean obedient assent; but here Mr. Bascom was unhappily mistaken. The proverbial obstinacy of the pig family is as nothing compared with the obstinacy of a cross-grained old man, whose narrow mind has never been illuminated by education. Daniel was beginning to feel jealous of his master's compassionate interest in the orphan girl. She was a sort of gentle clinging thing that might creep into an elderly bachelor's heart unawares, and make herself a comfortable nest there.

"We shall have fine carryings-on, and me and my old woman will be nowhere, if I don't put down my heel pretty strong upon this nonsense," Daniel muttered to himself, as he carried the breakfast-tray to the pantry.

Maria met him in the passage.

"Well, Mr. Skegg, what did my master say?" she asked breathlessly. "Did he see anything strange in the room?"

"No, girl. What should he see? He said you were a fool."

"Nothing disturbed him? And he slept there peacefully?" faltered Maria.

"Never slept better in his life. Now don't you begin to feel ashamed of yourself?"

"Yes," she answered meekly; "I am ashamed of being so full of fancies. I will go back to my room to-night, Mr. Skegg, if you like and I will never complain of it again."

"I hope you won't," snapped Skegg; "you've given us trouble enough already."

Maria sighed, and went about her work in saddest silence. The day wore slowly on, like all other days in that lifeless old house. The scholar sat in his study; Maria moved softly from room to room, sweeping and dusting in the cheerless solitude. The mid-day sun faded into the grey of afternoon, and evening came down like a blight upon the dull old house.

Throughout that day Maria and her master never met. Anyone who had been so far interested in the girl as to observe her appearance would have seen that she was unusually pale, and that her eyes had a resolute look, as of one who was resolved to face a painful ordeal. She ate hardly anything all day. She was curiously silent. Skegg and his wife put down both these symptoms to temper.

"She won't eat and she won't talk," said Daniel to the partner of his joys. "That means sulkiness, and I never allowed sulkiness to master me when I was a young man, and you tried it on as a young woman, and I'm not going to be conquered by sulkiness in my old age."

Bed-time came, and Maria bade the Skeggs a civil good-night, and went up to her lonely garret without a murmur.

The next morning came, and Mrs. Skegg looked in vain for her patient hand-maiden, when she wanted Maria's services in preparing the breakfast.

"The wench sleeps sound enough this morning," said the old woman. "Go and call her, Daniel. My poor legs can't stand them stairs."

"Your poor legs are getting uncommon useless," muttered Daniel testily, as he went to do his wife's behest.

He knocked at the door, and called Maria—once, twice, thrice, many times; but there was no reply. He tried the door, and found it locked. He shook the door violently, cold with fear.

Then he told himself that the girl had played him a trick. She had stolen away before daybreak, and left the door locked to frighten him. But, no; this could not be, for he could see the key in the lock when he knelt down and put his eye to the keyhole. The key prevented his seeing into the room.

"She's in there, laughing in her sleeve at me," he told himself; "but I'll soon be even with her."

There was a heavy bar on the staircase, which was intended to secure the shutters of the window that lighted the stairs. It was a detached bar, and always stood in a corner near the window, which it was but rarely employed to fasten. Daniel ran down to the landing, and seized upon this massive iron bar, and then ran back to the garret door.

One blow from the heavy bar shattered the old lock, which was the same lock the carter had broken with his strong fist seventy years before. The door flew open, and Daniel went into the attic which he had chosen for the stranger's bed-chamber.

Maria was hanging from the hook in the wall. She had contrived to cover her face decently with her handkerchief. She had hanged herself deliberately about an hour before Daniel found her, in the early grey of morning. The doctor, who was summoned from Holcroft, was able to declare the time at which she had slain herself, but there was no one who could say what sudden access of terror had impelled her to the desperate act, or under what slow torture of nervous apprehension her mind had given way. The coroner's jury returned the customary merciful verdict of "Temporary insanity."

The girl's melancholy fate darkened the rest of Michael Bascom's life. He fled from Wildheath Grange as from an accursed spot, and from the Skeggs as from the murderers of a harmless innocent girl. He ended his days at Oxford, where he found the society of congenial minds, and the books he loved. But the memory of Maria's sad face, and sadder death, was his abiding sorrow. Out of that deep shadow his soul was never lifted.

The Shadow Builder

Bram Stoker

1881

The lonely Shadow Builder watches ever in his lonely abode.

The walls are of cloud, and round and through them, changing ever as they come, pass the dim shades of all the things that have been.

This endless, shadowy, wheeling, moving circle is called THE PROCESSION OF THE DEAD PAST. In it everything is just as it has been in the great world. There is no change in any part; for each moment, as it passes, sends its shade into this dim Procession. Here there are moving people and events—cares—thoughts—follies—crimes— joys—sorrows—places—scenes—hopes and fears, and all that make the sum of life with all its lights and shadows. Every picture in nature where shadow dwells—and that is every one—has here its dim phantom.

Here are all pictures that are most fair and most sad to see—the passing gloom over a sunny cornfield when with the breeze comes the dark sway of the full ears as they bend and rise; the ripple on the glassy surface of a summer sea; the dark expanse that lies beyond and without the broad track of moonlight on the water; the lacework of glare and gloom that flickers over the road as one passes in autumn when the moonlight is falling through the naked branches of overhanging trees; the cool, restful shade under the

thick trees in summer time when the sun is flaming down
on the haymaker at work; the dark clouds that flit across
the moon, hiding her light, which leaps out again hollowly
and coldly; the gloom of violet and black that rises on
the horizon when rain is near in summer time; the dark
recesses and gloomy caverns where the waterfall hurls itself shrieking into the pool below,—all these shadow pictures, and a thousand others that come by night and day,
circle in the Procession among the things that have been.

Here, too, every act that any human being does, every
thought—good and bad—every wish, every hope—everything that is secret—is pictured, and becomes a lasting
record which cannot be blotted out; for at any time the
Shadow Builder may summon with his special hand any
one—sleeping or waking—to behold what is pictured of
the Dead Past, in the dim, mysterious distance which
encompasses his lonely abode.

In this ever-moving Procession of the Dead Past there
is but one place where the circling phantoms are not, and
where the cloudy walls are lost. There is here a great blackness, dense and deep, and full of gloom, and behind which
lies the great real world without.

This blackness is called THE GATE OF DREAD.

The Procession afar off takes from it its course, and
when passing on its way it circles again towards the darkness, the shadowy phantoms melt again into the mysterious gloom.

Sometimes the Shadow Builder passes through the vapoury walls of his abode and mingles in the ranks of the
Procession; and sometimes a figure summoned by the wave
of his spectral hand, with silent footfall stalks out of the
mist and pauses beside him. Sometimes from a sleeping
body the Shadow Builder summons a dreaming soul; then
for a time the quick and the dead stand face to face, and
men call it a dream of the Past. When this happens, friend

meets friend or foe meets foe; and over the soul of the dreamer comes a happy memory long vanished, or the troubled agony of remorse. But no spectre passes through the misty wall, save to the Shadow Builder alone; and no human being—even in a dream—can enter the dimness where the Procession moves along.

So lives the lonely Shadow Builder amid his gloom; and his habitation is peopled by a spectral past.

His only people are of the past; for though he creates shadows they dwell not with him. His children go out at once to their homes in the big world, and he knows them no more till, in the fulness of time, they join the Procession of the Dead Past, and reach, in turn, the misty walls of his home.

For the Shadow Builder there is not night nor day, nor season of the year; but for ever round his lonely dwelling passes the silent Procession of the Dead Past.

Sometimes he sits and muses with eyes fixed and staring, and seeing nothing; and then out at sea there is a cloudless calm or the black gloom of night. Towards the far north or south for long months together he never looks, and then the stillness of the arctic night reigns alone. When the dreamy eyes again become conscious, the hard silence softens into the sounds of life and light.

Sometimes, with set frown on his face and a hard look in the eyes, which flash and gleam dark lightnings, the Shadow Builder sways resolute to his task, and round the world the shadows troop thick and fast. Over the sea sweeps the blackness of the tempest; the dim lights flicker in the cots away upon the lonely moors; and even in the palaces of kings dark shadows pass and fly and glide over all things— yea, through the hearts of the kings themselves—for the Shadow Builder is then dread to look upon.

Now and again, with long whiles between, the Shadow Builder as he completes his task lingers over the work as though he loves it. His heart yearns to the children of his will; and he fain would keep even one shadow to be a companion to him in his loneliness. But the voice of the Great Present is ever ringing in his ears at such times, enjoining him to haste. The giant voice booms out,

"Onwards, onwards."

Whilst the words ring in the ears of the Shadow Builder the completed shadow fades from beneath his hands, and passing unseen through the Gate of Dread, mingles in the great world without, in which it is to play its part. When, in the fulness of time, this shadow comes into the ranks of the Procession of the Dead Past, the Shadow Builder knows it and remembers it; but in his dead heart there is no gleam of loving remembrance, for he can only love the Present, that slips ever from his grasp.

And oh! it is a lonely life which the Shadow Builder lives; and in the weird, sad, solemn, mysterious, silent gloom which encompasses him, he toils on ever at his lonely task.

But sometimes too the Shadow Builder has his joys. Baby shadows spring up, and sunny pictures, alight with sweetness and love, glide from under his touch, and are gone.

Before the Shadow Builder at his task lies a space wherein is neither light nor darkness, neither joy nor gloom. Whatsoever touches it fades away as sand heaps melt before the incoming tide, or like words writ on water. In it all things lose their being and become part of the great *Is-Not;* and this terrible line of mystery is called THE THRESHOLD. Whatsoever passes into it disappears; and whatsoever emerges from it is complete as it comes and passes into the great world as a thing to run its course. Before the Threshold the Shadow Builder himself is as naught; and in its absorbing might there is that which he cannot sway or rule.

When at his task he summons; and out of the impalpable nothingness of the Threshold there comes the object of his will. Sometimes the shadow bursts full and freshly and is suddenly lost in the gloom of the Gate of Dread; and sometimes it grows softly and faintly, getting fuller as it comes, and so melts away into the gloom.

The lonely Shadow Builder is working in his lonely abode; around him, beyond the vapoury walls, pressing onward as ever, is the circling Procession of the Dead Past. Storm and calm have each been summoned from the Threshold, and have gone; and now in this calm, wistful moment the Shadow Builder pauses at his task, and wishes and wishes till, to his lonely longing wistfulness, the nothingness of THE THRESHOLD sends an answer.

Forth from it grows the shadow of a Baby's foot, stepping with tottering gait out towards the world; then follows the little round body and the big head, and the Baby shadow moves onwards, swaying and balancing with uncertain step. Swift behind it come the Mother's hands stretched out in loving helpfulness, lest it should fall. One step—two—it totters, and is falling; but the Mother's arms are swift, and the gentle hands bear it firmly up. The Child turns and toddles again into its Mother's arms.

Again it strives to walk; and again the Mother's watchful hands are ready. This time it needs not the help; but when the race is over, the shadow Child turns again lovingly to its Mother's breast.

Once again it strives, and it walks boldly and firmly; but the Mother's hands quiver as they hang by her side, whilst a tear sweeps down the cheek, although that cheek is gladdened by a smile.

The Baby shadow turns, and goes a little way off. Then over the misty Nothing on which the shadows fall, flits the flickering shadow of a tiny hand waving; and onward, with firm tread, the shadow of the little feet moves out into the misty gloom of the Gate of Dread, and passes away.

But the Mother's shadow moves not. The hands are pressed to the heart, the loving face is upturned in prayer, and down the cheeks roll great tears. Then her head bows lower as the little feet pass beyond her ken; and lower and lower bends the weeping Mother till she lies prone. Even as he looks, the Shadow Builder sees the shadows fade away, away, and the terrible nothingness of the Threshold only is there.

Then presently in the Procession of the Dead Past circle round the misty walls the shadows that had been— the Mother and the Child.

Now from out the Threshold steps a Youth with brave and buoyant tread; and as on the misty veil his shadow falls, the dress and bearing proclaim him a sailor lad. Close to this shadow comes another—the Mother's. Older and thinner she is, as if with watching, but still the same. The old loving hands array prettily the knotted kerchief hanging loosely on the open throat; and the Boy's hands reach out, take the Mother's face between them, and draw it forward for a kiss. The Mother's arms fly round her Son, and in a close embrace they cling.

The Mother kisses her Boy again and again; and together they stand, as though to part were impossible.

Suddenly the Boy turns as though he heard a call. The Mother clings closer. He seems to remonstrate tenderly; but the loving arms hold tighter, till with gentle force he tears himself away. The Mother takes a step forward, and holds out the thin hands trembling in an agony of grief. The Boy stops; to one knee he bends, then, dashing away his tears, he waves his cap, and hurries on, while once again the Mother sinks to her knees, and weeps.

And so, slowly, once again, the shadows of the Mother and the Child grown greater in the fulness of time, pass out through the Gate of Dread, and circle among the phantoms in the Procession of the Dead Past—the Mother following hard upon the speeding footsteps of her Son.

In the long pause that follows, whilst the Shadow Builder watches, all seems changed. Out from the Threshold comes a mist, such as hangs sometimes over the surface of a tropic sea.

By little and little the mist rolls away, and forth advances, black and great, the prow of a mighty vessel. The shadows of the great sails lie faintly in the cool depths of the sea, as the sails flap idly in the breezeless air. Over the bulwark lean listless figures waiting for a wind to come. The mist on the sea melts slowly away; and by the dark shadows of men sheltering from the sunny glare and fanning themselves with their broad sailor hats, it is plain that the heat is terrible.

Now from far off, behind the ship, comes up over the horizon a black cloud no bigger than a man's hand, but sweeping on with terrible speed. Also, from far away, before her course, rises the edge of a coral reef, scarcely seen above the glassy water, but darkling the depths below.

Those on board see neither of these things, for they shelter under their awnings, and sigh for cool breezes.

Quicker and quicker comes the dark cloud, sweeping faster and faster, and growing blacker and blacker and vaster and vaster as it comes.

Then those on board seem to know the danger. Hurried shadows fly along the decks; up the shadows of the ladders hurry shadows of men. The flapping of the great sails ceases as one by one the willing hands draw them in.

But quicker than the hands of men can work sweeps the tempest.

Onwards it rushes, and terrible things come close behind; black darkness—towering waves that break in fury

and fly aloft—the spume of the sea swept heavenwards—
the great clouds wheeling in fury;—and in the centre of
these flying, whirling, maddening shadows, rocks the
shadow of the ship.

As the black darkness of the heavens encompasses all,
the rush of shadowy storm sweeps through the Gate of
Dread.

As he waits and looks and sees the cyclone whirling
amongst the shadows in the Procession of the Dead Past,
the Shadow Builder, even in his dead heart, feels a weight
of pain for the brave Sailor Boy tossed on the deep, and
the anxious Mother sitting lonely at home.

Again from the Threshold passes a shadow, growing deeper
as it comes, but very, very faint at first; for here the sun
is strong, and there is but little room for shadows on the
bare rock which seems to rise from the glare and the glitter
of the sea deeps round.

On the lonely rock a Sailor Boy stands; thin and gaunt
he is, and his clothing is but a few rags. Sheltering his
eyes with his hand, he looks out to sea, where, afar off, the
cloudless sky sinks to meet the burning sea; but no speck
over the horizon—no distant glitter of a white sail—gives
him a ray of hope.

Long, long he peers, till, wearied out, he sits down on
the rock and bows his head as if in despair for a time. As
the sea falls, he gathers from the rock the shellfish which
has come during the tide.

So the day wears on, and the night comes; and in the
tropic sky the stars hang like lamps.

In the cool silence of the night the forlorn Sailor Boy
rests—sleeps, and dreams. His dreams are of home—of
loving arms stretched out to meet him—of banquets
spread—of green fields and waving branches, and the sheltering happiness of his mother's love. For in his sleep the

Shadow Builder summons his dreaming soul, and shows him all these blessings passing ceaselessly in the Procession of the Dead Past, and so comforts him lest he should despair and die.

Thus wear on many weary days; and the sailor-boy lingers on the lonely rock.

Afar off he can just see a hill that seems to rise over the Water. One morning when the blackening sky and the sultry air promise a storm, the distant mountain seems nearer; and he thinks that he will try to reach it by swimming.

Whilst he is thus resolving, the storm rushes up over the horizon and sweeps him from the lonely rock. He swims with a bold heart; but just as his strength is done, he is cast by the fury of the storm on a beach of soft sand. The storm passes on its way and the waves leave him high and dry. He goes inland, where, in a cave in the rock, he finds shelter, and sinks to sleep.

The Shadow Builder, as he sees all this happen in the shadows on the clouds, and land, and sea, rejoices in his dead heart that the lonely mother perhaps will not wait in vain.

So time wears on, and many, many weary days pass. The Boy becomes a young Man, living in the lonely island; his beard has grown, and he is clothed in a dress of leaves. All day long, save when he is not working to get food to eat, he watches from the mountain top for a ship to come. As he stands looking out over the sea, the sun casts his shadow down the hillside, so that at evening, as it sinks low in the waters, the shadow of the lonely Sailor grows longer and longer, till at the last it makes a dark streak down the hill side, even to the water's edge.

The lonely Man's heart grows heavier and heavier as he waits and watches, whilst the weary time passes and the countless days and nights come and go.

Time comes when he begins to get feebler and feebler. At last he grows sick to death, and lingers long a-dying.

Then these shadows pass away.

Out from the Threshold grows the shadow of an old woman, thin and worn, sitting in a lonely cottage on a jutting cliff. In the window a lamp burns in the night time to welcome the Lost One should he ever return, and to guide him to his Mother's home. By the lamp the Mother watches, till, wearied out, she sinks to sleep.

As she sleeps the Shadow Builder summons her sleeping soul with the wave of his spectral hand.

She stands beside him in the lonely abode, whilst round them through the misty walls passes onward the Procession of the Dead Past.

As she looks, the Shadow Builder lifts his spectral hand to point to the vision of her Son.

But the Mother's eyes are quicker than even the spectral hand that evokes all the shadows of the rushing storm, and ere the hand is raised she sees her Son among the Shadows of the Past. The Mother's heart is filled with unspeakable joy, as she sees him alive and hale, although a prisoner amongst the tropic seas.

But alas! she knows not that in the dim Procession pass only the things that have been; and that although in the past the lonely Sailor lived, in the present—even at the moment—he may be dying or dead.

The Mother stretches out her arms to her Boy; but even as she does, her sleeping soul loses sight of the dim Procession and vanishes from the Shadow Builder's lonely abode. For when she knows that her Boy is alive, there follows a great pain that he is lonely and waits and watches for help; and the quick heart of the Mother is overcome with grief, and she wakes with a bitter cry.

Then as she rises and looks past the dying lamp out into the dawn, the Mother feels that she has seen a vision of her son in sleep, and that he lives and waits for help; and her heart glows with a great resolve.

Quickly then from the Threshold float many shadows.—

A lonely Mother speeding with flying feet to a distant city.

Grave men refusing, but not unkindly, a kneeling woman making an appeal with uplifted hands.

Hard men spurning a praying Mother from their doors.

A wild rabble of bad and thoughtless boys and girls hounding through the streets a hurrying woman.

A shadow of pain on a Mother's heart.

The upcoming of a black cloud of despair, but which hangs far off—for it cannot advance into the bright sunlight of the Mother's resolve.

Weary days with their own myriad shadows.

Lonely nights—black want—cold—hunger and pain; and through all these darkening shadows the swift moving shadow of the Mother's flying feet.

A long long line of such pictures come ever anigh in the Procession, till the dead heart of the Shadow Builder grows icy, and his burning eyes look out savagely on all who give pain and trial to the Mother's faithful heart.

And so all these shadows float out into a black mist, and are lost in the gloom of the Gate of Dread.

Another shadow grows out of the mist.—

An Old Man sits in his armchair. The firelight flickering throws his image, quaintly dancing, on the wall of the room. He is old, for the great shoulders are bowed, and the grand strong face is lined with years. There is another shadow in the room; it is the Mother's—she is standing by the table, and is telling her story; her thin hands point away where in the distance she knows her Son is a prisoner in the lonely seas.

The Old Man rises; the enthusiasm of the Mother's heart has touched him, and back to his memory rush the old love and energy and valour of his youth. The great hand rises, closes, and strikes the table with a mighty blow, as though declaring a binding promise. The Mother sinks to her knees,—she seizes the great hand and kisses it, and stands erect.

Other men come in—they receive orders—they hurry out.

Then come many shadows whose movement and swiftness and firm purpose mean life and hope.

At sunset, when the masts make long shadows on the harbour water, a big ship moves out on her journey to the tropic seas. Men's shadows quickly flit up and down the rigging and along the decks.

As the shadows wheel round the capstan bar the anchor rises; and into the sunset passes the great vessel.

In the bow, like a figure of Hope, stands the Mother, gazing with eager eyes on the far-off horizon.

Then this shadow fades.

A great ship sweeps along with white sails swelling to the breeze; at the bow stands the Mother, gazing ever out into the distance before her.

Storms come and the ship flies before the blast; but she swerves not, for the Mother, with outstretched hand, points the way, and the helmsman swaying beside his wheel obeys the hand.

So this shadow also passes.

The shadows of days and nights come on in quick succession; and the Mother seeks ever for her Son.

So the records of the prosperous journey melt into a faint, dim, misty shadow through which one figure alone stands clear—the watching Mother at the vessel's prow.

Now from the Threshold grow the shadows of the mountain island and of the ship drawing nigh. In the prow the Mother kneels, looking out and pointing. A boat is lowered. Men spring on board with eager feet; but before them all is the Mother. The boat nears the island; the water shallows, and on the hot white beach the men spring to land.

But in the boat's prow still the Mother sits. In her long anxious hours of agony she has seen in her dreams her Son standing afar off and watching; she has seen him wave his arms with a great joy as the ship rises over the horizon's edge; she has seen him standing on the beach waiting; she has seen him rushing through the surf so that the first thing that the lonely Sailor Boy should touch would be his Mother's loving hands.

But alas! for her dreams. No figure with joyous waving arms stands on the summit of the mountain—no eager figure stands at the water's edge or dashes to meet her through the surf. Her heart grows cold and chill with fear.

Has she indeed come too late?

The men leave the boat, comforting her as they go with shakings of the hand and kindly touches upon the shoulder. She motions them to haste and remains kneeling.

The time goes on. The men ascend the mountain; they search, but they find not the lost Sailor Boy, and with slow, halting feet they return to the boat.

The Mother hears them coming afar and rises to meet them. They hang their heads. The Mother's arms go up, tossed aloft in the anguish of despair, and she sinks swooning in the boat.

The Shadow Builder in an instant summons her spirit from her senseless clay, and points to a figure passing, without movement, in the Procession of the Dead Past.

Then quicker than light the Mother's soul flies back full of new-found joy.

She rises from the boat—she springs to land. The men follow wondering.

She rushes along the shore with flying feet; the sailors come close behind.

She stops opposite the entrance to a cave obscured with trailing brambles. Here, without turning, she motions to the men to wait. They pause and she passes within.

For a few moments grim darkness pours from the threshold; and then one sad, sad vision grows and passes.—

A dim, dark cave—a worn man lying prone, and a Mother in anguish bending over the cold clay. On the icy breast she lays her hand; but alas! she cannot feel the beat of the heart she loves.

With a wild, heart-stricken gesture, she flings herself upon the body of her Son and holds it close, close—as though the clasp of a Mother were stronger than the grasp of Death.

The dead heart of the Shadow Builder is alive with pain as he turns away from the sad picture, and with anxious eyes looks where from behind the Gate of Dread, the Mother and Child must come to join the ever-swelling ranks of the Procession of the Dead Past.

Slowly, slowly comes the shadow of the clay cold Mariner passing on.

But swifter than light come the Mother's flying feet. The arms so strong with love are stretched out—the thin hands grasp the passing shadow of her Son and tear him back beyond the Gate of Dread—to life—and liberty—and love.

The lonely Shadow Builder knows now that the Mother's arms are stronger than the grasp of Death.

The Magic Shadow
Arthur Quiller-Couch
1891

Once upon a time there was born a man-child with a magic
shadow.

His case was so rare that a number of doctors have
been disputing over it ever since and picking his parents'
histories and genealogies to bits, to find the cause. Their
inquiries do not help us much. The father drove a cab;
the mother was a charwoman and came of a consumptive
family. But these facts will not quite account for a magic
shadow. The birth took place on the night of a new moon,
down a narrow alley into which neither moon nor sun ever
penetrated beyond the third-story windows—and that is
why the parents were so long in discovering their child's
miraculous gift. The hospital-student who attended merely
remarked that the babe was small and sickly, and advised
the mother to drink sound port-wine while nursing him,—
which she could not afford.

Nevertheless, the boy struggled somehow through five
years of life, and was put into small-clothes. Two weeks
after this promotion his mother started off to scrub out a
big house in the fashionable quarter, and took him with
her: for the house possessed a wide garden, laid with turf
and lined with espaliers, sunflowers, and hollyhocks, and
as the month was August, and the family away in Scotland,
there seemed no harm in letting the child run about in

this paradise while she worked. A flight of steps descended from the drawing-room to the garden, and as she knelt on her mat in the cool room it was easy to keep an eye on him. Now and then she gazed out into the sunshine and called; and the boy stopped running about and nodded back, or shouted the report of some fresh discovery.

By-and-by a sulphur butterfly excited him so that he must run up the broad stone steps with the news. The woman laughed, looking at his flushed face, then down at his shoe-strings, which were untied: and then she jumped up, crying out sharply—"Stand still, child—stand still a moment!"

She might well stare. Her boy stood and smiled in the sun, and his shadow lay on the whitened steps. Only the silhouette was not that of a little breeched boy at all, but of a little girl in petticoats; and it wore long curls, whereas the charwoman's son was close-cropped.

The woman stepped out on the terrace to look closer. She twirled her son round and walked him down into the garden, and backwards and forwards, and stood him in all manner of positions and attitudes, and rubbed her eyes. But there was no mistake: the shadow was that of a little girl.

She hurried over her charing, and took the boy home for his father to see before sunset. As the matter seemed important, and she did not wish people in the street to notice anything strange, they rode back in an omnibus. They might have spared their haste, however, as the cab-driver did not reach home till supper-time, and then it was found that in the light of a candle, even when stuck inside a carriage-lamp, their son cast just an ordinary shadow. But next morning at sunrise they woke him up and carried him to the house-top, where the sunlight slanted between the chimney-stacks: and the shadow was that of a little girl.

The father scratched his head. "There's money in this, wife. We'll keep the thing close; and in a year or two he'll be fit to go round in a show and earn money to support our declining years."

With that the poor little one's misfortunes began. For they shut him in his room, nor allowed him to play with the other children in the alley—there was no knowing what harm might come to his precious shadow. On dark nights his father walked him out along the streets; and the boy saw many curious things under the gas-lamps, but never the little girl who inhabited his shadow. So that by degrees he forgot all about her. And his father kept silence.

Yet all the while she grew side by side with him, keeping pace with his years. And on his fifteenth birthday, when his parents took him out into the country and, in the sunshine there, revealed his secret, she was indeed a companion to be proud of—neat of figure, trim of ankle, with masses of waving hair; but whether blonde or brunette could not be told; and, alas! she had no eyes to look into.

"My son," said they, "the world lies before you. Only do not forget your parents, who conferred on you this remarkable shadow."

The youth promised, and went off to a showman. The showman gladly hired him; for, of course, a magic shadow was a rarity, though not so well paying as the Strong Man or the Fat Woman, for these were worth seeing every day, whereas for weeks at a time, in dull weather or foggy, our hero had no shadow at all. But he earned enough to keep himself and help the parents at home; and was considered a success.

One day, after five years of this, he sought the Strong Man, and sighed. For they had become close friends.

"I am in love," he confessed.

"With your shadow?"

"No."

"Not with the Fat Woman!" the Strong Man exclaimed, with a start of jealousy.

"No. I have seen her that I mean these three days in the Square, on her way to music lesson. She has dark brown eyes and wears yellow ribbons. I love her."

"You don't say so! She has never come to our performance, I hope."

"It has been foggy ever since we came to this town."

"Ah, to be sure. Then there's a chance: for, you see, she would never look at you if she knew of—of that other. Take my advice—go into society, always at night, when there is no danger; get introduced; dance with her; sing serenades under her window; then marry her. Afterwards—well, that's your affair."

So the youth went into society and met the girl he loved, and danced with her so vivaciously and sang serenades with such feeling beneath her window, that at last she felt he was all in all to her. Then the youth asked to be allowed to see her father, who was a retired colonel; and professed himself a man of substance. He said nothing of the Shadow: but it is true he had saved a certain amount. "Then to all intents and purposes you are a gentleman," said the retired colonel; and the wedding-day was fixed.

They were married in dull weather, and spent a delightful honeymoon. But when spring came and brighter days, the young wife began to feel lonely; for her husband locked himself, all the day long, in his study—to work, as he said. He seemed to be always at work; and whenever he consented to a holiday, it was sure to fall on the bleakest and dismalest day in the week.

"You are never so gay now as you were last Autumn. I am jealous of that work of yours. At least," she pleaded, "let me sit with you and share your affection with it."

But he laughed and denied her: and next day she peered in through the keyhole of his study.

That same evening she ran away from him: having seen the shadow of another woman by his side.

Then the poor man—for he had loved his wife—cursed the day of his birth and led an evil life. This lasted for ten years, and his wife died in her father's house, unforgiving.

On the day of her funeral, the man said to his shadow—"I see it all. We were made for each other, so let us marry. You have wrecked my life and now must save it. Only it is rather hard to marry a wife whom one can only see by sunlight and moonlight."

So they were married; and spent all their life in the open air, looking on the naked world and learning its secrets. And his shadow bore him children, in stony ways and on the bare mountain-side. And for every child that was born the man felt the pangs of it.

And at last he died and was judged: and being interrogated concerning his good deeds, began—

"We two—"

—and looked around for his shadow. A great light shone all about; but she was nowhere to be seen. In fact, she had passed before him, and his children remained on earth, where men already were heaping them with flowers and calling them divine.

Then the man folded his arms and lifted his chin.

"I beg your pardon," he said, "I am simply a sinner."

There are in this world certain men who create. The children of such are poems, and the half of their soul is female. For it is written that without woman no new thing shall come into the world.

A Shadow Cast Before

L. Frank Baum

1897

I am valet to his Majesty the Emperor. My family has served the royal household for nearly two centuries, and we regard the record with pardonable pride.

On my breast glitters an order to possess which many a nobleman would willingly forfeit his wealth, and the Great Emperor himself pinned it there!

I won it in this way.

Entering my master's room one morning to arouse him and serve his customary cup of chocolate, I found him in an especially happy mood, and he entertained me with a goodly number of harmless witticisms as I busied myself over his toilet.

While standing near the dressing table, which was covered with a broad cloth whose folds reached the carpet, I observed the drapery move, as though disturbed from beneath the table. The first time I thought it was my fancy, as no draught could penetrate the room, but as again the cloth swayed perceptibly, I walked to the table and raised the cover while I peered beneath.

The sight that met my gaze was so terrible and unexpected that I gave an involuntary cry.

Squatting under the table was a dark, hunched-backed figure, with evil eyes glowing like two coals, and grasping in its hand a long double-edged dirk!

Hearing my exclamation His Majesty asked, "What is it, you rascal?"

To act promptly is one of the attributes of my family. Without replying to the Emperor I quickly reached beneath the table to clutch and draw forth the vile assassin. My hand met with no resistance; the fellow eluded me. Seizing the edge of the table I thrust it violently aside, and at the same time threw myself bodily upon the spot where the intruder must be.

There was no one there, and I sprawled upon the floor full of consternation and cutting so ridiculous a figure that His Majesty lay back and roared in merriment.

"You ass! You idiot!" he gasped, between fits of laughter, "what in God's name are you trying to do?"

But I pass over my master's reproaches, the more readily that they seemed fully deserved. For although I searched every portion of the chamber, the man had positively disappeared. And when I came to reason upon the matter calmly, I saw how impossible it was that any intruder could have gained access to the royal apartments.

Still, the incident impressed me.

One week later the Emperor was playing at quoits in the garden and I stood by to return the rings as he cast them. Finally a quoit, having alighted upon its edge, rolled briskly without the court and stopped at the edge of a cluster of low shrubs.

Stooping over to secure the errant quoit my eyes penetrated the leafy foliage beside it, and I plainly saw concealed therein the figure of the hunch-back, again clasping the murderous-looking knife and scowling as his dark eyes met mine.

A number of the Emperor's body guard stood a few paces away. Keeping close watch of the bushes and determined that this time the villain should not escape me, I beckoned the soldiers to my side.

In an instant they had surrounded the shrub, while my eyes remained fastened upon the hunch-back. In one brief sentence I explained the position of the assassin, and at my word half a score of pikes were thrust into the bushes.

I own I expected to see them withdrawn reeking with the scoundrel's blood, and my amazement was supreme when the figure of the man vanished before my very eyes, and the pikes met with no resistance whatever!

Again I was forced to endure the ridicule of the courtiers and the soldiery, while my royal master angrily chided me as a visionary fool and intimated that I was fast outgrowing my usefulness.

Another week rolled away and one afternoon I accompanied his Majesty upon his daily ride. On our return to the palace my master dismounted, nodded gaily to the vast throng of subjects that stood by to gaze upon his benignant features, and started to walk up the avenue either side of which was densely lined with people eager for a near view of the Great Emperor.

I was but a step behind him when I saw, a few paces in advance, the misshapen form and scowling face of the hunch-back. His right hand was thrust within his bosom, and I knew intuitively that his fingers grasped the double-edged knife.

As we reached the fellow I pressed to the Emperor's side, and at the same instant the hunch-back sprang forward with a bound.

The sharp blade flashed in his uplifted hand, and that moment might have been my master's last. But I had been forewarned. In an instant my hands clutched the villain's throat, and the blow intended for the Emperor penetrated my breast as I bore the assassin to the ground.

He did not leave the spot alive; for, as the Emperor lifted me in his own august arms, a dozen pikes pinned the would-be murderer to the earth.

It is true I was never able afterward to serve my dear
master in person, but he sees that my life wants nothing
to render it more bright or contented, and if ever I am
tempted to deplore my uselessness, one glance at the glit-
tering order upon my breast restores my peace of mind.

I have since decided that the shadow of the calamity
which threatened my master was cast before, and twice I
was permitted in an occult way, to perceive the murderer,
in order that when the event transpired I might preserve
for Europe and for Christendom the greatest ruler of my
time.

The Shadow and the Flash

Jack London

1902

When I look back, I realise what a peculiar friendship it was. First, there was Lloyd Inwood, tall, slender, and finely knit, nervous and dark. And then Paul Tichlorne, tall, slender, and finely knit, nervous and blond. Each was the replica of the other in everything except colour. Lloyd's eyes were black; Paul's were blue. Under stress of excitement, the blood coursed olive in the face of Lloyd, crimson in the face of Paul. But outside this matter of colouring they were as like as two peas. Both were high-strung, prone to excessive tension and endurance, and they lived at concert pitch.

But there was a trio involved in this remarkable friendship, and the third was short, and fat, and chunky, and lazy, and, loath to say, it was I. Paul and Lloyd seemed born to rivalry with each other, and I to be peacemaker between them. We grew up together, the three of us, and full often have I received the angry blows each intended for the other. They were always competing, striving to outdo each other, and when entered upon some such struggle there was no limit either to their endeavours or passions.

This intense spirit of rivalry obtained in their studies and their games. If Paul memorised one canto of "Marmion," Lloyd memorised two cantos, Paul came back with three, and Lloyd again with four, till each knew the whole poem by heart. I remember an incident that occurred at the swimming hole—an incident tragically significant of the life-struggle between them. The boys had a game of diving to the bottom of a ten-foot pool and holding on by submerged roots to see who could stay under the longest. Paul and Lloyd allowed themselves to be bantered into making the descent together. When I saw their faces, set and determined, disappear in the water as they sank swiftly down, I felt a foreboding of something dreadful. The moments sped, the ripples died away, the face of the pool grew placid and untroubled, and neither black nor golden head broke surface in quest of air. We above grew anxious. The longest record of the longest-winded boy had been exceeded, and still there was no sign. Air bubbles trickled slowly upward, showing that the breath had been expelled from their lungs, and after that the bubbles ceased to trickle upward. Each second became interminable, and, unable longer to endure the suspense, I plunged into the water.

I found them down at the bottom, clutching tight to the roots, their heads not a foot apart, their eyes wide open, each glaring fixedly at the other. They were suffering frightful torment, writhing and twisting in the pangs of voluntary suffocation; for neither would let go and acknowledge himself beaten. I tried to break Paul's hold on the root, but he resisted me fiercely. Then I lost my breath and came to the surface, badly scared. I quickly explained the situation, and half a dozen of us went down and by main strength tore them loose. By the time we got them out, both were unconscious, and it was only after much barrel-rolling and rubbing and pounding that they finally came to their senses. They would have drowned there, had no one rescued them.

When Paul Tichlorne entered college, he let it be generally understood that he was going in for the social sciences. Lloyd Inwood, entering at the same time, elected to take the same course. But Paul had had it secretly in mind all the time to study the natural sciences, specialising on chemistry, and at the last moment he switched over. Though Lloyd had already arranged his year's work and attended the first lectures, he at once followed Paul's lead and went in for the natural sciences and especially for chemistry. Their rivalry soon became a noted thing throughout the university. Each was a spur to the other, and they went into chemistry deeper than did ever students before—so deep, in fact, that ere they took their sheepskins they could have stumped any chemistry or "cow college" professor in the institution, save "old" Moss, head of the department, and even him they puzzled and edified more than once. Lloyd's discovery of the "death bacillus" of the sea toad, and his experiments on it with potassium cyanide, sent his name and that of his university ringing round the world; nor was Paul a whit behind when he succeeded in producing laboratory colloids exhibiting amoeba-like activities, and when he cast new light upon the processes of fertilisation through his startling experiments with simple sodium chlorides and magnesium solutions on low forms of marine life.

It was in their undergraduate days, however, in the midst of their profoundest plunges into the mysteries of organic chemistry, that Doris Van Benschoten entered into their lives. Lloyd met her first, but within twenty-four hours Paul saw to it that he also made her acquaintance. Of course, they fell in love with her, and she became the only thing in life worth living for. They wooed her with equal ardour and fire, and so intense became their struggle for her that half the student-body took to wagering wildly on the result. Even "old" Moss, one day, after an astounding demonstration in his private laboratory by Paul, was guilty to the extent of a month's salary of backing him to become the bridegroom of Doris Van Benschoten.

In the end she solved the problem in her own way, to everybody's satisfaction except Paul's and Lloyd's. Getting them together, she said that she really could not choose between them because she loved them both equally well; and that, unfortunately, since polyandry was not permitted in the United States she would be compelled to forego the honour and happiness of marrying either of them. Each blamed the other for this lamentable outcome, and the bitterness between them grew more bitter.

But things came to a head enough. It was at my home, after they had taken their degrees and dropped out of the world's sight, that the beginning of the end came to pass. Both were men of means, with little inclination and no necessity for professional life. My friendship and their mutual animosity were the two things that linked them in any way together. While they were very often at my place, they made it a fastidious point to avoid each other on such visits, though it was inevitable, under the circumstances, that they should come upon each other occasionally.

On the day I have in recollection, Paul Tichlorne had been mooning all morning in my study over a current scientific review. This left me free to my own affairs, and I was out among my roses when Lloyd Inwood arrived. Clipping and pruning and tacking the climbers on the porch, with my mouth full of nails, and Lloyd following me about and lending a hand now and again, we fell to discussing the mythical race of invisible people, that strange and vagrant people the traditions of which have come down to us. Lloyd warmed to the talk in his nervous, jerky fashion, and was soon interrogating the physical properties and possibilities of invisibility. A perfectly black object, he contended, would elude and defy the acutest vision.

"Colour is a sensation," he was saying. "It has no objective reality. Without light, we can see neither colours nor objects themselves. All objects are black in the dark, and in the dark it is impossible to see them. If no light strikes upon them, then no light is flung back from them to the eye, and so we have no vision-evidence of their being."

"But we see black objects in daylight," I objected.

"Very true," he went on warmly. "And that is because they are not perfectly black. Were they perfectly black, absolutely black, as it were, we could not see them—ay, not in the blaze of a thousand suns could we see them! And so I say, with the right pigments, properly compounded, an absolutely black paint could be produced which would render invisible whatever it was applied to."

"It would be a remarkable discovery," I said noncommittally, for the whole thing seemed too fantastic for aught but speculative purposes.

"Remarkable!" Lloyd slapped me on the shoulder. "I should say so. Why, old chap, to coat myself with such a paint would be to put the world at my feet. The secrets of kings and courts would be mine, the machinations of diplomats and politicians, the play of stock-gamblers, the plans of trusts and corporations. I could keep my hand on the inner pulse of things and become the greatest power in the world. And I—" He broke off shortly, then added, "Well, I have begun my experiments, and I don't mind telling you that I'm right in line for it."

A laugh from the doorway startled us. Paul Tichlorne was standing there, a smile of mockery on his lips.

"You forget, my dear Lloyd," he said.

"Forget what?"

"You forget," Paul went on—"ah, you forget the shadow."

I saw Lloyd's face drop, but he answered sneeringly, "I can carry a sunshade, you know." Then he turned suddenly and fiercely upon him. "Look here, Paul, you'll keep out of this if you know what's good for you."

A rupture seemed imminent, but Paul laughed good-naturedly. "I wouldn't lay fingers on your dirty pigments. Succeed beyond your most sanguine expectations, yet you will always fetch up against the shadow. You can't get away from it. Now I shall go on the very opposite tack. In the very nature of my proposition the shadow will be eliminated—"

"Transparency!" ejaculated Lloyd, instantly. "But it can't be achieved."

"Oh, no; of course not." And Paul shrugged his shoulders and strolled off down the briar-rose path.

This was the beginning of it. Both men attacked the problem with all the tremendous energy for which they were noted, and with a rancour and bitterness that made me tremble for the success of either. Each trusted me to the utmost, and in the long weeks of experimentation that followed I was made a party to both sides, listening to their theorisings and witnessing their demonstrations. Never, by word or sign, did I convey to either the slightest hint of the other's progress, and they respected me for the seal I put upon my lips.

Lloyd Inwood, after prolonged and unintermittent application, when the tension upon his mind and body became too great to bear, had a strange way of obtaining relief. He attended prize fights. It was at one of these brutal exhibitions, whither he had dragged me in order to tell his latest results, that his theory received striking confirmation.

"Do you see that red-whiskered man?" he asked, pointing across the ring to the fifth tier of seats on the opposite side. "And do you see the next man to him, the one in the white hat? Well, there is quite a gap between them, is there not?"

"Certainly," I answered. "They are a seat apart. The gap is the unoccupied seat."

He leaned over to me and spoke seriously. "Between the red-whiskered man and the white-hatted man sits Ben Wasson. You have heard me speak of him. He is the cleverest pugilist of his weight in the country. He is also a Caribbean negro, full-blooded, and the blackest in the United States. He has on a black overcoat buttoned up. I saw him when he came in and took that seat. As soon as he sat down he disappeared. Watch closely; he may smile."

I was for crossing over to verify Lloyd's statement, but he restrained me. "Wait," he said.

I waited and watched, till the red-whiskered man turned his head as though addressing the unoccupied seat; and then, in that empty space, I saw the rolling whites of a pair of eyes and the white double-crescent of two rows of teeth, and for the instant I could make out a negro's face. But with the passing of the smile his visibility passed, and the chair seemed vacant as before.

"Were he perfectly black, you could sit alongside him and not see him," Lloyd said; and I confess the illustration was apt enough to make me well-nigh convinced.

I visited Lloyd's laboratory a number of times after that, and found him always deep in his search after the absolute black. His experiments covered all sorts of pigments, such as lamp-blacks, tars, carbonised vegetable matters, soots of oils and fats, and the various carbonised animal substances.

"White light is composed of the seven primary colours," he argued to me. "But it is itself, of itself, invisible. Only by being reflected from objects do it and the objects become visible. But only that portion of it that is reflected becomes visible. For instance, here is a blue tobacco-box. The white light strikes against it, and, with one exception, all its component colours—violet, indigo, green, yellow, orange, and red—are absorbed. The one exception is *blue*. It is not absorbed, but reflected. Therefore the tobacco-box gives us a sensation of blueness. We do not see the other colours because they are absorbed. We see only the blue. For the same reason grass is *green*. The green waves of white light are thrown upon our eyes."

"When we paint our houses, we do not apply colour to them," he said at another time. "What we do is to apply certain substances that have the property of absorbing from white light all the colours except those that we would have our houses appear. When a substance reflects all the colours to the eye, it seems to us white. When it absorbs all the colours, it is black. But, as I said before, we have as yet no perfect black. *All* the colours are not absorbed. The perfect black, guarding against high lights, will be utterly and absolutely invisible. Look at that, for example."

He pointed to the palette lying on his work-table. Different shades of black pigments were brushed on it. One, in particular, I could hardly see. It gave my eyes a blurring sensation, and I rubbed them and looked again.

"That," he said impressively, "is the blackest black you or any mortal man ever looked upon. But just you wait, and I'll have a black so black that no mortal man will be able to look upon it—*and see it!*"

On the other hand, I used to find Paul Tichlorne plunged as deeply into the study of light polarisation, diffraction, and interference, single and double refraction, and all manner of strange organic compounds.

"Transparency: a state or quality of body which permits all rays of light to pass through," he defined for me. "That is what I am seeking. Lloyd blunders up against the shadow with his perfect opaqueness. But I escape it. A transparent body casts no shadow; neither does it reflect light-waves—that is, the perfectly transparent does not. So, avoiding high lights, not only will such a body cast no shadow, but, since it reflects no light, it will also be invisible."

We were standing by the window at another time. Paul was engaged in polishing a number of lenses, which were ranged along the sill. Suddenly, after a pause in the conversation, he said, "Oh! I've dropped a lens. Stick your head out, old man, and see where it went to."

Out I started to thrust my head, but a sharp blow on the forehead caused me to recoil. I rubbed my bruised brow and gazed with reproachful inquiry at Paul, who was laughing in gleeful, boyish fashion.

"Well?" he said.

"Well?" I echoed.

"Why don't you investigate?" he demanded. And investigate I did. Before thrusting out my head, my senses, automatically active, had told me there was nothing there, that nothing intervened between me and out-of-doors, that the aperture of the window opening was utterly empty. I stretched forth my hand and felt a hard object, smooth and cool and flat, which my touch, out of its experience, told me to be glass. I looked again, but could see positively nothing.

"White quartzose sand," Paul rattled off, "sodic carbonate, slaked lime, cutlet, manganese peroxide—there you have it, the finest French plate glass, made by the great St. Gobain Company, who made the finest plate glass in the world, and this is the finest piece they ever made. It cost a king's ransom. But look at it! You can't see it. You don't know it's there till you run your head against it.

"Eh, old boy! That's merely an object-lesson—certain elements, in themselves opaque, yet so compounded as to give a resultant body which is transparent. But that is a matter of inorganic chemistry, you say. Very true. But I dare to assert, standing here on my two feet, that in the organic I can duplicate whatever occurs in the inorganic.

"Here!" He held a test-tube between me and the light, and I noted the cloudy or muddy liquid it contained. He emptied the contents of another test-tube into it, and almost instantly it became clear and sparkling.

"Or here!" With quick, nervous movements among his array of test-tubes, he turned a white solution to a wine colour, and a light yellow solution to a dark brown. He dropped a piece of litmus paper, the *rocella tinctoria,* into an acid, when it changed instantly to red, and on floating it in an alkali it turned as quickly to blue.

"The litmus paper is still the litmus paper," he enunciated in the formal manner of the lecturer. "I have not changed it into something else. Then what did I do? I merely changed the arrangement of its molecules. Where, at first, it absorbed all colours from the light but red, its molecular structure was so changed that it absorbed red and all colours except blue. And so it goes, *ad infinitum.* Now, what I purpose to do is this." He paused for a space. "I purpose to seek—ay, and to find—the proper reagents, which, acting upon the living organism, will bring about molecular changes analogous to those you have just witnessed. But these reagents, which I shall find, and for that matter, upon which I already have my hands, will not turn the living body to blue or red or black, but they will turn it to transparency. All light will pass through it. It will be invisible. It will cast no shadow."

A few weeks later I went hunting with Paul. He had been promising me for some time that I should have the pleasure of shooting over a wonderful dog—the most wonderful dog, in fact, that ever man shot over, so he averred, and continued to aver till my curiosity was aroused. But on the morning in question I was disappointed, for there was no dog in evidence.

"Don't see him about," Paul remarked unconcernedly, and we set off across the fields.

I could not imagine, at the time, what was ailing me, but I had a feeling of some impending and deadly illness. My nerves were all awry, and, from the astounding tricks they played me, my senses seemed to have run riot. Strange sounds disturbed me. At times I heard the swish-swish of grass being shoved aside, and once the patter of feet across a patch of stony ground.

"Did you hear anything, Paul?" I asked once.

But he shook his head, and thrust his feet steadily forward.

While climbing a fence, I heard the low, eager whine of a dog, apparently from within a couple of feet of me; but on looking about me I saw nothing.

I dropped to the ground, limp and trembling.

"Paul," I said, "we had better return to the house. I am afraid I am going to be sick."

"Nonsense, old man," he answered. "The sunshine has gone to your head like wine. You'll be all right. It's famous weather."

But, passing along a narrow path through a clump of cottonwoods, some object brushed against my legs and I stumbled and nearly fell. I looked with sudden anxiety at Paul.

"What's the matter?" he asked. "Tripping over your own feet?"

I kept my tongue between my teeth and plodded on, though sore perplexed and thoroughly satisfied that some acute and mysterious malady had attacked my nerves. So far my eyes had escaped; but, when we got to the open fields again, even my vision went back on me. Strange flashes of varicoloured, rainbow light began to appear and disappear on the path before me. Still, I managed to keep myself in hand, till the varicoloured lights persisted for a space of fully twenty seconds, dancing and flashing in continuous play. Then I sat down, weak and shaky.

"It's all up with me," I gasped, covering my eyes with my hands. "It has attacked my eyes. Paul, take me home."

But Paul laughed long and loud. "What did I tell you?—the most wonderful dog, eh? Well, what do you think?"

He turned partly from me and began to whistle. I heard the patter of feet, the panting of a heated animal, and the unmistakable yelp of a dog. Then Paul stooped down and apparently fondled the empty air.

"Here! Give me your fist."

And he rubbed my hand over the cold nose and jowls of a dog. A dog it certainly was, with the shape and the smooth, short coat of a pointer.

Suffice to say, I speedily recovered my spirits and control. Paul put a collar about the animal's neck and tied his handkerchief to its tail. And then was vouchsafed us the remarkable sight of an empty collar and a waving handkerchief cavorting over the fields. It was something to see that collar and handkerchief pin a bevy of quail in a clump of locusts and remain rigid and immovable till we had flushed the birds.

Now and again the dog emitted the varicoloured light-flashes I have mentioned. The one thing, Paul explained, which he had not anticipated and which he doubted could be overcome.

"They're a large family," he said, "these sun dogs, wind dogs, rainbows, halos, and perihelia. They are produced by refraction of light from mineral and ice crystals, from mist, rain, spray, and no end of things; and I am afraid they are the penalty I must pay for transparency. I escaped Lloyd's shadow only to fetch up against the rainbow flash."

A couple of days later, before the entrance to Paul's laboratory, I encountered a terrible stench. So overpowering was it that it was easy to discover the source—mass of putrescent matter on the doorstep which in general out-lines resembled a dog.

Paul was startled when he investigated my find. It was his invisible dog, or rather, what had been his invisible dog, for it was now plainly visible. It had been playing about but a few minutes before in all health and strength. Closer examination revealed that the skull had been crushed by some heavy blow. While it was strange that the animal should have been killed, the inexplicable thing was that it should so quickly decay.

"The reagents I injected into its system were harmless," Paul explained. "Yet they were powerful, and it appears that when death comes they force practically instantaneous disintegration. Remarkable! Most remarkable! Well, the only thing is not to die. They do not harm so long as one lives. But I do wonder who smashed in that dog's head."

Light, however, was thrown upon this when a frightened housemaid brought the news that Gaffer Bedshaw had that very morning, not more than an hour back, gone violently insane, and was strapped down at home, in the huntsman's lodge, where he raved of a battle with a ferocious and gigantic beast that he had encountered in the Tichlorne pasture. He claimed that the thing, whatever it was, was invisible, that with his own eyes he had seen that it was invisible; wherefore his tearful wife and daughters shook their heads, and wherefore he but waxed the more violent, and the gardener and the coachman tightened the straps by another hole.

Nor, while Paul Tichlorne was thus successfully mastering the problem of invisibility, was Lloyd Inwood a whit behind. I went over in answer to a message of his to come and see how he was getting on. Now his laboratory occupied an isolated situation in the midst of his vast grounds. It was built in a pleasant little glade, surrounded on all sides by a dense forest growth, and was to be gained by way of a winding and erratic path. But I have travelled that path so often as to know every foot of it, and conceive my surprise when I came upon the glade and found no laboratory. The quaint shed structure with its red sandstone chimney was not. Nor did it look as if it ever had been. There were no signs of ruin, no debris, nothing.

I started to walk across what had once been its site. "This," I said to myself, "should be where the step went up to the door." Barely were the words out of my mouth when I stubbed my toe on some obstacle, pitched forward, and butted my head into something that *felt* very much like a door. I reached out my hand. It *was* a door. I found the knob and turned it. And at once, as the door swung inward on its hinges, the whole interior of the laboratory impinged upon my vision. Greeting Lloyd, I closed the door and backed up the path a few paces. I could see nothing of the building. Returning and opening the door, at once all the furniture and every detail of the interior were visible. It was indeed startling, the sudden transition from void to light and form and colour.

"What do you think of it, eh?" Lloyd asked, wringing my hand. "I slapped a couple of coats of absolute black on the outside yesterday afternoon to see how it worked. How's your head? you bumped it pretty solidly, I imagine."

"Never mind that," he interrupted my congratulations. "I've something better for you to do."

While he talked he began to strip, and when he stood naked before me he thrust a pot and brush into my hand and said, "Here, give me a coat of this."

It was an oily, shellac-like stuff, which spread quickly and easily over the skin and dried immediately.

"Merely preliminary and precautionary," he explained when I had finished; "but now for the real stuff."

I picked up another pot he indicated, and glanced inside, but could see nothing.

"It's empty," I said.

"Stick your finger in it."

I obeyed, and was aware of a sensation of cool moistness. On withdrawing my hand I glanced at the forefinger, the one I had immersed, but it had disappeared. I moved and knew from the alternate tension and relaxation of the muscles that I moved it, but it defied my sense of sight. To all appearances I had been shorn of a finger; nor could I get any visual impression of it till I extended it under the skylight and saw its shadow plainly blotted on the floor.

Lloyd chuckled. "Now spread it on, and keep your eyes open."

I dipped the brush into the seemingly empty pot, and gave him a long stroke across his chest. With the passage of the brush the living flesh disappeared from beneath. I covered his right leg, and he was a one-legged man defying all laws of gravitation. And so, stroke by stroke, member by member, I painted Lloyd Inwood into nothingness. It was a creepy experience, and I was glad when naught remained in sight but his burning black eyes, poised apparently unsupported in mid-air.

"I have a refined and harmless solution for them," he said. "A fine spray with an air-brush, and presto! I am not."

This deftly accomplished, he said, "Now I shall move about, and do you tell me what sensations you experience."

"In the first place, I cannot see you," I said, and I could hear his gleeful laugh from the midst of the emptiness. "Of course," I continued, "you cannot escape your shadow, but that was to be expected. When you pass between my eye and an object, the object disappears, but so unusual and incomprehensible is its disappearance that it seems to me as though my eyes had blurred. When you move rapidly, I experience a bewildering succession of blurs. The blurring sensation makes my eyes ache and my brain tired."

"Have you any other warnings of my presence?" he asked.

"No, and yes," I answered. "When you are near me I have feelings similar to those produced by dank warehouses, gloomy crypts, and deep mines. And as sailors feel the loom of the land on dark nights, so I think I feel the loom of your body. But it is all very vague and intangible."

Long we talked that last morning in his laboratory; and when I turned to go, he put his unseen hand in mine with nervous grip, and said, "Now I shall conquer the world!" And I could not dare to tell him of Paul Tichlorne's equal success.

At home I found a note from Paul, asking me to come up immediately, and it was high noon when I came spinning up the driveway on my wheel. Paul called me from the tennis court, and I dismounted and went over. But the court was empty. As I stood there, gaping open-mouthed, a tennis ball struck me on the arm, and as I turned about, another whizzed past my ear. For aught I could see of my assailant, they came whirling at me from out of space, and right well was I peppered with them. But when the balls already flung at me began to come back for a second whack, I realised the situation. Seizing a racquet and keeping my eyes open, I quickly saw a rainbow flash appearing and disappearing and darting over the ground. I took out after it, and when I laid the racquet upon it for a half-dozen stout blows, Paul's voice rang out:

"Enough! Enough! Oh! Ouch! Stop! You're landing on my naked skin, you know! Ow! O-w-w! I'll be good! I'll be good! I only wanted you to see my metamorphosis," he said ruefully, and I imagined he was rubbing his hurts.

A few minutes later we were playing tennis—a handicap on my part, for I could have no knowledge of his position save when all the angles between himself, the sun, and me, were in proper conjunction. Then he flashed, and only then. But the flashes were more brilliant than the rainbow—purest blue, most delicate violet, brightest yellow, and all the intermediary shades, with the scintillant brilliancy of the diamond, dazzling, blinding, iridescent.

But in the midst of our play I felt a sudden cold chill, reminding me of deep mines and gloomy crypts, such a chill as I had experienced that very morning. The next moment, close to the net, I saw a ball rebound in mid-air and empty space, and at the same instant, a score of feet away, Paul Tichlorne emitted a rainbow flash. It could not be he from whom the ball had rebounded, and with sickening dread I realised that Lloyd Inwood had come upon the scene. To make sure, I looked for his shadow, and there it was, a shapeless blotch the girth of his body, (the sun was overhead), moving along the ground. I remembered his threat, and felt sure that all the long years of rivalry were about to culminate in uncanny battle.

I cried a warning to Paul, and heard a snarl as of a wild beast, and an answering snarl. I saw the dark blotch move swiftly across the court, and a brilliant burst of vari-coloured light moving with equal swiftness to meet it; and then shadow and flash came together and there was the sound of unseen blows. The net went down before my frightened eyes. I sprang toward the fighters, crying:

"For God's sake!"

But their locked bodies smote against my knees, and I was overthrown.

"You keep out of this, old man!" I heard the voice of Lloyd Inwood from out of the emptiness. And then Paul's voice crying, "Yes, we've had enough of peacemaking!"

From the sound of their voices I knew they had separated. I could not locate Paul, and so approached the shadow that represented Lloyd. But from the other side came a stunning blow on the point of my jaw, and I heard Paul scream angrily, "Now will you keep away?"

Then they came together again, the impact of their blows, their groans and gasps, and the swift flashings and shadow-movings telling plainly of the deadliness of the struggle.

I shouted for help, and Gaffer Bedshaw came running into the court. I could see, as he approached, that he was looking at me strangely, but he collided with the combatants and was hurled headlong to the ground. With despairing shriek and a cry of "O Lord, I've got 'em!" he sprang to his feet and tore madly out of the court.

I could do nothing, so I sat up, fascinated and power-less, and watched the struggle. The noonday sun beat down with dazzling brightness on the naked tennis court. And it was naked. All I could see was the blotch of shadow and the rainbow flashes, the dust rising from the invisible feet, the earth tearing up from beneath the straining foot-grips, and the wire screen bulge once or twice as their bodies hurled against it. That was all, and after a time even that ceased. There were no more flashes, and the shadow had become long and stationary; and I remembered their set boyish faces when they clung to the roots in the deep cool-ness of the pool.

They found me an hour afterward. Some inkling of what had happened got to the servants and they quitted the Tichlorne service in a body. Gaffer Bedshaw never recov-ered from the second shock he received, and is confined in a madhouse, hopelessly incurable. The secrets of their marvelous discoveries died with Paul and Lloyd, both lab-oratories being destroyed by grief-stricken relatives. As for myself, I no longer care for chemical research, and science is a tabooed topic in my household. I have returned to my roses. Nature's colours are good enough for me.

The Shadows on the Wall
Mary E. Wilkins Freeman
1903

"Henry had words with Edward in the study the night before Edward died," said Caroline Glynn.

She was elderly, tall, and harshly thin, with a hard co-
lourlessness of face. She spoke not with acrimony, but
with grave severity. Rebecca Ann Glynn, younger, stouter
and rosy of face between her crinkling puffs of gray hair,
gasped, by way of assent. She sat in a wide flounce of black
silk in the corner of the sofa, and rolled terrified eyes from
her sister Caroline to her sister Mrs. Stephen Brigham,
who had been Emma Glynn, the one beauty of the family.
She was beautiful still, with a large, splendid, full-blown
beauty; she filled a great rocking-chair with her superb
bulk of femininity, and swayed gently back and forth,
her black silks whispering and her black frills fluttering.
Even the shock of death (for her brother Edward lay dead
in the house,) could not disturb her outward serenity of
demeanour. She was grieved over the loss of her brother:
he had been the youngest, and she had been fond of him,
but never had Emma Brigham lost sight of her own importance amidst the waters of tribulation. She was always
awake to the consciousness of her own stability in the
midst of vicissitudes and the splendour of her permanent
bearing.

But even her expression of masterly placidity changed before her sister Caroline's announcement and her sister Rebecca Ann's gasp of terror and distress in response.

"I think Henry might have controlled his temper, when poor Edward was so near his end," said she with an asperity which disturbed slightly the roseate curves of her beautiful mouth.

"Of course he did not *know,*" murmured Rebecca Ann in a faint tone strangely out of keeping with her appearance.

One involuntarily looked again to be sure that such a feeble pipe came from that full-swelling chest.

"Of course he did not know it," said Caroline quickly. She turned on her sister with a strange sharp look of suspicion. "How could he have known it?" said she. Then she shrank as if from the other's possible answer. "Of course you and I both know he could not," said she conclusively, but her pale face was paler than it had been before.

Rebecca gasped again. The married sister, Mrs. Emma Brigham, was now sitting up straight in her chair; she had ceased rocking, and was eyeing them both intently with a sudden accentuation of family likeness in her face. Given one common intensity of emotion and similar lines showed forth, and the three sisters of one race were evident.

"What do you mean?" said she impartially to them both. Then she, too, seemed to shrink before a possible answer. She even laughed an evasive sort of laugh. "I guess you don't mean anything," said she, but her face wore still the expression of shrinking horror.

"Nobody means anything," said Caroline firmly. She rose and crossed the room toward the door with grim decisiveness.

"Where are you going?" asked Mrs. Brigham.

"I have something to see to," replied Caroline, and the others at once knew by her tone that she had some solemn and sad duty to perform in the chamber of death.

"Oh," said Mrs. Brigham.

After the door had closed behind Caroline, she turned to Rebecca.

"Did Henry have many words with him?" she asked.

"They were talking very loud," replied Rebecca evasively, yet with an answering gleam of ready response to the other's curiosity in the quick lift of her soft blue eyes.

Mrs. Brigham looked at her. She had not resumed rocking. She still sat up straight with a slight knitting of intensity on her fair forehead, between the pretty rippling curves of her auburn hair.

"Did you—hear anything?" she asked in a low voice with a glance toward the door.

"I was just across the hall in the south parlour, and that door was open and this door ajar," replied Rebecca with a slight flush.

"Then you must have—"

"I couldn't help it."

"Everything?"

"Most of it."

"What was it?"

"The old story."

"I suppose Henry was mad, as he always was, because Edward was living on here for nothing, when he had wasted all the money father left him."

Rebecca nodded with a fearful glance at the door.

When Emma spoke again her voice was still more hushed. "I know how he felt," said she. "He had always been so prudent himself, and worked hard at his profession, and there Edward had never done anything but spend, and it must have looked to him as if Edward was living at his expense, but he wasn't."

"No, he wasn't."

"It was the way father left the property—that all the children should have a home here—and he left money enough to buy the food and all if we had all come home."

"Yes."

"And Edward had a right here according to the terms of father's will, and Henry ought to have remembered it."

"Yes, he ought."

"Did he say hard things?"

"Pretty hard from what I heard."

"What?"

"I heard him tell Edward that he had no business here at all, and he thought he had better go away."

"What did Edward say?"

"That he would stay here as long as he lived and afterward, too, if he was a mind to, and he would like to see Henry get him out; and then—"

"What?"

"Then he laughed."

"What did Henry say."

"I didn't hear him say anything, but—"

"But what?"

"I saw him when he came out of this room."

"He looked mad?"

"You've seen him when he looked so."

Emma nodded; the expression of horror on her face had deepened.

"Do you remember that time he killed the cat because she had scratched him?"

"Yes. Don't!"

Then Caroline reentered the room. She went up to the stove in which a wood fire was burning—it was a cold, gloomy day of fall—and she warmed her hands, which were reddened from recent washing in cold water.

Mrs. Brigham looked at her and hesitated. She glanced at the door, which was still ajar, as it did not easily shut, being still swollen with the damp weather of the summer. She rose and pushed it together with a sharp thud which jarred the house. Rebecca started painfully with a half exclamation. Caroline looked at her disapprovingly.

"It is time you controlled your nerves, Rebecca," said she.

"I can't help it," replied Rebecca with almost a wail. "I am nervous. There's enough to make me so, the Lord knows."

"What do you mean by that?" asked Caroline with her old air of sharp suspicion, and something between challenge and dread of its being met.

Rebecca shrank.

"Nothing," said she.

"Then I wouldn't keep speaking in such a fashion."

Emma, returning from the closed door, said imperiously that it ought to be fixed, it shut so hard.

"It will shrink enough after we have had the fire a few days," replied Caroline. "If anything is done to it it will be too small; there will be a crack at the sill."

"I think Henry ought to be ashamed of himself for talking as he did to Edward," said Mrs. Brigham abruptly, but in an almost inaudible voice.

"Hush!" said Caroline, with a glance of actual fear at the closed door.

"Nobody can hear with the door shut."

"He must have heard it shut, and—"

"Well, I can say what I want to before he comes down, and I am not afraid of him."

"I don't know who is afraid of him! What reason is there for anybody to be afraid of Henry?" demanded Caroline.

Mrs. Brigham trembled before her sister's look. Rebecca gasped again. "There isn't any reason, of course. Why should there be?"

"I wouldn't speak so, then. Somebody might overhear you and think it was queer. Miranda Joy is in the south parlour sewing, you know."

"I thought she went upstairs to stitch on the machine."

"She did, but she has come down again."

"Well, she can't hear."

"I say again I think Henry ought to be ashamed of himself. I shouldn't think he'd ever get over it, having words with poor Edward the very night before he died. Edward was enough sight better disposition than Henry, with all his faults. I always thought a great deal of poor Edward, myself."

Mrs. Brigham passed a large fluff of handkerchief across her eyes; Rebecca sobbed outright.

"Rebecca," said Caroline admonishingly, keeping her mouth stiff and swallowing determinately.

"I never heard him speak a cross word, unless he spoke cross to Henry that last night. I don't know, but he did from what Rebecca overheard," said Emma.

"Not so much cross as sort of soft, and sweet, and aggravating," sniffled Rebecca.

"He never raised his voice," said Caroline; "but he had his way."

"He had a right to in this case."

"Yes, he did."

"He had as much of a right here as Henry," sobbed Rebecca, "and now he's gone, and he will never be in this home that poor father left him and the rest of us again."

"What do you really think ailed Edward?" asked Emma in hardly more than a whisper. She did not look at her sister.

Caroline sat down in a nearby armchair, and clutched the arms convulsively until her thin knuckles whitened.

"I told you," said she.

Rebecca held her handkerchief over her mouth, and looked at them above it with terrified, streaming eyes.

"I know you said that he had terrible pains in his stomach, and had spasms, but what do you think made him have them?"

"Henry called it gastric trouble. You know Edward has always had dyspepsia."

Mrs. Brigham hesitated a moment. "Was there any talk of an—examination?" said she.

Then Caroline turned on her fiercely.

"No," said she in a terrible voice. "No."

The three sisters' souls seemed to meet on one common ground of terrified understanding though their eyes. The old-fashioned latch of the door was heard to rattle, and a push from without made the door shake ineffectually. "It's Henry," Rebecca sighed rather than whispered. Mrs. Brigham settled herself after a noiseless rush across the floor into her rocking-chair again, and was swaying back and forth with her head comfortably leaning back, when the door at last yielded and Henry Glynn entered. He cast a covertly sharp, comprehensive glance at Mrs. Brigham with her elaborate calm; at Rebecca quietly huddled in the corner of the sofa with her handkerchief to her face and only one small reddened ear as attentive as a dog's uncovered and revealing her alertness for his presence; at Caroline sitting with a strained composure in her armchair by the stove. She met his eyes quite firmly with a look of inscrutable fear, and defiance of the fear and of him.

Henry Glynn looked more like this sister than the others. Both had the same hard delicacy of form and feature, both were tall and almost emaciated, both had a sparse growth of gray blond hair far back from high intellectual foreheads, both had an almost noble aquilinity of feature. They confronted each other with the pitiless immovability of two statues in whose marble lineaments emotions were fixed for all eternity.

Then Henry Glynn smiled and the smile transformed his face. He looked suddenly years younger, and an almost boyish recklessness and irresolution appeared in his face. He flung himself into a chair with a gesture which was bewildering from its incongruity with his general appearance. He leaned his head back, flung one leg over the other, and looked laughingly at Mrs. Brigham.

"I declare, Emma, you grow younger every year," he said.

She flushed a little, and her placid mouth widened at the corners. She was susceptible to praise.

"Our thoughts to-day ought to belong to the one of us who will *never* grow older," said Caroline in a hard voice.

Henry looked at her, still smiling. "Of course, we none of us forget that," said he, in a deep, gentle voice, "but we have to speak to the living, Caroline, and I have not seen Emma for a long time, and the living are as dear as the dead."

"Not to me," said Caroline.

She rose, and went abruptly out of the room again. Rebecca also rose and hurried after her, sobbing loudly.

Henry looked slowly after them.

"Caroline is completely unstrung," said he. Mrs. Brigham rocked. A confidence in him inspired by his manner was stealing over her. Out of that confidence she spoke quite easily and naturally.

"His death was very sudden," said she.

Henry's eyelids quivered slightly but his gaze was unswerving.

"Yes," said he; "it was very sudden. He was sick only a few hours."

"What did you call it?"

"Gastric."

"You did not think of an examination?"

"There was no need. I am perfectly certain as to the cause of his death."

Suddenly Mrs. Brigham felt a creep as of some live horror over her very soul. Her flesh prickled with cold, before an inflection of his voice. She rose, tottering on weak knees.

"Where are you going?" asked Henry in a strange, breathless voice.

Mrs. Brigham said something incoherent about some sewing which she had to do, some black for the funeral, and was out of the room. She went up to the front chamber which she occupied. Caroline was there. She went close to her and took her hands, and the two sisters looked at each other.

"Don't speak, don't, I won't have it!" said Caroline finally in an awful whisper.

"I won't," replied Emma.

That afternoon the three sisters were in the study, the large front room on the ground floor across the hall from the south parlour, when the dusk deepened.

Mrs. Brigham was hemming some black material. She sat close to the west window for the waning light. At last she laid her work on her lap.

"It's no use, I cannot see to sew another stitch until we have a light," said she.

Caroline, who was writing some letters at the table, turned to Rebecca, in her usual place on the sofa.

"Rebecca, you had better get a lamp," she said.

Rebecca started up; even in the dusk her face showed her agitation.

"It doesn't seem to me that we need a lamp quite yet," she said in a piteous, pleading voice like a child's.

"Yes, we do," returned Mrs. Brigham peremptorily. "We must have a light. I must finish this to-night or I can't go to the funeral, and I can't see to sew another stitch."

"Caroline can see to write letters, and she is farther from the window than you are," said Rebecca.

"Are you trying to save kerosene or are you lazy, Rebecca Glynn?" cried Mrs. Brigham. "I can go and get the light myself, but I have this work all in my lap."

Caroline's pen stopped scratching.

"Rebecca, we must have the light," said she.

"Had we better have it in here?" asked Rebecca weakly.

"Of course! Why not?" cried Caroline sternly.

"I am sure I don't want to take my sewing into the other room, when it is all cleaned up for to-morrow," said Mrs. Brigham.

"Why, I never heard such a to-do about lighting a lamp."

Rebecca rose and left the room. Presently she entered with a lamp—a large one with a white porcelain shade. She set it on a table, an old-fashioned card-table which was placed against the opposite wall from the window. That wall was clear of bookcases and books, which were only on three sides of the room. That opposite wall was taken up with three doors, the one small space being occupied by the table. Above the table on the old-fashioned paper, of a white satin gloss, traversed by an indeterminate green scroll, hung quite high a small gilt and black-framed ivory miniature taken in her girlhood of the mother of the family. When the lamp was set on the table beneath it, the tiny pretty face painted on the ivory seemed to gleam out with a look of intelligence.

"What have you put that lamp over there for?" asked Mrs. Brigham, with more of impatience than her voice usually revealed. "Why didn't you set it in the hall and have done with it. Neither Caroline nor I can see if it is on that table."

"I thought perhaps you would move," replied Rebecca hoarsely.

"If I do move, we can't both sit at that table. Caroline has her paper all spread around. Why don't you set the lamp on the study table in the middle of the room, then we can both see?"

Rebecca hesitated. Her face was very pale. She looked with an appeal that was fairly agonizing at her sister Caroline.

"Why don't you put the lamp on this table, as she says?" asked Caroline, almost fiercely. "Why do you act so, Rebecca?"

"I should think you *would* ask her that," said Mrs. Brigham. "She doesn't act like herself at all."

Rebecca took the lamp and set it on the table in the middle of the room without another word. Then she turned her back upon it quickly and seated herself on the sofa, and placed a hand over her eyes as if to shade them, and remained so.

"Does the light hurt your eyes, and is that the reason why you didn't want the lamp?" asked Mrs. Brigham kindly.

"I always like to sit in the dark," replied Rebecca chokingly. Then she snatched her handkerchief hastily from her pocket and began to weep. Caroline continued to write, Mrs. Brigham to sew.

Suddenly Mrs. Brigham as she sewed glanced at the opposite wall. The glance became a steady stare. She looked intently, her work suspended in her hands. Then she looked away again and took a few more stitches, then she looked again, and again turned to her task. At last she laid her work in her lap and stared concentratedly. She looked from the wall around the room, taking note of the various objects; she looked at the wall long and intently. Then she turned to her sisters.

"What *is* that?" said she.

"What?" asked Caroline harshly; her pen scratched loudly across the paper.

Rebecca gave one of her convulsive gasps.

"That strange shadow on the wall," replied Mrs. Brigham.

Rebecca sat with her face hidden: Caroline dipped her pen in the inkstand.

"Why don't you turn around and look?" asked Mrs. Brigham in a wondering and somewhat aggrieved way.

"I am in a hurry to finish this letter, if Mrs. Wilson Ebbit is going to get word in time to come to the funeral," replied Caroline shortly.

Mrs. Brigham rose, her work slipping to the floor, and she began walking around the room, moving various articles of furniture, with her eyes on the shadow.

Then suddenly she shrieked out:

"Look at this awful shadow! What is it? Caroline, look, look! Rebecca, look! *What is it?*"

All Mrs. Brigham's triumphant placidity was gone. Her handsome face was livid with horror. She stood stiffly pointing at the shadow.

"Look!" said she, pointing her finger at it. "Look! What is it?"

Then Rebecca burst out in a wild wail after a shuddering glance at the wall:

"Oh, Caroline, there it is again! There it is again!"

"Caroline Glynn, you look!" said Mrs. Brigham. "Look! What is that dreadful shadow?"

Caroline rose, turned, and stood confronting the wall.

"How should I know?" she said.

"It has been there every night since he died," cried Rebecca.

"Every night?"

"Yes. He died Thursday and this is Saturday; that makes three nights," said Caroline rigidly. She stood as if holding herself calm with a vise of concentrated will.

"It—it looks like—like—" stammered Mrs. Brigham in a tone of intense horror.

"I know what it looks like well enough," said Caroline. "I've got eyes in my head."

"It looks like Edward," burst out Rebecca in a sort of frenzy of fear. "Only—"

"Yes, it does," assented Mrs. Brigham, whose horror-stricken tone matched her sister's, "only— Oh, it is awful! What is it, Caroline?"

"I ask you again, how should I know?" replied Caroline. "I see it there like you. How should I know any more than you?"

"It *must* be something in the room," said Mrs. Brigham, staring wildly around.

"We moved everything in the room the first night it came," said Rebecca; "it is not anything in the room."

Caroline turned upon her with a sort of fury. "Of course it is something in the room," said she. "How you act! What do you mean by talking so? Of course it is something in the room."

"Of course, it is," agreed Mrs. Brigham, looking at Caroline suspiciously. "Of course it must be. It is only a coincidence. It just happens so. Perhaps it is that fold of the window curtain that makes it. It must be something in the room."

"It is not anything in the room," repeated Rebecca with obstinate horror.

The door opened suddenly and Henry Glynn entered. He began to speak, then his eyes followed the direction of the others'. He stood stock still staring at the shadow on the wall. It was life size and stretched across the white parallelogram of a door, half across the wall space on which the picture hung.

"What is that?" he demanded in a strange voice.

"It must be due to something in the room," Mrs. Brigham said faintly.

"It is not due to anything in the room," said Rebecca again with the shrill insistency of terror.

"How you act, Rebecca Glynn," said Caroline.

Henry Glynn stood and stared a moment longer. His face showed a gamut of emotions—horror, conviction, then furious incredulity. Suddenly he began hastening hither and thither about the room. He moved the furniture with fierce jerks, turning ever to see the effect upon the shadow on the wall. Not a line of its terrible outlines wavered.

"It must be something in the room!" he declared in a voice which seemed to snap like a lash.

His face changed. The inmost secrecy of his nature seemed evident until one almost lost sight of his lineaments. Rebecca stood close to her sofa, regarding him with woeful, fascinated eyes. Mrs. Brigham clutched Caroline's hand. They both stood in a corner out of his way. For a few moments he raged about the room like a caged wild animal. He moved every piece of furniture; when the moving of a piece did not affect the shadow, he flung it to the floor, the sisters watching.

Then suddenly he desisted. He laughed and began straightening the furniture which he had flung down.

"What an absurdity," he said easily. "Such a to-do about a shadow."

"That's so," assented Mrs. Brigham, in a scared voice which she tried to make natural. As she spoke she lifted a chair near her.

"I think you have broken the chair that Edward was so fond of," said Caroline.

Terror and wrath were struggling for expression on her face. Her mouth was set, her eyes shrinking. Henry lifted the chair with a show of anxiety.

"Just as good as ever," he said pleasantly. He laughed again, looking at his sisters. "Did I scare you?" he said. "I should think you might be used to me by this time. You know my way of wanting to leap to the bottom of a mystery, and that shadow does look—queer, like—and I thought if there was any way of accounting for it I would like to without any delay."

"You don't seem to have succeeded," remarked Caroline dryly, with a slight glance at the wall.

Henry's eyes followed hers and he quivered perceptibly.

"Oh, there is no accounting for shadows," he said, and he laughed again. "A man is a fool to try to account for shadows."

Then the supper bell rang, and they all left the room, but Henry kept his back to the wall, as did, indeed, the others.

Mrs. Brigham pressed close to Caroline as she crossed the hall. "He looked like a demon!" she breathed in her ear.

Henry led the way with an alert motion like a boy; Rebecca brought up the rear; she could scarcely walk, her knees trembled so.

"I can't sit in that room again this evening," she whispered to Caroline after supper.

"Very well, we will sit in the south room," replied Caroline. "I think we will sit in the south parlour," she said aloud; "it isn't as damp as the study, and I have a cold."

So they all sat in the south room with their sewing. Henry read the newspaper, his chair drawn close to the lamp on the table. About nine o'clock he rose abruptly and crossed the hall to the study. The three sisters looked at one another. Mrs. Brigham rose, folded her rustling skirts compactly around her, and began tiptoeing toward the door.

"What are you going to do?" inquired Rebecca agitatedly.

"I am going to see what he is about," replied Mrs. Brigham cautiously.

She pointed as she spoke to the study door across the hall; it was ajar. Henry had striven to pull it together behind him, but it had somehow swollen beyond the limit with curious speed. It was still ajar and a streak of light showed from top to bottom. The hall lamp was not lit.

"You had better stay where you are," said Caroline with guarded sharpness.

"I am going to see," repeated Mrs. Brigham firmly.

Then she folded her skirts so tightly that her bulk with its swelling curves was revealed in a black silk sheath, and she went with a slow toddle across the hall to the study door. She stood there, her eye at the crack.

In the south room Rebecca stopped sewing and sat watching with dilated eyes. Caroline sewed steadily. What Mrs. Brigham, standing at the crack in the study door, saw was this:

Henry Glynn, evidently reasoning that the source of the strange shadow must be between the table on which the lamp stood and the wall, was making systematic passes and thrusts all over and through the intervening space with an old sword which had belonged to his father. Not an inch was left unpierced. He seemed to have divided the space into mathematical sections. He brandished the sword with a sort of cold fury and calculation; the blade gave out flashes of light, the shadow remained unmoved. Mrs. Brigham, watching, felt herself cold with horror.

Finally Henry ceased and stood with the sword in hand and raised as if to strike, surveying the shadow on the wall threateningly. Mrs. Brigham toddled back across the hall and shut the south room door behind her before she related what she had seen.

"He looked like a demon!" she said again. "Have you got any of that old wine in the house, Caroline? I don't feel as if I could stand much more."

Indeed, she looked overcome. Her handsome placid face was worn and strained and pale.

"Yes, there's plenty," said Caroline; "you can have some when you go to bed."

"I think we had all better take some," said Mrs. Brigham. "Oh, my God, Caroline, what—"

"Don't ask and don't speak," said Caroline.

"No, I am not going to," replied Mrs. Brigham; "but—"
Rebecca moaned aloud.

"What are you doing that for?" asked Caroline harshly.

"Poor Edward," returned Rebecca.

"That is all you have to groan for," said Caroline.
"There is nothing else."

"I am going to bed," said Mrs. Brigham. "I sha'n't be
able to be at the funeral if I don't."

Soon the three sisters went to their chambers and the
south parlour was deserted. Caroline called to Henry in
the study to put out the light before he came upstairs.
They had been gone about an hour when he came into
the room bringing the lamp which had stood in the study.
He set it on the table and waited a few minutes, pacing
up and down. His face was terrible, his fair complexion
showed livid; his blue eyes seemed dark blanks of awful
reflections.

Then he took the lamp up and returned to the library.
He set the lamp on the centre table, and the shadow sprang
out on the wall. Again he studied the furniture and moved
it about, but deliberately, with none of his former frenzy.
Nothing affected the shadow. Then he returned to the
south room with the lamp and again waited. Again he
returned to the study and placed the lamp on the table,
and the shadow sprang out upon the wall. It was midnight
before he went upstairs. Mrs. Brigham and the other sisters, who could not sleep, heard him.

The next day was the funeral. That evening the family
sat in the south room. Some relatives were with them. Nobody entered the study until Henry carried a lamp in there
after the others had retired for the night. He saw again the
shadow on the wall leap to an awful life before the light.

The next morning at breakfast Henry Glynn announced
that he had to go to the city for three days. The sisters

looked at him with surprise. He very seldom left home, and just now his practice had been neglected on account of Edward's death. He was a physician.

"How can you leave your patients now?" asked Mrs. Brigham wonderingly.

"I don't know how to, but there is no other way," replied Henry easily. "I have had a telegram from Doctor Mitford."

"Consultation?" inquired Mrs. Brigham.

"I have business," replied Henry.

Doctor Mitford was an old classmate of his who lived in a neighbouring city and who occasionally called upon him in the case of a consultation.

After he had gone Mrs. Brigham said to Caroline that after all Henry had not said that he was going to consult with Doctor Mitford, and she thought it very strange.

"Everything is very strange," said Rebecca with a shudder.

"What do you mean?" inquired Caroline sharply.

"Nothing," replied Rebecca.

Nobody entered the library that day, nor the next, nor the next. The third day Henry was expected home, but he did not arrive and the last train from the city had come.

"I call it pretty queer work," said Mrs. Brigham. "The idea of a doctor leaving his patients for three days anyhow, at such a time as this, and I know he has some very sick ones; he said so. And the idea of a consultation lasting three days! There is no sense in it, and *now* he has not come. I don't understand it, for my part."

"I don't either," said Rebecca.

They were all in the south parlour. There was no light in the study opposite, and the door was ajar.

Presently Mrs. Brigham rose—she could not have told why; something seemed to impel her, some will outside her own. She went out of the room, again wrapping her rustling skirts around that she might pass noiselessly, and began pushing at the swollen door of the study.

"She has not got any lamp," said Rebecca in a shaking voice.

Caroline, who was writing letters, rose again, took a lamp (there were two in the room) and followed her sister. Rebecca had risen, but she stood trembling, not venturing to follow.

The doorbell rang, but the others did not hear it; it was on the south door on the other side of the house from the study. Rebecca, after hesitating until the bell rang the second time, went to the door; she remembered that the servant was out.

Caroline and her sister Emma entered the study. Caroline set the lamp on the table. They looked at the wall. "Oh, my God," gasped Mrs. Brigham, "there are—there are *two*—shadows." The sisters stood clutching each other, staring at the awful things on the wall. Then Rebecca came in, staggering, with a telegram in her hand. "Here is—a telegram," she gasped. "Henry is—dead."

The Portent of the Shadow

Edith Nesbit

1905

This is not an artistically rounded off ghost story and nothing is explained in it; and there seems to be no reason why any of it should have happened. But that is no reason why it should not be told. You must have noticed that all the real ghost stories you ever come close to are like this in these respects: no explanation, no logical coherence. Here is the story.

There were three of us—and another. But she had fainted suddenly at the second extra of the Christmas Dance, and had been put to bed in the dressing-room next to the room which we three shared. It had been one of those jolly old-fashioned dances, where nearly everybody stays the night, and the big country house is stretched to its utmost containing power; guests harbouring on sofas, couches, cots, and even mattresses on the floor. Some of the young men, even, I believe, slept on the great dining table. We had talked of our partners, as girls will, and then the stillness of the Manor House, broken only by the whisper of the wind in the cedar branches, and the scraping of their lean fingers against our window panes, had pricked us to such a luxurious confidence in our surroundings of bright chintz and candle-flame and firelight, that we had dared to talk of ghosts—in which, said we all, we did not believe one bit. We had told the story of the phantom coach, and the horribly strange bed, and the lady in the sacque, and the house in Berkeley Square. Not one of us believed in ghosts, but my heart, at least, seemed to leap to my throat and choke me, when a tap came to our door—a tap faint, but not to be mistaken.

"Who's there?" said the youngest of us, craning a lean neck towards the door. It opened slowly—and I give you my word the instant of suspense that followed is still reckoned among my life's least confident moments. Almost at once the door opened fully, and Miss Eastwich, my aunt's housekeeper, companion and general standby, looked in on us.

We all said "Come in," but she stood there. She was, at all normal hours, the most silent woman I have ever known. She stood and looked at us, and shivered a little. So did we—for in those days corridors were not warmed by hot-water pipes, and the air from the door was keen.

"I saw your light," she said at last, "and I thought it was late for you to be up—after all this gaiety. I thought perhaps—" her glance turned towards the door of the dressing-room.

"No," I said, "she's fast asleep." I should have added a "goodnight," but the youngest of us forestalled my speech. She did not know Miss Eastwich as we others did. Did not know how her persistent silence had built a wall round her, a wall that no one dared to break down with the commonplaces of talk or the littlenesses of mere human relationship. Miss Eastwich's silence had taught us to treat her as a machine, and as other than a machine we never dreamed of treating her. But the youngest of us had seen Miss Eastwich for the first time that day. She was young and crude and ill-balanced, and the victim of blind calf-like impulse. She was also the heiress of a rich tallow-chandler, but that has nothing to do with this part of the story. She jumped up from the hearthrug, her unsuitably rich silk, lace-trimmed dressing gown falling back from her lean neck, and ran to the door, and put an arm round Miss Eastwich's prim lisse-encircled neck. I gasped. I should as soon have dared embrace Cleopatra's Needle.

"Come in," said the youngest of use, "come in and get warm. There's lots of cocoa left." She drew Miss Eastwich in and shut the door.

The vivid light of pleasure in the housekeeper's pale eyes went through my heart like a knife. It would have been so easy to put an arm round her neck if one had only thought she wanted it. But it was not I who had thought that, and, indeed, my arm might not have brought the light invoked by the lean arm of the youngest of us.

"Now," the youngest went on eagerly, "you shall have the very biggest, nicest chair, and the cocoa pot's here on the hob as hot as hot, and we've all been telling ghost stories, only we don't believe in them a bit, and when you get warm you ought to tell one too."

Miss Eastwich, that model of decorum and decently done duties, tell a ghost story! The child was mad!

"You're sure I'm not in your way?" Miss Eastwich said, stretching her hands to the blaze. I wondered whether housekeepers have fires in their rooms even at Christmas time.

"Not a bit," I said it and I hope I said it as warmly as I felt it. "I—Miss Eastwich—I'd have asked you to come in other times—only I didn't think you'd care for girls' chatter."

The third girl, who was really of no account, and that's why I have not said anything about her before, poured cocoa for our guest; I put my fleecy Madeira shawl round her shoulders. I could not think of anything else to do for her, and I suddenly found myself wishing desperately to do something. The smile she gave us was quite pretty. People can smile prettily at 40 or 50, or even later, though girls don't realize this. It occurred to me, and this was another knife-thrust, that I had never seen Miss Eastwich smile—a real smile—before. The pale smiles of dutiful acquiescence were not of the same blood as this dimpling, happy transfiguring look.

"This is very pleasant," she said, and it seemed to me that I had never before heard her real voice. It did not please me to think that at the cost of cocoa and fire and my arms round her neck I might have heard this new voice any time these six years.

"We've been telling ghost stories," I said, "the worst of it is we don't believe in ghosts. No one anyone knows has ever seen one."

"It's always what somebody told somebody who told somebody, you know," said the youngest of us. "And you can't believe that, can you?"

"What the soldier said is not evidence," said Miss Eastwich. Will it be believed that the little Dickens quotation pierced me more keenly than the new smile or the new voice?

"And all ghost stories are so beautifully rounded off—a murder committed on the spot—or a hidden treasure or a warning—I think that makes them harder to believe. The most horrid ghost story I ever heard was one that was quite silly."

"Tell it."

"I can't—it doesn't sound anything to tell. Miss Eastwich ought to tell one."

"Oh, do!" said the youngest of us, and her salt-cellars loomed dark as she stretched her neck eagerly and laid an entreating arm on our guest's knee.

"The only thing that I ever knew of was—was hearsay," she said slowly, "at least half of it was."

I knew she would tell her story, and I knew she had never before told it, and I knew she was only telling it now because she was proud, and this seemed the only way to pay for the fire and the cocoa and the laying of that thin arm round her neck.

"Don't tell it," I said suddenly, "I know you'd rather not."

"I daresay it would bore you," she said meekly, and the youngest of us, who after all, did not understand everything, glared resentfully at me.

"We should just love it," she said, "do tell us. Never mind if it isn't a real proper fixed-up story. I'm certain anything you think ghostly would be quite too beautifully horrid for anything."

Miss Eastwich finished her cocoa and reached up to set the cup on the mantelpiece.

"It can't do any harm," she said to herself, "they don't believe in ghosts, and it wasn't exactly a ghost either. And they're all over twenty—they're not babies." There was a breathing time of hush and expectancy. The fire crackled and the gas flared higher because the billiard lights had been put out. We heard the steps and voices of the men going along the corridors.

"It is really hardly worth telling," Miss Eastwich said doubtfully, shading her faded face from the fire with her thin hand.

We all said, "Go on; oh, go on, do!"

"Well," she said, "twenty years ago, and more than that, I had two friends, and I loved them more than anything in the world. And they married each other."

She paused, and I knew just in what way she had loved each of them. The youngest of us said. "How awfully nice for you! Do go on."

She patted the youngest's shoulder, and I was glad that I had understood what the youngest of all hadn't. She went on.

"Well, after they married I didn't see much of them for a year or two, and then he wrote and asked me to come and stay, because his wife was ill, and I should cheer her up, and cheer him up as well, for it was a gloomy house, and he himself was growing gloomy too."

I knew as she spoke that she had every line of that letter by heart.

"Well, I went. The address was in Lee, near London, and in those days there were streets and streets of new villa-houses growing up round old brick mansions standing in their own grounds, with red walls round, you know, and a sort of flavor of coaching days and post-chaises and Blackheath highwaymen about them. He had said the house was gloomy, and it was called 'The Firs,' and I imagined my cab going through a dark winding shrubbery and drawing up in front of one of those sedate old square houses. Instead, we drew up in front of a large, smart villa, with iron railings, gay, encaustic tiles leading from the iron gate to the stained-glass-paneled door, and for shrubbery, only a few stunted cypresses and acubas in the tiny front garden. But inside it was all warm and welcoming. He met me at the door."

She was gazing into the fire, and I knew she had forgotten us. But the youngest girl of all still thought that it was to us she was telling her story.

"He met me at the door," she said again, "and thanked me for coming, and asked me to forgive the past."

"What past?" asked that high priestess of the inapropos, the youngest of all.

"Oh, I suppose he meant because they hadn't invited me before, or something," said Miss Eastwich, worriedly. "But it's a very dull story, I find, after all, and—"

"Do go on," I said. Then I kicked the youngest of us and got up to re-arrange Miss Eastwich's shawl, and said in blatant dumb show, over the shawled shoulders.

"Shut up, you little idiot!"

After another silence the housekeeper's new voice went on:

"They were very glad to see me, and I was very glad to be there. You girls now have such troops of friends, but these two were all I had, all I had ever had. Mabel wasn't exactly ill, only weak and excitable. I thought he seemed more ill than she did. She went to bed early, and before she went, she asked me to keep him company through his last pipe, so we went into the dining room and sat in the two armchairs on each side of the fireplace. They were covered with green leather, I remember. There were bronze groups of horses and a black marble clock on the mantel-piece—all wedding presents. He poured out some whisky for himself, but he hardly touched it. He sat looking into the fire. At last I said:

"'What's wrong? Mabel looks as well as you could expect.'

"He said 'Yes, but I don't know from one day to another that she won't begin to notice something wrong. That's why I wanted you to come. You were always so sensible and strong-minded, and Mabel's like a little bird, or a flower.'

"I said 'Yes, of course,' and waited for him to go on. I thought he must be in debt or in trouble of some sort. So I just waited. Presently he said:

"'Margaret, this is a very peculiar house.' He always called me Margaret; you see, we'd been such old friends. I told him I thought the house was very pretty, and fresh, and homelike, only a little too new, but that fault would mend with time. He said:

"'It is new; that's just it. We're the first people who've ever lived in it. If it were an old house, Margaret, I should think it was haunted.'

"I asked if he had seen anything. 'No,' he said, 'not yet.'

"'Heard, then?' said I.

"'No, nor heard either,' he said, 'but there's a sort of feeling, I can't describe it. I've seen nothing and I've heard nothing, but I've been so near to seeing and hearing! Just not, that's all. And something follows me about—only when I turn round there's never anything but my shadow. And I always feel that I shall see the thing, or hear it, next minute; but I never do, not quite, it's always just not visible.'

"I thought he'd been working rather hard, and I tried to cheer him up by making light of all this. 'It was just nerves,' I said. Then he said he had thought I could help him. and did I think anyone he had wronged could have laid a curse on him, and did I believe in curses? I said I didn't, and the only person anyone could have said he had wronged forgave him freely, I knew, if there was anything to forgive. So I told him this too."

It was I, not the youngest of us, who knew the name of that person wronged and forgiving.

"So then I said 'He ought to take Mabel away from the house and have a complete change.' But he said, 'No, Mabel had got everything in order, and he could never manage to get her away just now without explaining everything, and above all,' he said, 'she mustn't guess there's anything wrong. I daresay I shall not feel quite such a lunatic now you're here.'

"So we said 'Good-night.'"

"Is that all the story?" said the third girl, striving to convey that even as it stood it was a good story.

"That is only the beginning," said Miss Eastwich. "Whenever I was alone with him, he used to tell me the same thing over and over again, and at first when I began to notice things I tried to think that it was his talk that had upset my nerves. The odd thing was that it wasn't only at night—but in broad daylight, and particularly on the stairs and passages. On the staircase the feeling used to be so awful that I have had to bite my lips till they bled, to keep myself from running up the stairs at full speed. Only I knew if I did I should go mad at the top. There was always something behind me—exactly as he had said—something that one could just not see. And a sound that one could just not hear. There was a long corridor at the top of the house. I have sometimes almost seen something—you know how one sees things without looking—but if I turned round it seemed as if the thing dropped and melted into my shadow. There was a little window at the end of the corridor.

"Downstairs there was another corridor, something like it, with a cupboard at one end and the kitchen at the other. One night I went down into the kitchen to warm some milk for Mabel. The servants had gone to bed. As I stood by the fire waiting for the milk to boil I glanced through the open door and along the passage. I never could keep my eyes on what I was doing, in that house. The cupboard door was partly open; they used to keep empty bottles and things in it. And as I looked I knew that now it was not going to be 'almost' any more. Yet I said 'Mabel?' not because I thought it could be Mabel who was crouching down there, half in and half out of the cupboard. The thing was gray at first and then it was black. And when I whispered 'Mabel,' it seemed to sink down till it lay like a pool of ink on the floor, and then its edges drew in, and it seemed to flow, like ink, when you tilt up the paper you have spilt it on, and it flowed into the cupboard till it was all gathered into the shadow there. I saw it go quite plainly. The gas was full on in the kitchen. I screamed aloud, but even then I'm thankful to say I had enough sense to upset the boiling milk, so that when he came downstairs three steps at a time, I had the excuse for my scream of a scalded hand. The explanation was satisfactory to Mabel, but next night he said:

"'Why didn't you tell me? It was that cupboard. All the horror of the house comes out of that. Tell me, have you seen anything yet? Or is it only the nearly seeing and nearly hearing still?'

"I said. 'You must tell me first what you've seen.' He told me, and his eyes wandered as he spoke to the shadows by the curtains, and I turned up all three gaslights and lit the candles on the mantelpiece. Then we looked at each other and said we were both mad, and thanked God that Mabel was at least sane. For what he had seen was what I had seen.

"After that I hated to be alone with a shadow, because at any moment I might see something that would crouch and sink and lie like a black pool and then slowly draw itself into the shadow that was nearest. Often that shadow was my own. The thing came first at night, but afterwards there was no hour safe from it. I saw it at dawn, and at noon, in the dusk and in the firelight, and always it crouched and sank, and was a pool that flowed into some shadow and became part of it. And always I saw it with a straining of the eyes, a pricking and aching. It seemed as though I could only just see it, as if my sight, to see it, had to be strained to the uttermost. And still the sound was in the house, the sound that I could just not hear. At last one morning early I did hear it. It was close behind me, and it was only a sigh. It was worse than the thing that crept among the shadows.

"I don't know how I bore it. I couldn't have borne it if I hadn't been so fond of them both. But I knew in my heart that if he had no one to whom he could speak openly he would go mad, or tell Mabel. His was not a very strong character. Very sweet and kind and gentle, but not strong. He was always easily led. So I stayed on and bore up, and we were very cheerful and made little jokes and tried to be amusing when Mabel was with us. But when we were alone we did not try to be amusing.

"And sometimes a day or two would go by without our seeing or hearing anything, and we should perhaps have fancied that we had fancied what we had seen and heard, only there was always the feeling of there being something about the house that one could just not hear and not see. Sometimes we used to try not to talk about it, but generally we talked of nothing else at all. And the weeks went by, and Mabel's baby was born. The nurse and the doctor said that both mother and child were doing well. He and I sat late in the dining-room that night. We had neither of us seen or heard anything for three days—our anxiety about Mabel was lessened. We talked of the future: it seemed then so much brighter than the past. We arranged that the moment she was fit to be moved he should take her away to the sea, and I should superintend the moving of their furniture into the new house he had already chosen. He was gayer than I had seen him since his marriage—almost like his old self. When I said 'good-night' to him he said a lot of things about my having been a comfort to them both. I hadn't done anything much of course, but still I am glad he said that.

"Then I went upstairs—almost for the first time without that feeling of something following me. I listened at Mabel's room. Everything was quiet. I went on towards my own room, and in an instant I felt that there was something behind me. I turned. It was crouching there: it sank, and the black fluidness of it seemed to be sucked under the floor of Mabel's room.

"I went back. I opened the door a listening inch. All was still. And then I heard a sigh—close behind me. I opened the door and went in. The nurse and the baby were asleep. Mabel was asleep, too; she looked so pretty, like a tired child—the baby was cuddled up into one of her arms with its tiny head against her side. I prayed then that Mabel might never know the terrors that he and I had known—that those little ears might never hear any but pretty sounds, those dear eyes never see any but pretty sights. I did not dare to pray for a long time after that. Because my prayer was answered. She never saw, never heard anything more in this world. And now I could do nothing more for him or for her.

"When they had put her in her coffin I lighted wax candles round her, and laid the horrible white flowers that people will send, near to her, and then I saw he had followed me. I took his hand to lead him away.

"At the door we both turned. It seemed to us that we heard a sigh. He would have sprung to her side in I don't know what mad glad hope. But at that instant we both saw it. Between us and the coffin, first gray, then black, it crouched an instant, then sank and liquefied, and was gathered together and drawn till it ran into the nearest shadow. And the nearest shadow was the shadow of Mabel's coffin. I left the next day. His mother came. She had never liked me."

Miss Eastwich paused. I think she had quite forgotten us.

"Didn't you see him again?" asked the youngest of all.

"Only once," Miss Eastwich answered, "and something black crouched then between him and me. But it was only his second wife crying beside his coffin. It's not a cheerful story, is it? And it doesn't lead anywhere. I've never told anyone else. I think it was seeing his daughter that brought it all back."

She looked toward the dressing-room door. "Mabel's baby," said the youngest of all.

"Yes, and exactly like Mabel, only with his eyes."

The youngest of all had Miss Eastwich's hands and was petting them.

Suddenly the woman wrenched her hands away and stood at her gaunt height, hands clenched, eyes straining. She was looking at something that we could not see, and I know now what the man in the Bible meant when he said "the hair of my flesh stood up—"

What she saw seemed not quite to reach the height of the dressing-room door handle. Her eyes following it down, down, widened and widened. Mine followed hers, and all the nerves of my eyes seemed strained to the uttermost—and I almost saw—or did I quite see? I can't be certain. But we all heard the long-drawn, quivering sigh. And to each of us it seemed to be breathed just behind each.

It was I who caught up the candle—it dropped wax all over my trembling hands—it was I who was dragged by Miss Eastwich to the side of the girl who had fainted during the second extra. But it was the youngest of all whose lean arms were round the housekeeper when we turned away, and that have been round her many a time since in the new home where she keeps house for the youngest of us all.

The doctor, who came in the morning, said that Mabel's daughter had died of heart disease, which she inherited from her mother. That was what made her faint during the second extra. But I have sometimes wondered whether she may not have inherited something from her father. I have never been able to forget the look on her dead face.

The Shadow of Good Fortune

Nellie K. Blissett

1906

I

The woman sat by the bed, a figure of beautiful despair, with her long black hair streaming over her shoulders, and her head bent. Her hand held the burning fingers of little Sava, as he tossed about in uneasy sleep, broken by cries of pain, or terror; the shrill, complaining voice went to her heart. She did not understand all he said, and her very failure to comprehend those half-delirious words hurt her as nothing else in her short, hard life had done. It seemed to her that the one thing which fate had left her was escaping from her grasp into a land into which she could not follow it. Again and again came the cry she could not understand—the start of terror which puzzled her.

"Oh, mother, make them give it back—they have stolen it—they have put it in the ground! Oh, mother, I want it so—make them give it back to me! The boys laugh at me—do not let them laugh any more. I want it back—I want it back!"

"Sava, my darling, what have they stolen—what is it that you want?" But he did not seem to hear her voice, or to understand what she said. Still the little figure tossed to-and-fro under the shabby carpet coverlet which she vainly tried to keep over it; still the fretful cry rang in her

181

ears. Since sunrise she had sat there by the bed, motionless, terror-stricken; it was sunset when the door opened, and Madame Nikolich thrust her grizzled black head into the darkening room.

"The boy is sick, Militsa—eh?"

She looked up, with a gesture almost of relief, though Madame Nikolich was no friend of hers, but merely a very worldly landlady with a very sharp eye fixed upon the not always rosy possibilities of rent.

"Oh, he is very sick—I do not know what to do for him!"

Madame Nikolich came forward and stood at the foot of the bed, looking down not unkindly on the small, restless figure.

"Yes, he is certainly very sick. I will tell you what is the matter with him, Militsa. My Mika has just been talking about it. He says the workmen at the big house round the corner caught Sava two days ago and made him stand in the sunshine while they built his shadow into the foundations—you know, it brings a house good-fortune when a living shadow is caught and built into it. But the person who has lost the shadow very often dies—so many people have told me that." Militsa shrank nearer to the bed. Sava lifted his rutiled curls from the pillow, and raised once more that beseeching cry.

"They have stolen it and put it in the ground. Oh, give it back to me—give it back!"

Militsa shivered; Anna Nikolich nodded in dismal triumph.

"There—do you hear what he says? That is what I told you—they have stolen his shadow, and put it into Bora Jovanovich's fine new house. It will bring Bora Jovanovich good fortune, no doubt, but I think you will lose the child."

Militsa turned upon the other woman like a tempest, with a swift, passionate, protective movement towards Sava.

"No—no—not that!" she said. "He is all I have—there is nothing else in the world for me. I will not lose him—I cannot."

Anna Nikolich turned towards the door. When she reached it, she paused for a moment, and looked back.

"I will send Mika up with some supper for you," she said; "and—and the rent may stand over for this week."

Militsa sank down beside the bed without a word of gratitude. The other's kindness struck her like a curse—if Anna Nikolich could be generous, Sava must indeed be far gone.

The darkness came down upon the miserable little room; Mika, shy and solemn-eyed, brought the supper Militsa could not eat, and went away again. Still she crouched by the bed; still the child's restless cry went on.

"Oh, give it back—make them give it back to me!"

She rose suddenly, and bent over the child for a moment.

"Sava, you shall have it back if you will lie quite still until—until I bring it to you. Do you hear me—do you understand? You shall have it if you will lie still, and go to sleep."

For the first time that day her voice seemed to reach him. His great black eyes rested with a look of comprehension on her face as she bent lamp in hand, over the bed.

"You will bring it back?" he murmured sleepily, and sank back almost contentedly upon the pillow.

As she stole down the narrow stairs, for the first time that day the restless cry was still.

II

Bora Jovanovich sat in his office—the finest office in Palatz, for he was the richest man in the town. He was thinking a little of his wealth, and his success, as he sat there in the morning sunshine with his pen tracing idle patterns on the blotting-pad before him. He thought of the poor mountain village where he was born, and which he had left seven years ago to come down to Palatz and find favor in the eyes of the greatest merchant in the place, and marry his only daughter, and succeed, in due course, to all his riches. Jovanovich sighed as he thought, so perhaps he did not find the contemplation of his success altogether satisfactory. It was spring, and the soft air blowing through the open window seemed to blow from the blue hills of his home. He remembered the sighing pines, and the cool white foam of the waterfall by which he had walked with the popadia's (priest's wife) pretty niece in those far off days. His wife had brought him riches and success, but he had loved one curl on the black head of the popadia's niece better than he had loved the whole body of the rich merchant's daughter. Now that his wife was dead he was a lonely man in the house where his father-in-law had lived. Perhaps it was for this reason that he had set himself to build a new and more splendid house, which should be all his own, and hold no memory of the woman who had bought him—perhaps it pleased him this morning to remember that at the corner of the market-place the walls of his new home were already rising fast. There was a tap at the door, and Bora Jovanovich roused himself abruptly from the dream into which he had fallen. A workman in a greasy blouse answered his invitation to enter, and then stood tongue-tied in the door-way regarding the great man of Palatz with a frightened eye.

"The house—" he stammered at last.

Bora Jovanovich laid down his pen. "What has happened to it?"

"It's no fault of ours," the man said sullenly. "Yesterday it was the same—half our day's work undone. And to-day the wall is down again. We do not understand it."

"Who pulls the wall down?"

"How should we know?" The man's tone was half fierce, half frightened. "Some one comes—at night—and pulls down half of what we do by day."

Bora Jovanovich sat silent, looking at the workman at the door; and the same thought was in the minds of both. No one in Palatz—that is to say, no one merely human—would care to interfere with the rich man's house.

"You had better keep watch," Jovanovich said.

The man shifted his weight from one foot to the other. The prospect of keeping watch did not seem to appeal to him.

"You need not trouble," Bora Jovanovich said, with a touch of scorn. He was clever enough to know that it is best not to give orders when you are certain they will not be obeyed.

But that night, when the house was asleep, he muffled himself in a cloak and slipped out and made his way to the market-place. It was a dark night, for heavy clouds came and went before a pale moon. Palatz was asleep; and Bora Jovanovich groped his way down into the foundations of his new house and sat there waiting, wrapped to the ears in his cloak.

He waited a long time and at last fell asleep and dreamed that he was roaming the forests of his home, with the popadia's pretty niece beside him; but she wept all the time, and the great tears ran down her face and fell on the pine-needles, and he tried in vain to comfort her.

He woke with a start, shivering. The dew was cold on his hands. He thought of the tears of the popadia's niece. He heard her crying still—or—no, the crying was no dream. In the darkness he heard a voice which murmured "Sava! Oh, Sava, stay with me!" He heard the sobbing of a woman, and it seemed to him that he knew the sound.

The moon came from behind a cloud and flung a doubtful light around. Close to him a woman knelt, trying to pull down the wall with torn and bleeding fingers. Her black hair fell curling on her shoulders as once, long ago, the hair of the popadia's niece had curled in the little mountain village where he was born.

Bora Jovanovich went and stood beside the kneeling figure. It looked up at him. In the moonlight he saw the great tears rolling down its face.

"Militsa!"

She did not pause from her labor, but tore still at the resisting bricks. He saw the blood running down her fingers as the tears ran down her face. Her voice rose to a piteous cry.

"Oh, Bora, save him—save Sava! They have built his shadow into the walls, and unless I give it back to him he will die. And, since you went away, I have nothing else. Save Sava—help me to save Sava!"

Bora Jovanovich looked at her. It was not the cold night air which made him tremble.

"Who is Sava?"

Her black head was bent over the torn fingers which clutched still at the wall. Her voice died to a sob.

"Sava is—all you left me when you went away. Save him—help me to find his shadow in the wall."

Bora Jovanovich said nothing. In silence he knelt down by her side and began, with shaking fingers, to tear down the walls of the new house in which there were to be no memories and no regrets.

III

In the fine new house at the corner of the market place, which is not so very new now, Bora Jovanovich, the richest man in Palatz, lives with his wife, who was once the popadia's niece. Every one envies them their prosperity; some, it may be, envy them the children who run in and out, laughing, and shaking their black curls in the sun. Nothing but happiness has come to them in the new house. "As lucky as Bora Jovanovich's new house" has become a proverb in Palatz. But it is a proverb which is never quoted in his presence, for Palatz has learned that he does not like it.

For sometimes at night, when the black-haired children are still, Bora Jovanovich and his wife remember another child who does not run in and out with the others. They remember a little shadow which was built into the foundations of their house and upon which their happiness has risen, like a house which human hands did not build. It lies buried still—perhaps in their hearts, perhaps in the walls of the new house on the market-place—the shadow of a living soul, which they remember as the Shadow of Good Fortune.

The Shadow-Dance

Bernard Capes

1915

"Yes, it was a rum start," said the modish young man.

He was a modern version of the crutch and toothpick genus, a derivative from the "Gaiety boy" of the Nellie Farren epoch, very spotless, very superior, very—fundamentally and combatively—simple. I don't know how he had found his way into Carleon's rooms and our company, but Carleon had a liking for odd characters. He was a collector, as it were, of human pottery, and to the collector, as we know, primitive examples are of especial interest.

The bait in this instance, I think, had been Bridge, which, since some formal "Ducdame" must serve for calling fools into a circle, was our common pretext for assembling for an orgy of talk. We had played, however, for insignificant stakes and, on the whole, irreverently as regarded the sanctity of the game; and the young man was palpably bored. He thought us, without question, outsiders, and not altogether good form; and it was even a relief to him when the desultory play languished, and conversation became general in its place.

Somebody—I don't remember on what provocation—had referred to the now historic affair of the Hungarian Ballet, which, the rage in London for a season, had voluntarily closed its own career a week before the date advertised for its termination; and the modish young man, it appeared, was the only one of us all who had happened to be present in the theatre on the occasion of the final performance. He told us so; and added that "it was a rum start."

"The abrupt finish was due, of course," said Carleon, bending forward, hectic, bright-eyed, and hugging himself, as was his wont, "to Kaunitz's death. She was the bright particular 'draw.' It would have been nothing without her. Besides, there was the tragedy. What was the 'rum start'? Tell us."

"The way it ended that night," said the young man. He was a little abashed by the sudden concentration of interest on himself; but carried it off with *sang-froid*. Only a slight flush of pink on his youthful cheek, as he flicked the ash from his cigarette with the delicate little finger of the hand that held it, confessed to a certain uneasy self-consciousness.

"I have heard something about it," said Carleon. "Give us your version."

"I'm no hand at describing things," responded the young man, committed and at bay; "never wrote a line of description in my life, nor wanted to. It was the *Shadow-Dance,* you know—the last thing on the programme. I dare say some of you have seen Kaunitz in it."

One or two of us had. It was incomparably the most beautiful, the most mystic, idyll achieved by even that superlative dancer; a fantasia of moonlight, supported by an ethereal, only half-revealed, shimmer of attendant sylphids.

"Yes," said Carleon eagerly.

"Well, you know," said the young man, "there is a sort of dance first, in and out of the shadows, a mysterious, gossamery kind of business, with nobody made out exactly, and the moon slowly rising behind the trees. And then, suddenly, the moon reaches a gap in the branches, and—

and it's full moon, don't you know, a regular white blaze of it, and all the shapes have vanished; only you sort of guess them, get a hint of their arms and faces hiding behind the leaves and under the shrubs and things. And that was the time when Kaunitz ought to have come on."

"Didn't she come on?"

"Not at first; not when she ought to. There was a devil of a pause, and you could see something was wrong. And after a bit there was a sort of rustle in the house, and people began to cough; and the music slipped round to the beginning again; and they danced it all over a second time, until it came to the full moonlight—and there she was this time all right—how, I don't know, for I hadn't seen her enter."

"How did she dance—when she *did* appear?"

The young man blew the ash from his cigarette. "Oh, I don't know!" he said.

"You must know. Wasn't it something quite out of the common? You called it a rum start, you remember."

"Well, if you insist upon it, it was—the most extraordinary thing I ever witnessed—more like what they describe the Pepper's Ghost business than anything else I can think. She was here, there, anywhere; seemingly independent of what d'ye call—gravitation, you know; she seemed to jump and hang in the air before she came down. And there was another thing. The idea was to dance to her own shadow, you see—follow it, run away from it, flirt with it—and it was the business of the moon, or the limelight man, to keep the shadow going."

"Well?"

"Well, there was no shadow—not a sign of one."

"That may have been the limelight man's fault."

"Very likely; but I don't think so. There was something odd about it all; and most in the way she went."

"How was that?"

"Why, she just gave a spring, and was gone."

Carleon sank back, with a sigh as if of repletion, and sat softly cracking his fingers together.

"Didn't you notice anything strange about the house, the audience?" he said—"people crying out; girls crouching and hiding their faces, for instance?"

"Perhaps, now I think of it," answered the modish youth. "I noticed, anyhow, that the curtain came down with a bang, and that there seemed a sort of general flurry and stampede of things, both behind it and on our side."

"Well, as to that, it is a fact, though you may not know it, that after that night the company absolutely refused to complete its engagement on any terms."

"I dare say. They had lost Kaunitz."

"To be sure they had. She was already lying dead in her dressing-room when the *Shadow-Dance* began."

"Not when it began?"

"So, anyhow, it was whispered."

"I say," said the young man, looking rather white; "I'm not going to believe that, you know."

The Shadow

Gwendolyn Ranger Wormser

1918

He was colossally vain.

He lived with his wife Ellen, in the small house on Peach Tree Road.

There was nothing pretentious about the house; there were any number of similar houses along the line of Peach Tree Road. For that matter the house was the kind planted innumerable times in the numerous suburbs of the large city. Still, it was his house. His own. That meant a lot to him whenever he thought of it; and he thought of it often enough. He liked to feel the thing actually belonged to him. It emphasized his being to himself.

The house was a two-storied affair built of wood and white washed. A green mansard roof came down over the small green shuttered upper windows. On the lower floor the windows were somewhat larger with the same solid wooden green shutters. A gravel path led up to the front door. Two drooping willow trees stood on either side of the wicker gate.

Before the time when his aunt had died and had left him the house he had not been particularly successful. At the age of forty-one he had found himself a hard-working journalist and nothing more. He had had no ambition to ever be anything else. He was at all times so utterly confident that the work he was doing was quite right; chiefly because it was the work that he was doing. No man had a more unbounded faith in himself. At that time he had not been conscious of his lack of success. Now, of course, he looked back on it all as a period of development; something which had prepared him for this that was even then destined to come.

He told himself that in this small house, away from the surrounding clatter and nuisances of the city, he had found time to write; to be himself; to really express what he knew himself to be.

He had become tremendously well known in that space of six years. No one ever doubted the genius of Jasper Wald. He wrote as a man writes who is actually inspired. His books were read with interest and surprisingly favorable comment. There was something different; something singularly appealing in all of Jasper Wald's works.

At that time his conceit was inordinate. It extended to a sort of personal, physical vanity. In itself that was grotesque. There was absolutely nothing attractive in the loosely jointed, stoop-shouldered body of him; or for that matter in the narrow head covered with sparse blond gray hair. The eyes of him were of rather a washed blue and bulged a bit from out their sockets; the nose was a singularly squat affair, at the same time too long. The mouth was unpleasantly small with lips so colorless and thin that the line of it was like some weird mark. Yet he was vain of his appearance. But then his egoism was the keynote of his entire being.

Some people could not forgive it in him; even when they acknowledged him as a writer and praised his work. The man in literature was spoken of as a mystic, a poet, a possessor of subtlety that was close to genius. In actual life, Jasper Wald was an out and out materialist.

As for his wife, Ellen:

She was rather a tall woman; thin but not ungraceful. Her features were good, very regular, still somewhat nondescript. All but her eyes. Her eyes were strange; green in color, and so heavily lidded that one could rarely see the expression of them. Then, too, she had an odd manner of moving. There never seemed to be any effort or any abruptness in whatever she did. Even her walk was sinuous.

He had married her when they both were young. Through his persistent habit of ignoring her she had been dwarfed into a nonentity. To have looked at the woman one would have said that hers was a distinctive personality unbelievably suppressed. It would not have been possible for any one living with Jasper Wald to have asserted himself. Perhaps she had learned that years before. Certainly his was the character which predominated; domineered through the encouragement of his own egoism.

Her attitude toward him was perpetually one of self-effacement. She stood for his conceit in a peculiarly passive way. If it ever irritated her she gave no sign. And he kept right on with his semi-indulgent manner of patronizing her stupidity. That is, when he noticed her at all.

She was essential to him in so far as she supplied all of his physical wants. Those in themselves were of great importance to Jasper Wald. There was no companionship between them. Jasper Wald could never have indulged in companionship of any kind. He had put himself far beyond that. To his way of thinking he was a super being who had no need whatever for the rest of man. He was all self-sufficient.

If there had ever been love between them in those days when they had first come together they had both of them completely lost sight of it. He in his complacent conceit; she in her monotonous negation.

And as time went on, and as his work became greater Jasper Wald grew even further away from the sort of thing he wrote; so that it was more than ever difficult for those who knew him to disassociate him from his writings. There was always the temptation to try to find some of his literary idealism in himself; to find some of his prosaic realism in his works.

On one occasion Delafield, his publisher, came to him; to the house on Peach Tree Road. It was a peculiarity of Jasper Wald's to persistently refuse any request to leave his home. It was the one thing about which he was superstitious. He had never by word or thought attributed his success to anyone or anything outside of himself. He had made his name in this house and he would not leave it.

Delafield's visit came at a time just after Jasper Wald's last book had been published.

Sitting in the square, simply furnished living room, Delafield for all his enthusiasm for the author had felt a certain inexplicable disgust.

"It's great, Wald; there's genius to it. We'll have it run through its second edition a week after we put it on the market."

"I don't doubt that;" Jasper Wald's tone was matter-of-fact in his confidence. "Not for a moment."

Delafield bit off the end of his cigar.

"When will your next one be ready?"

He asked it abruptly.

"Oh, I don't know," Jasper Wald had pulled leisurely at his pipe. "Whenever I make up my mind to it, I suppose. It's going to be the biggest thing I've tackled yet, Delafield."

"Well—" Delafield got up to go. "It can't be too soon. You'll have a barrel of money before you get done. Genius doesn't usually pay that way, either. But—;" he could not help himself. "You've got the knack of the thing. Heaven

knows where you get it; but it's the knowledge we all need
that comes from—"

He broke off quite suddenly as Ellen Wald came into
the room.

"I didn't know;" she said uncertainly. "I thought you
were alone."

"My wife, Delafield." Jasper Wald made the introduction impatiently. "Ellen, this is Mr. Delafield, who pub-
lishes my books."

She came toward them and held out her hand to Delafield. He could not help but noticing her odd manner of
moving.

"Good evening," she said.

Delafield had not known that Jasper Wald was married.
It was almost impossible for him to imagine anyone living with this man. He looked at the woman curiously. He
had the feeling that her individuality had been stultified.
It did not surprise him. Jasper Wald could have accomplished that. It would have been difficult to have matched
him with as flagrantly material a person as he himself was.
Only that sort of person would have stood a chance with
him. Any other would have had to fall flat. She had fallen
flat. Delafield knew that the moment he looked at her.

"Why, I didn't know;" Delafield took her hand in his.
"You never told me, Wald, that you were married."

"Didn't I? No, of course not.—But, about the new
book, Delafield."

Delafield dropped her hand. He had never felt anything
quite as inert as that hand. It impressed the nondescript
quality of her upon him even more strongly than had her
appearance.

"Your husband has promised me another book, Mrs.
Wald." He spoke slowly. He felt he had to speak that way
or she would not understand him. "Your husband is a great
author, Mrs. Wald."

"Yes."

"Why don't you say, genius, Delafield, and be done
with it? Why don't you make a clean breast of it with—
genius?"

"I've got to be going."

Delafield felt a strange irritation. The man was a fool.
For what reason under the sun could this woman with
those half closed eyes let herself be dominated by him?
The two of them got on his nerves.

"Won't you stay to dinner?"

Jasper Wald was obviously anxious for a chance to speak
of himself.

"Sorry, Wald. I've got to be getting on."

Delafield still watched the woman. She stood there
quite silent.

"I thought you might have something to say about that
book of mine."

"No— There's nothing more." Delafield started for the
door. "I've just told you that it's full of the sort of knowledge all of us are in need of. I can't say more, you know. I
suppose that knowledge is what constitutes genius; but—"
He was staring now full into those bulging blue eyes—
"Lord, man, where, where d'you get it from?"

Glancing at the woman, Delafield saw that she was
looking straight at him. Her eyes met his in a way which
he was completely at a loss to explain. There was something eerie about it.

"Where does he get it?"

She repeated his question stupidly and once again the
heavy lids came down over those strange green eyes, hiding all expression.

Jasper Wald drew in his breath.

"I write it," he said.

After that Delafield left them both severely alone.
The woman puzzled him. He could not tolerate the man,

Jasper Wald, and he could not for worlds have the genius of Jasper Wald hurt or slighted in any way. He knew how big it was. It often left him breathless. But the man; he would have liked to have hit him that day in the living room in the house on Peach Tree Road; to have kicked him into some sort of a realization as to what an utter little rat he was.

And so, because of his physical make-up, people stayed away from Jasper Wald. Not that he avoided people; not that he wanted to live the life of a recluse. He never made any attempt to conceal his living from the general public. He was too much of the egoist to attempt concealment of any kind. So his life was known to any man, woman or child who cared for the knowledge. His life of narrow selfishness, of tranquil complacency; of colossal conceit. And of genius.

He always wrote in the evenings, did Jasper Wald. And often he would keep at his writing well on into the morning.

He liked to sit there in the square, old-fashioned living room with its wide window that gave out upon Peach Tree Road.

When he had first moved into the house as an obscure, hard-working journalist he had placed the desk against the window ledge so that he could look directly out of the window without moving. And he had kept the desk there. He was just a bit insistent about it. Then, too, he liked the blind up so that he could stare out into the evening and at the house opposite.

For all his impossible vanity there must have been imbedded deep down in the small, hard soul of the man some excessive, frantic hunger of self-recognition by others. A potential desire to accomplish an assertion of self that could in no way be denied; a fundamental energy which had in some way made possible the work, but which he

could never admit for fear that it might evade the importance of himself.

The house opposite interested him tremendously. Sitting there in an abstract fit of musing, he watched it as one
subconsciously watches a place that has one's attention.

To all outward appearances the house across the way
was heavily boarded up and closed. It had always been
closed since the time that Jasper Wald had come to live in
Peach Tree Road. Yet every evening in the window directly
facing his he had seen the shadow of a man moving to
and fro; to and fro, beyond the drawn blind. He would sit
there watching the dark, undefined shadow until he felt
that he had to work, and then the whole thing would slip
from his mind until the following evening when he would
again be at his desk.

Strangely enough he had never mentioned the presence
of the shadow to anyone. There was about it a certain mysterious unreality. That much he, Jasper Wald, was capable
of knowing. It was the one thing outside of himself that
gripped at his intelligence.

During all those six years he had waited at his desk
each night for the coming of the shadow. And when it
came he had started to work. He never explained the thing
to himself. He never thought he had to explain anything
to his own understanding. Had he tried, he would have
been utterly at a loss for an explanation. So Jasper Wald
had come to look upon the shadow as a sign of luck; a
superstition-fostered thing that epitomized his genius to
himself.

Naturally it had not always been that way. The first
time that Jasper Wald had felt the shadow he had experienced an uncanny sense of terror. That had been before he
had really seen it.

He had been standing there beside the window just
after he and Ellen had moved into their home, looking out

at the closed house opposite. He had felt a queer oppression which he readily interpreted as the vibration of his new environment. When the thing had persisted he had become a bit uneasy. The sense of oppression so utterly unknown to him had changed to one which grew upon him; as if he were being forced out of himself in some uncanny manner.

There was about it all a curious sensation of remoteness of self and at the same time a weird consciousness of the haunting permeation of something invisible and dynamic.

He never thought back to that evening without a positive horror. The whole thing was so completely alien to him.

It had been with a great sense of relief that he had, finally, been able to see and to rivet his attention upon the shadow there against the blind of the house opposite. He had clinched his thought onto it. And the other thing had left him; had lessened in its maddening oppression.

That evening he had started to write. He had felt that writing was a thing he had to do. It was entirely because of his first fear that he kept the knowledge of the shadow to himself.

Cock sure as he was of himself, thoroughly certain of his genius, and inordinately vain of his success, there was one thing about it all that Jasper Wald could not quite make out. Not for worlds would he have admitted it. Still there was the one thing. And the one thing was that Jasper Wald could not understand the kind of thought behind what he himself wrote.

It was late one summer evening that Jasper Wald sat at his desk in the square living room; his pen was in his hand; a pile of blank paper made a white patch on the dark wood before him. His blue eyes that bulged a bit looked out into the graying half light. The green of the lawn was matted with dark shadows. A mist of shadows were pressed into the faint lined leaves of the two drooping willow trees on either side of the wicker gate. An unreal light held in the sky.

His eyes were fixed on the one window of the house opposite. With his pen in his hand, Jasper Wald waited.

From somewhere in the house came the chimes of a clock striking the half hour.

Starting from his chair, Jasper Wald went to the side of the desk and leaned far out of the window. A wave of heat came up to him from the earth. His eyes stared intently at the window opposite.

The door behind him was thrown open. He turned to see Ellen's tall, not ungraceful, figure standing in the doorway. Her two hands grasped the bowl of a lighted lamp.

"I don't need that."

Jasper Wald told it to her impatiently.

She came a step into the room.

"It's dark in here, Jasper."

"But I don't need any more light, Ellen. I don't need it, I tell you!"

"It's dark in here, Jasper."

"All right, then; put the thing down. I can't take up my time arguing with you. How can a man write in a place like this, anyway? Have you no consideration? Must I always be disturbed? Have you no respect for genius?"

She came a step further toward the center of the room.

"Genius,—Jasper?"

"My genius, Ellen. Mine."

He watched her cross the room with that odd, sinuous moving of hers and place the lamp in the center of his desk. And then he saw her go to a chair within its light and, sitting down, pick up some sewing which she had left there.

He went back and sat at his desk.

He had made up his mind that this new book of his would be something big; something bigger than he had ever done before. He wanted to write a stupendous thing.

He caught up his pen and dipped it in the ink.

She startled him with a quick cough.

"Can't you be still?" He turned toward her. "You know I can't write if I'm bothered. You don't have to sit in here if you're going to cough your head off. There're plenty of other rooms in the house."

She half rose from her chair.

"D'you want me to go?"

"Oh, sit there," he muttered irritably. "Only, for heaven's sake be still!"

"Yes, Jasper."

All of his books had brought him fame; but this one; this one would bring him fame with something else. This book would be the great work that would show to people the staggering power of one man's mind; his mind.

His eyes that stared at the window of the house opposite came back to be pile of blank paper which made a white patch on the dark wood before him.

Without any definite idea he began to write. A word. A sentence. A paragraph.

He tore the thing up without stopping to read it.

Ellen's dull-toned voice came to him through the stillness of the room.

"Anything wrong, Jasper?"

"Wrong? What should be wrong?"

"I don't know."

He began to write again.

He looked out of his window at the window of the house opposite.

He went on with his writing till he had covered the whole page. Again he tore the paper up and threw it from him.

"I'm going, Jasper."

He turned to see her standing in the center of the room, her heavily lidded eyes fixed on the floor.

"I told you you could stay here!"

"I'd best be going, Jasper."

"Sit down, over there; and do be still."

"I seem to bother you. You haven't started to write. Is it because I'm here, Jasper?"

"You!" He snorted contemptuously. "What've you got to do with it?"

"I don't know," she said quietly, and she went back to her chair.

Again his eyes were fixed on that one window. He leaned forward quickly. His hands gripped the chair's arms on either side of him. His brows drew down together above the bulging blue eyes.

Thrown on the clear blank of the window blind, moving to and fro across it, went the shadow.

With a sharp sigh of relief Jasper Wald began to write.

It was not until he had gotten far down the page that he became suddenly conscious of Ellen standing directly behind him.

He looked over at the window. The shadow was still there.

"What is it? What d'you want?"

The lamplight brought out her features, good and very regular and still somewhat nondescript. The lamplight showed her strange green eyes and beneath the heavy lids the lamplight brought out in a glinting streak the expression of the eyes themselves.

"What made you do that, Jasper?"

"I'm trying to write. You keep interrupting me. What are you talking about? Made me do what?"

"Made you write, Jasper."

"Don't I always write?"

"Yes, Jasper. Always. All of a sudden—; like that."

"Well, what of it?"

"What makes you do it, Jasper?"

"Oh, Lord, can't you leave me alone?"

"D'you know what makes you do it, Jasper?"

"Of course I know."

"Well, what?"

"My—it's my inspiration!"

"That comes"; she spoke slowly. "Every night when you look out of the window. That's how it comes, Jasper."

"Look out of the window? Why shouldn't I look out of the window?"

"What is it you see? Over there; in that house; in that one window?"

He looked across the way at the shadow moving to and fro against the window blind.

He started to his feet so suddenly that his chair crashed to the floor behind him. He faced her angrily.

"What under the sun's the matter with you?"

"Nothing."

"Then why can't you leave me alone?"

"I want to know, Jasper."

"You don't know what you want."

"Yes, Jasper; I—want—to—know—"

"Leave the room," he said furiously. "Leave the room! I've got to write!"

She started for the door.

"You've got to write?" Her words came back to him across the length of the room with a curious insistence. "*You've*—got—to—write, Jasper?"

He waited until the door closed behind her and then he went back to his desk.

What had she meant by that last question of hers? Didn't she know that he had to write? Didn't she realize that he had to write?

And this book of his; this book that was to be the biggest thing that he had yet done.

"Ellen," he called. "Ellen!"

He heard her feet coming toward him along the passageway.

She came back into the room as though nothing had happened.

"Yes, Jasper?"

"What—what did you mean by that, Ellen? By what you just said?"

She faced him in the center of the room.

"I've been wanting to tell you, Jasper."

"Well?"

Her hands hung quite quietly at her sides.

"I've put up with you for a long time, Jasper. I haven't said very much, you know."

"What?" He stuttered.

"Oh, yes," she went on evenly. "If it weren't for your vanity you'd have realized long ago what a contemptible little man you really are."

He interrupted her.

"Ellen!"

His tone was astonished.

"You're so full of yourself that you can't see anything else. You're so full of that genius—; of—yours—"

"You don't have to speak of that—; you can leave that out of it—; you've nothing to do with it—; with my genius."

"Your genius." She laughed then. "It's your genius, Jasper, that has nothing to do with you!"

"Nothing—to—do—with—me?"

"No, Jasper. I haven't been blind."

"Blind?"

"I've seen, Jasper; sitting here night after night in this room with you; I've seen."

"What?"

"Over there—; in the house opposite."

"You mean—"

"And you can't write without it, Jasper! You couldn't write before and you can't write now without it. It isn't you. It isn't you who writes. It's something—something working through you. And you call it your own. Jasper, you're a fool!"

"Ellen, how dare you!"

"Dare!"

She spoke the word disdainfully. He had never in his whole life seen her this way; he had never thought to see her like this; but then, he had never given Ellen much thought of any kind.

"It's you who're the fool." He was furious. "It's I who've always been the brains; if you could you'd have hampered me with your stupidity. But you couldn't. I shut you quite outside. I nurtured my own genius. If I'd have left things to you, I'd have been down and out by now; and that's all there is to it."

"No!" Her voice rang through the room. "I won't let you say that, Jasper. I'll tell you the truth now. And take it or leave it as you will. You won't be able to get away from it. Not if I tell you the truth, Jasper. There'll be no getting away from it!"

"Truth—; about what?"

"You and your genius. I wouldn't have told you but it's no good going on like this. I thought there was some hope for you; I couldn't think any human being would be as self-satisfied, as disgustingly material as you are. Why, if you have a soul, but you haven't, and I thought—God, how I hoped!"

He started to speak. He could not find his voice.

She went on presently in that quiet, monotonous voice which had been hers for so many years.

"You left me alone; I wouldn't have complained; I wouldn't complain now if you had some excuse for it. It all made me different. There's no use in telling you how; you couldn't understand. But I got to feeling things I'd never felt before; and then I saw things. And after a while I found I could bring those things to me. And that night, the first night we moved in here—"

He interrupted her in spite of himself.

"What of that night? What?"

"That night when you were standing there at the window I got down on my knees and prayed. I brought something to you that night. And you called the genius yours." She broke off and was silent for a second. "I brought it to you because I wanted you to be great. I thought with all that energy of yours for writing that if it could work through you, you'd be big. But you were too small for it! You tried to make it a thing of your own. And I've held on to it. For six years I've kept it here with you; and now it's going. I'm letting it go back again. You're too small; you can't ever be anything but just—you!"

He walked over to his desk, and sank down into the arm chair.

"I don't—know—what—you're—talking—about."

"You do! And if you don't, why do you look out of the window there every night? Why d'you wait for it to come, before you start to write?"

His exclamation was involuntary.

"The shadow!"

"Yes. Its shadow—; from this room where I kept it—casting—over—there—its—shadow."

So that was what she meant. The superstition-fostered thing that epitomized his genius to himself. The shadow that he had come to look upon as a sign of luck. But it was nonsense. It wasn't possible; not such rot as that. It was his mind; the big creative mind of him that wrote.

"Have you said all you're going to say?"

For a second her gaze met his and then the heavy lids came down again over those strange green eyes, hiding all expression.

"Yes, Jasper."

He looked out of the window. His eyes stared through the night beyond the two shadowy, drooping willow trees on either side of the wicker gate and over at the house opposite. He caught his breath. The yellow light from the lamp on his desk played across the clear blank of the window blind across the way. The shadow had gone.

"Ellen—" His voice was hoarse. "Ellen!"

"What is it?"

"It's not there, Ellen—; six years; now—; why, Ellen—"

She went and sat down in the chair beside the desk.

"Yes."

"It isn't there! I tell you—"

"I thought it could make no difference to you!"

"It was—lucky—Ellen."

"Oh, lucky, Jasper?"

He made an effort to pull himself together.

"It won't make any difference to me—not to my writing; not to my genius."

After the silence of a moment her voice came to him in its low even measure.

"Then—; write!"

"Of course." His tone was high pitched, hysterical. "Naturally I'll write."

"Write, Jasper."

He caught up his pen and dipped it in the ink. He drew the white pile of paper nearer to him.

"Jasper—"

"How can I work if you don't stop talking? How can I do anything? How can I write?"

"Are—you—writing—Jasper? Are—you—?"

He did not answer her.

"Because;" she went on very quietly. "It's gone back, Jasper. It's—gone—now—"

His pen went to and fro; to and fro across the page. His figure was bent well over the desk. Every now and again, without moving, his bulging blue eyes would lift themselves to the clear blank blind of the window opposite and then they would come back and fix themselves intently upon the white page of paper which he was so busily covering with stupid, meaningless little drawings.

Daylight Shadows

Arthur J. Burks

1925

I had been told by a more experienced officer than myself that only a fool would attempt the passage of Neiba
Desert after 10 o'clock in the morning. No white man,
afoot, could bear up under the terrible heat, and there are
few Dominican mules that can carry with ease a bulk as
great as mine. Neiba Desert, in the heart of the tropics, is
a hundred feet below the level of the sea.

But what youngster ever listened to the advice of his
elders! I never had, and because I did not in this instance,
I qualified for the first rank among fools.

We, a tenderfoot pharmacist's mate and myself, left
Barahona at 5 o'clock in the morning, intent on reaching
Las Salinas in time to make the crossing in the cool of the
morning. We rode a pair of Dominican mules that were
too small for us. But, even so, we should have made it,
had we not tarried overlong in Cabral to listen to the rau-
cous cries of the natives in the marketplace—until it was
8 o'clock by the sun.

We pulled out finally, after breakfasting on Dominican coffee, which is nectar fit for the gods after one has
acquired the taste for it. We reached the branching of the
road at about 9, and it was 10 o'clock exactly when we
gave the mules their last chance at water just Neibaward
from Las Salinas. We filled our canteens there, after which

we gave our mounts a breathing space ere we struck out through the thorn-tree studded waste of sand.

I shall never forget that momentous first glance toward Neiba. Just behind us to the south were the broad reaches of the Bahoruco mountains, while away ahead we could see the blue outline of the distant Cordilleras. We could not see the town of Neiba because of the fringe of palm-trees which hide her from view, even as they disclose her whereabouts. Even at that distance, which must have been very great, we could see that the palm-trees bowed and beckoned to us, as if they urged us ahead with promises of hospitality upon arrival.

We started blithely on our way. My companion was a pharmacist's mate in Uncle Sam's navy, and we talked of some of his queer experiences in hospital wards during the war, I remember. This was during the first hour, only, of the crossing. There was a dim trail through the sand, and the dust came up in clouds, filling our eyes and nostrils with fine layers of the stuff. The heat was almost unbearable. It must have been 104 degrees Fahrenheit even then. And we had just started. The palm-trees looked no nearer. The Cordilleras were just as blue as at first. Our talking died away to oppressive silence. We drank often from our canteens, and we did not try to spare the water. Those palm-trees looked much closer than they really were, although we had been warned that their beckoning was treacherous—like that of *Die Lorelei*. Our water was gone before we had half completed the passage.

Two hours more.

Half an hour after the water gave out we were slumped low in our saddles, our shirts pulled up about our necks to keep the heat from frying our brains, and our mules were creeping along with their heads hanging almost into the trail. They were very tired, and the dust had built gray coats on their sweat-drenched hides.

My companion, who had been but a few weeks out of
the states, rode along without a glance to right or left. He
was feeling the heat more than I was. It was tough on him.
Another hour passed, with the palm-trees seemingly no
nearer. I saw that his gaze was fixed steadfastly upon them.
Once when their fronded heads bowed and beckoned to
us, he raised his hand and waved, as if he answered their
silent greeting. He listened. Then he laughed—a laugh
that was as dry as footfalls in the leaves of autumn. I knew
without looking that his lips had begun to crack and that
his tongue was swelling in his mouth.

I began to see queer things. A lizard scrambled from
beneath a thorn-tree and stopped in the trail ahead, his
yellow throat moving in the heat like a bellows. Before my
eyes, as we approached, he swelled in size until he was not
a lizard, but an iguana—not an iguana, but a dinosaur—a
monster. He did not move as my mule approached, but
ducked his serpentine head as if, like the ostrich, he would
hide it in the sand. He kept on swelling until, just as the
mule's hoof must strike him, he covered the entire road,
and his body stretched away in the desert on either side.
But the mule never noticed. Nor did my companion. The
mule's foot struck without a jar. In a flash the monster
vanished. I looked back after we had passed. There was
only a greenish smear in the footprint, which was rapidly
filling with dust. I laughed, loud and long, but my companion did not turn around.

When I had looked back I had lowered my head so
that my gaze was upon the ground beneath. I noticed a
strange thing. Neither myself, my companion, nor the
mules, cast a sign of a shadow upon the sand beneath us! I
pinched myself and it hurt. I struck spurs to the mule and
he grunted dismally. Real enough. But why were there no
shadows? I bent over to look beneath the animal I rode.
Still no shadow! The pharmacist's mate looked at me then.

We laughed in each other's faces and neither knew why the other laughed.

My mule stopped. His sides were moving rapidly out and in—out and in, as if he could not stop them. His breath came groaning from drooling lips; slobbers made cakes of sand and dried at once, leaving little hills like the workings of certain kinds of yellow-jackets. I knew at once that the mule could proceed no farther. I alighted and attempted to pull the creature along. Not to be done.

My lips were cracked and bleeding. My tongue protruded from between sand-gritted teeth. I addressed the pharmacist's mate in a weird kind of croak:

"Go on to Neiba. and tell the *guardia* to come back out for me. Your mule can make it. You never could do it afoot if I took your mule. I don't know that I can do it myself, but my chances are better than yours. Beat it!"

"Just so, sir. Certainly! It was to me that they beckoned, anyway. They have no welcome for you in Neiba. The greeting was for me."

What was the fool talking about? And why did he laugh like a croaking raven as he set spurs to his mule and moved on up the trail? I stood and watched him until he mingled with the heat waves, vanishing into the shimmering stuff like a creature from the pit.

Once more I tried to pull the mule along. It was no use, but my knees were knocking together and I was weak as a cat before I gave it up and tied my mule in the dubious shade of a thorn-tree, where it was hotter even than out in the sunlight.

I started on afoot. I came to myself at the end of a hundred yards or so, to see that I was heading back toward Las Salinas. That would never do! Two hundred yards of needless walking when I needed every ounce of my strength!

The mate would never reach Neiba, I felt sure. He was already crazy from the heat. He'd be bound to try a short cut and leave his bones to bleach in the sun. I had to make it on in. I need not look for the arrival of *guardia* soldiers. The pharmacist's mate would never get in to tell them. He was too crazy.

I had to laugh when I thought about it. Then I looked down and turned clear around once. Not a shade of a shadow! Pretty good, that, I thought. Shade of a shadow! Ha! ha! Carefully, solemnly, I raised one foot at a time, looking under each one. No shadow.

I started on again, saying, "Eeny, meeny, miny, mo" to make sure I got started in the right direction this time. Queer how I had gotten turned around while turning around looking for the shade of my shadow! Ha! ha! ha!

I stumbled along, cursing to myself because my scuffling feet stirred up dust which flew into my nostrils. I didn't hear myself curse. My tongue was so big now that no sound could get out. But I should be all right in a brace of minutes. There was a sparkling stream crossing the trail right up there ahead of me. Queer, too, that—the officer who had given me that crazy advice had told me that there were no streams between Las Salinas and Neiba. But I could see it, couldn't I? Sure! I stumbled along until I reached its very edge, flung myself down and pressed my lips to its cooling surface. They came away coated with burning sand, some of which worked past my lips, past my swollen tongue, and into my mouth. I tried to expel the grains, but there wasn't enough moisture in my mouth. I had to stumble on with the gritty grains scratching me terribly. Somebody had placed the stream there as a kind of funny joke; but whoever had done it had hauled it away just when I would have slaked my thirst! Very poor joke.

I looked back at the mule. He brayed at me with the note of a croaking raven. I turned at looked at the palm-trees that beckoned me on to Neiba. I could almost hear the whispering of the fronds. But the Cordilleras were as blue as ever. Where was that dratted pharmacist's mate? Damn him!

I looked once more for my shadow. No shadow. Then I knew that I was nearing the end. The thought brough me back to a semblance of reason for a few minutes. I was suffering the torments of the utterly damned. How many a poor fool had left his bones to bleach in this desert in days gone by? There must have been many of them, surely. But not if they remained on the road. Someone would surely come along and find them. Only the poor fool who wandered off the trail left his bones to bleach. I had better sense. I would stick to the trail.

But where was the trail! I saw trails now which led to every point of the compass. Follow the beckoning of the palm-trees? There were palm-trees all around me. But some of them were thorn-trees! I couldn't for the life of me tell the difference. Eeny, meeny, miny, mo! Straight ahead. I looked for my shadow again and could not find it.

But all at once there were shadows all around me! But where were the bodies that caused the shadows! The substance which was the father of the shadows! I saw not a single upright creature. Only those shadows, flat on the ground, that danced and eddied around me. The shadows of human beings! But where were the human beings! I looked more closely at the shadows. Arms, legs, heads, bodies—all were there. But the substance which caused them? None to be seen. No solid bodies. The shadows were whole and perfectly formed. But stay! They weren't entirely whole. In each and every shadow there were three bright spots, marking two eyes and a gash of a mouth to each shadow, where the sun shone through the substance I could not see!

I stopped dead in my tracks as an idea came to me. The shadows, which were increasing at an alarming rate, paused, radiating out from me like the spokes of a wheel, and thumbed shadow noses at me with shadow thumbs. My idea was this: I, who was human and alive, cast no shadow. Therefore these shadows must be the shadows of those who had ceased to exist. It was perfectly reasonable, like a proposition in geometry. The living cast no shadow, therefore that which cast a shadow must be dead and gone! It followed, as a corollary, that I should cast a shadow only after I had died!

Queer about this desert. Lizards that were iguanas; iguanas that were dinosaurs; streams that did not exist: shadows of the desert dead! Why did the shadows gather about me! Were they inviting me to join the ranks of those who were able to cast shadows? Were the dead who had died in Neiba asking me to join them! Or were they taunting me because they knew I must join them whether I willed it or no?

"But you haven't got me yet!" I croaked to the shadows. "I am still of those who cast no shadows! See? Look about me and see if there be even the sign of a shadow!"

And I looked down to satisfy myself that I spoke truth.

My God! I didn't cast a shadow, no: but right where my shadow would have been had there been a shadow was a thin pencil mark of darkness, as if someone had drawn a black line about my shadow's outline and then jerked the shadow away! Like that practical joker who had jerked the stream away when I would have slaked my thirst.

I paused for a moment, studying that weird outline, while the real shadows kept thumbing their noses at me. There was a heavier shadow among those real shadows— the shadow of a fat man who had died. Fat men are said to be jolly. I looked at the fat man as I recalled this. The spot where the right eye would have been, had it been a person instead of a shadow, closed slowly and strangely, in a terrible and horrifying wink! The bright eye opened again and the bright gash of a mouth widened into a terrible, ghastly, silent grin!

I screamed and ran, closing my eyes to shut out the shadows. I fell to my knees and slumped forward on my stomach, crawling slowly ahead through the scorching sand. It burned my hands and body. Hellfire rushed into my nostrils from the desert floor. I dragged myself to my feet, then fell and lay still for a long time. I opened my eyes to see that the shadows were dancing in hellish glee upon my chest! All thumbed their noses except the fat man. He winked, and grinned with that bright gash of a mouth.

I arose and looked at my own shadow. I could call it that now, for there was only the bright outline of a miniature of myself, within that other outline of black. I was almost a shadow. I closed my eyes again and stumbled ahead.

Suddenly I met three Dominican women riding toward me on three burros piled high with gourds. Filled with water, I knew, for the gourds were dripping precious moisture upon the gray coats of the burros. I raised a hand beseechingly and pointed to my swollen throat. The women crossed themselves and shied away from me. I tried to run toward them and the burros bolted. One of the women called back to me:

"Go back to Barahona, or on to Neiba, if you wish water! There is more than you can drink, ever, in either place!"

Surely, that was truth! Stupid of me! I would go on to Neiba. That's where I had started for, wasn't it?

I walked on, stumbling, falling, crawling forward on my stomach like a snake—rising and going forward with feet that were heavy as lead. Molten lead.

Where were the palm-trees? I could not see them. And this trail was not a trail at all. It was the snaky trace of a

lizard! No, of an iguana! Or a dinosaur. I don't know. I'll
follow it anyway. My shadow tells me that there isn't much
time. The miniature within the outline isn't a miniature
any more—just a weirdly shaped spray of blinding light,
growing smaller. And there are other shadows all about
me—countless numbers of them.

What is that up ahead there? Another stream? But I
shan't be disappointed if it isn't; I'll have a look anyway.
I'm going in that direction. I stumble into the stream. It
is real! I feel its coolness creep up over my shoetops, creep
into my shoes and harden the molten lead which compose
my feet. I fall face downward in the stream and drink—
drink—drink! The water is green because the cattle use it
overmuch, but it is nectar for all that—nectar superior to
the best Dominican coffee.

I crawl out on the bank and look at my shadow. There
is only a spot of light in its center now. To be cheated,
after I have reached water at last!

But whence come these other shadows? They are shadows of black soldiers, and they are upright instead of
flat on the ground. I am not to be fooled. I'm all turned
around, I know that, but I am not crazy yet. They look
at me queerly, hesitantly, as they approach. One man, a
sergeant, is in the lead, and he is running toward me with
swift strides. He stops just before me and his shadow blots
out the spray of light which is all that stands between me
and the desert dead.

"Curse you! Curse you!" I cry, slashing out with my
fist; "would you relegate me to the shadows after I have
slaked my thirst and am able to go on! I don't want to be
a shadow, I tell you!"

My fist takes him in the mouth, and I see the red blood
start as total darkness closes around me, filling the world
itself with shadow.

I came to myself in the *guardia* barracks at Neiba. The sergeant sat opposite me, wiping his lips with a soiled handkerchief.

"Where am I?" I asked feebly. "Did the pharmacist's mate get in all right? How did I get here?"

He smiled at me and answered in Spanish.

"You are in Neiba. Yes, he got in all right. We brought you in, after tracking you halfway to Lake Enriquillo, toward which, leaving the trail, you were wandering. You were unconscious, flat on the desert floor, and licking up sand with your swollen tongue, which, sticking through between your teeth, was so big that it wouldn't carry the sand into your mouth! It kept rolling off your tongue and you mumbled to yourself as if cursing. I caught the words 'cattle' and 'shadows'. Then you hit me in the mouth. That's all!"

It was enough.

The Shadow of the Tower
Mihaly Babeti
1926

I have meditated a long while about the person to whom I should send these notes and observations. I first thought of simply sending them to a scientist, but I soon abandoned that idea. I am a scientist of sorts myself, so I know how unbelieving these people are; they would not take my story seriously.

Perhaps, with witnesses chosen amongst my friends, or making them watch the phenomenon themselves, waiting for it to occur again, months hence perhaps. . . .

But who would do that for me? I haven't the time.

The Almighty has passed sentence on me; He has counted the hours I have to live, Glory be to His name.

Happy are those that can accept the will of the Lord, so that is why I am writing to you, Sir; you, whose calling is to relate and explain creeds and symbols.

The thing that happened to me will not enrich humanity's treasure of knowledge; science will have nothing to do with such things. Indeed she is afraid of them, as if she was treading on forbidden ground. It belongs to the kingdom of fables—fables are sent to us by God, and He sends very few.

It was one fine summer evening at the convent of Szentmarton. The carriage was waiting for me at the station, for it was a long distance from there to the old convent, miles away from everything. It was the home of old and crippled priests, unable to teach or to administer a parish, who lived near God in that retired part of the world.

It would have been impossible to have found anywhere a spot more favorable to meditation. I was going there as an invalid, although I brought with me books and scientific notes I wanted to finish while I was in that retreat. The great calm that accompanies the twilight had descended like a mantle upon the hills when I first beheld the old convent. It was a monument dating from Bela the Third, with a strange tower, which seemed to have been left unfinished by the builder. In the background was the wonderful deep blue of the sky. The monotonous rumble of the carriage wheels mingled with the melancholy chirping of the crickets. In front of me, the driver swayed to and fro, his black coat and cocked hat making him look like an undertaker. We were going along slowly like a black boat sailing across a calm sea.

"O God, if Thy will is that this is my last journey, I accept Thy will," was my prayer.

An hour later I was sitting in the calm atmosphere of the convent refectory among the old priests. Some of them were friends of long standing with whom I had lived in other convents.

They inquired about those they used to know. We talked of old times, then strolled out into the garden to enjoy the beautiful evening. The garden paths wound under the trees in the shadows and the sharp outlines of the convent stood out against the sky. It was only then that I noticed the tower was quite apart from the rest of the building, so that it was possible to walk right round it, and the extraordinary shape of the unfinished building roused my curiosity.

"Now the tower is abandoned and the gardener uses it as a tool shed," the superior told me when I inquired about it.

Our colleague, the professor of comparative philology, told me that there was a story associated with the tower— it is a legend very similar to that of "Kelemen-the-Mason": A young girl was entombed alive within these walls.

The old Hungarian legend of "Kelemen-the-Mason" is a story of a nobleman who built with his own hands a tower—but his work was always miraculously destroyed as he went on. One day he heard the voice of God saying, "You will be allowed to finish your tower if you entomb therein the first woman who passes this way." The nobleman took the risk. His wife was the first woman who passed, and she fell a victim to his ambition.

"O Lord, thou hast sent very few fables to mankind; that of Kelemen-the-Mason and this one that is so like it. We are in a very primitive country where legends still live."

I came out of my arched roofed cell keener than ever to see by daylight the strange abode where henceforth I was to live. I walked through many dark passages, and was blinded by the glare of the light on reaching the open. It seemed to me that a myriad of bees were humming in the sunshine, and I was dazzled by the blue sky above the garden, which appeared as an immense sea of flowers melting into the sky on the horizon.

The air was laden with a sweet perfume and the golden light overshadowed the earth's beautiful cloak of flowers. In the cool clear morning air the mysterious tower cast its shadow over all this splendor with its wealth of color.

As I gazed on a red flower, a butterfly suddenly flew away. And all this splendor seemed to sing praises to the glory of our Creator.

I sat in the sun with my breviary, and offered thanks to the Lord for having directed my steps towards this place, which was a Paradise. I thanked him for the flowers, the butterflies, and for the beautiful old designs on the

convent walls, which seemed to smile as they basked in
the sunshine; for the sun itself, for the strange old tower
and the graceful silhouette of the gardener's wife leaning
over to water the flowers, all these wonders were pleasant
to my eyes. A wide open space encircled the tower and
there were flower beds running wild through lack of care,
for nobody ever came that way. My colleagues remained in
their rooms, and, when leaving, used the street door. Only
in the evening did they venture near the tower. I, being
a guest, passed my morning near the tower, only leaving
when the convent bell rang for lunch. When I was tired
of reading, I enjoyed the splendor of the garden or talked
to the gardener's wife, whose naïve simplicity was most
refreshing.

The monotony of autumn had fallen upon us, and the
sunny days had passed. I hardly noticed in the end that
I scarcely read, as I sat there with my book lying on my
knees, dazzled by the sun. The garden seemed to have a
strange power over me; I tried to free myself, and find
another lonely spot, but invariably came back and sat
in front of the tower, in the midst of the silent joy of
the flowers, bathing in the sea of brilliant light. Behind
me, the sunflowers were swinging their yellow heads, and
the multicolored balls on the blue garden railings held
my gaze. I was like a person hypnotized and I could not
move until the tinkle of the lunch bell released me. The
strange tower rose in front of me; above it the sun with its
blinding rays seemed to form part of the tower, and vanish
in the distance, but its shadow, like a gigantic needle, cast
its sinister darkness on the quivering flowers.

As midday drew nearer the effect became more phantom-like.

Yes, phantom-like. Have you ever noticed, Sir, that
there is something phantom-like about the hour of noon,
as there is midnight—all movement ceases, everything is

quiet—the world seems to pause and wait; there is a great silence, a great dread; nature stops breathing; the merciless sunlight does not lessen the ghostly effect. On the contrary, everything being lit up, nothing can be hidden, there is no shelter, no shade. The world is naked, a prey to the great danger that it feels approaching. The very light does not seem natural, it is a brilliant white glare like that of a full moon. The great calm and loneliness are then awful. Often I sat on the garden bench, like a downcast beast, without a thought, but conscious of some inexplicable fear. I thought it might be the effect of the sun. The sun has impassibly followed its course across the sky, its burning rays mercilessly revealing every detail. Alone in the midst of this light, the tower cast its deep shadow, like a huge black tombstone. I experienced a moment of bestial stupidity and bewilderment until I rose and staggered along like a drunkard to the convent, where I had lunch within the cool walls. And the afternoon passed in a heavy torpor.

Oh, these noon hours! It is of these moments that I will tell you.

The day had begun as usual. I was talking to the gardener's wife, who had brought her little girl out into the sun.

The pebbles on the path were scrunching under the wheels of the perambulator, where a pale, pretty face could be seen lying on the pillow. "My darling is ill," said the woman, who, herself, looked so frail that one would doubt whether she were a peasant.

"The sunshine will do her a lot of good," I replied. And really, at that moment, the sun seemed kind and well disposed. The morning air was warm, and light shadows were flitting over the golden hills. It was with pleasure that I took up my book, and when I was reading, I forgot the midday numbness. I read for a while, then the book dropped into my lap, and I looked around to gaze upon the pleasing scene, which seemed ever new to me. The young woman, wanting to return to her duties, seemed to hesitate as to whether she could leave the child in the open or take her indoors, and so I offered to look after the little one. I must confess (it may seem ridiculous to you), that my old priest's heart was delighted to have, if only for an hour, so fatherly a task.

The child was lying silent, the sun rose higher and higher and the usual torpidity overcame me. The many hued balls shone strangely throwing back distorted reflections; my gaze wandered dazzled by the richness and variety of the colors. The garden seemed to sway before my eyes; things met and mingled confusedly, the tower seemed to sway against the blue sky; a wasp danced, flew and droned before me from left to right, high and low in the vibrating furnace. I closed my eyes.

I closed my eyes. . . . Bright darkness, warm and velvety, overcame my brain like a soft helmet, blue-and-red spots with rainbow borders swarmed before me, one of them shot up so high, but I could not follow it—the droning was dying down, noon was near.

Suddenly a frightened wail came forth from the perambulator. I opened my eyes, scared. Oh, the phantom-like noon was around me. I felt as if I had alighted on another planet. The inexorable dazzling white light, hovering over everything, the awful silence and the only shadow that of the tower across the garden and, in the shadow of the tower, the perambulator, and in the perambulator, as if she felt the eeriness of the hour, the child was crying.

All of a sudden, I felt afraid and my heart galloped beneath my cassock. I soon knew the reason for this agitation. The carriage had not been in the shade of the tower, in fact, it had been very far away. I glanced towards the sun and the other shadow thrown across the grass, then I looked at the shadow of the tower. There was absolutely no doubt about it, the shadow was not in the direction that it should have been according to all optical laws. Just follow, you will see. The sun was above the tower, a little to the left, and thus the shadow should have fallen as the others did, to the right, whereas it fell to the left, right over the child's perambulator.

I do not know, Sir, if you can imagine how horrified I was. I am a man of science and used to scientific experiments, but there was no possibility of accounting for this strange occurrence, no other light existed that could cause the shadow to deviate in such a way. To tell you the truth, I never tried to fathom the mystery. I sat there amazed and stupefied before what could only be described as a miracle.

Noon was indeed more fantastical than midnight. All around, the brilliant light flooded everything, and all the shadows were on the right—there was no darkness, no mysterious shelter or any possible hiding place, everything was clear, pure and irrefutable.

My dread increased every instant as I watched the huge black phantasmagorial shadow extending across the gravel of the path, like an immense black sheet on the perambulator. In the midday silence, the child was crying, a piteous frightened wail, as if she knew that the shadow cast across her was unnatural. It was as though the single blue-black spot, the only shadow in contradiction with nature, gave a strange signification to the midday heat, the silence of the birds hidden in the bushes and to the cries of the little girl.

I was so overcome by the strange sight that I could neither move nor speak until the gardener's wife, hearing her child crying, ran out and without looking my way, rushed madly up to the perambulator. Her behavior was like that of an animal afraid for its young (it is often so with women), and, snatching up the child, she ran into the house.

Thoughtfully, I followed her with my eyes and I could not help connecting the strange shadow, the child's cries and the mother's animal-like fright. I should have liked to have known that it was all an illusion, but the shadow was still there in its unnatural position.

The lunch bell startled me back to sanity. As I went through the dark-walled passages, the red-and-green spots still danced before my eyes, and strange thoughts haunted me, but when I reached the cool white refectory, the restful calm drove away the terrified impression of which I was then beginning to be ashamed. How could I have related my adventure to these happy old priests? I began to doubt. I had perhaps been dreaming, but to make sure whether I had or not, I made up my mind to find some plausible excuse to bring some one to watch the phenomenon. But in the afternoon clouds drew a thick gray veil across the sky, and, when a pale light shone through a thinner part of the veil causing feeble shadows, I could see that that of the tower was in its usual place.

Had it been a dream after all, or had my eyes been dazzled by the brightness of the sun, so that I had seen things which did not exist? I really could not believe either one or the other of these explanations. In trying to solve the problem, I lost all peace, and my thoughts obstinately came back to the tower. Closing my eyes again, I could recall the vision, resembling a picture with a big mistake in perspective which caught my eyes and prevented me from noticing anything else. My memory recalled more details and I remembered that, not only did the shadow fall in an unusual direction but was much longer than it should have been in proportion to the length of the other shadows. The way it had grown and spread was simply miraculous, otherwise it could never have reached the perambulator. I could only think of the whole occurrence as having actually happened, and I wanted it, yet dreaded, to happen again.

However, the sky was overcast for several days and autumn seemed to be really with us. At a loose end, I would sit in my room with my books, my old complaint would come back, and my temper was bad. I would have given anything to see the sun and feel its warmth again.

One morning, however, I saw the blue sky through the railings of my cell and the rays of sunshine on the floor. I was seized with sudden fright and I knew that in a few hours I would go down to the mysterious garden and sit before the tower with the strange shadow.

The first morning, I was disappointed yet inwardly pleased. The shadow followed the sun and did not for one moment show any inclination to deviate from the beaten track, everything was normal. The day after nothing happened, the sun had come out again; and bathed the earth with light and heat. St. Martin's Summer was here, I sat in my usual place, and the days were no different from the first one I had passed at the convent. The only change was that many dead leaves fell faster and faster; they lay strewn about the paths in spite of the efforts of the gardener's wife who tried to sweep them away.

When the red rust of autumn mingled with the bright red of the last flower, the perambulator was no longer brought out, for the child had passed away the day after the strange happening which I have related. She is among the angels of the Lord.

I tried to resist the superstitious thought connected with this death, and I was beginning to be sure that the midday glare of the sun had hallucinated me, and that I had been a victim of an optical illusion. Yet, at other times, I was convinced that some strange presentiment had caused me to imagine that I had seen the shadow, and then I began to think quite rationally. This showed that I was less distressed.

However, one day, as I sat reading in my usual place, when summer heat had become autumnal warmth, a great calm reigned, and I was alone at the foot of the tall sunflowers. Lord, the old dog, was warming himself in the sun; and on the grass a pigeon was strutting about; further away I could see the russet apples gleaming on the branches of a low apple tree. I looked up and gazed laughingly at the peaceful picture and then turned to the shadow of the tower. "You'll no longer deceive me," I said to the shadow. "The great light that dazzles and distorts things has faded, and shadows must play no more tricks."

I had scarcely thought this when the shadow moved. Yes, Sir, just as I am telling you, the shadow described a big half circle to the right, then swayed back several times like an immense pendulum. Do you understand? Everything was calm, and the other shadows were quite still, as was the tower against the sky.

Yet the shadow was oscillating as if a huge lantern was being swung to and fro behind the tower, or as if the sun was swaying. I watched very closely but it was the only thing moving; it was more and more mysterious. The shadow spread across the lawn, across the road, from left to right, and stretched and shrank itself like the arm of a monstrous cuttle-fish.

How can I describe the terror of the moment? The pigeon, flapping its wings wildly, flew towards the apple tree; the dog got up and whined, the wild flowers shuddered. The shadow seemed to crunch the gravel as if it was heavy; the grass bowed down before it and bounced back again and a tamarind tree bent beneath the weight. Suddenly the shadow in one last swing threw itself over the spot where the dog was lying and Lord jumped up, mouth open and panting, watching the shadow stretching towards him. It fell on him like a huge black hand and stopped.

The dog, like a wounded animal, fell with an awful death rattle and then ran away howling. I cannot describe what I felt like and I passed the evening in prayer. I had a vision of the young woman who had been entombed alive in the tower. Oh! Lord! (I prayed), if the story is true give peace to her soul!

But there was no peace for my soul. Being a priest, I have always believed in miracles, and I have never made the mistake of scientists who think that they can rule the universe with their human mathematics. All the same, there is a big margin between believing in miracles and seeing them. I confess that my thoughts were upset. God's ways are unfathomable, the consequence of a crime is terrible; generation after generation we still feel them and even the innocent are victims. I thought of the sick child I had seen cry in the shade of the tower on the eve of his death.

Next day I anxiously looked around for the dog. The poor beast had "broken its pipe." "It is a very old dog," said the gardener. My heart stopped beating, and as I anxiously glanced at the tower I felt myself getting worse and I recall the words my doctor had spoken and they seemed to have a hidden and awful meaning. Something warned me to stay away from the tower, and yet once more, on one sunny morning, an invisible and irresistible force guided my steps to my usual place; I could not leave it before noon. The autumnal scene affected me deeply, it fascinated me, and although my health was failing, I thought of the healing faculties of the light. We had a glorious autumn, greenish gold virgin threads were floating through the warm air and all living things were enjoying the last fine days. But, alas! they were not restful days for me, for I could feel the strange and deep pains within me and I thought of death drawing near. I obstinately wrote, wanting to finish a part of my work before the angel of death appeared before me. What could a miserable worm like me do before the Creator? The Lord does not use exterior forces to keep us from acting against His will. He sends our very soul against ourselves. Happy are they who accept His Will. The Lord hath said unto His servant, "I no longer need your work," and He made my soul anxious so that I should abandon my task, and He put before me, like His own finger, a fatal sign, the strange tower, so that I could gaze at it in anguish for hours.

At any moment I was expecting to see the shadow move and fall upon me. Then came the day . . . with a large swing the shadow moved. Very still I waited and prayed and I did not try to flee, but my heart beat very hard as the shadow oscillated two or three times, stretched out, shrank back, curled up before the bushes and then fell on me, hiding the sun from my eyes.

I confess that as I write my heart still thumps and I beg the Lord to forgive me my sins and make me one of His chosen ones. . . . I am already on my way to that place from whence there can be no return.

The Shadows

Henry S. Whitehead

1927

I did not begin to see the shadows until I had lived in Old Morris' house for more than a week. Old Morris, dead and gone these many years, had been the scion of a still earlier Irish settler in Santa Cruz, of a family which had come into the island when the Danes, failing to colonize its rich acres, had opened it, in the middle of the Eighteenth Century, to colonists; and younger sons of Irish, Scottish, and English gentry had taken up sugar estates and commenced that baronial life which lasted for a century and which declined after the abolition of slavery and the German bounty on beet sugar had started the long process of West Indian commercial decadence. Mr. Morris' youth had been spent in the French islands.

The shadows were at first so vague that I attributed them wholly to the slight weakness which began to affect my eyes in early childhood, and which, while never materially interfering with the enjoyment of life in general, had necessitated the use of glasses when I used my eyes to read or write. My first experience of them was about 1 o'clock in the morning. I had been at a "Gentlemen's Party" at Hacker's house, "Emerald," as some poetic-minded ancestor of Hacker's had named the family estate three miles out of Christiansted, the northerly town, built on the site of the ancient abandoned French town of Bassin.

I had come home from the party and was undressing in my bedroom, which is one of two rooms on the westerly side of the house which stands at the edge of the old "Sunday Market". These two bedrooms open on the market-place, and I had chosen them, rather than the more airy rooms on the other side, because of the space outside. I like to look out on trees in the early mornings, whenever possible, and the ancient market-place is overshadowed with the foliage of hundred-year-old mahogany trees, and a few gnarled "otaheites" and Chinese-bean trees.

I had nearly finished undressing, had noted that my servant had let down and properly fastened the mosquito netting, and had stepped into the other bedroom to open the jalousies so that I might get as much of the night-breeze as possible circulating through the house. I was coming back through the doorway between the two bed-rooms, and taking off my dressing gown, at the moment, when the first faint perception of what I have called "the shadows" made itself apparent. It was very dark, just after switching off the electric light in that front bedroom. I had, in fact, to feel for the doorway. In this I experienced some difficulty, and my eyes had not fully adjusted them-selves to the thin starlight seeping in through the slanted jalousies of my own room when I passed through the doorway and groped my way toward the great mahogany four-poster in which I was about to lie down for my be-lated rest.

I saw the nearest post looming before me, closer than I had expected. Putting out my hand, I grasped—nothing. I winked in some surprise, and peered through the slightly increasing light, as my eyes adjusted themselves to the sudden change. Yes, surely,—there was the corner of the bedstead just in front of my face! By now my eyes were sufficiently attuned to the amount of light from outside to see a little plainer. I was puzzled. The bed was not where

I had supposed it to be. What could have happened? That the servants should have moved my bed without orders to do so was incredible. Besides, I had undressed, in full electric light in that room, not more than a few minutes ago, and then the bed was standing exactly where it had been since I had had it moved into that room a week before. I kicked, gently, before me with a slippered foot, against the place where that bedpost appeared to be standing—and my foot met no resistance.

I stepped over to the light in my own room, and snapped the button. In the sudden glare, everything readjusted itself to normal. There stood my bed, and here in their accustomed places about the room were ranged the chairs, the polished wardrobe (we do not use cupboards in the West India Islands), the mahogany dressing table,—even my clothes which I had hung over a chair where Albertina my servant would find them in the morning and put them (they were of white drill) into the soiled-clothes bag in the morning.

I shook my head. Light and shadow in these islands seem, somehow, different from what they are like at home in the United States! The tricks they play are different tricks, somehow.

I snapped off the light again, and in the ensuing dead blackness, I crawled in under the loose edge of the mosquito netting, tucked it along under the edge of the mattress on that side, adjusted my pillows and the sheets, and settled myself for a good sleep. Even to a moderate man, these gentlemen's parties are rather wearing sometimes. They invariably last too long. I closed my eyes and was asleep before I could have put these last ideas into words.

In the morning the recollection of the experience with the bed-being-in-the-wrong-place was gone. I jumped out of bed and into my shower bath at half-past 6, for I had

promised O'Brien, captain of the U. S. Marines, to go out
with him to the rifle range at La Grande Princesse that
morning and look over the butts with him. I like O'Brien,
and I am not uninterested in the efficiency of Uncle Sam's
Marines, but my chief objective was to watch the pelicans.
Out there on the glorious beach of Estate Grande Princesse ("Big Princess" as the Black People call it), a colony
of pelicans make their home, and it is a never-ending
source of amusement to me to watch them fish. A Caribbean pelican is probably the most graceful flier we have
in these latitudes,— barring not even the hurricane bird,
that describer of noble arcs and parabolas,—and the most
insanely, absurdly awkward creature on land that Providence has cared in a light-hearted moment to create!

I expressed my interest in Captain O'Brien's latest im-
provements, and while he was talking shop to one of his
lieutenants and half a dozen enlisted men he has camped
out there, I slipped down to the beach to watch the pelicans fish. Three or four of them were describing curves
and turns of indescribable complexity and perfect grace
over the green water of the reef-enclosed white beach. Ever
and again one would stop short in the air, fold himself up
like a jackknife, turn head downward, his great pouched
bill extended like the head of a cruel spear, and drop like
a plummet into the water, emerging an instant later with
the pouch distended with a fish.

I stayed a trifle too long,—for my eyes. Driving back I
observed that I had picked up several sun-spots, and when
I arrived home I polished a set of yellowish sun-spectacles
I keep for such emergencies and put them on.

The east side of the house had been shaded against
the pouring morning sunlight, and in this double shade I
looked to see my eyes clear up. The sun-spots persisted,
however, in that annoying, recurrent way they have,—
almost disappearing and then returning in undiminished

kaleidoscopic grotesqueness,—those strange blocks and parcels of pure color changing as one winks from indigo to brown and from brown to orange and then to a blinding turquoise-blue, according to some eery natural law of physics, within the fluids of the eye itself.

The sun-spots were so persistent that morning that I decided to keep my eyes closed for some considerable time and see if that would allow them to run their course and wear themselves out. Blue and mauve grotesques of the vague, general shape of diving pelicans swam and jumped inside my eyes. It was very annoying. I called to Albertina.

"Albertina," said I, when she had come to the door, "please go into my bedroom and close all the jalousies tight. Keep out all the light you can, please."

"Ahl roight, sir," replied the obedient Albertina, and I heard her slapping the jalousie-blinds together with sharp little clicks.

"De jalousie ahl close, sir," reported Albertina. I thanked her, and proceeded with half-shut eyes into the bedroom, which, not yet invaded with afternoon's sunlight and closely shuttered, offered an appearance of deep twilight. I lay, face down, across the bed, a pillow under my face, and my eyes buried in darkness.

Very gradually, the diving pelican faded out, to a cube, to a dim, recurrent blur, to nothingness. I raised my head and rolled over on my side, placing the pillow back where it belonged. And as I opened my eyes on the dim room, there stood, in faint, shadowy outline, in the opposite corner of the room, away from the outside wall on the market-place side, the huge, Danish bedstead I had vaguely noted the night before, or rather, early that morning.

It was the most curious sensation, looking at that bed in the dimness of the room. I was reminded of those fourth-dimensional tales which are so popular nowadays, for the bed impinged, spatially, on my large bureau, and the curious thing was that I could see the bureau at the same time! I rubbed my eyes, a little unwisely, but not enough to bring back the pelican sun-spots into them, for I remembered and desisted pretty promptly. I looked, fixedly, at the great bed, and it blurred and dimmed and faded out of my vision.

Again, I was greatly puzzled, and I went over to where it seemed to stand and walked through it,—it being no longer visible to my now restored vision, free of the effects of the sun-spots,—and then I went out into the "hall"—a West Indian drawing room is called "the hall"—and sat down to think over this strange phenomenon. I could not account for it. If it had been poor Prentice, now! Prentice attended all the "gentlemen's parties" to which he was invited with a kind of religious regularity, and had to be helped into his ear with a similar regularity, a regularity which was verging on the monotonous nowadays, as the invitations became more and more strained. No,—in my case it was, if there was anything certain about it, assuredly not the effects of strong liquors, for barring an occasional sociable swizzel I retained here in my West Indian residence my American convictions that moderation in such matters was a reasonable virtue. I reasoned out the matter of the phantom bedstead,—for so I was already thinking of it,—as far as I was able. That it was a phantom of defective eyesight I had no reasonable doubt. I had had my eyes examined in New York three months before, and the oculist had pleased me greatly by assuring me that there were no visible indications of deterioration. In fact, Dr. Jusserand had said at that time that my eyes were stronger, sounder, than when he had made his last examination six months before.

Perhaps this conviction,—that the appearance was due to my own physical shortcoming, accounts for the fact that I was not (what shall I say?) *disturbed,* by what I saw, or thought I saw. Confront the most thoroughgoing materialist with a ghost, and he will act precisely like anyone else; like any normal human being who believes in the material world as the outward and visible sign of something which animates it. All normal human beings, it seems to me, are sacramentalists!

I was, for this reason, able to think clearly about the phenomenon. My mind was not clouded and bemused with fear, and its known physiological effects. I can, quite easily, record what I "saw" in the course of the next few days. The bed was clearer to my vision and apprehension than it had been. It seemed to have grown in visibility; in a kind of substantialness, if there is such a word! It appeared more *material* than it had before, less shadowy.

I looked about the room and saw other furniture: a huge, old-fashioned mahogany bureau with men's heads carved on the knuckles of the front legs, Danish fashion. There is precisely such carving on pieces in the museum in Copenhagen, they tell me, those who have seen my drawing of it. I was actually able to do that, and had completed a kind of plan-picture of the room, putting in all the shadow-furniture, and leaving my own, actual furniture out. Thank the God in whom I devoutly believe,—and know to be more powerful than the Powers of Evil,—I was able to finish that rather elaborate drawing before . . . Well, I must not "run ahead of my story".

That night when I was ready to retire, and had once more opened up the jalousies of the front bedroom, and had switched off the light, I looked, naturally enough under the circumstances, for the outlines of that ghostly furniture. They were much clearer now. I studied them with a certain sense of almost "scientific" detachment. It was, even then, apparent to me that no weakness of the strange complexity which is the human eye could reasonably

account for the presence of a well-defined set of mahogany
furniture in a room already furnished with real furniture!
But I was by now sufficiently accustomed to it to be able
to examine it all without that always-disturbing element
of fear,—strangeness. I looked at the bedstead and the
"roll-back" chairs, and the great bureau, and a ghostly,
huge, and quaintly carved wardrobe, studying their outlines, noting their relative positions. It was on that occasion that it occurred to me that it would be of interest to
make some kind of drawing of them. I looked the harder
after that, fixing the details and the relations of them all
in my mind, and then I went into the hall and got some
paper and a pencil and set to work.

It was hard work, this of reproducing something which
I was well aware was some kind of an "apparition", especially after looking at the furniture in the dark bedroom,
switching on the light in another room and then trying to
reproduce. I could not, of course, make a direct comparison. I mean it was impossible to look at my drawing and
then look at the furniture. There was always a necessary
interval between the two processes. I persisted through
several evenings, and even for a couple of evenings fell
into the custom of going into my bedroom in the evening's
darkness, looking at what was there, and then attempting
to reproduce it. After five or six days, I had a fair plan, in
considerable detail, of the arrangement of this strange furniture in my bedroom,— a plan or drawing which would
be recognizable if there were anyone now alive who remembered such an arrangement of such furniture. It will
be apparent that a story had been growing up in my mind,
or, at least, that I had come to some kind of conviction
that what I "saw" was a reproduction of something that
had once existed in that same detail and that precise order!

On the seventh night, there came an interruption.

I had, by that time, finished my work, pretty well. I had drawn the room as it would have looked with that furniture in it, and had gone over the whole with India ink, very carefully. As a drawing, the thing was finished, so far as my indifferent skill as a draftsman would permit.

That seventh evening, I was looking over the appearance of the room, such qualms as the eeriness of the situation might have otherwise produced reduced to next-to-nothing partly by my interest, in part by having become accustomed to it all. I was making, this evening, as careful a comparison as possible between my remembered work on paper and the detailed appearance of the room. By now, the furniture stood out clearly, in a kind of light of its own which I can roughly compare only to "phosphorescence." It was not, quite, that. But that will serve, lame as it is, and trite perhaps, to indicate what I mean. I suppose the appearance of the room was something like what a cat "sees" when she arches her back,—as Algernon Blackwood has pointed out, in John *Silence*,—and rubs against the imaginary legs of some personage entirely invisible to the man in the armchair who idly wonders what has taken possession of his house-pet.

I was, as I say, studying the detail. I could not find that I had left out anything salient. The detail was, too, quite clear now. There were no blurred outlines as there had been on the first few nights. My own, material furniture had, so to speak, sunk back into invisibility, which was sensible enough, seeing that I had put the room in as nearly perfect darkness as I could, and there was no moon to interfere, those nights.

I had run my eyes all around it, up and down the twisted legs of the great bureau, along the carved ornamentation of the top of the wardrobe, along the lines of the chairs, and had come back to the bed. It was at this point of my checking-up that I got what I must describe as the first "shock" of the entire experience.

Something moved, beside the bed.

I peered, carefully, straining my eyes to catch what it might be. It had been something bulky, a slow-moving object, on the far side of the bed, blurred, somewhat, just as the original outlines had been blurred in the beginning of my week's experience. The now strong and clear outlines of the bed, and what I might describe as its ethereal substance, stood between me and it. Besides, the vision of the slow-moving mass was further obscured by a ghostly mosquito-net, which had been one of the last of the details to come into the scope of my strange night-vision.

Those folds of the mosquito-netting moved,—waved, before my eyes.

Someone, it might almost be imagined, was getting into that bed!

I sat, petrified. This was a bit too much for me. I could feel the little chills run up and down my spine. My scalp prickled. I put my hands on my knees, and pressed hard. I drew several deep breaths. "All-overish" is an old New England expression, once much used by spinsters, I believe, resident in that intellectual section of the United States. Whatever the precise connotation of the term, that was the way I felt. I could feel the reactive sensation, I mean, of that particular portion of the whole experience, in every part of my being,—body, mind, and soul! It was,—paralyzing. I reached up a hand that was trembling violently,—I could barely control it, and the fingers, when they touched the hard-rubber button, felt numb,— and switched on the bedroom light, and spent the next ten minutes recovering.

That night, when I came to retire, I dreaded,—actually dreaded,—what might come to my vision when I snapped off the light. This, however, I managed to reason out with myself. I used several arguments—nothing had so far occurred to annoy or injure me; if this were to be a cumulative experience, if something were to be "revealed" to me by this deliberate process of slow materialization which had been progressing for the last week or so, then it might as well be for some good and useful purpose. I might be, in a sense, the agent of Providence! If it were otherwise; if it were the evil work of some discarnate spirit, or something of the sort, well, every Sunday since my childhood, in church, I had recited the Creed, and so admitted, along with the clergy and the rest of the congregation, that God our Father had created all things,—visible *and invisible!* If it were this part of His creation at work, for *any* purpose, then He was stronger than they. I said a brief prayer before turning off that light, and put my trust in Him. It may appear to some a bit old-fashioned,—even Victorian! But He does not change along with the current fashions of human thought about Him, and this "human thought," and "the modern mind," and all the rest of it, does not mean the vast, the overwhelming majority of people. It involves only a few dozen prideful "intellectuals" at best, or worst!

I switched off the light, and, already clearer, I saw what must have been Old Morris, getting into bed.

I had interviewed old Mr. Bonesteel, the chief government surveyor, a gentleman of parts and much experience, a West Indian born on this island. Mr. Bonesteel, in response to my guarded enquiries,—for I had, of course, already suspected Old Morris; was not my house still called his?— had stated that he remembered Old Morris well, in his own remote youth. His description of that personage and this apparition tallied. This, undoubtedly, was Old Morris. That it was *someone,* was apparent. I felt, somehow, rather relieved to realize that it was he. I knew something about him, you see. Mr. Bonesteel had given me a good description and many anecdotes, quite freely, and as though he enjoyed being called on for information about one of the old-timers like Morris. He had been more reticent, guarded, in fact, when I pressed him for details of Morris' end. That there had been some obscurity,— intentional or otherwise, I could never ascertain,—about the old man, I had already known. Such casual enquiries as I had made on other occasions through natural interest in the person whose name still clung to my house sixty years or more since he had lived in it, had never got me any-where. I had only gathered what Mr. Bonesteel's more am-ple account corroborated: that Morris had been eccentric, in some ways, amusingly so. That he had been extraordi-narily well-to-do. That he gave occasional large parties, which, contrary to the custom of the hospitable island of St. Croix, were always required to come to a conclu-sion well before midnight. Why, there was a story of Old Morris almost literally getting rid of a few reluctant guests, by one device or another, from these parties, a circum-stance on which hinged several of the amusing anecdotes of that eccentric person!

Old Morris, as I knew, had not always lived on St. Croix. His youth had been spent in Martinique, in the then smaller and less important town of Fort-de-France. That, of course, was many years before the terrific calam-ity of the destruction of St. Pierre had taken place, by the eruption of Mt. Pelée. Old Morris, coming to St. Croix in young middle-age,—forty-five or thereabouts,—had already been accounted a rich man. He had been engaged in no business. He was not a planter, not a storekeeper, had no profession. Where he produced his affluence was one of the local mysteries. His age, it seemed, was the other.

"I suppose," Mr. Bonesteel had said, "that Morris was nearer a hundred than ninety, when he,—ah,—died. I was a child of about eight at that time. I shall be seventy next

August-month. That, you see, would be about sixty-two years ago, about 1861, or about the time your Civil War was beginning. Now my father has told me,—he died when I was nineteen,—that Old Morris looked exactly the same when he was a boy! Extraordinary. The Black People used to say—" Mr. Bonesteel fell silent, and his eyes had an old man's dim, far-away look.

"The Black People have some very strange beliefs, Mr. Bonesteel," said I, attempting to prompt him. "A good many of them I have heard about myself, and they interest me very much. What particular—"

Mr. Bonesteel turned his mild, blue eyes upon me, reflectively.

"You must drop in at my house one of these days, Mr. Stewart," said he, mildly. "I have some rare old rum that I'd be glad to have you sample, sir! There's not much of it on the island these days, since Uncle Sam turned his prohibition laws loose on us in 1922."

"Thank you very much indeed, Mr. Bonesteel," I replied. "I shall take the first occasion to do so, sir; not that I care especially for 'old rum' except a spoonful in a cup of tea, or in pudding sauce, perhaps; but the pleasure of your company, sir, is always an inducement."

Mr. Bonesteel bowed to me gravely, and I returned his bow from where I sat in his airy office in Government House.

"Would you object to mentioning what that 'belief' was, sir?"

A slightly pained expression replaced my old friend's look of hospitality.

"All that is a lot of foolishness!" said he, with something like asperity. He looked at me, contemplatively.

"Not that I believe in such things, you must understand. Still, a man sees a good many things in these islands, in a lifetime, you know! Well, the Black People—"

Mr. Bonesteel looked apprehensively about him, as though reluctant to have one of his clerks overhear what he was about to say, and leaned toward me from his chair, lowering his voice to a whisper.

"They said,—it was a remark here and a kind of hint there, you must understand; nothing definite,—that Morris had interfered, down there in Martinique, with some of their queer doings, offended the Zombi,—something of the kind; that Morris had made some kind of conditions—oh, it was very vague, and probably all mixed up!—you know, whereby he was to have a long life and all the money he wanted,—something like that,—and afterward. . .

"Well, Mr. Stewart, you just ask somebody, sometime, about Morris' death."

Not another word about Old Morris could I extract out of Mr. Bonesteel.

But of course he had me aroused. I tried Despard, who lives on the other end of the island, a man educated at the Sorbonne, and who knows, it is said, everything there is to know about the island and its affairs.

It was much the same with Mr. Despard, who is an entirely different kind of person; younger, for one thing, than my old friend the government surveyor.

Mr. Despard smiled, a kind of wry smile. "Old Morris!" said he, reflectively, and paused.

"Might I venture to ask—no offense, my dear sir!—why you wish to rake up such an old matter as Old Morris' death?"

I was a bit nonplussed, I confess. Mr. Despard had been perfectly courteous, as he always is, but, somehow, I had not expected such an intervention on his part.

"Why," said I, "I should find it hard to tell you, precisely, Mr. Despard. It is not that I am averse to being frank in the face of such an enquiry as yours, sir. I was not aware that there was anything important,—serious, as your tone implies,—about that matter. Put it down to mere curiosity if you will, and answer or not, as you wish, sir."

I was, perhaps, a little nettled at this unexpected, and, as it then seemed to me, finicky obstruction being placed in my way. What could there be in such a case for this formal reticence,—these verbal safeguards? If it were a "jumbee" story, there was no importance to it. If otherwise, well, I might be regarded by Despard as a person of reasonable discretion. Perhaps Despard was some relative of Old Morris, and there was something a bit off-color about his death. That, too, might account for Mr. Bonesteel's reticence.

"By the way," I enquired, noting Despard's reticence, "might I ask another question, Mr. Despard?"

"Certainly, Mr. Stewart."

"I do not wish to impress you as idly or unduly curious, but—are you and Mr. Bonesteel related in any way?"

"No, sir. We are not related in any way at all, sir."

"Thank you, Mr. Despard," said I, and, bowing to each other after the fashion set here by the Danes, we parted.

I had not learned a thing about Old Morris' death.

I went in to see Mrs. Heidenklang. Here, if anywhere, I should find out what was intriguing me.

Mrs. Heidenklang is an ancient Creole lady, relict of a prosperous storekeeper, who lives, surrounded by a certain state of her own, propped up in bed in an environment of a stupendous quantity of lacy things and gauzy ruffles. I did not intend to mention Old Morris to her, but only to get some information about the Zombi, if that should be possible.

I found the old lady, surrounded by her ruffles and lace things, in one of her good days. Her health has been precarious for twenty years!

It was not difficult to get her talking about the Zombi.

"Yes," said Mrs. Heidenklang, "it is extraordinary how the old beliefs and the old words cling in their minds! Why, Mr. Stewart, I was hearing about a trial in the police court a few days ago. One old Black woman had summoned another for abusive language. On the witness stand the complaining old woman said: 'She cahl me a wuthless ole Cartagene, sir!' Now, think of that! Carthage was destroyed 'way back in the days of Cato the Elder, you know, Mr. Stewart! The greatest town of all Africa. To be a Carthaginian meant to be a sea-robber,—a pirate; that is, a thief. One old woman on this island, more than two thousand years afterward, wishes to call another a thief, and the word 'Cartagene' is the word she naturally uses! I suppose that has persisted on the West Coast and throughout all those village dialects in Africa without a break, all these centuries! The Zombi of the French islands? Yes, Mr. Stewart. There are some extraordinary beliefs. Why, perhaps you've heard mention made of Old Morris, Mr. Stewart. He used to live in your house, you know?"

I held my breath. Here was a possible trove. I nodded my head. I did not dare to speak!

"Well, Old Morris, you see, lived most of his earlier days in Martinique, and, it is said, he had a somewhat adventurous life there, Mr. Stewart. Just what he did or how he got himself involved, seems never to have been made clear, but—in some way, Mr. Stewart, the Black People believe, Morris got himself involved with a very powerful 'Jumbee', and that is where what I said about the persistence of ancient beliefs comes in. Look on that table there, among those photographs, Mr. Stewart. There! that's the place. I wish I were able to get up and assist you. These maids! Everything askew, I have no doubt! Do you observe a kind of fish-headed thing, about as big as the palm of your hand? Yes! that is it!"

I found the "fish-headed thing" and carried it over to Mrs. Heidenklang. She took it in her hand and looked at it. It lacked a nose, but otherwise it was intact, a strange, uncouth-looking little godling, made of anciently-polished volcanic stone, with huge, protruding eyes, small, human-like ears, and what must have been a nose like a Tortola jackfish, or a black witch-bird, with its parrot beak.

"Now that," continued Mrs. Heidenklang, "is one of the very ancient household gods of the aborigines of Martinique, and you will observe the likeness in the idea to the *Lares* and *Penates* of your school-Latin days. Whether this is a *lar* or a *penate,* I can not tell," and the old lady paused to smile at her little joke, "but at any rate he is a representation of something very powerful,—a fish-god of the Caribs. There's something Egyptian about the idea, too, I've always suspected; and, Mr. Stewart, a Carib or an Arawak Indian,—there were both in these islands, you know,—looked much like an ancient Egyptian; perhaps half like your Zuni or Aztec Indians, and half Egyptian, would be a fair statement of his appearance. These fish-gods had men's bodies, you see, precisely like the hawk-headed and jackal-headed deities of ancient Egypt.

"It was one of those, the Black People say, with which Mr. Morris got himself mixed up,—'Gahd knows' as they say,—how! And, Mr. Stewart, they say, his death was terrible! The particulars I've never heard, but my father knew, and he was sick for several days after seeing Mr. Morris' body. Extraordinary, isn't it? And when are you coming this way again, Mr. Stewart? Do drop in and call on an old lady."

I felt that I was progressing.

The next time I saw Mr. Bonesteel, which was that very evening, I stopped him on the street and asked for a word with him.

"What was the date, or the approximate date, Mr. Bone-steel, of Mr. Morris' death? Could you recall that, sir?"

Sir Bonesteel paused and considered.

"It was just before Christmas," said he. "I remember it not so much by Christmas as by the races, which always take place the day after Christmas. Morris had entered his sorrel mare Santurce, and, as he left no heirs, there was no one who 'owned' Santurce, and she had to be withdrawn from the races. It affected the betting very materially and a good many persons were annoyed about it, but there wasn't anything that could be done."

I thanked Mr. Bonesteel, and not without reason, for his answer had fitted into something that had been grow-ing in my mind. Christmas was only eight days off. This drama of the furniture and Old Morris getting into bed, I had thought (and not unnaturally, it seems to me), might be a kind of re-enactment of the tragedy of his death. If I had the courage to watch, night after night, I might be relieved of the necessity of asking any questions. I might witness whatever had occurred, in some weird reproduc-tion, engineered, God knows how!

For three nights now, I had seen the phenomenon of Old Morris getting into bed repeated, and each time it was clearer. I had sketched him into my drawing, a short, squat figure, rather stooped and fat, but possessed of a strange, gorillalike energy. His movements, as he walked toward the bed, seized the edge of the mosquito-netting and climbed in, were, somehow, full of power, which was the more apparent since these were ordinary motions. One could not help imagining that Old Morris would have been a tough customer to tackle, for all his alleged age!

This evening, at the hour when this phenomenon was accustomed to enact itself, that is, about 11 o'clock, I watched again. The scene was very much clearer, and I observed something I had not noticed before. Old Morris' *simulacrum* paused just before seizing the edge of the netting, raised its eyes, and began, with its right hand, a motion precisely like one who is about to sign himself with the cross. The motion was abruptly arrested, however, only the first of the four touches on the body being made.

I saw, too, something of the expression of the face that night, for the first time. At the moment of making the arrested sign, it was one of despairing horror. Immediately afterward, as this motion appeared to be abandoned for the abrupt clutching of the lower edge of the mosquito-net, it changed into a look of ferocious stubbornness, of almost savage self-confidence. I lost the facial expression as the appearance sank down upon the bed and pulled the ghostly bedclothes over itself.

Three nights later, when all this had become as greatly intensified as had the clearing-up process that had affec-ted the furniture, I observed another motion, or what might be taken for the faint foreshadowing of another mo-tion. This was not on the part of Old Morris. It made itself apparent as lightly and elusively as the swift flight of a moth across the reflection of a lamp, over near the bedroom door (the doors in my house are more than ten feet high, in four- teen-foot-high walls), a mere flicker of something,—something entering the room. I looked, and peered at that corner, straining my eyes, but nothing could I sec save what I might describe as an intensification of the black shadow in that corner near the door, vaguely formed like a slim human figure, though grossly out of all human proportion. The vague shadow looked purple against the black. It was about ten feet high, and otherwise as though cast by an incredibly tall, thin human being.

I made nothing of it then; and again, despite all this cumulative experience with the strange shadows of my bedroom, attributed this last phenomenon to my eyes. It was too vague to be at that time accounted otherwise than as a mere subjective effect.

But the night following, I watched for it at the proper moment in the sequence of Old Morris' movements as he got into bed, and this time it was distinctly clearer. The shadow, it was, of some monstrous shape, ten feet tall, long, angular, of vaguely human appearance, though even in its merely shadowed form, somehow cruelly, strangely inhuman! I can not describe the cold horror of its realization. The head-part was, relatively to the proportions of the body, short and broad, like a pumpkin head of a "man" made of sticks by boys, to frighten passers-by on Hallowe'en.

The next evening I was out again to an entertainment at the residence of one of my hospitable friends, and arrived home after midnight. There stood the ghostly furniture, there on the bed was the form of the apparently sleeping Old Morris, and there in the corner stood the shadow, little changed from last night's appearance.

The next night would be pretty close to the date of Old Morris' death. It would be that night, or the next at latest, according to Mr. Bonesteel's statement. The next day I could not avoid the sensation of something impending!

I entered my room and turned off the light a little before 11, seated myself, and waited.

The furniture tonight was, to my vision, absolutely indistinguishable from reality. This statement may sound somewhat strange, for it will be remembered that I was sitting in the dark. Approximating terms again, I may say, however, that the furniture was visible in a light of its own, a kind of "phosphorescence", which apparently emanated from it. Certainly there was no natural source of light. Perhaps I may express the matter thus: that light and darkness were *reversed* in the case of this ghostly bed, bureau, wardrobe, and chairs. When actual light was turned on, they disappeared. In darkness, which, of course, is the absence of physical light, they emerged. That is the nearest I can get to it. At any rate, tonight the furniture was entirely, perfectly, visible to me.

Old Morris came in at the usual time. I could see him with a clarity exactly comparable to what I have said about the furniture. He made his slight pause, his arrested motion of the right hand, and then, as usual, cast from him, according to his expression, the desire for that protective gesture, and reached a hard-looking, gnarled fist out to take hold of the mosquito-netting.

As he did so, a fearful thing leaped upon him, a thing out of the corner by the high doorway,—the dreadful, purplish shadow-thing. I had not been looking in that direction, and while I had not forgotten this newest of the strange items in this fantasmagoria which had been repeating itself before my eyes for many nights, I was wholly unprepared for its sudden appearance and malignant activity.

I have said the shadow was purplish against black. Now that it had taken form, as the furniture and Old Morris himself had taken form, I observed that this purplish coloration was actual. It was a glistening, humanlike, almost metallic-appearing thing, certainly ten feet high, completely covered with great, iridescent fish-scales, each perhaps four square inches in area, which shimmered as it leaped across the room. I saw it for only a matter of a second or two. I saw it clutch surely and with a deadly malignity, the hunched body of Old Morris, from behind, just, you will remember, as the old man was about to climb into his bed. The dreadful thing turned him about as a wasp turns a fly, in great, flail-like, glistening arms, and never, to the day of my death, do I ever expect to be free of the look on Old Morris' face,—a look of a lost soul

who knows that there is no hope for him in this world or
the next,—as the great, squat, rounded head, a head precisely like that of Mrs. Heidenklang's little fish-jumbee,
descended, revealing to my horrified sight one glimpse of
a huge, scythelike parrotbeak which it used, with a nod-
ding motion of the ugly head, to plunge into its writhing
victim's breast, with a tearing motion like the barracoota
when it attacks and tears. . . .

I fainted then, for that was the last of the fearful picture which I can remember.

I awakened a little after 1 o'clock, in a dark and empty
room, peopled by no ghosts, and with my own, more
commonplace, mahogany furniture thinly outlined in the
faint light of the new moon which was shining cleanly in
a starry sky. The fresh night-wind stirred the netting of
my bed. I rose, shakily, and went and leaned out of the
window, and lit and puffed rapidly at a cigarette, which
perhaps did something to settle my jangling nerves.

The next morning, with a feeling of loathing which
has gradually worn itself out in the course of the months
which have now elapsed since my dreadful experience, I
took up my drawing again, and added as well as I could
the fearful scene I had witnessed. The completed picture
was a horror, crude as is my work in this direction. I wanted to destroy it, but I did not, and I laid it away under
some unused clothing in one of the large drawers of my
bedroom wardrobe.

Three days later, just after Christmas, I observed Mr.
Despard's car driving through the streets, the driver being
alone. I stopped the boy and asked him where Mr. Despard
was at the moment. The driver told me Mr. Despard was
having breakfast,—the West Indian midday meal,—with
Mr. Bonesteel at that gentleman's house on the Prince's
Cross Street. I thanked him and went home. I took out

the drawing, folded it, and placed it in the inside breast pocket of my coat, and started for Bonesteel's house.

I arrived fifteen minutes or so before the breakfast hour, and was pleasantly received by my old friend and his guest. Mr. Bonesteel pressed me to join them at breakfast, but I declined.

Mr. Bonesteel brought in a swizzel, compounded of his very old rum, and after partaking of this in ceremonious fashion, I engaged the attention of both gentlemen.

"Gentlemen," said I, "I trust that you will not regard me as too much of a bore, but I have, I believe, a legitimate reason for asking you if you will tell me the manner in which the gentleman known as Old Morris, who once occupied my house, met his death."

I stopped there, and immediately discovered that I had thrown my kind old host into a state of embarrassed confusion. Glancing at Mr. Despard, I saw at once that if I had not actually offended him, I had, by my question, at least put him "on his dignity." He was looking at me severely, rather, and I confess that for a moment I felt a bit like a schoolboy. Mr. Bonesteel caught something of this atmosphere, and looked helplessly at Despard. Both men shifted uneasily in their chairs; each waited for the other to speak.

Despard, at last, cleared his throat.

"You will excuse me, Mr. Stewart," said he, slowly, "but you have asked a question which for certain reasons, no one, aware of the circumstances, would desire to answer. The reasons are, briefly, that Mr. Morris, in certain respects, was—what shall I say, not to do the matter an injustice?—well, perhaps I might say he was abnormal. I do not mean that he was crazy. He was, though, eccentric. His end was such that stating it would open up a considerable argument, one which agitated this island for a long time after he was found dead. By a kind of general consent, that matter is taboo on the island. That will explain to you why no one wishes to answer your question. I am free to say that Mr. Bonesteel here, in considerable distress, told me that you had asked it of him. You also asked me about it not long ago. I can add only that the manner of Mr. Morris' end was such that—" Mr. Despard hesitated, and looked down, a frown on his brow, at his shoe, which he tapped nervously on the tiled floor of the gallery where we were seated.

"Old Morris, Mr. Stewart," he resumed, after a moment's reflection, in which, I imagined, he was carefully choosing his words, "was, to put it plainly, murdered! There was much discussion over the identity of the murderer, but the most of it, the unpleasant part of the discussion, was rather whether he was killed by human agency or not! Perhaps you will see now, sir, the difficulty of the matter. To admit that he was murdered by an ordinary murderer is, to my mind, an impossibility. To assert that some other agency, something ab-human, killed him, opens up the question of one's belief, one's credulity. 'Magic' and occult agencies are, as you are aware, strongly intrenched in the minds of the ignorant people of these islands. None of us cares to admit a similar belief. Does that satisfy you, Mr. Stewart, and will you let the matter rest there, sir?"

I drew out the picture, and, without unfolding it, laid it across my knees. I nodded to Mr. Despard, and, turning to our host, asked:

"As a child, Mr. Bonesteel, were you familiar with the arrangement of Mr. Morris' bedroom?"

"Yes, sir," replied Mr. Bonesteel, and added: "Everybody was! Persons who had never been in the old man's house, crowded in when—" I intercepted a kind of warning look passing from Despard to the speaker. Mr. Bonesteel, looking much embarrassed, looked at me in that

helpless fashion I have already mentioned, and remarked
that it was hot weather these days!

"Then," said I, "perhaps you will recognize its arrangement and even some of the details of its furnishing," and I
unfolded the picture and handed it to Mr. Bonesteel.

If I had anticipated its effect upon the old man, I would
have been more discreet, but I confess I was nettled by
their attitude. By handing it to Mr. Bonesteel (I could not
give it to both of them at once) I did the natural thing,
for he was our host. The old man looked at what I had
handed him, and (this is the only way I can describe what
happened) became, suddenly, as though petrified. His eyes
bulged out of his head, his lower jaw dropped and hung
open. The paper slipped from his nerveless grasp and fluttered and zigzagged to the floor, landing at Despard's feet.
Despard stooped and picked it up, ostensibly to restore
it to me, but in doing so, he glanced at it, and had *his*
reaction. He leaped frantically to his feet, and positively
goggled at the picture, then at me. Oh, I was having my
little revenge for their reticence, right enough!

"My God!" shouted Despard. "My God, Mr. Stewart,
where did you get such a thing?"

Mr. Bonesteel drew in a deep breath, the first, it seemed,
for sixty seconds, and added his word.

"Oh my God!" muttered the old man, shakily. "Mr.
Stewart, Mr. Stewart! what is it, what is it? where—"

"It is a Martinique fish-zombi, what is known to professional occult investigators like Elliott O'Donnell and
William Hope Hodgson as an 'elemental'," I explained,
calmly. "It is a representation of how poor Mr. Morris
actually met his death; until now, as I understand it, a
purely conjectural matter. Christiansted is built on the
ruins of French Bassin, you will remember," I added. "It is
a very likely spot for an 'elemental'!"

"But, but," almost shouted Mr. Despard, "Mr. Stewart, where did you get this, its—"

"I made it," said I, quietly, folding up the picture and placing it back in my inside pocket.

"But how—?" this from both Despard and Bonesteel, speaking in unison.

"I saw it happen, you see," I replied, taking my hat, bowing formally to both gentlemen, and murmuring my regret at not being able to remain for breakfast, I departed.

And as I reached the bottom of Mr. Bonesteel's gallery steps and turned along the street in the direction of Old Morris' house, where I live, I could hear their voices speaking together:

"But how, how—?" This was Bonesteel.

"Why, why—?" And that was Despard.

Devouring Shadows

N. J. O'Neail

1932

How, or why, should I begin a statement of such a nature as this —a chronicle probably the most vital in the history of the human race; and yet one which, if so, can probably never be read by human eye; which, in fact, if ever so read, must stand self-confuted, the frenzied product of a madman's brain?

It is strange, that in the face of so overwhelming, so inescapable a horror, I should turn almost mechanically to pen and paper, as though by sharing my fears I should halve their intensity, or lighten the burden of numbing horror which weighs upon my soul. Should I not rather be upon my knees, in supplication to my Creator? Or is it blasphemy to dream that any plea of mine, or of any human creature, could avert the looming, inevitable cataclysm?

In any event, it is to my tablets that I have turned, like Hamlet, in a frenzied hope to face what may befall, with a sane mind. And there remains always the bare possibility that this record may yet be read—perhaps by eyes of which this world has never dreamed.

It is by agreement with Parfitt that I have undertaken so to apply my few remaining hours—Parfitt, who first, I believe, of any upon earth sensed the appalling truth; or he, at any rate, who first unfolded the vision to my shuddering and recoiling mind.

It is less than a week since the shadows beneath whose pall we cower today, like chickens when a hawk far overhead casts its black outline upon the ground—first fell like the nebulous, menacing tentacles of some cosmic monster, upon an unsuspecting earth.

It was upon a sunny June morning, when the scents of early summer languorously filled the air, and the placid buzzing of a bee outside my window came to my ears above the hubbub of the street traffic below, that the first inkling of the horror came to me—through the columns of my morning newspaper:

SOLID SHADOWS
FALL ON LONDON;
MYSTIFY SAVANTS

London, June 6—Meteorologists, astronomers and scientists confess themselves completely mystified by unique shadow formations, which fell over London yesterday.

The peculiarity lies in the fact that the shadows appear to possess depth, in place of the flatness of an ordinary shadow; that is, they are patches of darkness, not only lying upon the ground or on whatever surface they fall, but rising upward from it for a height of several feet, as though they were solid substances.

There was considerably more to the dispatches, detailing the prevalence of the shadows throughout the English capital. Apparently they had first been observed in Trafalgar Square, near Nelson's monument, and had spread thence until by evening virtually the whole city was knee-deep in the mysterious "solid shadows."

Each shadow was described as being nearly one hundred yards in length, several yards in width and rising from the surface on which it fell, for several feet. They were irregular and indistinct in outline, but all were practically identical in general shape and size. *And in no case was any actual object visible which might have cast such a shadow.*

There were also interviews with a number of scientists, who confessed themselves unable to explain the phenomenon. Some spoke vaguely of some atmospheric abnormality which might produce such an eccentric obscuration of the sunlight; some tried—rather feebly, I thought—to trace a connection with a recent outbreak of sun spots; and some inclined to the view that the "shadows" were some unusual fog formation, although June is far removed from London's foggy season, and the weather had been warm and dry.

The phenomenon was of only passing interest to me, although it occurred to me as I finished reading, that Parfitt—Roger Middleton Parfitt, former professor of astronomy and physics in Columbia University, and now engaged in private research—would find in it an irresistible challenge, and that he would be capable of plucking the heart from its mystery, if any man were.

In that I was all too correct, as subsequent events established. Meanwhile, however, the matter escaped my mind until twelve hours later, when a flaring black headline in an evening newspaper, caught my eye:

PANIC SPREADS AS MYSTERY SHADOWS SHROUD ALL EUROPE

Beneath were dispatches telling of the appearance of the mysterious shadows in practically every country of

Europe, as well as over the whole of the British Isles. They had risen like a tide of darkness over every capital, every city of any magnitude, and thousands of smaller communities. Panics were reported in several rural sections of France, Italy and the Balkan nations, where the populace had been terror-stricken by the phenomenon.

In some places, the shadows had become visible with the first rays of sunrise; in others they had fallen at intervals during the day. In every case, however, they were motionless, and identical in size and outline with those which had first appeared in London. And as before, nothing was visible which might have caused them.

There were columns of interviews now, with practically everyone whom the press could by any stretch of the imagination term "scientists," although I looked in vain for any statement from Parfitt. And the majority of the interviews were meaningless, for everyone admitted inability to fathom the mystery. The theories of "air streaks," sun spots and fog were all re-threshed. One eminent physicist advanced the possibility of the earth's having passed through the gaseous tail of some other astral body, and of patches of the vapor having clung to it. Another anonymous authority pinned his faith to some mysterious, sunlight-repelling rays emanating from within the earth. Another commentator ventured the argument that the sun's heat was dying out, and that this in some unexplained manner produced the phenomenon. Even more fantastic was the suggestion—possibly the product of a newspaperman's imagination—that the shadows were caused by a fleet of airplanes, constructed of some invisible material; a theory which, apart from its extravagant improbability, offered no explanation of the so-called solidity of the shadows, which was their peculiarity.

The thing was of increasing, but still only casual, interest to me—but next morning the ominous shadow bands fell upon North America.

Dreams in which intangible things clutched at me like a nebula of doom had broken my sleep, and I awoke slowly, to a vague consciousness of oppression, which was more physical than mental. I naturally set the sensation down to the effect of my dreams; and then, as the last mists of slumber cleared from my mind, I suddenly stared aghast.

The clean, clear sunlight streamed through the upper half of my bedroom window, but the lower half was obscured as though by a volume of blade mist, which crept across the floor, up the side of my bed, and lay full across my chest, terminating on the inner wall of the room.

I raised myself in bed and stared at the puzzling obscuration. It was just as described in the cabled reports: an apparent shadow formation, which possessed volume, instead of mere surface area. Its outline was at once vague and yet dearly defined; that is, I could not distinguish its actual shape, but I could see clearly that it was a coherent formation, divided distinctly from, and not merging gradually with, the sunlight above it.

It was black and opaque, like an ordinary shadow falling upon an ordinary surface. I thrust my hand into it, and saw that it was partly obscured, but still visible, just as though I had laid it upon the surface of an ordinary shadow.

Whatever might be the explanation of the phenomenon, I was satisfied already that it could not be that of fog. My hand encountered no sensation of dampness, or of cold or warmth; and no fog could retain such coherent form in such juxtaposition to clear morning sunlight.

I crossed from my bed to the window, and gazed outside. The formation appeared to bend at right angles, like a stove-pipe elbow. It lay like the trunk of a tree, against the outer wall of the building, and at the street level ran across the road. Whatever caused it, had it been a normal shadow, should have been visible over the roof of the apartment house opposite; but nothing which could have accounted for it met my eyes.

Now for the first time I became conscious that the nebulous formation which had entered my room was but one of a multitude. Similar solid black streaks crossed and recrossed the street at frequent intervals. Some lay across the roofs of buildings, and others climbed their walls. Ordinary shadows were visible on the street, also, and beside them the other formations appeared like bloated monstrosities from some nether world.

Even as I finished dressing, the newsboys in the streets below were crying the first extra editions of the afternoon newspapers, which were almost inarticulate in their efforts to broadcast the phenomenon. For the shadows had fallen, not only over the whole of New York, but over almost every other center in the eastern half of North America; and, as the day progressed, they swept westward in pace with the progress of the sun.

Still struggling against the vague forebodings which clutched at my mind, I hastened to the penthouse laboratory which Parfitt occupied, on the roof of a skyscraper near the water's edge. I found my friend wan-eyed, at a desk littered, as was the floor for yards about, with paper, scribbled with unintelligible mathematical formulae.

"Parfitt," I exclaimed, almost in the moment that I opened the door, "what on earth do these shadows mean?"

"Hello, Farquhar," Parfitt rejoined in peculiarly listless tones. "As for your question, the only answer I can give you, with all civility, is that it's none of your business."

"I'm sorry if I've intruded," I apologized somewhat stiffly. "But you might at least have asked me a little more politely to get out."

"Sit down," my friend urged. "I assure you, I had no intention of being discourteous."

"I can see you've been rather busy," I conceded.

"Since six o'clock last evening, without food or sleep," he replied casually.

"On—this thing?" I inquired.

"On it—or at least skirting the fringe of it, as near as the human brain can come to the heart of it," Parfitt answered.

"Then you know, or suspect, the cause?"

"Yes," he replied. "It isn't the cause that's the problem; it's the effect—and the remedy—that are beyond us."

"Then what on earth is it?" I insisted.

"It is probably nothing on earth—in the sense that we are on earth," my friend rejoined.

"You're not suggesting that it is a supernatural manifestation of some kind?" I ejaculated.

"Supernatural—I don't know," the astronomer confessed. "It's certainly supernormal, at least. I told you a few moments ago it was none of your business, Farquhar. I'll take that back. You're a man of sound nerves, and of better than average intelligence; perhaps the truth won't alarm you. The fact is that we are witnessing for the first time, I think, in human history, an active manifestation from the fourth dimension."

"Just what do you mean by the fourth dimension?" I demanded.

"That I don't know," Parfitt admitted. "We haven't got much nearer an understanding of it, since Einstein propounded his theory, nearly fifty years ago—back in the first quarter of the Twentieth Century. But the scientific world has come to accept, almost as it accepts that two and two always make four, which might be difficult of proof—that there is a fourth dimension; and very possibly a fifth, and perhaps many more."

"But what have these shadows to do with the fourth dimension?" I persisted.

"Isn't it obvious?" my companion countered. "Of course, we have lived so long in a three-dimensional world that it is difficult to conceive of any other. For instance—can you conceive of a two-dimensional object?"

"In theory, certainly," I replied. "As a concrete object, it is more difficult. Even a sheet of paper, of course, has three dimensions. It is hard to visualize an object of only two."

"What about—a shadow?" my companion suggested.

Now, for the first time, a glimmering of the truth dawned upon my mind.

"A shadow, I grant you, has no thickness," I admitted. "In that sense it is two-dimensional. But it is not an object; it is merely the absence of direct light upon a surface."

"True," Parfitt nodded. "A shadow is not an object. It is, we might say, a reflection—but it is the reflection of a three-dimensional object.

"Now today, the greater part of the world's surface, probably, is dotted with shadows which have, apparently, three dimensions, instead of two. Is the inference not inescapable? A two-dimensional shadow, a three-dimensional object; a three-dimensional shadow, a four-dimensional object."

"But, good heavens!" I exclaimed. "What do they mean? And what causes them?"

"Your first question, no one can answer," Parfitt replied. "Perhaps it is as well. Your second, I thought I had answered; they are caused by objects or beings, in the fourth dimension."

"But where are those objects, or beings?" I demurred. "If we can see the shadows, why not the original? They must be close at hand, to produce the shadows."

"Again, perhaps it is as well that we can not see them," my companion murmured. "But it is quite possible that the original objects may be near at hand, and yet invisible

to us. I do not imply that they are transparent, or anything of that nature, for if so, they would cast little or no
shadow. Yet they may be quite near, and yet beyond our
range of vision.

"By way of example, take the two-dimensional conception once more. Imagine, if you can, a sentient creature,
of two dimensions, living on a surface of two dimensions.
It is difficult to conceive, in reality, of such a thing; but,
for the sake of argument, let us assume it.

"That creature would be conscious only of two dimensions—let us say, those of length and width. Of height he
would have no conception. He might grasp vaguely at the
possibility of a third dimension, just as we do of a fourth,
but would be unable to visualize it. An object a fraction of
an inch above him would be absolutely invisible to him—
absolutely beyond his range of vision. Yet he could see a
shadow cast by that object upon his surface world.

"Therefore the objects causing these shadows may be
very near and yet beyond our range of vision. On the other
hand, they may be distant, not in space, but in time. We
know that there is a relation between space and time, in
the fourth dimension; therefore, these shadows may come
from the past or from the future-much more probably from
the future, since there has never been a similar known
phenomenon in the past."

By now my brain was reeling with the utter strangeness
of the conception which Parfitt's words unfolded. At first
I would almost have termed it incredible; and then gradually came the conviction that his theory not only might be
possible, but must almost inevitably be the truth.

"And what are the fourth-dimensional objects?" I asked.
"Are they animate or inanimate, human, or what?"

"No one can say, as yet," Parfitt answered. "My own
impression is that they are probably animate. Such a sudden manifestation, in such numerical strength, seems to

indicate a deliberate intent. That they are human, judged by any of our standards, I gravely doubt."

"The shadows are motionless, except that they move in conformity with the movement of the sun," I pointed out. "That might indicate that they are caused by inanimate objects."

"Not necessarily," Parfitt replied. "A period of twenty-four hours may be but a moment in the fourth dimension."

"How do you know that the fourth-dimensional world is inhabited?" I questioned him.

"Mainly by inference," my companion rejoined. "Since the three-dimensional world is inhabited, surely it follows that the four-dimensional world—necessarily a much more complex universe—is, also."

"And by what sort of creatures?"

"No one can say, but probably by beings very different from the human race. For example, return for a moment to the two-dimensional being which we hypothesized a few moments ago. Imagine what incredible, what incomprehensive monsters we beings of three dimensions must be to him; and the four-dimensional creatures may—in fact, almost certainly would—be equally so to us."

"This is an alarming theory of yours, Parfitt," I gasped. "Imagine the sensation the newspapers would make of it."

"They must never hear of it—unless developments render it absolutely imperative," the scientist declared.

"But what is the meaning of this manifestation?"

Parfitt replied with a weary shrug of the shoulders.

"That is beyond all human conjecture," he confessed. "We have no standard by which to judge it; it is unprecedented in human history. I trust it may prove a friendly one, but, I confess, I have grave misgivings."

"Still more alarming!" I exclaimed. "If it is hostile—"

"If it is hostile," Parfitt replied solemnly, "the world is facing the most deadly peril of its existence. Can you picture the consequences—the physical world which we know utterly at the mercy of creatures which we can not even see, of whose nature and powers we are in utter ignorance?

"It's a conception too horrible to be faced, Farquhar— and yet it may have to be. That's why I'm pledging you to secrecy. The very suggestion of such a thing might mean madness to the world; and the reality might mean far worse. I've been toiling all night, trying to find a solution, to evolve a formula which would make the fourth dimension visible to our eyes; but all in vain, and perhaps as well, too, for God alone knows what vista of unspeakable horror it might unfold.

"Do you realize, Farquhar, that within the shades of the fourth dimension may lurk all the obscene monstrosities with which the mind of man has peopled the unseen world—all those, and perhaps worse? Suppose that all the hideous deities of a score of pagan mythologies had actual, living prototypes—and there's no proof that they hadn't; the weight of evidence is rather in the other direction, for it isn't logical that the mind of man should conjure such saprophytic blasphemies out of nothing.

"The ancient Egyptians weren't fools, nor the immeasurably more ancient Atlanteans; they had a clearer perception of worlds unseen than we of today, whose eyes are dazzled by the feeble rays of rudimentary, material science. Mankind, in every generation since the mind first functioned, has sensed the actual existence of occult powers of awful potentiality. Sorcerers and demonologists, so called, have trafficked with those powers in every age.

"I'm not an alarmist, Farquhar; I hope and pray that what I've just pictured may not be the truth; but we are confronted, in the words of Grover Cleveland, with a condition, and not a theory. Thus far, I grant you, the shadows have done no harm; they may not do any harm, but some unfathomable purpose must lie beyond their sudden appearance."

Parfitt had no need to caution me to keep so soul-searing a secret; but even without that knowledge, the world that evening lay beneath a pall of apprehension.

By sunset, the shadows had made their appearance on practically every section of the globe. They lay aslant the Rockies, the Andes, and the Himalayas; they traversed the surface of the Sahara Desert, and darkened the midsummer snows as far north as Herschel Island, within the Arctic Circle. They fell alike on the African veldt and the Australian bush, and even spread their inexplicable lengths upon the waters of the seven seas.

The phenomenon was the feature of the day in the evening newspapers. Cable and telegraphic dispatches from every continent told of its manifestations, and speculated vainly as to the cause. There were reports of panics in half a dozen countries, and as I read them, I realized, more even than before, the necessity for the secrecy which Parfitt had impressed upon me. If the mere appearance of the shadows had power to rouse such alarm in human breasts, to what abysses of madness and despair might a realization of what they really portended lead?

In the Transylvania region of Rumania, peasants by thousands had fled from the fields, proclaiming that the end of the world was at hand. Many had fired their homes, and military forces were on guard in half a dozen centers against possible outbreaks of terrorism or sabotage.

In France and Austria also, the peasants were flocking to the cities, although in more orderly manner. From China and Tibet came word of weird rites performed in Buddhist temples and monasteries. In India, scores of natives hurled themselves into the Ganges, and from the

interior of Africa came ominous rumors of human sacrifices offered up to strange and almost forgotten tribal
gods.

There were other demonstrations of alarm in the Latin-
American republics, and in some sections of England and
the United States also. Both scientists and government
officials, however, published assurances that there was no
cause for alarm in the situation. "While admitting their
inability to explain the shadows, they insisted that these
must be of some natural origin, and that there was no reason to believe that they portended disaster of any nature.

Experiments conducted in a dozen different centers, in
an effort to determine the nature and cause of the shadows, brought no results but negative ones, which resulted
in the shattering of most of the theories previously advanced. Scientists satisfied themselves that the phenomenon was not produced by fog, mist or emanations of
any known ray or radio-active disturbance; nor could any
abnormal conditions be detected in the atmosphere.

It is the natural tendency of the human mind, however,
to shrink always from the unknown, and all assurances
as to the non-existence of danger failed to allay a growing sense of disquietude. Nightfall, bringing with it the
obliteration of the shadows, came as a welcome temporary
respite; for to many, ostrich-like, it appeared that since
the shadows were no longer visible, they were no longer in
existence.

One point impressed itself upon me that night—namely,
that no three-dimension shadows were cast by electric
lights or other forms of artificial illumination. I could
not bring myself to believe that the silent watchers from
the unseen world had actually departed with the coming
of darkness; therefore, I reasoned, they were probably
beyond the radius of man's artificial luminances.

Next morning, however, the shadows were in evidence once more in identically the same positions as twenty-four hours earlier, which would have strengthened my belief that they were caused by inanimate objects, were it not for Parfitt's assurance that time, as measured in our world, might be a negligible element in the realm of the fourth dimension.

And now came swift and sudden confirmation of his prediction; for a cable, received in New York at ten a.m., brought tidings which struck fresh dread to human hearts throughout the world.

The shadows were in motion, in London—"advancing like a phantom legion upon the city," as one writer, who had unwittingly plumbed nearer to the truth than he realized, phrased it.

Like sinuous serpents, they were gliding silently, but therefore the more ominously, over the capital of the British empire. The movement was not coordinated, or in unison; the shadows drifted in various directions, as though each were indeed the reflection of a conscious entity. Within an hour, every surface in London, whether vertical or horizontal, was a-shimmer with the creeping black patches, which frequently crossed and blended together, like rivulets converging in a common stream.

They writhed in sinister silence alike across the historic pavement of Whitehall and through the most leprous lanes of Limehouse; tossed upon the surface of the Thames as it lapped at the wharves of Wapping, circled the mighty dome of St. Paul's and scaled the walls of Buckingham Palace, where the octogenarian monarch, Edward VIII, had died three months before, and where his niece Elizabeth today reigned, as had another queen of that name four centuries before.

And now, many observers claimed to discern in the outline of the moving shadows a grotesque, but still visible, resemblance to the human form. Magnified and distorted though they were, their manner of movement was roughly comparable to the stride of a bipedal being; and occasionally, from the main bulk of the blackness, a pseudopod-like length of shade swung suddenly out, as might an arm attached to a body. Other onlookers disputed the resemblance and set it down as mere imagination, inspired by the fact that the shadows were moving.

The wave of apprehension which had swept the world in the preceding forty-eight hours now clutched more firmly at London's heart. The venerable prime ministress, Dame Megan Lloyd George, issued a proclamation in which she counseled the nation against alarm or hysteria; but the unrest spread, particularly among the Oriental colonies of the east end, where there were violent outbreaks of suicide, mutilation and unnamable rites and orgies.

I sought Parfitt out that night, and found him as though he had not moved from his desk in the last thirty-six hours. He was more wan and haggard than on the preceding day, and the litter of paper now carpeted the entire room.

"It's no use, Farquhar," he groaned. "I've tried every known formula and angle, and developed a dozen new ones, but they all fall short. The damnable thing seems to hover illusively, maddeningly, just beyond my reach, just round the corner from human eyesight and human understanding. If I could only turn that corner—"

"You're overdoing this task, Parfitt," I cautioned him. "I don't know just what you're groping for—"

"Nor do I," he exclaimed. "That's the agony of it. 'Groping' is the word— groping into blackness more unfathomable than those damned shadows. What I'm seeking is some channel of communication with the unseen world—some means of peering into the fourth dimension and seeing what all this means. But I fear it's futile. As I said yesterday, our two-dimensional man, with his two-dimensional brain, couldn't be expected to visualize the actual nature of the third dimension; and we, I suppose, are limited in turn, in our powers of perception."

"Of course you have seen today's cables—" I ventured.

"Yes, and talked for an hour to Greenwich observatory," Parfitt replied.

"Does this strengthen your belief that the shadows are those of living creatures?" I asked.

"Yes," he answered, "although I had little doubt of it before. Therefore, to that extent, there is nothing additionally alarming in the fact of their being in motion. But there's no doubt that they are spreading panic; and if the mere shadows do that, what will the actual substance do?"

"What do you suggest?"

"I don't know—I'm not sure that I want to know, though I've been toiling for days to do so. And it is more than possible that no one may ever know. I haven't the faintest conception whether the fourth-dimension creatures are human, beast or spirit—although presumably not the latter, since they cast shadows. Of what their coming may mean, I have an idea—one that I dare not divulge, one that it would be futile to divulge; for if it is wrong, it is far better that it never be known; and if it is right, no human power could avert what I fear."

Next morning, the shadows were in motion throughout Europe, and in the late afternoon they commenced to writhe and glide across North America, like the fingers of a giant hand which planned to crush the entire earth within its grasp, as I might crush an egg.

The New World, prepared by the preceding day's tidings from London, gave comparatively little manifestation of increased alarm, although thousands of persons thronged the churches of city, village, and countryside, to pray for deliverance from any disaster which might be in store.

There were no public services of intercession, however; for the clergy, almost as a unit—and perhaps feigning a confidence which they lacked inwardly, in order to reassure the public—refused to recognize the shadows as a source of even potential peril.

Again the newspapers were filled with columns of fruitless speculation as to the significance of the newest manifestation; but I noted that there was no suggestion even faintly resembling that which, on Parfitt's assurance, I believed to be the truth. Practically all scientists of any repute confessed themselves completely mystified; although some, I believe, by now must have grasped the meaning of the menace, as Parfitt had done, but refrained, as he did, from confiding so soul-searing a secret to the world at large— even though the onrushing culmination of that secret was then only a few hours distant.

At midnight I stood with Parfitt, gazing from his observatory window upon the throbbing city's night life, far below, where millions pursued the path of pleasure, either heedless of the shadow menace, or else seeking forgetfulness. A myriad pinpoints of light outlined faintly the lower thoroughfares along which motor cars sped, and the elevated paths above, reserved for pedestrians. On the right, a luminous aurora rose from Broadway's kaleidoscope. From the distance came the hoarse siren of a steamer somewhere in the sound, and overhead an occasional airplane hovered like a droning firefly.

The very familiarity of the scene seemed, somehow, to reassure me against the nebulous forebodings which had assailed my mind for days. It was impossible to conceive of any serious disaster intruding upon a world so firmly founded as ours.

At that moment, Parfitt was speaking:

"Sir Jason Singleton, director of the Greenwich observatory, is to call me early in the morning—within two or three hours. I sounded him on the subject yesterday, and he appears to have formed the same conclusions as myself. We must watch London, for it is reasonable to assume that future developments will occur there first, as they have in the past."

It was three o'clock in the morning—eight o'clock by Greenwich time—when the call light upon the radio-phone apparatus in the laboratory flashed alternately blue and red—London's call signal. Parfitt was at the phone instantly, simultaneously pressing the button which completed the television circuit, so that upon the screen that stood against the wall, I beheld the bearded figure of Sir Jason Singleton, seated at his desk.

Although television has been in practical use for nearly forty years, never have I seen an apparatus which functioned so perfectly as Parfitt's. I could detect every movement of the British astronomer's lips, could almost read the words which they framed, as clearly as though he sat before me in the flesh, instead of being three thousand miles distant.

From Parfitt's words I realized that he and Singleton had exchanged views, and that they were in agreement. Then, as I watched, I became aware that a shapeless black outline—one of the shadows—had stretched serpent-like across the British scientist's desk, apparently penetrating through a window which was beyond the radius of the television apparatus.

Sir Jason had apparently asked what steps could be taken to face the situation, for I heard Parfitt reply:

"What steps are possible? How can we act against a danger, of the very nature of which we are unaware? How can we conjecture when or where or how it will strike—"

And at that instant it struck.

At the recollection of those first few, soul-shattering seconds of horror, I still quiver as I write. For in a twinkling, as I gazed upon the television screen, I beheld a sudden movement of the shadow-mass on the Englishman's desk. It seemed to coil itself, tentacle-like, about his figure, and in the flashing of an eye Sir Jason Singleton had vanished, as though obliterated by a giant eraser.

Parfitt had seen the thing, even as I had; for as I sprang from my chair with an ejaculation of horror on my lips, he was calling hoarsely into the radiophone:

"Singleton—Singleton! Where are you, man? For God's sake, speak to me—the world's safety depends on it!"

Dazed at the suddenness of what I had beheld, I stared over his shoulder at the television screen. The interior of Sir Jason's office was clearly visible. The chair in which he had sat was unmoved; the radiophone stood upon his desk, the earphones still swaying from whatever force had torn them from Singleton's head. But the scientist himself had vanished, and with him, the shadow.

Now Parfitt was tearing at the dials and switches of the radiophone, in a frenzy that seemed half madness and half despair, still calling incoherently upon Singleton. When he finally thrust the apparatus aside and rose to face me, his face was ashen with the anguish of a man who has read, not alone his own death sentence, but that of a world.

"It's come, Farquhar," he said dully. "I didn't foresee that it would come in this form; but then, who could?"

"In God's name," I ejaculated, "what has happened, and what does it mean?"

"The creatures of the fourth dimension have struck— and it means the world's doom," Parfitt answered. "You saw what happened? Singleton was snatched out of sight, as though by a giant, invisible hand—snatched not only out of sight, but out of all human ken—snatched, in short, into the fourth dimension."

"What will become of him?" I demanded.

"How can we tell?" my companion groaned. "It may be immediate annihilation—some horrible metamorphosis—anything. But it's not Singleton alone. The creatures of the fourth dimension haven't singled out one man for their attack, be assured of that. They may have struck at hundreds—millions! They may have wiped out all England, and may be advancing on us at this very moment—a shadow army that will devour the world."

The contemplation of such a crushing, cosmic catastrophe seemed somehow to chill me less than the sight of Singleton's disappearance had done. It may be that the first shock had numbed my mental consciousness, or it may be that my mind recoiled from the effort to envision a doom so all-devouring as that which Parfitt's words foretold.

"This is what I have vaguely feared since the first appearance of the shadows," my companion went on. "You may say it was my duty to warn the world—but of what use would such a warning have been? What means of defense can we take against such a foe which we can not even see, a foe which reaches out from the infinity of a dimension beyond our ken, to wipe our race from the earth? Even now, when we know how it has struck, when we know that it may strike again at any moment, what can we do?

"We can not flee from the shadows, for they are everywhere—and understand, of course, that it is not the shadows themselves, but the beings which cause them, that are the menace. We might hide from the shadows by immuring ourselves in rooms or caverns where no sunlight could penetrate; but we can not hide from the fourth-dimensional beings themselves. We can not even fortify ourselves against them. They, presumably, can enter a locked room, through the medium of the fourth dimension, as easily as we could step into a two-dimensional-plane through the medium of the third dimension—that is, from above it."

With a sudden gesture of determination he turned again to the radiophone, and for several minutes dialed frenziedly; then he turned to me once more.

"I can't raise London," he said, tonelessly. "Cullinan, Bywater, Hereward-Evans—none of them answers."

A call to the government radio bureau confirmed our worst fears. All wireless communication with London had been mysteriously and abruptly severed, shortly after three a. m.; and simultaneously even the now almost-obsolete undersea cables had suddenly "gone dead." Britain's capital was isolated from the world overseas.

And so, upon an unsuspecting world, the blow which Parfitt, and perhaps others, had foreseen but had been powerless to avert, had fallen,

Upon the numbing agony of the next few hours of darkness, as Parfitt conferred frantically with scientists of three continents, I can not dwell; for already I have lingered too long upon this history, and my labors, futile, probably, in any case, must necessarily be so, unless I complete them before the blow falls here.

All of Parfitt's calls to London were unavailing, but he finally succeeded in communicating with two Scottish physicists, the pallor of whose horror-stricken visages was apparent even on the television screen. And not without reason, for the story which they unfolded to us, across three thousand miles of space, was one of stark, blood-chilling terror, such as human ears had never heard before.

In a word, the city of London, with its twenty million inhabitants, had been wiped clean of human life, so far as outside observations could reveal; and, more, lay at that moment in the grip of a holocaust of destruction more ruthless even than that through which it had passed in the world war of 1947.

There had been no word of warning, not even time for panic; in the twinkling of an eye, apparently, the hovering shadows had snatched twenty million human beings out of visible existence, as though they had been drawn relentlessly into the maw of a gigantic vacuum. From homes and offices and streets and moving vehicles alike, every living soul had been tom, seemingly by ruthless, unseen hands.

And in the wake of that annihilation, the most incredible in human history, had come swiftly and inevitably an inferno of chaos. Motor cars by hundreds of thousands, speeding along thousands of streets, became unguided juggernauts of destruction as the controlling hands vanished from their wheels; they crashed and collided with one smother, and spread sheets of flaming gasoline on roadway and sidewalk.

A half-dozen airplanes, left suddenly pilotless in mid-air over the city, hurtled in flames to earth. Railway trains leaped their tracks and piled masses of tangled steel wreckage on every side. Boilers left untended in a hundred factories burst in belching eruptions of destruction; elevators crashed, and scores of towering structures already lay leveled in ruins. A score of barges ran amok upon the Thames, shattered themselves against its piers or against one another, and vanished beneath its waters.

And, following closely on that deluge of devastation, terror had swept like wildfire throughout the British Isles. In the streets of virtually every town and city, mobs ran rampant; some calling upon all they met to kneel and await the end of the world in prayer; others proclaiming an orgy of carousal and debauchery; and many seeking the nearest means of self-destruction.

With its royal family and the heads of its government wiped out of existence, the nation lay for the moment as though paralyzed beneath the blow which had struck it. A half-dozen cabinet ministers chanced to be absent from London, however, as Parliament was in the middle of its Whitsuntide recess; and these, under the leadership of Sir Fulford Treleaven, chancellor of the exchequer, summoned an emergency council of state in Liverpool, in a deter-mined effort to face the crisis.

Martial law was proclaimed throughout the country, and every available military unit was mobilized and dispatched to strategic points, in an effort to restore order. Rigid cen-sorship was imposed upon telephones, telegraphs, cables and radiophones; and a manifesto was broadcast, calling upon all to remain calm and to "carry on" with the normal affairs of everyday life. Any exodus of refugees from or to any community was forbidden, for fear that congestion in the larger centers might only result in increased panics, and in food shortages. Preparations were made to com-mandeer all food supplies and to ration them on a wartime basis, if such a step appeared necessary.

Whatever the nature of the disaster which had obliter-ated all human life from the nation's capital, the manifes-to pointed out, there was no certainty that it would strike at other points; and if it did, there was no known means of meeting it; therefore alarms of any nature could only intensify the gravity of the situation.

Even before these precautions could be put into force, however, virtually every roadway throughout the country was black with streams of refugees, country-dwellers seek-ing safety in the cities and townspeople hastening to the open spaces.

Thousands who had relatives in London converged upon that metropolis of doom in a frenzied effort to learn the fate of their loved ones. A few entered the city before a military cordon could be thrown about it; entered it, and vanished as had those whom they sought. A venturesome aviator flew over the capital, and his empty plane crashed in a flaming parabola a few minutes later.

Stark, cosmic annihilation had gripped the heart of the British Empire, and no one knew at what moment it might spread throughout the entire world.

"It is probably only a matter of hours, at most," Parfitt assured me. "It was logical that the blow should fall on London first, since the shadows first made their appearance there. It took them thirty-six hours to spread over the world, in the first place; but the interval in which they commenced to move was shorter, and the present interval—the world's last breathing-spell—may prove shorter yet."

It was now only daybreak, but already Parfitt had chartered a special aerocar in which to speed to Washington for a conference with the cabinet.

Never before, in all the world's history, has the sun risen upon such a day as this—the last, in all probability, which human eye shall ever see. The shadows still lay over us, writhing and contorting now like a colossal den of angry serpents; but an even blacker pall of terror and anguish hovered over every heart and mind.

Immediately upon recognizing the extent of the disaster which had overtaken London, the government clapped a ban of censorship upon all radio stations and newspapers throughout the United States; but too late, for already the tidings had spread that London was cut off from the world, and a score of rumors, all well-nigh as fantastic and alarming as the unguessed truth, ran like wildfire across the continent; and all seized upon the certainty that there was some deadly connection between the shadows and what had followed.

Parfitt and I, as it chanced, had not been the only eye-witnesses in the United States of the striking of the

blow. A radiophone operator in one of the morning newspaper offices, who had been in conversation with his
bureau in London, was carried semi-conscious from his
machine, babbling deliriously of a black cloud which had
engulfed the man with whom he was conversing three
thousand miles away. Had the thing occurred during the
day, hundreds of eyes must have witnessed it on television
screens.

By eight o'clock, the streets of downtown New York
were jammed with frenzied men and women, demanding
to know the truth. Mobs attempted to fight their way
into several newspaper offices and radio stations to obtain
information, but were repulsed by the police, reinforced
by hastily recruited squads of state troopers.

In the city's foreign districts, pandemonium reigned.
Thousands of aliens, of a score of races, assembled in
raving, inarticulate groups, and alternately prayed and
blasphemed. Several persons were trampled to death in
a stampede to enter an East Side church; and an aged
woman, screaming for news of her two daughters in London, hurled herself from a tenth-story window.

And the developments of every hour piled fresh fuel
upon the flames of panic. By nine o'clock, communication
with every point in the British Isles was cut off. Some believed it had been severed as a form of censorship, by the
British authorities; but I, with the recollection of what
we had seen still agonizingly fresh upon me, knew otherwise; knew that the horror was spreading, and that all
England, Scotland and Ireland were probably, by now, the
same smoldering, lifeless shambles that London had become a few hours earlier.

At ten o'clock, Paris failed to respond to the signals
of the world; and a few minutes later, sudden, ominous
silence cut short radio messages from two steamers and a
transatlantic air liner.

At noon, Parfitt returned from Washington, after a two-hour conference with the cabinet, in which he had convinced them of the actual nature of the fate which lies before us, and had offered what suggestions he could—not as to averting the inevitable, but as to the most advisable means of facing it.

And an hour later the President of the United States delivered by radio the most momentous message ever addressed by the chief executive to the nation.

It seemed to me that he had aged ten years in as many hours, as I beheld his face, sunken, set and careworn, on the television screen; seamed, not with personal fear, but with the appalling realization of what lay before his nation and the world.

"Citizens of the United States," his voice came with forced calmness, "the world is faced today with a danger which has never arisen in its history before.

"What that danger is, exactly, we do not know. It is a manifestation beyond human understanding. But it has apparently destroyed all human life in the British Isles, and in other parts of the world. There is grave reason to fear that it may do the same here.

"It is beyond human power to avert the disaster. If it comes, it will come. If we are spared, it will be by the will of God. But nothing can be gained, and much unnecessary suffering can be caused, by needless panic. In an hour of crisis such as the world has never faced before, my plea to you is—be calm.

"If death comes, there is every reason to believe that it will be instantaneous and painless; a more merciful death than most of us could anticipate in the ordinary course of nature. We can not flee from it; we can best await it in calmness, committing our souls to our Maker, and bearing in mind that 'Cowards die many times before their deaths; the valiant only taste of death but once'."

New York is as a city of living dead, as I complete these pages. By government decree, transportation and industry have been halted, in an effort at least to avert the chaotic destruction which followed the snuffing out of human life in London—and presumably throughout the Old World; for in the last few hours we have been unable to communicate with any point outside North America.

Not a factory wheel is turning throughout the United States; not an airplane, train or motor car is in motion; every possible fire has been extinguished. Scarcely a footfall sounds upon the streets, for everyone is within his home, in obedience to the president's plea. The panic-stricken mobs have at last been dispersed, and the stillness of the tomb broods already over the city and the nation.

What purpose these precautions can serve is admittedly uncertain; for if man is to vanish from the earth, what matter whether the walls and towers of this mechanical civilization are unimpaired? At least we have done what we can.

I am making six copies of this document, upon parchment, chemically treated to render it more durable. These I shall enclose in hermetically sealed cylinders of ferro-aluminum; and these cylinders I shall set afloat in the river, if indeed time remains. And thus a record of man's last days upon earth, and of the nature of the end of his reign, may be preserved, for what eyes I know not, to read upon what distant shore I know not.

Upon my desk, and upon the floor, upon the city outside and over all the world, so far as I know, the shadows still writhe as I cease to write. The sun is sinking in an arc of crimson beauty, and with it, the sun of mankind. A faint breeze rustles in the trees, and brings the scents of early summer to my window.

Oh, God, it would be sweet to live!

Epilogue
(By Quarus Nahal, official astronomer-historian
of the planet Mars)

The voyage to the planet Terrestria, successfully completed last year by the Martian research expedition, confirms
the opinion of our scientists that there is no animate life
upon that planet, nor has been for centuries.

The expedition, however, uncovered highly interesting—if authentic—evidence that a race of beings of some
culture and civilization may once have populated Terrestria. Charred and crumbling ruins of stone and metallic
structures, which may once have been the dwelling-places
of such beings, were noted; and enclosed in a hermetically
sealed cylinder was a document, of which the foregoing is
an approximate translation—a translation completed only
after twelve months of arduous study, since the document
is written in a language and an alphabet entirely foreign
to any known here.

Whether this chronicle actually portrays the manner
in which life was wiped from the planet must remain in
doubt; but the context of the translation is at least con-
sistent with the circumstances under which the document
was found.

The Double Shadow

Clark Ashton Smith

1933

My name is Pharpetron, among those who have known me in Poseidonis; but even I, the last and most forward pupil of the wise Avyctes, know not the name of that which I am fated to become ere to-morrow. Therefore, by the ebbing silver lamps, in my master's marble house above the loud, ever-ravening sea, I write this tale with a hasty hand, scrawling an ink of wizard virtue on the grey, priceless, antique parchment of dragons. And having written, I shall enclose the pages in a sealed cylinder of orichalchum, and shall cast the cylinder from a high window into the sea, lest that which I am doomed to become should haply destroy the writing. And it may be that mariners from Lephara, passing to Umb and Pneor in their tall triremes, will find the cylinder; or fishers will draw it from the wave in their seines of byssus; and having read my story, men will learn the truth and take warning; and no man's feet, henceforward, will approach the pale and demon-haunted house of Avyctes.

For six years, I have dwelt apart with the aged master, forgetting youth and its wonted desires in the study of arcanic things. Together, we have delved more deeply than all others before us in an interdicted lore; we have solved the keyless hieroglyphs that guard ante-human formulae; we have talked with the prehistoric dead; we have called up the dwellers in sealed crypts, in fearful abysses beyond space. Few are the sons of mankind who have cared to seek us out among the desolate, wind-worn crags; and many, but nameless, are the visitants who have come to us from further bourns of place and time.

Stern and white as a tomb, older than the memory of the dead, and built by men or devils beyond the recording of myth, is the mansion in which we dwell. Far below, on black, naked reefs, the northern sea climbs and roars indomitably, or ebbs with a ceaseless murmur as of armies of baffled demons; and the house is filled evermore, like a hollow-sounding sepulcher, with the drear echo of its tumultuous voices; and the winds wail in dismal wrath around the high towers, but shake them not. On the seaward side, the mansion rises sheerly from the straight-falling cliff; but on the other sides there are narrow terraces, grown with dwarfish, crooked cedars that bow always beneath the gale. Giant marble monsters guard the landward portals; and huge marble women ward the strait porticoes above the sea; and mighty statues and mummies stand everywhere in the chambers and along the halls. But, saving these, and the spirits we have summoned, there is none to companion us; and liches and shadows have been the servitors of our daily needs.

All men have heard the fame of Avyctes, the sole surviving pupil of that Malygris who tyrannized in his necromancy over Susran from a tower of sable stone; Malygris, who lay dead for years while men believed him living; who, lying thus, still uttered potent spells and dire oracles with decaying lips. But Avyctes lusted not for temporal power in the manner of Malygris; and having learned all that the elder sorcerer could teach him, withdrew from the cities of Poseidonis to seek another and vaster dominion; and I, the youth Pharpetron, in the latter years of Avyctes, was permitted to join him in this solitude; and since then, I

have shared his austerities and vigils and evocations . . . a
nd now, likewise, I must share the weird doom that has
come in answer to his summoning.

Not without terror (since man is but mortal) did I, the
neophyte, behold at first the abhorrent and tremendous
faces of them that obeyed Avyctes: the genii of the sea and
earth, of the stars and the heavens, who passed to and fro
in his marmorean halls. I shuddered at the black writhing
of submundane things from the many-volumed smoke of
the braziers; I cried in horror at the grey foulnesses, colossal, without form, that crowded malignly about the drawn
circle of seven colors, threatening unspeakable trespass on
us that stood at the center. Not without revulsion did I
drink wine that was poured by cadavers, and eat bread that
was purveyed by phantoms. But use and custom dulled
the strangeness, destroyed the fear; and in time I believed
implicitly that Avyctes was the lord of all incantations and
exorcisms, with infallible power to dismiss the beings he
evoked.

Well had it had been for Avyctes—and for me—if the master had contented himself with the lore preserved from
Atlantis and Thule, or brought over from Mu and Maya-
pan. Surely this should have been enough: for in the ivory-
sheeted books of Thule there were blood-writ runes that
would call the demons of the fifth and seventh planets, if
spoken aloud at the hour of their ascent; and the sorcerers
of Mu had left record of a process whereby the doors of
far-future time could be unlocked; and our fathers, the
Atlanteans, had known the road between the atoms and the
path into far stars, and had held speech with the spirits
of the sun. But Avyctes thirsted for a darker knowledge, a
deeper empery; and into his hands, in the third year of my
novitiate, there came the mirror-bright tablet of the lost
serpent-people.

Strange, and apparently fortuitous, was our finding of the tablet. At certain hours, when the tide had fallen from the steep rocks, we were wont to descend by cavern-hidden stairs to a cliff-walled crescent beach behind the promontory on which stood the house of Avyctes. There, on the dun, wet sands, beyond the foamy tongues of the surf, would lie the worn and curious driftage of alien shores, and trove that hurricanes had cast up from unsounded deeps. And there we had found the purple and sanguine volutes of great shells, and rude lumps of ambergris, and white flowers of perpetually blooming coral; and once, the barbaric idol of green brass that had been the figurehead of a galley from far hyperboreal isles.

There had been a great storm, such as must have riven the sea to its nethermost profound; but the tempest had gone by with morning, and the heavens were cloudless on that fatal day when we found the tablet, and the demon winds were hushed among the high crags and chasms; and the sea lisped with a low whisper, like the rustle of gowns of samite trailed by fleeing maidens on the sand. And just beyond the ebbing wave, in a tangle of russet sea-weed, we beheld a thing that glittered with blinding sun-like brilliance. And running forward, I plucked it from the wrack before the wave's return, and bore it to Avyctes.

The tablet was wrought of some nameless metal, like never-rusting iron, but heavier. It had the form of a triangle and was broader at the widest than a man's heart. On one side it was wholly blank; and Avyctes and I, in turn, beheld our features mirrored strangely, like the drawn, pallid features of the dead, in its burnished surface. On the other side many rows of small crooked ciphers were incised deeply in the metal, as if by the action of some mordant acid; and these ciphers were not the pictorial symbols or alphabetic characters of any language known to the master or to me.

Of the tablet's age and origin, likewise, we could form no conjecture; and our erudition was altogether baffled. For many days thereafter we studied the writing and held argument that came to no issue. And night by night, in a high chamber closed against the perennial winds, we pondered over the dazzling triangle by the tall straight flames of silver lamps. For Avyctes deemed that knowledge of rare value (or haply some secret of an alien or elder magic) was holden by the clueless crooked ciphers. Then, since all our scholarship was in vain, the master sought another divination, and had recourse to wizardy and necromancy. But at first, among the devils and phantoms that answered our interrogation, none could tell us aught concerning the tablet. And any other than Avyctes would have despaired in the end . . . and well would it have been if he had despaired, and had sought no longer to decipher the writing.

The months and years went by with a slow thundering of seas on the dark rocks, and a headlong clamor of winds around the white towers. Still we continued our delvings and evocations; and further, always further we went into lampless realms of space and spirit; learning, perchance, to unlock the hithermost of the manifold infinities. And at whiles, Avyctes would resume his pondering of the sea-found tablet; or would question some visitant from other spheres of time and place regarding its interpretation.

At last, by the use of a chance formula, in idle experiment, he summoned up the dim, tenuous ghost of a sorcerer from prehistoric years; and the ghost, in a thin whisper of uncouth, forgotten speech, informed us that the letters on the tablet were those of a language of the serpent-men, whose primordial continent had sunk aeons before the lifting of Hyperborea from the ooze. But the ghost could tell us naught of their significance; for, even in his time, the serpent-people had become a dubious legend; and their

deep, ante-human lore and sorcery were things irretrievable
by man.

Now, in all the books of conjuration owned by Avyctes,
there was no spell whereby we could call the lost serpent-
men from their fabulous epoch. But there was an old
Lemurian formula, recondite and uncertain, by which the
shadow of a dead man could be sent into years posterior
to those of his own life-time, and could be recalled after
an interim by the wizard. And the shade, being wholly
insubstantial, would suffer no harm from the temporal
transition, and would remember, for the information of
the wizard, that which he had been instructed to learn
during the journey.

So, having called again the ghost of the prehistoric
sorcerer, whose name was Ybith, Avyctes made a singular
use of several very ardent gums and combustible fragments
of fossil wood; and he and I, reciting the responses to the
formula, sent the thin spirit of Ybith into the far ages of
the serpent-men.

And after a time which the master deemed sufficient,
we performed the curious rites of incantation that would
recall Ybith from his alienage. And the rites were successful; and Ybith stood before us again, like a blown vapor
that is nigh to vanishing. And in words that were faint as
the last echo of perishing memories, the specter told us
the key to the meaning of the letters, which he had learned
in the primeval past; and after this, we questioned Ybith
no more, but suffered him to return unto slumber and
oblivion.

Then, knowing the import of the tiny, twisted ciphers,
we read the writing on the tablet and made thereof a trans-
literation, though not without labor and difficulty, since
the very phonetics of the serpent tongue, and the symbols
and ideas expressed in the writing, were somewhat alien to

those of mankind. And when we had mastered the inscription, we found that it contained the formula for a certain evocation which, no doubt, had been used by the serpent sorcerers. But the object of the evocation was not named; nor was there any clue to the nature or identity of that which would come in answer to the rites. And moreover there was no corresponding rite of exorcism nor spell of dismissal.

Great was the jubilation of Avyctes, deeming that we had learned a lore beyond the memory or prevision of man. And though I sought to dissuade him, he resolved to employ the evocation, arguing that our discovery was no chance thing but was fatefully predestined from the beginning. And he seemed to think lightly of the menace that might be brought upon us by the conjuration of things whose nativity and attributes were wholly obscure. "For," said Avyctes, "I have called up, in all the years of my sorcery, no god or devil, no demon or lich or shadow, which I could not control and dismiss at will. And I am loath to believe that any power or spirit beyond the subversion of my spells could have been summoned by a race of serpents, whatever their skill in demonism and necromancy."

So, seeing that he was obstinate, and acknowledging him for my master in all ways, I consented to aid Avyctes in the experiment, though not without dire misgivings. And then we gathered together, in the chamber of conjuration, at the specified hour and configuration of the stars, the equivalents of sundry rare materials that the tablet had instructed us to use in the ritual.

Of much that we did, and of certain agents that we employed, it were better not to tell; nor shall I record the shrill, sibilant words, difficult for beings not born of serpents to articulate, whose intonation formed a signal part of the ceremony. Toward the last, we drew a triangle on the marble floor with the fresh blood of birds; and

Avyctes stood at one angle, and I at another; and the gaunt umber mummy of an Atlantean warrior, whose name had been Oigos, was stationed at the third angle. And standing thus, Avyctes and I held tapers of corpse-tallow in our hands, till the tapers had burned down between our fingers as into a socket. And in the outstretched palms of the mummy of Oigos, as if in shallow thuribles, talc and asbestos burned, ignited by a strange fire whereof we knew the secret. At one side we had traced on the floor an infrangible ellipse, made by an endless linked repetition of the twelve unspeakable Signs of Oumor, to which we could retire if the visitant should prove inimical or rebellious. We waited while the pole-circling stars went over, as had been prescribed. Then, when the tapers had gone out between our seared fingers, and the talc and asbestos were wholly consumed in the mummy's eaten palms, Avyctes uttered a single word whose sense was obscure to us; and Oigos, being animated by sorcery and subject to our will, repeated the word after a given interval, in tones that were hollow as a tomb-born echo; and I in my turn also repeated it.

Now, in the chamber of evocation, before beginning the ritual, we had opened a small window giving upon the sea, and had likewise left open a high door on the hall to landward, lest that which came in answer to us should require a spatial mode of entrance. And during the ceremony, the sea became still and there was no wind, and it seemed that all things were hushed in awful expectation of the nameless visitor. But after all was done, and the last word had been repeated by Oigos and me, we stood and waited vainly for a visible sign or other manifestation. The lamps burned stilly in the midnight room; and no shadows fell, other than were cast by ourselves and Oigos and by the great marble women along the walls. And in the magic mirrors we had placed cunningly, to reflect those that were otherwise unseen, we beheld no breath or trace of any image.

At this, after a reasonable interim, Avyctes was sorely disappointed, deeming that the evocation had failed of its purpose; and I, having the same thought, was secretly relieved. And we questioned the mummy of Oigos, to learn if he had perceived in the room, with such senses as are peculiar to the dead, the sure token or doubtful proof of a presence undescried by us the living. And the mummy gave a necromantic answer, saying that there was nothing.

"Verily," said Avyctes, "it were useless to wait longer. For surely in some way we have misunderstood the purport of the writing, or have failed to duplicate the matters used in the evocation, or the correct intonement of the words. Or it may be that in the lapse of so many aeons, the thing that was formerly wont to respond has long ceased to exist, or has altered in its attributes so that the spell is now void and valueless."

To this I assented readily, hoping that the matter was at an end. So, after erasing the blood-marked triangle and the sacred ellipse of the linked Signs of Oumor, and after dismissing Oigos to his wonted place among other mummies, we retired to sleep. And in the days that followed, we resumed our habitual studies, but made no mention to each other of the strange triangular tablet or the vain formula.

Even as before, our days went on; and the sea climbed and roared in white fury on the cliffs, and the winds wailed by in their unseen, sullen wrath, bowing the dark cedars as witches are bowed by the breath of Taaran, god of evil. Almost, in the marvel of new tests and cantraips, I forgot the ineffectual conjuration, and I deemed that Avyctes had also forgotten it.

All things were as of yore, to our sorcerous perception; and there was naught to trouble us in our wisdom and power and serenity, which we deemed secure above the sovereignty of kings. Reading the horoscopic stars, we found no future ill in their aspect; nor was any shadow of bale foreshown to us through geomancy, or other modes of divination such as we employed. And our familiars, though grisly and dreadful to mortal gaze, were wholly obedient to us the masters.

Then, on a clear summer afternoon, we walked, as was often our custom, on the marble terrace behind the house. In robes of ocean-purple, we paced among the windy trees with their blown, crooked shadows; and there, following us as we went to and fro, I saw the blue shadow of Avyctes and my own shadow on the marble; and between them, an adumbration that was not wrought by any of the cedars. And I was greatly startled, but spoke not of the matter to Avyctes, and observed the unknown shadow with covert care.

I saw that it followed closely the shadow of Avyctes, keeping ever the same distance. And it fluttered not in the wind, but moved with a flowing as of some heavy, thick, putrescent liquid; and its color was not blue nor purple nor black, nor any other hue to which man's eyes are habituated, but a hue as of some unearthly purulence; and its form was altogether monstrous, having a squat head and a long, undulant body, without similitude to beast or devil.

Avyctes heeded not the shadow; and still I feared to speak, though I thought it an ill thing for the master to be companioned thus. And I moved closer to him, in order to detect by touch or other perception the invisible presence that had cast the adumbration. But the air was void to sunward of the shadow; and I found nothing opposite the sun nor in any oblique direction, though I searched closely, knowing that certain beings cast their shadows thus.

After a while, at the customary hour, we returned by the coiling stairs and monster-flanked portals into the high house. And I saw that the strange adumbration moved ever

behind the shadow of Avyctes, falling horrible and unbroken on the steps and passing clearly separate and distinct
amid the long umbrages of the towering monsters. And in
the dim halls beyond the sun, where shadows should not
have been, I beheld with terror the distorted loathly blot,
having a pestilent, unnamable hue, that followed Avyctes as
if in lieu of his own extinguished shadow. And all that day,
everywhere that we went, at the table served by specters,
or in the mummy-warded room of volumes and books, the
thing pursued Avyctes, clinging to him even as leprosy to
the leper. And still the master had perceived it not; and
still I forbore to warn him, hoping that the visitant would
withdraw in its own time, going obscurely as it had come.

But at midnight, when we sat together by the silver
lamps, pondering the blood-writ runes of Hyperborea, I
saw that the shadow had drawn closer to the shadow of
Avyctes, towering behind his chair on the wall between
the huge sculptured women and the mummies. And the
thing was a streaming ooze of charnel pollution, a foul-
ness beyond the black leprosies of hell; and I could bear
it no more; and I cried out in my fear and loathing, and
informed the master of its presence.

Beholding now the shadow, Avyctes considered it closely
and in silence; and there was neither fear nor awe nor
abhorrence in the deep, graven wrinkles of his visage. And
he said to me at last: "This thing is a mystery beyond
my lore; but never, in all the practice of my art, has any
shadow come to me unbidden. And since all others of our
evocations have found answer ere this, I must deem that
the shadow is a veritable entity, or the sign of an entity,
that has come in belated response to the formula of the
serpent-sorcerers, which we thought powerless and void.
And I think it well that we should now repair to the
chamber of conjuration, and interrogate the shadow in

such manner as we may, to inquire its nativity and purpose."

We went forthwith into the chamber of conjuration,
and made such preparations as were both necessary and
possible. And when we were prepared to question it, the
unknown shadow had drawn closer still to the shadow of
Avyctes, so that the clear space between the two was no
wider than the thickness of a necromancer's rod.

Now, in all ways that were feasible, we interrogated
the shadow, speaking through our own lips and the lips
of mummies and statues. But there was no determinable
answer; and calling certain of the devils and phantoms
that were our familiars, we made question through the
mouths of these, but without result. And all the while,
our magic mirrors were void of any reflection of a presence
that might have cast the shadow; and they that had been
our spokesmen could detect nothing in the room. And
there was no spell, it seemed, that had power upon the
visitant. So Avyctes became troubled; and drawing on the
floor with blood and ashes the ellipse of Oumor, wherein
no demon nor spirit may intrude, he retired to its center.
But still within the ellipse, like a flowing taint of liquid corruption, the shadow followed his shadow; and the
space between the two was no wider than the thickness of
a wizard's pen.

Now, on the face of Avyctes, horror had graven new
wrinkles; and his brow was beaded with a deathly sweat.
For he knew, even as I, that this was a thing beyond all
laws, and foreboding naught but disaster and evil. And he
cried to me in a shaken voice, and said:

"I have no knowledge of this thing nor its intention
toward me, and no power to stay its progress. Go forth and
leave me now; for I would not that any man should witness
the defeat of my sorcery and the doom that may follow
thereupon. Also, it were well to depart while there is time,

lest you too should become the quarry of the shadow and be compelled to share its menace."

Though terror had fastened upon my inmost soul, I was loath to leave Avyctes. But I had sworn to obey his will at all times and in every respect; and moreover I knew myself doubly powerless against the adumbration, since Avyctes himself was impotent.

So, bidding him farewell, I went forth with trembling limbs from the haunted chamber; and peering back from the threshold, I saw that the alien umbrage, creeping like a noisome blotch on the floor, had touched the shadow of Avyctes. And at that moment the master shrieked aloud like one in nightmare; and his face was no longer the face of Avyctes but was contorted and convulsed like that of some helpless madman who wrestles with an unseen incubus. And I looked no more, but fled along the dim outer hall and through the high portals giving upon the terrace.

A red moon, ominous and gibbous, had declined above the terrace and the crags; and the shadows of the cedars were elongated in the moon; and they wavered in the gale like the blown cloaks of enchanters. And stooping against the gale, I fled across the terrace toward the outer stairs that led to a steep path in the riven waste of rocks and chasms behind Avyctes' house. I neared the terrace edge, running with the speed of fear; but I could not reach the topmost outer stair; for at every step the marble flowed beneath me, fleeing like a pale horizon before the seeker. And though I raced and panted without pause, I could draw no nearer to the terrace edge.

At length I desisted, seeing that an unknown spell had altered the very space about the house of Avyctes, so that none could escape therefrom to landward. So, resigning myself in despair to whatever might befall, I returned toward the house. And climbing the white stairs in the low,

level beams of the crag-caught moon, I saw a figure that
awaited me in the portals. And I knew by the trailing robe
of sea-purple, but by no other token, that the figure was
Avyctes. For the face was no longer in its entirety the face
of man, but was become a loathly fluid amalgam of human
features with a thing not to be identified on earth. The
transfiguration was ghastlier than death or the changes of
decay; and the face was already hued with the nameless,
corrupt and purulent color of the strange shadow, and had
taken on, in respect to its outlines, a partial likeness to the
squat profile of the shadow. The hands of the figure were
not those of any terrene being; and the shape beneath the
robe had lengthened with a nauseous undulant pliancy;
and the face and fingers seemed to drip in the moonlight with a deliquescent corruption. And the pursuing
umbrage, like a thickly flowing blight, had corroded and
distorted the very shadow of Avyctes, which was now
double in a manner not to be narrated here.

Fain would I have cried or spoken aloud; but horror
had dried up the fount of speech. And the thing that had
been Avyctes beckoned me in silence, uttering no word
from its living and putrescent lips. And with eyes that
were no longer eyes, but had become an oozing abomination, it peered steadily upon me. And it clutched my
shoulder closely with the soft leprosy of its fingers, and
led me half-swooning with revulsion along the hall, and
into that room where the mummy of Oigos, who had
assisted us in the threefold incantation of the serpent-men,
was stationed with several of his fellows.

By the lamps which illumed the chamber, burning with
pale, still, perpetual flames, I saw that the mummies stood
erect along the wall in their exanimate repose, each in
his wonted place with his tall shadow beside him. But
the great, gaunt shadow of Oigos on the marble wall was
companioned by an adumbration similar in all respects

to the evil thing that had followed the master and was now incorporate with him. I remembered that Oigos had performed his share of the ritual, and had repeated an unknown stated word in turn after Avyctes; and so I knew that the horror had come to Oigos in turn, and would wreak itself upon the dead even as on the living. For the foul, anonymous thing that we had called in our presumption could manifest itself to mortal ken in no other way than this. We had drawn it from unfathomable depths of time and space, using ignorantly a dire formula; and the thing had come at its own chosen hour, to stamp itself in abomination uttermost on the evocators.

Since then, the night has ebbed away, and a second day has gone by like a sluggish ooze of horror. . . . I have seen the complete identification of the shadow with the flesh and the shadow of Avyctes . . . and also I have seen the slow encroachment of that other umbrage, mingling itself with the lank shadow and the sere, bituminous body of Oigos, and turning them to a similitude of the thing which Avyctes has become. And I have heard the mummy cry out like a living man in great pain and fear, as with the throes of a second dissolution, at the impingement of the shadow. And long since it has grown silent, like the other horror, and I know not its thoughts or its intent. . . . And verily I know not if the thing that has come to us be one or several; nor if its avatar will rest complete with the three that summoned it forth into time, or be extended to others.

But these things, and much else, I shall soon know; for now, in turn, there is a shadow that follows mine, drawing ever closer. The air congeals and curdles with an unseen fear; and they that were our familiars have fled from the mansion; and the great marble women seem to tremble where they stand along the walls. But the horror that was Avyctes, and the second horror that was Oigos, have left me not, and neither do they tremble. And with eyes that are not eyes, they seem to brood and watch, waiting till I too shall become as they. And their stillness is more terrible than if they had rended me limb from limb. And there are strange voices in the wind, and alien roarings upon the sea; and the walls quiver like a thin veil in the black breath of remote abysses.

So, knowing that the time is brief, I have shut myself in the room of volumes and books and have written this account. And I have taken the bright triangular tablet, whose solution was our undoing, and have cast it from the window into the sea, hoping that none will find it after us. And now I must make an end, and enclose this writing in the sealed cylinder of orichalchum, and fling it forth to drift upon the wave. For the space between my shadow and the shadow of the horror is straitened momently. . . . and the space is no wider than the thickness of a wizard's pen.

A Disembodied Shadow

Kenneth B. Pritchard

1934

(A True Experience)

Everyone has seen shadows, but I'll wager that there are exceedingly few who have seen the kind I did, beside those who were with me at the time it happened.

You have read weird stories of shadows, or of people who cast none. What I am about to relate is true; I have witnesses to prove it.

It was twilight of a summer day in the year '27 or '28. Our little group was gathered in the rear of our homes— we called it the backyard, though it was composed of roadways. We were talking and the stars began to peep out of the skies. The street lamps began to glow, and the windows of the surrounding houses began to show lights. And thus, the stage was set.

Our eyes wandered. About fifteen feet away lay a large shadow.

It was mainly because of its size that I thought it might have been caused by a friend of mine sitting by a window in a nearby building. I became curious; thinking I could attract his attention so he would come and join us, I walked to a point of vantage. There was no one by the window, yet the shadow persisted in remaining!

Upon looking further, being fully aroused, I could find no cause for its existence. There was no possible, or probable source of blocked light. I did not forget the sun, the stars, or the sky itself. I found no flaw; the heavens and all ordinary light were normal. But there was a shadow covering an area of from 100 to 150 square feet.

The others gave it up. We could draw no satisfactory conclusion. I can tell you that it was an eerie feeling I had in observing a disembodied shadow. My mind went riot with thoughts of time travelers, visitors from space, etc.

Since then, I have tried to think of it as being caused by a kink in an otherwise clear atmosphere; but my reason seems to tell me differently. What was it? What strange thing had occurred that evening? Was this planet of ours visited by some half-seen beings from another world?

The Shadow on the Screen

Henry Kuttner

1938

Torture Master was being given a sneak preview at a Beverly Hills theatre. Somehow, when my credit line, "Directed by Peter Haviland," was flashed on the screen, a little chill of apprehension shook me, despite the applause that came from a receptive audience. When you've been in the picture game for a long time you get these hunches; I've often spotted a dud flicker before a hundred feet have been reeled off. Yet *Torture Master* was no worse than a dozen similar films I'd handled in the past few years.

But it was formula, box-office formula. I could see that. The star was all right; the make-up department had done a good job; the dialogue was unusually smooth. Yet the film was obviously box-office, and not the sort of film I'd have liked to direct.

After watching a reel unwind amid an encouraging scattering of applause, I got up and went to the lobby. Some of the gang from Summit Pictures were lounging there, smoking and commenting on the picture. Ann Howard, who played the heroine in *Torture Master,* noticed my scowl and pulled me into a corner. She was that rare type, a girl who will screen well without a lot of the yellow greasepaint that makes you look like an animated corpse. She was small, and her hair and eyes and skin were brown—I'd like to have seen her play *Peter Pan*. That type, you know.

I had occasionally proposed to her, but she never took me seriously. As a matter of fact, I myself didn't know how serious I was about it. Now she led me into the bar and ordered sidecars.

"Don't look so miserable, Pete," she said over the rim of her glass. "The picture's going over. It'll gross enough to suit the boss, and it won't hurt my reputation."

Well, that was right. Ann had a fat part, and she'd made the most of it. And the picture would be good box-office; Universal's *Night Key,* with Karloff, had been released a few months ago, and the audiences were ripe for another horror.

"I know," I told her, signaling the bartender to refill my glass. "But I get tired of these damn hokumy pics. Lord, how I'd like to do another *Cabinet of Doctor Caligari!*"

"Or another *Ape of God,*" Ann suggested.

I shrugged. "Even that, maybe. There's so much chance for development of the weird on the screen, Ann—and no producer will stand for a genuinely good picture of that type. They call it arty, and say it'll flop. If I branched out on my own—well, Hecht and MacArthur tried it, and they're back on the Hollywood payroll now."

Someone Ann knew came up and engaged her in conversation. I saw a man beckoning, and with a hasty apology left Ann to join him. It was Andy Worth, Hollywood's dirtiest columnist. I knew him for a double-crosser and a skunk, but I also knew that he could get more inside information than a brace of Winchells. He was a short, fat chap with a meticulously cultivated mustache and sleeky pomaded black hair. Worth fancied himself as a ladies' man, and spent a great deal of his time trying to blackmail actresses into having affairs with him.

That didn't make him a villain, of course. I like any-body who can carry on an intelligent conversation for ten minutes, and Worth could do that. He fingered his mustache and said, "I heard you talking about *Ape of God*. A coincidence, Pete."

"Yeah?" I was cautious. I had to be, with this walking scandal-sheet. "How's that."

He took a deep breath. "Well, you understand that I haven't got the real lowdown, and it's all hearsay—but I've found a picture that'll make the weirdest flicker ever canned look sick."

I suspected a gag. "Okay, what is it? *Torture Master?*"

"Eh? No—though Blake's yarn deserved better adaptation than your boys gave it. No, Pete, the one I'm talking about isn't for general release—isn't completed, in fact. I saw a few rushes of it. A one-man affair; title's *The Nameless*. Arnold Keene's doing it."

Worth sat back and watched how I took that. And I must have shown my amazement. For it was Arnold Keene who had directed the notorious *Ape of God,* which had wrecked his promising career in films. The public doesn't know that picture. It never was released. Summit junked it. And they had good cause, although it was one of the most amazingly effective weird films I've ever seen. Keene had shot most of it down in Mexico, and he'd been able to assume virtual dictatorship of the location troupe. Several Mexicans had died at the time, and there had been some ugly rumors, but it had all been hushed up. I'd talked with several people who had been down near Taxco with Keene, and they spoke of the man with peculiar horror. He had been willing to sacrifice almost anything to make *Ape of God* a masterpiece of its type.

It was an unusual picture—there was no question about that. There's only one master print of the film, and it's kept in a locked vault at Summit. Very few have seen it. For what Machen had done in weird literature, Keene had done on the screen—and it was literally amazing.

I said to Worth, "Arnold Keene, eh? I've always had a sneaking sympathy for the man. But I thought he'd died long ago."

"Oh, no. He bought a place near Tujunga and went into hiding. He didn't have much dough after the blow-up, you know, and it took him about five years to get together enough *dinero* to start his *Nameless*. He always said *Ape of God* was a failure, and that he intended to do a film that would be a masterpiece of weirdness. Well, he's done it. He's canned a film that's—unearthly, I tell you it made my flesh creep."

"Who's the star?" I asked.

"Unknowns. Russian trick, you know. The real star is a—a shadow."

I stared at him.

"That's right, Pete. The shadow of something that's never shown on the screen. Doesn't sound like much, eh? But you ought to see it!"

"I'd like to," I told him. "In fact, I'll do just that. Maybe he'll release it through Summit."

Worth chuckled. "No chance. No studio would release that flicker. I'm not even going to play it up in my dirt sheet. This is the real McCoy, Pete."

"What's Keene's address?" I asked.

Worth gave it to me. "But don't go out till Wednesday night," he said. "The rough prints 'll be ready then, or most of them. And keep it under you hat, of course."

A group of autograph hunters came up just then, and Worth and I were separated. It didn't matter. I'd got all the information I needed. My mind was seething with fantastic surmises. Keene was one of the great geniuses of the screen, and his talent lay in the direction of the macabre. Unlike book publishers, the studios catered to no small, discriminating audiences. A film must suit everybody.

Finally I broke away and took Ann to a dance at Bel-Air. But I hadn't forgotten Keene, and the next night I was too impatient to wait. I telephoned Worth, but he was out. Oddly enough, I was unable to get in touch with him during the next few days; even his paper couldn't help me. A furious editor told me the Associated Press had been sending him hourly telegrams asking for Worth's copy; but the man had vanished completely. I had a hunch.

It was Tuesday night when I drove out of the studio and took a short cut through Griffith Park, past the Planetarium, to Glendale. From there I went on to Tujunga, to the address Worth had given me. Once or twice I had an uneasy suspicion that a black coupé was trailing me, but I couldn't be sure.

Arnold Keen's house was in a little canyon back in the Tujunga mountains. I had to follow a winding dirt road for several miles, and ford a stream or two, before I reached it. The place was built against the side of the canyon, and a man stood on the porch and watched me as I braked my car to a stop.

It was Arnold Keene. I recognized him immediately. He was a slender man under middle height, with a closely cropped bristle of gray hair; his face was coldly austere. There had been a rumor that Keene had at one time been an officer in Prussia before he came to Hollywood and Americanized his name, and, scrutinizing him, I could well believe it. His eyes were like pale blue marbles, curiously shallow.

He said, "Peter Haviland? I did not expect you until tomorrow night."

I shook hands. "Sorry if I intrude," I apologized. "The fact is, I got impatient after what Worth told me about your film. He isn't hear, by any chance?"

The shallow eyes were unreadable. "No. But come in. Luckily, the developing took less time than I had anticipated. I need only a few more shots to complete my task."

He ushered me into the house, which was thoroughly modern and comfortably furnished. Under the influence of good cognac my suspicions began to dissolve. I told Keene I had always admired his *Ape of God*.

He made a wry grimace. "Amateurish, Haviland. I depended too much on hokum in that film. Merely devil-worship, a reincarnated Gilles de Rais, and sadism. That isn't true weirdness."

I was interested. "That's correct. But the film had genuine power—"

"Man has nothing of the weird in him intrinsically. It is only the hints of the utterly abnormal and unhuman that give one the true feeling of weirdness. That, and human reactions to such supernatural phenomena. Look at any great weird work—*The Horla,* which tells of a man's reaction to a creation utterly alien, Blackwood's *Willows,* Machen's *Black Seal,* Lovecraft's *Color Out of Space*—all of these deal with the absolutely alien influencing normal lives. Sadism and death may contribute, but alone they cannot produce the true, intangible atmosphere of weirdness."

I had read all these tales. "But you can't film the indescribable. How could you show the invisible beings of *The Willows?*"

Keene hesitated. "I think I'll let my film answer that. I have a projection room downstairs—"

The bell rang sharply. I could not help noticing the quick glance Keene darted at me. With an apologetic gesture he went out and presently returned with Ann Howard at his side. She was smiling rather shakily.

"Did you forget our date, Pete?" she asked me.

I blinked, and suddenly remembered. Two weeks ago I had promised to take Ann to an affair in Laguna Beach this evening, but in my preoccupation with Keene's picture the date had slipped my mind. I stammered apologies.

"Oh, that's all right," she broke in. "I'd much rather stay here—that is, if Mr. Keene doesn't mind. His picture—"

"You know about it?"

"I told her," Keene said. "When she explained why she had come, I took the liberty of inviting her to stay to watch the film. I did not want her to drag you away, you see," he finished, smiling. "Some cognac for Miss—eh?"

I introduced them.

"For Miss Howard, and then *The Nameless.*"

At his words a tiny warning note seemed to throb in my brain. I had been fingering a heavy metal paperweight, and now, as Keene's attention was momentarily diverted to the sideboard, I slipped it, on a sudden impulse, into my pocket. It would be no defense, though, against a gun.

What was wrong with me, I wondered? An atmosphere of distrust and suspicion seemed to have sprung out of nothing. As Keene ushered us down into his projection room, the skin of my back seemed to crawl with the expectation of attack. It was inexplicable, but definitely unpleasant.

Keene was busy for a time in the projection booth, and then he joined us.

"Modern machinery is a blessing," he said with heavy jocularity. "I can be as lazy as I wish. I needed no help with the shooting, once the automatic cameras were installed. The projector, too, is automatic."

I felt Ann move closer to me in the gloom. I put my arm around her and said, "It helps, yes. What about releasing the picture, Mr. Keene?"

There was a harsh note in his voice. "It will not be released. The world is uneducated, not ready for it. In a hundred years, perhaps, it will achieve the fame it deserves. I am doing it for posterity, and for the sake of creating a weird masterpiece on the screen."

With a muffled click the projector began to operate, and a title flashed on the screen: *The Nameless.*

Keene's voice came out of the darkness. "It's a silent film, except for one sequence at the start. Sound adds nothing to weirdness, and it helps to destroy the illusion of reality. Later, suitable music will be dubbed in."

I did not answer. For a book had flashed on the gray oblong before us—that amazing tour de force, *The Circus of Doctor Lao.* A hand opened it, and a long finger followed the lines as a toneless voice read:

"These are the sports, the offthrows of the universe instead of the species; these are the weird children of the lust of the spheres. Mysticism explains them where science cannot. Listen: when that great mysterious fecundity that peopled the worlds at the command of the gods had done with its birth-giving, when the celestial midwives all had left, when life had begun in the universe, the primal womb-thing found itself still unexhausted, its loins still potent. So that awful fertility tossed on its couch in a final fierce outbreak of life-giving and gave birth to these nightmare beings, these abortions of the world."

The voice ceased. The book faded, and there swam into view a mass of tumbled ruins. The ages had pitted the man-carved rocks with cracks and scars; the bas-relief figures were scarcely recognizable. I was reminded of certain ruins I had seen in Yucatan.

The camera swung down. The ruins seemed to grow larger. A yawning hole gaped in the earth.

Beside me Keene said, "The site of a ruined temple. Watch, now."

The effect was that of moving forward into the depths of a subterranean pit. For a moment the screen was in darkness; then a stray beam of sunlight rested on an idol that stood in what was apparently an underground cavern. A narrow crack of light showed in the roof. The idol was starkly hideous.

I got only a flashing glimpse, but the impression on my mind was that of a bulky, ovoid shape like a pineapple or a pine-cone. The thing had certain doubtful features which lent it a definitely unpleasant appearance; but it was gone in a flash, dissolving into a brightly lighted drawing-room, thronged with gay couples.

The story proper began at that point. None of the actors or actresses was known to me; Keene must have hired them and worked secretly in his house. Most of the interiors and a few of the exteriors seemed to have been taken in this very canyon. The director had used the "parallel" trick which saves so much money for studios yearly. I'd often done it myself. It simply means that the story is tied in with real life as closely as possible; that is, when I had a troupe working up at Lake Arrowhead last winter, and an unexpected snowfall changed the scene, I had the continuity rewritten so that the necessary scenes could take place in snow. Similarly, Keene had paralleled his own experiences—sometimes almost too closely.

The Nameless told of a man, ostracized by his fellows because of his fanatical passion for the morbid and bizarre, who determined to create a work of art—a living master-piece of sheer weirdness. He had experimented before by directing films that were sufficiently unusual to stir up considerable comment. But this did not satisfy him. It was acting—and he wanted something more than that. No one can convincingly fake reaction to horror, not even the most talented actor, he contended. The genuine emotion must be felt in order to be transferred to the screen.

It was here that *The Nameless* ceased to parallel Keene's own experiences, and branched out into sheer fantasy. The protagonist in the film was Keene himself, but this was not unusual, as directors often act in their own productions. And, by deft montage shots, the audience learned that Keene in his search for authenticity had gone down into Mexico, and had, with the aid of an ancient scroll, found the site of a ruined Aztec temple. And here, as I say, reality was left behind as the film entered a morbid and extraordinary phase.

There was a god hidden beneath this ruined temple—a long-forgotten god, which had been worshipped even before the Aztecs had sprung from the womb of the centuries. At least, the natives had considered it a god, and had erected a temple in its honor, but Keene hinted that the thing was actually a survival, one of the "offthrows of the universe," unique and baroque, which had come down through the eons in an existence totally alien to mankind. The creature was never actually seen on the screen, save for a few brief glimpses in the shadowed, underground temple. It was roughly barrel-shaped, and perhaps ten feet high, studded with odd spiky projections. The chief feature was a gem set in the thing's rounded apex—a smoothly polished jewel as large as a child's head. It was in this gem that the being's life was supposed to have its focus.

It was not dead, but neither was it alive, in the accepted sense of that term. When the Aztecs had filled the temple with the hot stench of blood the thing had lived, and the jewel had flamed with unearthly radiance. But with the passage of time the sacrifices had ceased, and the being had sunk into a state of coma akin to hibernation. In the picture Keene brought it to life.

He transported it secretly to his home, and there, in an underground room hollowed beneath the house, he placed the monster-god. The room was built with an eye for the purpose for which Keene intended it; automatic cameras and clever lighting features were installed, so that pictures could be shot from several different angles at once, and pieced together later as Keene cut the film. And now there entered something of the touch of genius which had made Keene famous.

He was clever, I had always realized that. Yet in the scenes that were next unfolded I admired not so much the technical tricks—which were familiar enough to me—as the marvelously clever way in which Keene had managed to inject realism into the acting. His characters did not act—they *lived*.

Or, rather, they died. For in the picture they were thrust into the underground room to die horribly as sacrifices to the monster-god from the Aztec temple. Sacrifice was supposed to bring the thing to life, to cause the jewel in which its existence was bound to flare with fantastic splendor. The first sacrifice was, I think, the most effective.

The underground room in which the god was hidden was large, but quite vacant, save for a curtained alcove which held the idol. A barred doorway led to the upper room, and here Keene appeared on the screen, revolver in hand, herding before him a man—overall-clad, with a stubble of black beard on his stolid face. Keene swung open the door, motioned his captive into the great room. He closed the barred door, and through the grating could be seen busy at a switchboard.

Light flared. The man stood near the bars, and then, at Keene's gesture with his weapon, moved forward slowly to the far wall. He stood there, staring around vaguely, dull apprehension in his face. Light threw his shadow in bold relief on the wall.

Then another shadow leaped into existence beside him.

It was barrel-shaped, gigantic, studded with blunt spikes, and capped by a round dark blob—the life-jewel. The shadow of the monster god! The man saw it. He turned.

Stark horror sprang into his face, and at sight of that utterly ghastly and realistic expression a chill struck through me. This was almost too convincing. The man could not be merely acting.

But, if he was, his acting was superb, and so was Keene's direction. The shadow on the wall stirred, and a thrill of movement shook it. It rocked and seemed to rise, supported by a dozen tentacular appendages that uncoiled from beneath its base. The spikes—changed. They lengthened. They coiled and writhed, hideously worm-like.

It wasn't the metamorphosis of the shadow that held me motionless in my chair. Rather, it was the appalling expression of sheer horror on the man's face. He stood gaping as the shadow toppled and swayed on the wall, growing larger and larger. Then he fled, his mouth an open square of terror. The shadow paused, with an odd air of indecision, and slipped slowly along the wall out of range of the camera.

But there were other cameras, and Keene had used his cutting-shears deftly. The movements of the man were mirrored on the screen; the glaring lights swung and flared; and ever the grim shadow crawled hideously across the wall. The thing that cast it was never shown—just the shadow, and it was a dramatically effective trick. Too many directors, I knew, could not have resisted the temptation to show the monster, thus destroying the illusion—for papier-mâché and rubber, no matter how cleverly constructed, cannot convincingly ape reality.

At last the shadows merged—the gigantic swaying thing with its coiling tentacles, and the black shadow of the man that was caught and lifted, struggling and kicking frantically. The shadows merged—and the man did not reappear. Only the dark blob capping the great shadow faded and flickered, as though strange light were streaming from it; the light that was fed by sacrifice, the jewel that was—life.

Beside me there came a rustle. I felt Ann stir and move closer in the gloom. Keene's voice came from some distance away.

"There were several more sacrifice scenes, Haviland, but I haven't patched them in yet, except for the one you'll see in a moment now. As I said, the film isn't finished."

I did not answer. My eyes were on the screen as the fantastic tale unfolded. The pictured Keene was bringing another victim to his cavern, a short, fat man with sleekly pomaded black hair. I did not see his face until he had been imprisoned in the cave, and then, abruptly, there came a close-up shot, probably done with a telescopic lens. His plump face, with its tiny mustache, leaped into gigantic visibility, and I recognized Andy Worth.

It was the missing columnist, but for the first time I saw his veneer of sophistication lacking. Naked fear crawled in his eyes, and I leaned forward in my seat as the ghastly barrel-shaped shadow sprang out on the wall. Worth saw it, and the expression on his face was shocking. I pushed back my chair and got up as the lights came on. The screen went blank.

Arnold Keene was standing by the door, erect and military as ever. He had a gun in his hand, and its muzzle was aimed at my stomach.

"You had better sit down, Haviland," he said quietly. "You too, Miss Howard. I've something to tell you—and I don't wish to be melodramatic about it. This gun"—he glanced at it wryly—"is necessary. There are a few things you must know, Haviland, for a reason you'll understand later."

I said, "There'll be some visitors here for you soon, Keene. You don't think I'd neglect normal precautions!"

He shrugged. "You're lying, of course. Also you're unarmed, or you'd have had your gun out by now. I didn't expect you until tomorrow night, but I'm prepared. In a word, what I have to tell you is this: the film you just saw is a record of actual events."

Ann's teeth sank into her lip, but I didn't say anything. I waited, and Keene resumed.

"Whether you believe me or not doesn't matter, for you'll have to believe in a few minutes. I told you something of my motive, my desire to create a genuine masterpiece of weirdness. That's what I've done, or will have done before tomorrow. Quite a number of vagrants and laborers have disappeared, and the columnist, Worth, as well; but I took care to leave no clues. You'll be the last to vanish—you and this girl."

"You'll never be able to show the film," I told him.

"What of it? You're a hack, Haviland, and you can't understand what it means to create a masterpiece. Is a work of art any less beautiful because it's hidden? I'll see the picture—and after I'm dead the world will see it, and realize my genius even though they may fear and hate its expression. The reactions of my unwilling actors—that's the trick. As a director, you should know that there's no substitute for realism. The reactions were not faked—that was obvious enough. The first sacrifice was that of a clod— an unintelligent moron, whose fears were largely superstitious. The next sacrifice was of a higher type—a vagrant who came begging to my door some months ago. You will complete the group, for you'll know just what you're facing, and your attempt to rationalize your fear will lend an interesting touch. Both of you will stand up, with your hands in the air, and precede me into this passage."

All this came out tonelessly and swiftly, quite as though it were a rehearsed speech. His hand slid over the wall beside him, and a black oblong widened in the oak paneling. I stood up.

"Do as he says, Ann," I said. "Maybe I can—"

"No, you can't," Keene interrupted, gesturing impatiently with his weapon. "You won't have the chance. Hurry up."

We went through the opening in the wall and Keene followed, touching a stud that flooded the passage with light. It was a narrow tunnel that slanted down through solid rock for perhaps ten feet to a steep stairway. He herded us down this, after sliding the panel shut.

"It's well hidden," he said, indicating metal sheathing—indeed, the entire corridor was lined with metal plates. "This lever opens it from within, but no one but me can find the spring which opens it from without. The police could wreck the house without discovering this passage."

That seemed worth remembering, but of little practical value at the moment. Ann and I went down the stairway until it ended in another short passage. Our way was blocked by a door of steel bars, which Keene unlocked with a key he took from his pocket. The passage where we stood was dimly lighted; there were several chairs here; and the space beyond the barred door was not lighted at all.

Keene opened the door and gestured me through it. He locked it behind me and turned to Ann. Her face, I saw, was paper-white in the pale glow.

What happened after that brought an angry curse to my lips. Without warning Keene swung the automatic in a short, vicious arc, smashing it against Ann's head.

She saw it coming too late, and her upflung hand failed to ward off the blow. She dropped without a sound, a little trickle of blood oozing from her temple. Keene stepped over her body to a switchboard set in the rock wall.

Light lanced with intolerable brilliance into my eyes. I shut them tightly, opening them after a moment to stare around apprehensively. I recognized my surroundings. I was in the cave of sacrifice, the underground den I had seen on the screen. Cameras high up on the walls began to operate as I discovered them. From various points blinding arc-lights streamed down upon me.

A gray curtain shielded a space on the far wall, but this was drawn upward to reveal a deep alcove. There was an object within that niche—a barrel-shaped thing ten feet high, studded with spikes, and crowned with a jewel that pulsed and glittered with cold flame. It was gray and varnished-looking, and it was the original of Keene's Aztec god.

Somehow I felt oddly reassured as I examined the thing. It was a model, of course, inanimate and dead; for certainly no life of any kind could exist in such an abnormality. Keene might have installed machinery of some sort within it, however.

"You see, Haviland," Keene said from beyond the bars, "the thing actually exists. I got on the trail of it in an old parchment I found in the Huntington Library. It had been considered merely an interesting bit of folk-lore, but I saw something else in it. When I was making *Ape of God* in Mexico I discovered the ruined temple, and what lay forgotten behind the altar."

He touched a switch, and light streamed out from the alcove behind the thing. Swiftly I turned. On the wall behind me was my own shadow, grotesquely elongated, and beside it was the squat, amorphous patch of blackness I had seen on the screen upstairs.

My back was toward Keene, and my fingers crept into my pocket, touching the metal paperweight I had dropped there earlier that evening. Briefly I considered the possibility of hurling the thing at Keene, and then decided against it. The bars were too close together, and the man would shoot me at any sign of dangerous hostility.

My eyes were drawn to the shadow on the wall. It was moving.

It rocked slightly, and lifted. The spikes lengthened. The thing was no longer inanimate and dead, and as I swung about, stark amazement gripping me, I saw the incredible metamorphosis that had taken place in the thing that cast the shadow.

It was no longer barrel-shaped. A dozen smooth, glistening appendages, ending in flat pads, supported the snake-thin body. And all over that grayish upright pole tentacles sprouted and lengthened, writhing into ghastly life as the horror awakened. Keene had not lied, and the monstrous survival he had brought from the Aztec temple was lumbering from the alcove, its myriad tentacles alive with frightful hunger!

Keene saved me. He saw me standing motionless with abysmal fear in the path of that gigantic, nightmare being, and realizing that he was being cheated of his picture, the man shouted at me to run. His hoarse voice broke the spell that held me unmoving, and I whirled and fled across the cave to the barred door. Skin ripped from my hands as I tore at the bars.

"Run!" Keene yelled at me, his shallow eyes blazing. "It can't move fast! Look out—"

A writhing, snake-like thing lashed out, and a sickening musky stencil filled my nostrils. I leaped away, racing across the cave again. The arc-lights died and others flared into being as Keene manipulated the switchboard. He was adjusting the lights, so that our shadows would not be lost—so that in the climax of *The Nameless* the shadow of that ghastly horror would be thrown on the cave wall beside me.

It was an infernal game of tag we played there, in those shifting lights that glared down while the camera lenses watched dispassionately. I fled and dodged with my pulses thundering and blood pounding in my temples, and ever the grim shadow moved slowly across the walls, while my legs began to ache with the strain. For hours, perhaps, or eons, I fled.

There would come brief periods of respite when I would cling to the bars, cursing Keene, but he would not answer. His hands flickered over the switchboard as he adjusted the arc-lights, and his eyes never paused in their roving examination of the cave. In the end it was this that saved me.

For Keene did not see Ann stir and open her eyes. He did not see the girl, after a swift glance around, get quietly to her feet. Luckily she was behind Keene, and he did not turn.

I tried to keep my eyes away from Ann, but I do not think I succeeded. At the last moment I saw Keene's face change, and he started back; but the chair in Ann's hands crashed down and splintered on the man's head. He fell to his knees, clawing at the air, and then collapsed inertly.

I was on the far side of the cave, and my attention was momentarily diverted from the monster. I had been watching it from the corner of my eye, expecting to be able to dodge and leap away before it came too close; but it lumbered forward with a sudden burst of speed. Although I tried to spring clear I failed; a tentacle whipped about my legs and sent me sprawling. As I tried to roll away another smooth gray coil got my left arm.

Intolerable agony dug into my shoulder as I was lifted. I heard Ann scream, and a gun barked angrily. Bullets plopped into the smooth flesh of the monster, but it paid no attention. I was lifted through a welter of coiling, ropy tentacles, until just above me was the flaming jewel in which the creature's life was centered.

Remembrance of Keene's words spurred me to action; this might be the monster's vulnerable point. The paper-weight was still in my pocket, and I clawed it out desperately. I hurled it with all my strength at the shining gem. And the jewel shattered!

There came a shrill vibration, like the tinkling of count-less tiny crystalline bells. Piercingly sweet, it shrilled in my ears, and died away quickly. And suddenly nothing existed but light.

It was as though the shattering of the gem had released a sea of incandescent flame imprisoned within it. The glare of the arc-lights faded beside this flood of silvery radiance that bathed me. The cold glory of Arcturus, the blaze of tropical moonlight, were in the light.

Swiftly it faded and fled away. I felt myself dropping, and pain lanced into my wrenched shoulder as I struck the ground. I heard Ann's voice.

Dazedly I got up, expecting to see the monster towering above me. But it was gone. In its place, a few feet away, was the barrel-shaped thing I had first seen in the alcove. There was a gaping cavity in the rounded apex where the jewel had been. And, somehow, I sensed that the creature was no longer deadly, no longer a horror.

I saw Ann. She was still holding Keene's gun, and in her other hand was the key with which she had unlocked the door. She came running toward me, and I went swiftly to meet her.

I took the gun and made sure it was loaded. "Come on," I said, curtly. "We're getting out of here."

Ann's fingers were gripping my arm tightly as we went through the door, past the prone figure of Keene, and up the stairway. The lever behind the panel was not difficult to operate, and I followed Ann through the opening into the theater. Then I paused, listening.

Ann turned, watching me, a question in her eyes. "What is it, Pete?"

"Listen," I said. "Get the cans of film from the projec-tion booth. We'll take them with us and burn them."

"But—you're not—"

"I'll be with you in a minute," I told her, and swung the panel shut.

I went down the stairs swiftly and very quietly, my gun ready and my ears alert for the low muttering I had heard from below.

Keene was no longer unconscious. He was standing beside the switchboard with his back to me, and over his shoulder I could see the shadow of the monster-god sprawling on the wall, inert and lifeless. Keene was chanting something, in a language I did not know, and his hands were moving in strange gestures.

God knows what unearthly powers Keene had acquired in his search for horror! For as I stood there, watching the patch of blackness on the cave wall, I saw a little shudder rock that barrel-shaped shadow of horror, while a single spike abruptly lengthened into a tentacle that groped out furtively and drew back and vanished.

Then I killed Arnold Keene.

Afraid of His Shadow

Dorothy Donnell Calhoun

1941

The smoking-room of the club was gray with twilight, and nearly deserted. In one corner an elderly man, showing perhaps sixty-five years in his lined, thoughtful face, sat buried in the "Revue Philosophique." Behind him a group of young members stretched their long legs around the dying fire, in desultory chat of one thing and another. Presently, led perhaps by a chance remark on the waning light, the talk touched, strangely enough, on fear.

"I wonder how many of us, if we were quite truthful, would not confess to some sort of fear," mused the young novelist. His glance about the group was whimsical. "Don't worry, I'm not thinking of third-degreeing any of you for copy, but it just occurred to me. I'll wager there isn't a man among us or anywhere else who hasn't some pet private dread locked away in his own soul where even his wife doesn't know of its presence."

"What do you mean by fear?" objected his neighbor. "The bravest man I ever knew was an army captain, with a V. C. for gallantry in ten engagements, who confessed to me once that he had a deadly horror of cats!"

"That proves my point." The novelist puffed his brier complacently. "Cats, the toothache, death, ridicule—it doesn't matter what. That poor devil of a policeman who was stripped of his shield the other day for failing to follow an armed thief into a dark cellarway was probably no worse a coward at heart than you or I. We're luckier in never having come up against our own particular phobia, that's all."

"Do you remember the verse of Coleridge's about a man walking along a lonely road?" hesitated a third voice. The young physician leaned forward to light his cigar on his neighbor's. "Let's see, how does it run?

> 'And having once looked round, walks on,
> and no more turns his head
> Because he knows a frightful fiend doth
> close behind him tread.'

"Do you know, I've thought of that sometimes when I was driving through the country at midnight? And, well, you couldn't hire me to look around for love or money at that moment!"

"Fear of the darkness seems to be born in us." nodded the novelist. "I suppose there wasn't a night when I was a child that I felt really safe going upstairs to bed."

"But did you ever hear of a man who was afraid of the light?" asked a deep voice unexpectedly from behind them. The gray-haired man stood on the outskirts of the group, dimly sketched against the grayness.

"I trust you will pardon my intrusion," he went on, almost shyly. "I am a stranger here—an old member. I happened to overhear your conversation, and it singularly interests me."

"No apologies, sir; draw up your chair and welcome," the physician assured him heartily. "We'll be everlastingly grateful if you can spin us a new yarn. We're stale on each other's stories. Have a cigar."

"No, thanks, I don't smoke." The stranger settled back in the leather armchair, and gazed steadily into the glowing coals. It was almost as though the light hurt his eyes, yet he forced himself to look at it. The unusual in his attitude whetted the appetite of the group for strange disclosures. Finally, without taking his gaze from the fire, he began to talk in a level, colorless voice.

"The man I was thinking about when I spoke just now used to live in this town." He glanced an instant about the circle. "I wonder—perhaps you may have heard of him. He left before your times, I suppose; almost thirty years ago. The name was Peter Van Dorn."

"Van Dorn?" The novelist leaned forward interestedly. "There was a Van Dorn I've heard my father speak of; a wealthy young rake who left his gay life suddenly without any explanation and became a hermit. People said it was the fault of the girl he was in love with."

"People were wrong," said the stranger slowly. "Peter Van Dorn suffered from no one's fault but his own. You will wonder how I know this story. You see, I was a friend and schoolmate of the man, and he told me the truth that the world only guessed and gossiped about. The real reason Peter became a recluse was because he was afraid. I said when I joined you that he was afraid of the light, but that is not quite accurate. He was afraid of what the light might show him, and that was his own shadow!"

A stir ran around the group. On the tips of half a dozen cigars the ashes gathered. Only the stranger seemed unmoved by his own words.

"You were right when you summed up the man's character, just now—'young rake.' Yet, the Van Dorns belonged to one of the oldest families in the State. There were governors among them before the line dwindled down to Peter. And up to the time he went to college, and then to a foreign university, the lad was harmless enough; a slight, pretty youngster, with girl's hair and eyes. Even then, Eleanor Hammond, daughter of the old judge, was his sweetheart in a childish fashion, and everyone supposed that Peter would come home in a few years, marry her, and settle down.

"But five years went by, six, and seven, and all of Peter that returned were sly rumors and shreds of gossip that drift in the wake of a careless young blackguard; gossip of gambling, drinking, and gay companions, though nothing worse. Then, one day, on the heels of the tales, appeared Peter himself, broadened and thickened into a fine figure of a man, with no hint of evil in his frank ways.

"By that time Eleanor Hammond was a lovely woman of twenty-five, with more suitors than you could count, but none of them favored. She could have married well a dozen times, but she hadn't, and as soon as Peter came upon the scene it was plain that she had kept the thankless young scoundrel's image in her pure heart all these years.

"It was on a moonlight evening, a month later, that he asked her to marry him; one of those white, unstirring nights when every twig is doubled by its shadow, like a cameo on the grass. For a moment after the question had left his lips she did not answer, then she raised her head and looked him straight in the eyes.

"'Are you coming to me quite free, Peter?' she asked him slowly.

"'There is nothing or no one else in the wide world with a claim on me,' he told her. 'Not a shadow even, sweetheart, between you and me.'

"But before the words were out of his mouth, the sudden horror in her eyes warned him, and following their shrinking gaze he saw it—the Thing on the grass where his shadow should have been, black and distinct in the white pools of the moon. He did not know, he told me, how long he stood there staring—staring, or just when she went. It was the sound of a door closing that broke the spell at last, for he knew that with that door he was shut out from her, from love and happiness, he and the Thing on the grass, in a world where the darkness that hides sin and horrors is kinder than the day.

"Like a lost soul, Peter Van Dorn fled from the tell-tale moon, plunging into the grove, over tree-stumps, through close-growing bushes, panting like a hounded animal, moaning, muttering, beating his breast. In a close covert of evergreens—as the spicy smell told him—he stopped and cast a hunted look behind; but the shadows of the woods had erased the Thing he feared.

"He drew long, sobbing breaths and tried to think the matter over calmly. It was impossible, against nature, reason, belief—yet it was true! He had seen it—she had seen.

"There had been no mistaking the slender figure, the fragile, piquant profile, every line the same. Yet she was dead; she and the child that had shamed her.

"'It is a bad dream!' cried Peter aloud. 'Why, such things cannot happen in this world!'

"But when later he had to cross a field of white, pure moonlight, he did it on a run, hands clasped across his eyes.

"She wrote the next day. My friend showed me the letter, kissed almost illegible. 'I do not pretend to judge you,' she wrote sadly, 'I do not even question. Yet, with that between us, Peter, I can never marry you. If it were an illusion, some strange freak of the leaves! But, Peter, Peter, where was your own shadow on the grass?'

"At the end there was a hint of hope. 'If it goes away— that black woman-shadow, Peter, come to me, for I have waited a long time for you, and I will wait longer. And, dear, if you can make any reparation, do so.'

"But Peter Van Dorn sat in his darkened room, and knew without hope that the shadow of his old sin would never let him go to her.

"Tongues clacked, of course. People said he was crazy to shut himself up in his darkened house, and one of his chums who had gone to expostulate with him, ratified this belief.

"'Peter, old man,' he had begun, jovially, 'what are you doing, shut up with the shadows—'

"He had not finished his sentence, he said, for Peter had sprung to him, gripping his arm with frenzied fingers like claws. 'Shadows—where?' he had gasped. 'What light?' And then, with a wild cry of despair, 'What would you do if you had lost your shadow?'

"After that, you may believe, no one was anxious to visit Peter. His servants left, telling strange tales of how their master refused to have a lamp, or so much as a candle, lighted in the room with him. Soon there was fresher gossip to occupy people's tongues, and they left off wondering about poor Peter. Sometimes a man, coming home late on a clouded night, would see a shadowy figure slipping along furtively in the covert of the buildings; but for ten years Peter Van Dorn lived, the ghost of himself, hidden from the eyes of mankind and the revelation of the sun. Always, he told me, he felt the Thing with him, ready to spring out in the place of his shadow whenever he dared the light, but he never saw it during that time. Then, one day, he heard somehow that Eleanor Hammond was dying. Well—he went to her.

"The old judge met him at the door, as naturally as though he had seen him yesterday.

"'She has been calling for you, Peter,' he told him, 'come in.'

"The sick-room was darkened. On the pillow was a whiter blur that Peter knew for her face. Kneeling by the bedside, he cried like a child. He thought, you see, that she was dead, she lay so still; but it was not so. The door behind opened suddenly to admit the physician, also the father carrying an oil-lamp in his shaking, veined old hands.

"The room sprang into lights and shadows, and the dying woman opened her eyes with a great cry.

"'Your shadow has come back, Peter!' she said. 'The other one is gone. There is nothing between us now, my dear, my dear!'

"Even as she spoke she fell back, dead. And Peter saw the old lost shadow of himself rise up and stagger before him from the room. From that hour, the shadow of the woman he had wronged never returned, for she, dead, had had her triumph, and had kept what was hers."

The stranger's voice sank to a whisper. The coals in the grate fell apart with a hiss and flared into a brief glow. In the circle several men started up and cast furtive looks over their shoulders. The stranger laughed grimly.

"It never fails," he mused aloud, as though to himself. "I have told that story many times, and at the end there is always some one who looks hurriedly over his shoulder for his own shadow! Strange how conscience makes us cowards."

"You had not finished," interposed the novelist hastily. "What became of Peter afterward?"

"He went to foreign lands in search of forgetfulness," said the deep voice tonelessly; "then gave up the search and came home. But always he preferred the darkness to the light, for he was afraid of his own shadow the rest of his days."

The novelist knocked his pipe against the chimney-piece with a hand that was not quite steady.

"That's quite a good yarn, friend," he yawned carelessly. "But altogether too strained to be true. Of course, you admit it is only a yarn?"

The stranger rose and faced him. In the fire-flicker they saw the lines in his face and the infinite sadness in his tired eyes.

"Yes, yes, of course it is fiction," he assented wearily. "As you say, it is too strained to be true."

The soft-footed butler of the club had entered as they were speaking, and now, suddenly, without warning, the room sprang into warm light from the two great chandeliers.

With a sharp cry the gray-haired stranger covered his eyes with his hands.

"Turn off the light!" he cried. "I am afraid!"

Night of Impossible Shadows
Allison V. Harding
1945

My first reaction to Paul's telegram was one of exasperated annoyance. He had sent me an airmail special a few weeks ago begging me to come to his country home, that it was a matter of great urgency and he must see me right away. I wrote back and refused as politely and tactfully as I could, explaining that even "a lawyer needs a vacation once a year," which was just what I intended taking, and—had he forgotten my bride of less than a year, Elaine?

My reply was final, or was meant to be, and then my golden-haired wife brought me the yellow envelope.

"One of your paroled clients, Mr. Anderson?" she kidded me.

I ripped it open and frowned at the "Valley Lake" sender's address.

"Come immediately. Must see you. Life or death. Bring Elaine." It was signed simply "Paul."

I would have dismissed the thing, for after all my three-week vacation was very precious to me. I wanted every minute of it, and with Elaine. But she, standing on tiptoe looking over my shoulder, intervened, or was it fate?

"Jim," she said, "what an intriguing note! Is he serious? And where is Valley Lake?"

Before I could marshal my forces, she had a map out and her carmine-tipped finger was pointing at a spot in the upper reaches of the state. Even on the map the area looked desolate.

"Let's go," she said. "It'll be fun. He's asked me."

I had a hundred objections and she a hundred answers. Paul Okerdon was hardly my choice of a host for a carefree twenty-one-day vacation.

I had known him in college and afterward as a major and experimenter in electronic science. He was cynical, disillusioned, a chronic scoffer, but withal, witty, highly intelligent, and at times, excellent company. It may seem strange that one who is studying the law and another whose interests were along the lines of science should have found a common meeting ground. That common meeting ground was the occult. All manner of things beyond normal. He had read extensively on the subject; I, less extensively, and perhaps my tastes were less highbrow. He was amused that during my college years I never missed a horror film that came to our local theatre near the campus.

Recollections of our talks floated back to me. He had maintained that we were in the infancy of our knowledge of this thing "Life," of all that went on and all around us. That it was merely the ignorant and the cowardly who scoffed at any novel suggestion, however outré or outlandish.

Paul Okerdon had a small income of his own. He stoutly maintained that he would work at no repetitious, unspectacular little jobs in construction companies or engineering firms. He had ideas of his own and was going to indulge both himself and his ideas. We exchanged letters often after graduation, but as the years passed, we saw each other less and less frequently.

He grew strangely diffident, it seemed, and I, well, I was immersed in my increasing law work. Then he wrote me he was taking a sixty-acre place in Valley Lake, several hundred miles upstate. He urged me to come and see him

in his new home. I think I might have but I was so very
busy, and then I met Elaine and soon afterward we were
married. He had written me a formal little congratulatory
note but I hadn't heard from him again. That is, until now.

Elaine seemed so terribly excited about the idea that
I found even my own mental reservations disappearing.
After all, why not go up and visit the old fellow? I hadn't
seen him in a long while. He probably had highly contro-
versial new theories on occultism he wanted to talk over
with me. I dismissed the almost hysterical urgency of his
telegram as being typical of Paul, who could command
a wide range of sympathy-getting procedures to gain his
own ends.

That evening I wired him that we were coming, and the
next morning after an early breakfast we packed my coupé
and started off. I hadn't been out of the city for three years
except for very occasional weekends and I must confess my
thoughts were on the glories and attractions of a tree and
some green grass rather than on Paul.

Elaine chattered at my side with road maps spread
out on knees. We followed State Highway 1 faithfully all
morning, and at lunch time when we pulled up at the side
of the road for sandwiches and thermos coffee that we'd
brought with us, we figured we were halfway there. Elaine
sniffed delightedly at the country air with her exquisite
little nose.

"It's a treat to be out here, Jim. You and your dusty old
law tomes!"

I agreed with her. We took our time eating and then
started off again. As the afternoon wore on, I noticed that
the green, lush countryside, although in no way losing its
beauty, grew more desolate, more primitive even. What
houses there were seemed much fewer and farther between.

"How near are we, Honey?" I asked Elaine.

She crinkled up her blue eyes and squinted at the map. We rumbled over a rude wooden bridge, its planks shaking to the weight of our car. She indicated something on the map.

"That must be this, Jimmy, the bridge we just went over. It can't be so very many more miles."

The road was narrower now. The concrete had ended back beyond the creek we'd crossed. This highway was dirt. In my rear-vision mirror I could see how clearly the mark of our tire treads stood out, as though other autos had not been along for some time. The trees grew closer to the road here, and the late afternoon sun dropped behind them leaving the highway crisscrossed with long, sentrylike shadows. Elaine shivered a little and pulled on her coat.

"It's chilly up here, Jim."

"When the sun goes down," I said. "You're used to the hot pavements, gal!"

But I felt the chillier air myself and rolled the window up halfway on my side. The gold and light blue seemed to be squeezed out of the sky. Purple took its place and twilight came on us with the suddenness of an August thunderstorm. Almost involuntarily I speeded up, and the coupé jounced along the crude road.

I fumbled in my suit pocket for Paul's letter. His instructions were explicit: "Follow the dirt road until you come to a long hill. You go up to the top and then down about halfway. On the right you'll see two iron gateposts. There's a rusted sign but I'm sure you'll be able to make out 'Valley Lake Estate.'"

Elaine frowned at the letter. For the first time something seemed to strike her.

"He seems awfully upset about something, Jim, and that telegram! You don't think he's ill?"

"Why send for me, darling?" I replied. "I'm not a doctor."

"But you've told me yourself, you're probably his closest friend."

"Simply because Paul *hasn't* other friends, to my knowledge. I'm not the closest. Once perhaps. But you've come between us!"

Elaine giggled, "You mean those musty old law tomes."

My coupé nosed its way onto the hill road and began to climb. It took second gear to get up to the top, and the car moving at slow speed, rolled over the brow. In the twilight we had a wonderful view of the countryside below. It stretched out in front of us in patterns of green and brown, seemingly lush, unbroken wilderness.

"Why, it's like a jungle!" Elaine gasped.

I was thinking myself it looked as though no living creature dwelt here, or could or would want to.

My auto picked up speed as we rolled downhill. I braked gently around a corner, and then suddenly coming in sight on the right were the iron gateposts. Even in the increasingly dim light, we could make out the legend on one of the iron plates, "Valley Lake Lodge."

As we passed through the gates and down an even narrower dirt road, the trees seemed to close more tightly around us. It was dark enough for me to use my headlight. The birch and elm trees gave way to evergreens, I noticed, and then my car lights picked up something ahead. We turned to run parallel to water.

"Suppose that's Valley Lake," Elaine suggested in a hushed voice. "Sort of a spooky place, Jim, don't you think?"

I felt her soft shoulder pressing closer to me and I patted her arm reassuringly.

"We ought to see Paul's place pretty soon. He's really got a chunk of land here."

Needles from the evergreens muted our car tires and we seemed to steal on silent rubber tiptoes deeper into a strange wilderness. And then the tunnel of trees through which we'd been riding opened out. The road curved sharply to the right and swept toward a large dark bulge of house that loomed up out of the early evening.

"There it is!" I said with an attempt at cheerfulness.

The place did look gloomy. There was one light high up in a wing. A small pinpoint of yellow. The rest was dark, forbidding. It was a trick of the light, I knew, mixed with fatigue from our long journey, but the structure looked like some huge loathsome monster, waiting to spring as we came out of the forest toward it.

"Golly! Jim, it's like one of those silly movies you drag me to! I don't think any man lives here. We'll probably find a dragon!"

I laughed appreciatively.

"If Paul's turned himself into a dragon, he's done more in this line than I ever thought he could! No, I'm afraid it's just his odd, egotistical way. He's probably even forgotten we're to arrive."

We pulled up in front of the steps that piled one upon another onto the porch. I got out and slammed the car door and came around to Elaine's side.

"I hope a big meal's waiting for us," I commented.

"It's so dark," she said. "Jim, he isn't, well, crazy or anything, is he?"

"As a lawyer, I can assure you Paul Okerdon was never insane in the legal sense of the word. That's all that can be said for a lot of us. Look at me and my musty old tomes!"

I feigned a jocularity I did not feel. Elaine was clinging to my arm and we mounted the stairs onto the dark porch. Our eyes, growing accustomed to the gloom, found the door and the black button set at one side. I thumbed it, and inside somewhere a bell sounded sharply. We heard steps and then a light flooded the porch. We grinned at each other.

"Some dragon!" I murmured. I could see Elaine was relieved.

"Hello Paul!" I called.

The door was thrown back and my erstwhile college companion stood before us. I reached for his hand instinctively. And although he returned my clasp, somehow the coldness of his fingers tempered my enthusiasm. I introduced Elaine and he led us inside. I could see my wife had recovered from any doubts she'd had about the place, but an edge of uneasiness crept into my mind. As Paul stood before us in the great hall, his face was, well, Paul's. But it was as though a great conflict had raged in the man for some time. I am trained to notice such things in court, and quite obviously to one like myself who had known him for so long, Paul was highly elated about something— and at the same time also in deadly fear.

With conventional small-talk out of the way, Paul showed us our room, a large dark-paneled chamber made more depressing by its ancient mahogany furniture, its windows revealing nothing but the rustling blackness of trees at the corner of the house. I felt the driveway should be down there somewhere but it was too dark to see even the outline of our coupé. Elaine was humming in the background as she unpacked the bags.

When we had readied ourselves to go downstairs, we found Paul bustling in the large old-fashioned kitchen like any suburban housewife.

"Can't get anybody nowadays, especially to work way out in the country like this, as I wrote Jim in one of my letters," he explained to Elaine.

"Now let me do things," Elaine said, her attention already attracted by a sizzling pot on the stove that needed water added.

"No, no, please," Paul smiled with a charming diffidence that I remembered from earlier days. "Just because I'm without a staff and entourage is no fair excuse to press my guests into service."

But Elaine made herself helpful and I leaned against the white enamel table chatting about this and that. With dinner ready Elaine led the way toward the dining room. Paul followed and I brought up the rear with a fistful of silver which made me feel useful but much to Elaine's amusement.

As we pushed out of the kitchen through the planked pantry door into a little serving hall, I noticed that the light from behind threw Paul's and my moving shadow against the wall and he stopped suddenly as though surprised or in fear. I know, because I almost rammed into his back with my handful of knives and forks. He didn't answer to the small joke I made but I thought no more about it—at the time.

The meal was pleasant. When a man cooks well, and Paul did, he is usually exceptional, and our long trip had made us hungry. We talked of old classmates out of the past, gone from one's life and the small tragedy of it. Then we adjourned to the living room, a room even larger than the dining chamber, with a high ceiling and a small balcony on two sides. The evening passed quickly and I found myself stifling yawns. The country air will do that to a man who's been in the city too long.

Paul had spoken superficially of his own interest in psychic and occult research. Elaine tied in a reference to me, pointing a finger accusingly.

"Jim's work has none of the elements of intrigue and adventure that keeps a man young. The law turns you old before your time, Paul," she mocked me pityingly. "Look, he's yawning already!"

But Paul's expression as he looked at me was one very hard to describe. I think envy is the nearest I can come to an evaluation.

"Say," I broke in, "I've got to stick my car somewhere, Paul. This castle must have some sort of a garage. Even a shed'll do."

"Of course," replied Paul, rising. "How stupid of me to forget. C'mon, Jim. Will you excuse us a moment, Elaine?"

We went through the great hall out onto the porch, and Paul produced a small flashlight.

"Golly," I said, "I didn't know it could get as black as this! I miss those electric signs!"

Paul played the thin beam of light across the drive to the car. I got in. He followed.

"Half a turn around the center," he directed, "then there's another gravel drive leading to the right. There's a big shed at the end of that."

I started the coupé's motor and we moved away in gear. The headlights picked up the turn, and then a few yards further a square shed at road's end.

"You've still got room for a couple of stagecoaches here," I joked with the coupé put away in the big barn. "Got your torch?"

Paul nodded. I switched off the lights.

As I did so, I felt his hand suddenly on my shoulder.

"Did you see that?" he hissed, and the thin beam of the pocket-flash played around the huge shed making grotesque and gigantic shadows.

"What!" I demanded.

His grip on my arm slackened and fell away. His silence was ominous. The beam caught the painted white inside of the shed door. As we were about to pass outside, I saw Paul's face. It was ashen in the light that reflected back. His skin bloodless, something had shaken him to the innermost of his very being. Outside of the rude structure, the starless darkness settled around us, the torch beam small in the gloom. A pinpoint of light showed ahead, far ahead. I hadn't realized the house was so distant. Paul's steps beside me quickened.

"What's wrong, Paul? What did you see?" I questioned again.

His only answer was to turn his head and look back. Although nothing could have been seen in the impenetrable gloom behind us, I followed suit and cold apprehension needled up and down my back. Paul's steps speeded up almost into a half run. His breath had the sound of a fleeing animal and I was caught up in the spirit of fright.

We reached the circular driveway and then finally the porch steps loomed ahead. I slackened speed abruptly.

"For God's sake, man, what was all that about!" I exploded, more than a little ashamed of myself.

Paul slowed too, and my eyes grown more accustomed to the darkness could make out the dejection of his figure.

"I . . . I'm terribly sorry, Jim."

He took my hand and squeezed it.

"Won't you put it down to a man who's lived too long alone out here? I guess my nerves are jumpy. Silly of me."

His laugh was forced and his fingers in my hand had the same coldness I had noticed before. Fear causes that. We climbed the porch steps and went inside. Soon after, Elaine and I went upstairs to our room. The open windows let in cool fragrant air as we settled ourselves for bed. The last thing in the world I wanted was to suggest any fear thoughts to Elaine. In fact, the happiest part of our vacation so far was the enjoyment my citified wife seemed to be getting out of this country visit.

With the light out I shut my eyes but sleep was elusive. Long after I heard my wife's breathing become regular in slumber I lay on my back, thinking, staring up at the ceiling. Paul's actions this night had been strange, to say the least. I wondered if living alone had affected his mind. The thought of sleeping in the same house with someone unbalanced was not conducive to restfulness.

The late moon threw thin gray light into the room, shadowing bedposts, chairs, and bureau. There was the occasional chirp of a cricket or humming noise of other small insects from outside, and then I heard a faint noise in the corridor outside our bedroom. There was no sound for a second and then the heavy iron handle turned and the door began to open, so slowly at first I thought it a trick of my staring eyes. I raised myself higher in bed. Then the opening was large enough for me to see Paul's figure touched by a shaft of moonlight, standing there solemnly. He raised his fingers to his lips and then motioned me to come. I silently slipped my bare feet into slippers and stole out of the room. Elaine still slept.

I followed Paul down the long gloomy corridor lit by one small bulb, down the stairs that led to his room. It was not until we were inside with the door closed that he spoke.

"I had to talk to you, Jim, and right away. I hoped to pass off the earlier events of tonight but my resolution . . ." he made a hopeless little gesture ". . . well, it didn't work out, did it?"

I nodded. "I want you to tell me, Paul. I want to help you."

If the man were unbalanced, this would be the only way to handle him. One side of his bedchamber was lined with bookcases, and here and there I spotted a familiar title. Books of pseudo-science, of psychical research. There were many more I did not recognize. We sat down, Paul facing me. He began speaking.

"As you know, I have been interested in the unusual, the outré, Jim. I'm not going to bore you with a lot of scientific folderol because a lawyer is even less of a mathematician than I am. But as you may have guessed, knowing me of old, I took this place, frankly, because I wanted to be undisturbed in my experiments. Now that you've driven here yourself, I think you will believe it when I tell you that this is one of the most out-of-the-way spots in our section of the country."

I nodded, wondering what would come next.

"I had no set idea when I came here, but there were many that I wished to follow up. The creation of some Frankenstein monster is spectacular but thoroughly impractical. My interests were directed toward other fields, yet as I now have found out, nonetheless spectacular." He stopped.,

"Well, go ahead," I urged. "Tell me more about it, Paul."

The man's enthusiasm grew as he talked on.

"I became interested in light, not as a scientist for my training is not profound in that direction, but in its relation to the psychic, to the occult. Light simply is a form of imagery which, by its action upon our organs of vision produces sight. Without taxing your legal mind, Jim, I think you can grasp that light is transmitted by undulations of the ether, a sort of radiant energy."

I bobbed my head. "Fine, but what—?"

Paul raised his hand.

"The next step in the study of light, the logical progression, was the study of shadow. Shadow we know as a sort of obscurity or shade within defined limits in a space from which rays are thrown off by an interposed body. I think you can visualize shadow easily as the image made by such an obscure space on some intercepting service, a wall or ceiling. You follow me, Jim?"

"To the limits of my legal mind," I grinned, but Paul Okerdon had no time for humor.

"I have discovered something that you with your conventional mind will not accept, for I with my willingness to believe almost anything, would not accept—at first! No, not until its truth was forced upon me."

I leaned forward in my chair. "What is it?"

"A shadow, Jim, is not a detached secondary visual experience. It is something of its own, a living entity in some peculiar way, whose purposes for reasons not yet apparent to me, have been served best by subordinating itself by mimicking and imitating man."

"You mean . . ." I started with a frown.

"I mean that your shadow, my shadow is not a meaningless harmless little patch of darkness and nothingness. It's something far more ordered, more sinister, more progressive than any of us have ever guessed."

I settled back in my chair, studying Paul's face. My worst fears were realized. He was obviously unbalanced. I censured myself for bringing my wife hundreds of miles to live under the same roof with a lunatic.

"I can see the five-letter word 'doubt' written across your face, Jim," and Paul's smile was not a pleasant one. "There has always been doubt of those who discovered anything new and revolutionary."

"You've been out here too long, old mam. You need to get away from this place. Come into the city and see people. Forget your dabblings in the occult arts for a while." I realized I'd said the wrong thing as his face clouded.

"Dabblings in the occult arts!" he repeated after me. "I pray to God another had discovered what I have uncovered instead of me!"

"Mankind has lived with its shadows for many centuries, Paul. What do you think is going to be different?"

"I don't know. I just don't know," he replied miserably. "But this place here, Jim. It's haunted by them."

"By what?"

"By shadows. Shadows without any rime or reason. Without the God-created form of human or animal structure that should give them being. Shadows that are independent of us and that have a malign, monstrous power of their own. I feel I'm a prisoner here now with this knowledge."

"That's absurd!" I burst out. "You're talking like a little boy afraid of a graveyard!"

My restraint was gone.

"I suppose you realize, Paul, that you're giving every indication of having worked much too hard and of having been alone much too long."

"You mean you think . . ." he tapped his own forehead significantly and smiled. "No, Jim, I'm afraid not. Perhaps it was selfish of me to have you come up here. Yes, it was, but I had to have someone I could trust, someone I had known out of the past. I boasted we were friends, you know. I like to think of you as the best one I have. You know about me and my past and the type of unusual research I've always been interested in. I had thought I could impart some of this discovery to you before whatever revenge was meant for me was meted out. This would make for some permanent record the means of my death, date, time, in a way to certificate it.

"But now, Jim, I'm very much afraid that through my eagerness, my selfishness if you will, I have gotten you and your lovely young wife into almost the same predicament I am in.

"These shadow forces are more powerful than I thought. I'm afraid, Jim, we're all prisoners here now till some form of death relieves our vigil."

The man was obviously insane. I believed it now with my whole heart. His threats against me and Elaine were typical. I knew I must josh him into a more reasonable mood.

"Come on now, Paul," I slapped his knee. "Don't let this thing get you down. You're coming back to the city with us."

"Even after what I've told you?" He looked at me penetratingly. "You don't believe me?"

"Of course not," I said. "I don't think you really do either, Paul. You're far too sensible, too intelligent, to be afraid of, well, afraid of shadows."

There was silence then between us, a silence that seemed to come from every corner of the huge old house.

And then shattering the silence with soul-shocking suddenness came a shriek of mortal terror. In an instant I was on my feet and out the door, dashing up the stairs toward the screams.

"Elaine!" I cried, "I'm coming!"

Paul was at my heels. I burst into our bedroom and rushed over to where my wife was sitting upright in bed. The table lamp beside her was on. I took her in my arms and cushioned her blonde head against my shoulders, soothing her sobs. Paul stood gravely by.

"What's the matter, darling?"

"Oh, Jim," she gasped. "Something so horrible! It must have been some sort of awful nightmare!"

"What was it?" whispered Paul.

"Something in the room," Elaine replied against my chest. "Something huge and horrible. It was so real though, darling." She turned her frightened face upward toward me and I kissed her forehead tenderly.

"It seemed to envelop me, to smother me. It was like . . . like a huge black distorted shadow!"

I turned my head and found Paul's eyes boring into my own. There was a smile on his face not nice to see and I again squeezed Elaine's head protectively to my shoulder. My mind worked at top speed as I stood there trying to control my own emotions. I looked again at Paul. His face was a mask now, as he leaned against the bureau watching us.

"Is there anything I can do?" he asked me.

"Thanks, no. Elaine's had a fright. Anyone can have a mean nightmare like that."

Paul's acknowledgement was the suggestion of an enigmatic smile. Elaine had regained her composure now.

"I'm sorry," she said simply.

Paul withdrew then. My wrist-watch said one o'clock. I came to a quick decision. This was no place for Elaine, for us. I told my wife some of what had happened earlier, omitting the details of Okerdon's talk about the shadows.

"He's ill mentally," I summed up. "I'm afraid our coming here has been the very worst thing. It's disturbed him and upset him. I'm for slipping out."

My wife looked at me wide-eyed.

"You mean to leave now, in the middle of the night?"

My overwrought nerves gave way a bit then and I blurted out, "Your experience, Elaine. It may not have been entirely a dream!"

Her face paled again but I felt a sense of growing urgency. I was convinced that we were in the greatest peril, only of precisely what sort, I was not sure.

"You mean someone *was* in this room? But who, Jim?"

I shook my head. Far better to let Elaine think of this in a logical, normal manner than even consider the outré possibilities of the situation. What fiendish forces were at work in this accursed place, I did not know, but Paul was a man of tremendous intellect, of resources beyond normal. It was my job to get my wife out of here as soon as possible.

"We'd better dress," I said, and Elaine did so without further questioning.

It was then I turned to the bureau. My car keys were missing and Paul had been leaning there not long ago! Elaine had followed the direction of my eyes. I could see her quick mind had grasped the situation as my gaze came back to her face.

I walked to the door and was not entirely surprised to find it locked on the outside. Anger welled up in me and I rattled the heavy fixture in my hand and pounded on the thick panel.

"Okerdon!" I yelled. "Let us out of here! What's the matter with you, man! Is this some stupid sort of joke?"

I knew better but this was the only way to talk to him. Paul's steps came along the hall and paused outside.

"Ah, Jim," he said. "I didn't want you to do anything rash like leaving hurriedly, so I took the precaution of shutting the door. Believe me, you're better off in there. Your quick mind has probably considered the window as an avenue of escape. I daresay, you and your pretty wife could make it that way, but there are things outside, Jim, things I fear you would not like, and I, as you have no doubt already noticed, also took the precaution of removing your car keys. It would be quite impossible to walk to the nearest house. There is no 'nearest' house."

His laugh punctuated the sentence, confirming my belief that we were in the house of a maniac. I thought back to the previous evening, to our experience in the shed.

Certainly Paul seemed compelled by some fear greater than anything of a subjective nature.

Elaine was at my side, her finger at her lips. She had her purse, and on her own key ring was a duplicate ignition key for the coupé. My wife often drove and we both kept a set. I smiled. It was the first card we had held all evening, but my exultation was short-lived.

The table light dimmed, dipped twice, and then flickered out. The sudden blackness was stifling. The thin rays from the moon outside shone feebly here and there.

But Paul's reaction outside the door was truly horrible. An animal sound in his throat grew to vile curses and entreaties. Heathen prayers and threats. I could make out little that was intelligible, but now and then I could understand a phrase:

"Don't! Don't! Destroy them, take them! Let me alone! Don't!"

I heard the sound of a striking match and a flicker of yellow light came under the door. Okerdon had been caught without his flashlight apparently.

I headed quickly to the window, guiding Elaine with me. There was a tree limb barely out of reach. The noise from the hall kept up. I stretched mightily for the limb and made it. I reached my hand back for Elaine, grasped hers.

"Come on," I ordered, and she forced herself away from the window-sill with her other arm.

Paul's screams were now accompanied by a tremendous knocking on the door. Almost as an afterthought I could hear metal scraping. He had inserted the key. I completed our trapeze act, lowering Elaine to the ground and dropping by her side myself. I turned and looked up then.

Paul came to the window, his face framed in the yellow flicker of a match. He screamed at us and I expected any minute he would vault from the window in pursuit. Pushing Elaine behind me I was fully prepared to fight, but Okerdon remained there in the window.

"Don't go out there!" he screamed. "For God's sake don't leave me. Jim, please!"

The match flickered and died and I heard the frenzied scraping as he lit another. The man's face above us was frightening beyond description. Madness is one thing, but lunacy induced by stark, raving fear is far more horrible.

I heard Elaine give a little cry. She had covered her face up with her hands. I turned away then and we started along the circular drive. Paul's shrieks and entreaties rose and fell. Some were to us, others to something else, begging them not to take him, not to destroy him. Indistinctly, every now and then he screamed one word over and over again. Elaine heard it and looked up at me.

"Shadows!" she shuddered.

The gravel crunched beneath our feet as we hurried. I knew the direction, but it was a considerable distance to the shed. My straining eyes could barely discern the turn-out path from this we were on. Our quick steps took us out from beyond the shadow of the great house. The moon seemed to rise up behind its bulk and the way was somewhat brighter. The mansion we'd fled from was completely dark except for the flicker of light that was Paul in the window, calling, crying, cursing.

It was Elaine strangely who noticed it first. She grabbed my wrist tightly.

"Jim!"

Close behind where none should be was a long thin shadow! A second appeared. This was a bulky, monstrous one. I turned my head even though I knew there would be nothing behind to have caused these shadows.

"Run!" My voice rose. "Run like hell, Elaine! Don't look back! Get your keys out and give them to me!"

We sped over the gravel. Then the shadows behind us, coming closer, taking all shapes and forms, reaching out tenuous, monstrous appendages toward us, and behind Paul Okerdon shrieked and yelled.

The dim outline of the shed was ahead. I fairly pushed Elaine before me. The door was only a few yards away.

"Jim!" Elaine sobbed and staggered a bit.

Oh God! I had felt it too, something soft as cotton, yet with strength, touching, gripping for a moment on my flying legs, shaking me off balance for a second.

"Keep on!" I screamed, and we flung ourselves forward.

I gave Elaine a last push toward the door and threw myself after her against the increasing weight of a soft velvet pressure on my shoulder, another at my thigh, soft yet iron in strength, reaching out, groping and a third tight-vised at my left wrist. I hurled myself forward and the resistance slipped away.

We leaped into the car. I switched on the lights, cranked the motor, and accelerated madly out of the garage.

"Keep the windows up," I yelled, and as we headed toward the great circular drive; soft things plopped and swished at the glass.

We were running through patches of dark and light. There was a stripedness on each side of us and the car bumped and jerked a few times, but I kept the coupé in second gear, the gas to the floor. Only when we reached the drive did I notice the flames climbing out of the window where we had last seen Paul, shooting up the front of the old house.

Before we had gone a hundred yards more, the fire had spread and the old mansion was a flaming pyre. The flames lit up the desolate forest we passed through and even When we reached the iron gate and headed out on the country road, the flames were still visible behind us in the sky. There was no use turning back, even if we had dared. Paul was by now beyond any human help.

We sped through the lonely countryside for miles, and finally it was safe to slacken speed. I put my arm around Elaine, and tried to quiet her shaking.

"Darling," I said, "it was a terrible experience but we're through it."

"But the shadows," she cried. "Jim, things like that can't be! But we *saw* them. I . . . I *felt* something!"

"We were wrought up," I argued. "Paul's collapse was shocking to both of us, poor devil. But as for anything else, that was imagination, darling. You've got to forget it."

My own mind had already started to reject the memories of our sprint across the grounds, our race against the shadows!

As I squeezed Elaine with my right arm, my left wrist gave a painful twinge. I looked at it in the dashlight. It was bruised severely. The welts were red and angry, raised around my wrist in perfect symmetry . . . unlike anything I had ever seen before!

The Third Shadow

H. Russell Wakefield

1950

"And the other man on the rope, Andrew," I asked, "did you ever encounter him?"

He gave me a quick glance and tapped the ash from his cigarette.

"Well, *is* there such a one?" he asked, smiling.

"I've many times read of him," I replied. "Didn't Smythe actually see him on the Brenva Face and again on that last dread lap of Everest?"

Sir Andrew paused before replying.

No one glancing casually at that eminent and superbly discreet civil servant, Sir Andrew Poursuivant, would have guessed that in his day and prime he had been the second-best amateur mountaineer of all time, with a dozen first ascents to his immortal fame, and many more than a dozen of the closest looks at death vouchsafed to any man. One who had leaped almost from the womb on to his first hill, a gravity defier by right of birth, soon to revolutionise the technique of rock-climbing and later to write two of the very finest books on his exquisite art. Yet there was something about that uncompromising buttress, his chin, the superbly modelled arête, his nose, those unflinching blue tarns, his eyes, and the high, wide cliff of his brow, to persuade the reader of faces that here was a born man of action, endowed with that strange and strangely named faculty, presence of mind, which ever finds in great emergency and peril the stimulus to a will and a cunning to meet and conquer them.

We were seated in my state room in the *Queen Elizabeth* bound for New York, he for some recurrent brawl, I on the interminable quest for dollars. The big tub was pitching hard into a nor-west blizzard and creaking her vast length.

I am but an honorary member of the corps of mountaineers, having no "head" for the game. But I love it dearly by proxy, and as the sage tells us, "He who *thinks on* Himalcha shall have pardon for all sins," and the same is true, I hope, of lesser ranges.

I dined with Sir Andrew perhaps half-a-dozen times a year and usually persuaded him on these felicitous occasions to tell me some great tale of the past. Hence on this felicitous occasion my "fishing" enquiry.

"Yes, so I remember," he presently said, "but are there not nice, plausible explanations for that? The illusions consequent on great height, great strain? You may remember Smythe, who is highly psychic, saw something else from Everest, very strange wings beating the icy air."

"He isn't the only one," I said, "it's a well-documented tradition."

"It is, I agree. Guides, too, have known his presence, and always at moments of great stress and danger, and he has left them when these moments passed. And if they do not pass, the fanciful might suggest he meets them on the Other Side. But who he is no one knows. I grant you, also, I myself have sometimes felt that over, say twelve thousand feet, one moves into a realm where nothing is quite the same, or, perhaps, and more likely, it is just one's mind that changes and becomes more susceptible and exposed to—well, certain *oddities.*"

"But you have never encountered this particular oddi-
ty?" I insisted.

"What an importunate bag-man you are!"

"I believe you have, Andrew, and you must tell me of
it!"

"That is not quite so," he replied, "but—it will be thirty-
five long years ago next June, I did once have a very terrible experience that had associated with it certain sub-
sidiary experiences somewhat recalcitrant to explanation."

"That is a very cautious pronouncement, Andrew!"

"Phrased in the jargon of my trade, Bill."

"And you are going to relate it to me?"

"I suppose so. I've never actually told it to another, and
it will give me no pleasure to rouse it from my memory.
But perhaps I owe it you."

"Fill your glass, mind that lurch, and proceed."

"I haven't told it before," said Sir Andrew, "partly
because it's distasteful to recall, and partly, for the reason that the prudent sea-captain turns his blind eye on a
sea serpent and keeps a buttoned lip over the glimpse he
caught; no one much appreciates the grin of incredulous
derision."

"I promise to keep a straight face," I assured him.

"Yes, I rather think you will. Well, all those years ago,
in that remote and golden time, I knew and climbed with
a man I will call 'Brown.' He was about my age. He had
inherited considerable position and fortune and he was
heir, also, to that irresistible and consuming passion for
high places, their conquest and company, which, given the
least opportunity, will never be denied, and only decrepi-
tude or death can frustrate. Technically, he was a master in
all departments, a finished cragsman and just as expert on
snow and ice. But there was just occasionally an unmas-
tered streak of recklessness in him which flawed him as a

leader, and everyone, including myself, preferred to have
him lower down the rope.

"It was, perhaps, due to one of these feckless seizures
that, after our fourth season together, he proposed to a
wench, who replied promptly in the affirmative. He was
a smallish fellow, though immensely lithe, active, strong
and tough. She was not far short of six feet and tipped
the beam at one hundred and sixty-eight pounds, mostly
muscle. With what suicidal folly, my dear Bill, do these
infatuate pigmies, like certain miserable male insects,
doom themselves with such Boadiceas, and how pitilessly
and jocundly do those monsters pounce upon their prey!
This particular specimen was terribly, viciously, 'County',
immensely handsome, and intolerably authoritarian.
Speaking evil of the dead is often the only revenge permitted us and I have no intention of refraining from saying that I have seldom, almost certainly *never* disliked
anyone more than Hecate Quorn. Besides being massive
and menacing to the nth degree, she was endowed with a
reverberating contralto which loaned a fearsomely oracu-
late air to her insistent spate of edicts. Marry for lust and
repent in haste, the oldest, saddest lesson in the world, and
one my poor friend had almost instantly to learn. Once
she'd gripped him in her red remorseless maw, she bullied
him incessantly and appeared to dominate him beyond
hope of release. Such an old story I need enlarge upon no
more! How many of our old friends have we watched fall
prostrate before these daughters of Masrur!

"She demanded that he should at least attempt to teach
her to climb, and females of her build are seldom much
good at the game, particularly if they are late beginners.
She was no exception, and her nerve turned out to be surprisingly more suspect on a steepish slope than her ghastly
assurance on the level would have suggested. Poor Brown
plugged away at it, because he feared, if she chucked her

hand in, he would never see summer snow again. He did his very desperate best. He hired Fritz Mann, the huskiest and best-tempered of all the Chamonix guides, and between them on one searing and memorable occasion they shoved and pulled and hauled and slid her on feet and rump to creditably near the summit of Mt. Blanc. She loathed the ordeal, but she refused to give in, just because she knew poor Brown was longing to join up with a good party, and have some fun. I need say no more, you have sufficient imagination fully to realise the melancholy and humiliating pass of my sad friend. And, of course, it wasn't only in Haute-Savoie and Valais she made his life hell, it was at least purgatory for the rest of the year; his was eternal punishment, one might say. A harsh sentence for a moment's indiscretion!"

"What about those occasional feckless flashes?" I asked; "had she quenched and overlaid those, too?"

"Permit me to tell this story my own way and pour me out another drink. In the second summer after their marriage the Browns had preceded me by a few days to the Montenvert, which, doubtless you recall, is a hotel overlooking the Mer de Glâce, three thousand feet above Chamonix. When I arrived there late one evening I found the place in a turmoil, and Brown apparently almost out of his mind. Hecate had fallen down a crevasse that morning and, as a matter of fact, her body was never recovered. I took him to my room, gave him a stiff drink, and he blurted out his sorry tale. He had taken her out on the Mer de Glâce for a morning's training, he said, determined to take no risks whatsoever. They had wandered a little way up the glacier, perhaps rather further than he'd intended. He'd cut some steps for her to practice on, and so forth. Presently he'd encountered a crevasse, crossed by a snowbridge, which he'd tested and found perfectly reliable. He'd passed over himself, but, when she followed, she'd gone straight through, the rope had snapped—and that was that. They'd lowered a guide, but the hole went down forever and it was quite hopeless. Hecate must have died instantly; that was the only assuaging thought.

"'Should that rope have gone, Arthur?' I asked. 'Can I see it?'

"He produced it. It was poor stuff, an Austrian make, which had once been very popular but had been found unreliable and the cause of several accidents. There was also old bruising near the break. It wasn't a reassuring bit of stuff. 'I realise' said Brown hurriedly, 'I shouldn't have kept that piece. As you know, I'm a stickler for perfection in a rope. But we were just having a little easy work and, as that rope's light and she always found it so hard to manage one, I took it along. I'd no intention of actually having to trust to it. We were just turning back when it happened. I swear to you that bridge seemed absolutely sound.'

"'She was a good deal heavier than you, Arthur,' I said.

"'I know, but I made every allowance for that.'

"'I quite understand,' I said. 'Well, it's just too bad,' or words to that effect. I was rather at a loss for appropriate expressions. He was obviously acting a part. I didn't blame him, he had to. He had to appear heavy with grief when he was feeling, in a sense, as light as mountain air. He got a shade tight that evening, and his efforts to sustain two such conflicting moods would have amused a more cynical and detached observer than myself. Besides, I foresaw the troubles ahead.

"The French held an enquiry, of course, and inevitably exonerated him completely, then I took him home to face the music, which, as I'd expected, was strident and loud enough. How far was it justified? I asked myself. He should, perhaps, not have taken Hecate up so far. Even if that rope hadn't gone, he'd never have been able to pull her up by himself—it would have taken two very strong men to have done that. He could merely have held her there, and she would, I suppose have died of slow strangulation, unless help had quickly come. Yet there is always risk, however prudently you try to play that game: it is the first of its rules and nothing will ever eliminate it. You must take my word for all this, which is rather outside your sphere of judgment. All the same the condition of that rope—and I wasn't the only one to examine it—didn't help things. Still, all that wouldn't have mattered nearly so much if he'd been a happily married man. I needn't dwell on that. Anyway the dirty rumour followed him home and resounded there."

"What was your candid opinion, Andrew?" I said.

"I must ask you," he replied, "to believe a rather hard thing, that I had and have no opinion, candid or otherwise. It *could* have been a pure accident. All could have happened exactly as he said it did. I've no valid reason to suppose otherwise. He may have been a bit careless: I might have been so myself. One takes such practice mornings rather lightly. There *is* risk, as I've said, but it's miniscule compared with the real thing. The expert mountaineer develops an exquisitely nice and certain 'feel' for degrees of danger, it is the condition precedent of his survival,—and adjusts his whole personality to changing degrees. He must take the small ones in his stride. The errors of judgment, if any, that Brown committed were petty and excusable. His reason for taking that rope was sensible enough in a way."

"Yes," I put in, "I can more or less understand all that, but you actually knew him well and you're a shrewd judge of character. You were in a privileged position to decide."

"Was I? A very learned judge once told me he'd find it far easier to decide the guilt or innocence of an absolute stranger than of a close friend; the personal equation confuses the problem and pollutes the understanding. I think he was perfectly right. Anyway I am shrewd enough to know when I am baffled, and I have always felt the balance of probability was peculiarly nicely poised. In a word, I have no opinion."

"Well, I have," I proclaimed. "I think he had a sudden fearful temptation. I don't think it was exactly premeditated, yet always, as it were, at the back of his mind. He realised that bridge would go when she had her weight on it, knew a swift, reckless temptation, and let it rip. I think he'd kept that rotten rope because he'd always felt in a vague half-repressed way, it might, as they say, 'come in handy one day'."

Sir Andrew shrugged his shoulders. "Very subtle, no doubt," he said, "and you may be right. But I know I shall never be able to decide. Perhaps it is that personal equation, for I was always very fond of him, and he saved my life more than once at the greatest peril to his own; and since his marriage, that ordeal of thumb-screw and rack, I had developed profound sympathy for him. Hecate was far better dead. I greeted his release with a saturnine cheer. We will leave that point.

"Well, he had to face a very bad time. Hecate's relatives were many and influential and they pulled no punches, no stabs in the back, rather. No one, of course, actually cried: 'Murder!' in public, but such terms as 'Darned odd!', 'Very happy release!' 'Accidents *must* happen!' and so on, were in lively currency.

"Very few people comprehend the first thing about mountaineering, just sultry, celluloid visions of high-altitude villains slashing ropes, so this sepsis found receptive blood-streams. I did my best to foster antibodies and rallied my fellow-climbers to the defence. But we were hopelessly outnumbered and out-gunned, and it was lucky for poor Brown he had more than sufficient private means to retire from public life to his estate and his farming,

and insulate himself to some extent against the slings and
arrows which were so freely and cruelly flying about.

"I spent a week-end with him in April and was shocked
at his appearance: even life with Hecate had never reduced
him to such a pass. His nerves were forever on the jump,
he had those glaring insomniac eyes, he was drinking far
more and eating far less than was good for him; he looked
a driven, haunted man."

"Haunted?" I asked.

"I know what you mean," said Sir Andrew, "but I don't
think I can be more definite. I will say, however, I found
the atmosphere of the house unquiet and was very glad to
quit it. Anyway, something had to be done.

"'You must start climbing again, Arthur,' I said.

"'Never! My nerve's gone!' he replied.

"'Nonsense!' I said. 'We'll leave on June 3rd for Chamonix. You must conquer all this and at the very place which
tests you most starkly. You will be amongst friends. It will
be a superb nerve tonic. This tittle-tattle will inevitably
die down—it has started to do so already, I fancy. There
is nothing to fear, as you'll discover once you're fit again.
Come back to your first, your greatest, your only real love!'

"'What will people say?' he muttered uncertainly.

"'What say they, let them say! Actually I think it'll
be very good propaganda: no one'd believe a guilty man
would return to the scene of such a crime. My dear Arthur,
you're a bit young to die, aren't you! If you stay moping
here you'll be in the family vault in a couple of years. I'll
get the tickets and we'll dine together at the Alpine Club
on June the second at eight p.m. precisely.'

"To this he promptly agreed and his fickle spirits rose.
So the fourth of June saw us entering the Montenvert,
where our reception was cordial enough.

"It took him over a week, far longer than usual, to get
back to anything like his old standard, but I'd expected

that. On the ninth day I decided it was time for a crucial test of his recovery. It was no use frittering about, he'd got to face the hard thing, something far tougher than the practice grounds.

"After some deliberation I chose the Dent du Géant for the trial run. It was an old friend of ours, and the last time we'd done it, four years before, we'd simply raced to the aluminum Madonna which more or less adorns its summit. The Géant, I will remind you, is a needle, some thirteen thousand feet high, situated towards the southern rim of that great and glorious lake of ice, part French, part Swiss, part Italian, from which rise some of the most renowned peaks in the world, and of those the acknowledged monarchs are the Grandes Jurasses, the Grépon Aiguilles and, of course, the Mont Blanc Massiv itself. It is sacred ground to our fraternity and the very words ring like a silver peal. The Géant culminates in a grotesque colossal 'tooth' of rock, some of which is in a fairly advanced state of decay. These things are relative, of course, it will almost certainly be standing there, somewhat diminished, in five thousand years time. It provides an interesting enough climb, not, in my view, one of the most severe, but sheer and exposed enough. Nowadays, I understand, the livelier sections are so festooned with spikes and cords that it resembles the fruit of the union of a porcupine and a puppet. But I have not revisited it for years and, for very sure, I never shall again.

"Brown agreed with my choice, which he declared himself competent to tackle, so off we went late on a promising morning and made our leisurely way up and across the ice to the hat. He seemed in pretty good shape, and once, when a most towering and displeasing sérac fell almost dead on our line, he kept his head, his footing and his life. Yet somehow I didn't quite like the look of him. He didn't improve as the day wore on and, to tell the truth, I didn't either."

Here Sir Andrew paused, lit a cigarette, and continued more slowly. "You are not familiar with such matters, but I will try and explain the cause of my increasing preoccupation. We were, of course, roped almost all day, and from very early on I began to experience those intimations—it is difficult to find the precise, inevitable word—which were increasingly to disturb and perplex me on that tragic expedition. It is extremely hard to make them plain and plausible to you, who have never been hitched to a manila. When merely pursuing a more or less untrammelled course over ice it is our custom to keep the rope neither trailing nor quite taut, but always—I speak as leader—of course, one is very conscious of the presence and pressure of the man behind. Now—how shall I put it? Well, over and over again it seemed to me as if that rope was behaving oddly, as though the 'pull' I experienced was inconsistent with the distance Brown was keeping behind me, as though something else was exercising pressure nearer to me. Do I make myself at all plain?"

"I think so," I replied. "You mean, as though there was someone tied to that rope between you and Brown."

"Nothing like so definite and distinct as that. Imagine if you were driving a car and you continually got the impression the brakes were coming on and off, though you knew they were not. You would be puzzled and somewhat disconcerted. I'm afraid that analogy isn't very illuminating. It was just that I was conscious of some inexplicable anomaly connected with our roped progress that day. I remember I kept glancing round in search of an explanation. I tried to convince myself it was due to Brown's somewhat inept, sluggish and erratic performance, but I was not altogether successful in this attribution. To make it worse a thick mist came on in the afternoon and this increased our difficulties, delayed us considerably, and intensified my sombre and rather defeatist mood.

"Certain pious, but, in my view, misguided persons, profess to find in the presence, the atmosphere, of these doomed Titans, evidence for a benevolent Providence, and a beneficent cosmic principle. I am not enrolled in their ranks. At best these eminences seem aloof and neutral, at worst, viciously and virulently hostile—I reverse the pathetic fallacy. That is, to a spirited man, half their appeal. Only once in a long while have I been lulled into a sense of their goodwill. And if one must endow them with a Pantheon, I would people it with the fickle and malicious denizens of Olympus and Valhalla, and not the allegedly philanthropic triad of heaven. In no place is the working of a ruthless, blind causality more starkly shewn. And never, for some reason, have I felt that oppressive sense of malignity more acutely than during the last four hours of our climb that day, as we forced our groping way through a nightmare world of ice-pillars, many of them as high and ponderous as the Statue of Liberty, destined each one of them soon to fall with a thunder like the crack of doom. And all the while I was bothered with that rope. Several times, as I glanced round through the murk, I seemed to sense Brown almost at my heels, when he was thirty feet away. Once I actually saw him, as I thought, near enough to touch. It was a displeasing illusion."

"Were you scared?" I asked.

"I was certainly keyed-up and troubled. I am never scared, I think, when actually on the move. It was just that there was a noxious puzzle I couldn't solve. We were in no great danger, just experiencing the endemic risks inherent in all such places. But I was mainly responsible for the safety of us both and my mode of securing that safety was impaired."

"I imagine," I said, "that the rope establishes, as it were, some psychic bond between those it links."

"An unexpectedly percipient remark," replied Sir Andrew. "That is precisely the case. The rope makes the fate of one the fate of all; and each betrays along its strands his spiritual state; his hopes, anxieties, good cheer, or lack of confidence. So I could feel Brown's hesitation and poor craftsmanship, as well as this inexplicable interruption of my proper connection with him.

"When we eventually reached the hut I had in no way elucidated the problem. I didn't like the look of Brown; he was far more tired than he should have been and his nerves were sparking again. He put the best face he could on it, as good mountaineers are trained to do, and declared a night's rest would put him right. I hoped for the best."

"Did you mention your trouble with the rope?"

"I did not," said Sir Andrew shortly. "For one thing, it might have been purely subjective. For another, what was there to say? And the first duty of the mountaineer is to keep his fears to himself, unless they are liable to imperil his comrades. Never lower the 'psychic temperature' if it can possibly be avoided. Yet somehow, I cannot define precisely how, I gained the impression he had noticed something and that this was partly the cause of his malaise.

"The hut was full, but not unpleasantly so, with young Italians for the most part, and we secured good sleeping places. Then we fed and lay down. It was a night of evil memory. Brown went to sleep almost at once, to sleep and to dream, and to tell of his dreams. He was, apparently, well, beyond all doubt, dreaming of Hecate and—how shall I put it?—in contact, in debate with her. And what made it far more trying to the listener, he was mimicking her voice with perfect virtuosity. This was at once horrible and ludicrous, the most pestilential and disintegrating combination of all, in my opinion. He was, it seemed, pleading with her to leave him alone, to spare him, and she was ruthlessly refusing. I say 'it seemed,' because the repulsive surge of words was blurred, and only at times articulate; just sufficient to give, as it were, the sense of the dialogue. But that was more than enough. The sleep-hungry Italians were naturally and vociferously infuriated, and I was compelled to rouse Brown over and over again, but each time he relapsed into that vilely haunted sleep. Once he raised himself on his elbow and thrust out blindly with his arms. And Hecate's minatory contralto spewed from his throat, while the Italians mocked and cursed. It was a bestial pandemonium.

"The Italians left early, loud in their execrations of us. One of them, his black eyes wide with fear and anger, shook his lantern in my face and exclaimed 'Who is this woman!' 'What woman?' I replied. He shrugged his shoulders and said: 'That is for you to say. I do not think I would climb the Géant with him if I were you! Good luck, Signore, *I think you will need it!*' Then they clattered off, and at four o'clock we followed them.

"I know now I should have taken that Italian's advice and got Brown back by the easiest and quickest route to the hotel, but when I tentatively suggested it, he almost hysterically implored me to carry on. 'If I fail this time,' he said, 'I shall never climb again, I know it! I *must* conquer it!' I was very tired, my judgment and resolution were at a disgracefully low ebb, and I half surrendered. I decided we would go up some of the way to a ledge or platform I remembered, at about the twelve thousand foot level, rest, eat, and turn back.

"We had a tiresome climb up the glacier, Brown in very poor form, and that nuisance on the rope beginning again almost at once. We crossed the big crevasse where the glacier meets the lower rocks and began to ascend. There was still some mist, but it thinned as the sun rose. I led and Brown, making very heavy weather, followed. The difference between his performance this time and that other I have mentioned, was gross and terrifying. I remember doubting if he would ever be a climber again and realising I had made a shocking error in going on. I had to nurse him with the greatest care and there was always that harassing behaviour of the rope. Only those with expert knowledge of such work could realise the great and deadly difference it made. I could never be quite sure when I had it properly firm on Brown, and he was climbing like a nervous novice. My own standard of the day was, not surprisingly, none too high. I'd had a damned bad, worried night and my mind was fussed and preoccupied. Usually one climbs half-subconsciously, that is the sign-manual of the expert, a rhythmic selection and seizure of 'holds,' with only now and again a fully controlled operation of will and decision. But now I was at full stretch all the time and ever ready for Brown to slip. Over and over again I was forced to belay the rope to some coign of vantage and coax and ease him up, and there was forever that strong interruption between us. The Géant was beating us hands down all the time and I hadn't felt so outclassed since my first season in the Alps. The light became most sinister and garish, the sun striking through the brume, creating a potent and prismed dazzle. So much so that more than once I fancied I saw Brown's outline duplicated, or rather revealed at different levels. And several times it seemed his head appeared just below me when he was still struggling far down. And then there were our shadows, cast huge on the snow-face across the gulf, vast and distorted by those strange rays.

"That there were *three* such shadows, now stationary, now in motion, was an irresistible illusion. There was mine, there was the lesser one of Brown, and there was another in between us. What was causing it? This fascinating and extraordinary puzzle served somewhat to distract my mind

from its heavy and intensifying anxiety. At last, to my vast
relief, I glanced up and saw that hospitable little platform
not more than sixty feet above me. Once there, the worst
would be, I thought, over, for I could lower Brown down
more easily than get him up.

"I shouted down to him. 'We're nearly there!', but he
made no reply. I shouted again and listened carefully. And
then I could hear him talking, using alternatively *his* voice
and Hecate's.

"I cannot describe to you the kind of ghostly fear
which then seized me. There was I fifteen hundred feet
up on a pretty sheer precipice with someone whose mind
had clearly gone, on my rope. And I had to get him, first
to the ledge, then try and restore him to a condition in
which descent might be possible. I could never leave him
there; we must survive or die together. First, I must reach
that platform. I set myself to it, and for the time being he
continued to climb, clumsily and mechanically, and carrying on that insane dialogue, yet *he kept moving!* But for
how much longer would that mechanism continue to func-
tion and bring him to his holds? I conquered my fear and
rallied again that essential detachment of spirit without
which we were both certainly doomed.

"So I set myself with the utmost care to reach that ledge.
Between me and it was a stretch of the Géant's rottenest
rock, which I suddenly remembered well. It is spiked and
roped now, I believe. When that gneiss is bad, it is very,
very evil indeed. Mercifully, the mist was not freezing
or we should have been dead ere then. How I cursed my
insensate folly, the one great criminal blunder of my
climbing career! This rush of rage may have saved me, for
just when I was struggling up that infamous forty-five feet
I got a fearful jerk from the rope. I was right out, attack-
ing a short over-hang, exposed a hundred per cent, and
how I sustained that jerk I shall never know. I even drove

my teeth into the rock. It was one of those super-human efforts only possible to a powerful, fully-trained man at the peak of his physical perfection when he knows that failure means immediate death. Somehow then he draws out his final erg of strength and resilience.

"At last I reached the ledge, belayed like lightning, gasped for breath and looked down. As I did so, Brown ceased to climb, screamed, and then a torrent of wild, incoherent words spewed from his mouth. I yelled at him encouragement and assurance, but he paid no heed. And, though he was stationary, clawing to his holds, the rope was still under pressure, working and sounding on the belay. No explanation of that has ever been vouchsafed me. For a moment my glance flickered out across the great gulf on to the dazzling slope opposite; and there were my shadow and Brown's, and another which seemed still on the move and reaching down towards him.

"I could see his body trembling in every muscle and I knew he must go at any second. I shouted down wildly again and again, telling him I had him firm and that he could take his time, but again he paid no heed. I couldn't get him up, I must go down to him. There was just one possible way which, a shade technical, I will not describe to you. Nor is there need or point in doing so, for suddenly Brown relinquished all holds and swung out. As my eye followed him, once more it caught those shadows, and now there were but two, Brown's hideously enlarged. For a moment he hung there screaming and thrashing out with his arms, his whole body in violent motion. And then he began to spin most horribly, faster and faster, and almost it seemed, in the visual chaos of that whirl, as though there were two bodies lashed and struggling in each other's arms. Then somehow in his writhings he worked free of the rope and fell two thousand feet to his death on the glacier below, leaving my shadow alone gigantic on the snow.

"That is all, and I want no questions, because I know I should have no answers for them and I am off to bed. As for your original question, I've done my best to answer it. But remember this, perchance such questions can never quite be answered."

GRAVEN IMAGES

Classic Stories of
Ghastly Paintings and
Dreadful Effigies

Edited by Chad Arment

COACHWHIPBOOKS.COM (PRINT)
COACHWHIP.COM (EPUB)

CATS OF SHADOW,
CLAWS OF DARKNESS

Stories of Were-Cats, Ghost Cats,
and Other Supernatural Felines

COACHWHIP PUBLICATIONS
ALSO AVAILABLE

COACHWHIPBOOKS.COM (PRINT)
COACHWHIP.COM (EPUB)

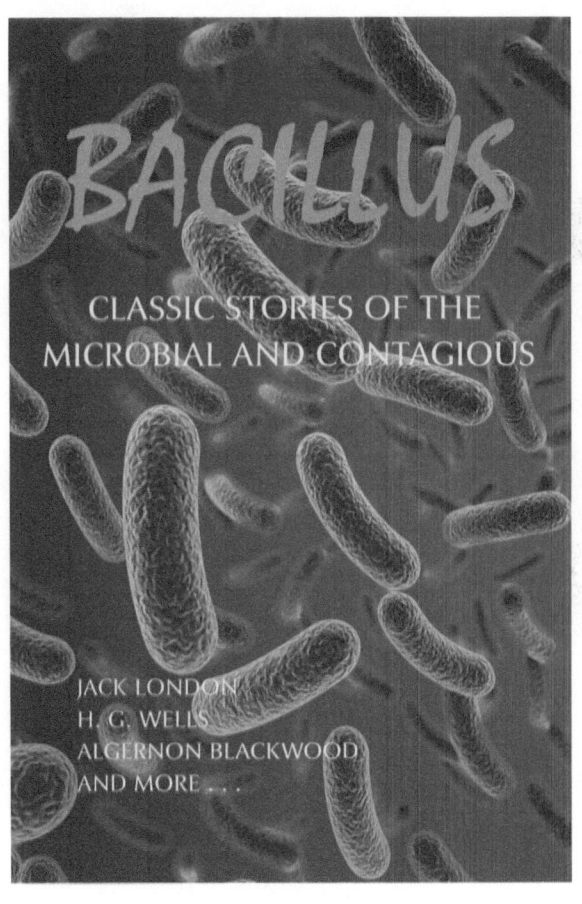

TRAVELS THROUGH
LOST WORLDS

THE LIVING DEATH
IN AMUNDSEN'S TENT
DROME

JOHN MARTIN LEAHY

COACHWHIP PUBLICATIONS
ALSO AVAILABLE

CRIMINAL ROGUES 1

The Exploits of Danby Croker
R. Austin Freeman

A Prince of Swindlers
Guy Boothby

OTHER LIFE

An Anthology of
Non-Terrestrial Biology

www.ingramcontent.com/pod-product-compliance
Lightning Source LLC
Chambersburg PA
CBHW022141010726
47493CB00002B/291